PRAISE FOR *STARRING ADELE ASTAIRE*

"Eliza Knight's *Starring Adele Astaire* strikes the perfect chord illustrating Adele Astaire's professional success as half of a dynamic dancing duo with her brother, Fred, and her personal trials and tribulations of attaining love and a family of her own. Knight crafts an intimate sensation that adeptly places readers in the footlights along America's Great White Way and London's West End theaters, among chorus dancers jostling for stardom, privileged royals, and the glamour of nonstop parties with a dapper and debonair entourage of A-listers. At the center of it all is Adele Astaire, an entertainer who wins the hearts of everyone with her dancing prowess, showmanship, perseverance, and dedication to service. A great read!"

—Monica Chenault-Kilgore, author of
Long Gone, Come Home

"Just as Adele Astaire received standing ovations for her performances, so too does Eliza Knight deserve to be similarly acclaimed for this book. I can't believe I'd never heard of this incredible woman, and I loved how the novel shone a well-deserved spotlight on this less famous but exceptionally talented Astaire sibling. Bravo Eliza Knight—and please take a bow. You've written a showstopper of a story."

—Natasha Lester, *New York Times* bestselling author of
The Paris Orphan

"From the stages of Hollywood to the war front, *Starring Adele Astaire* dances with life and emotion, paying homage to a largely overlooked persona in Hollywood's illustrious lineup of characters. Knight's admiration for Adele Astaire—her talent and her passions, onstage and off—shines in this touching and compelling tale of a woman who strives to realize her dreams. A winner!"

—Heather Webb, *USA Today* bestselling author of *Strangers in the Night*

"Impeccably researched and beautifully written, *Starring Adele Astaire* is a peek behind the curtain of what it was like to be a woman and a performer in the 1920s to1940s. Eliza Knight explores the timeless question of whether a woman can truly have it all in this fascinating novel filled with love, heartbreak, resilience, and, ultimately, friendship."

—Jillian Cantor, *USA Today* bestselling author of *Beautiful Little Fools*

"Long before Ginger Rogers came along, Fred Astaire's dance partner was his sister, Adele, who positively dazzles in Eliza Knight's latest work of historical fiction. We follow the spirited Adele from New York to London and beyond as she takes a young dancer under her wing. As their friendship grows, the women learn to juggle fame, love, loss, and the devastation of war. Knight's fan will surely appreciate how she once again seamlessly weaves her research into this rich tale, delivering another winner!"

—Renée Rosen, author of *The Social Graces*

"*Starring Adele Astaire* peels back the layers of Adele Astaire's life beyond the stage while highlighting how ferociously an intrepid dreamer must fight for an edge into the spotlight. Eliza Knight's in-depth research brings these stories to life in exquisite, vibrant detail that will captivate readers everywhere."

—Madeline Martin, *New York Times* and internationally bestselling author of *The Last Bookshop in London*

"Be swept away to London and New York between the wars with *Starring Adele Astaire*, a bittersweet true-life tale of one of the early twentieth century's greatest dancers and most famous siblings. Author Knight has penned a lovely, evocative, and inspiring story about personal choice and sacrifice set during the headiness of the 1920s and the increasingly dark days of the Depression and war ahead. Ambition, family duty, sibling rivalry, classism, ill-fated love, and maternal loss are just some of Adele's struggles when she decides to leave the stage for marriage into one of England's most illustrious titled families. By so deftly and compassionately bringing Adele to life, Knight gives us a most memorable and vital heroine for any age."

—Natalie Jenner, internationally bestselling author of *The Jane Austen Society* and *Bloomsbury Girls*

"*Starring Adele Astaire* tells the riveting tale of an enormously talented performer who steps away from the spotlight into a world of romance, friendship, adventure, and survival. Adele Astaire's remarkable life is center stage in this wonderfully researched, lavishly told novel."

—Denny S. Bryce, bestselling author of *Wild Women and the Blues*

STARRING ADELE ASTAIRE

ALSO BY ELIZA KNIGHT

STARRING ADELE ASTAIRE

A NOVEL

ELIZA KNIGHT

wm

WILLIAM MORROW

An Imprint of HarperCollinsPublishers

HarperCollins books may be purchased for educational, business, or sales promotional use. For information, please email the Special Markets Department at SPsales@harpercollins.com.

FIRST EDITION

Designed by Diahann Sturge
Newspaper background © Here / Shutterstock
Geometric pattern background © BK_graphic / Shutterstock

Library of Congress Cataloging-in-Publication Data has been applied for.

ISBN 978-0-06-320920-6

23 24 25 26 27 LBC 5 4 3 2 1

For every artist who dared to dream, and every woman who dared to buck the status quo. You are our past, our present, and our future.

STARRING ADELE ASTAIRE

PART ONE

HOOFING IT TO FAME

"Heaven doesn't send every generation an Adele Astaire. . . . She's one of God's few women who can be both funny and bewitching . . ."
—ASHTON STEVENS, *CHICAGO HERALD-EXAMINER*

CHAPTER ONE

ADELE

THE LIMELIGHT

London's West End is about to be taken over by American brother-and-sister duo Fred and Adele Astaire. While our friends across the pond seem captivated by the performers, who reportedly enchant their audiences the way a snake charmer hypnotizes his cobra, what our more civilized spectators will think remains to be seen . . .

March 1923
New York City

The colossal steamship *Aquitania* loomed at the pier, its four great red-and-black stacks puffing clouds of grayish-white smoke. My breath mirrored those hazy swirls, and I tucked my fur stole around my neck. The ocean liner was massive, its many decks lined with hundreds of windows and portholes. A floating skyscraper, if there were such a thing.

I wondered, as I stared at the streamlined floating tank—all the layers on top of one another and each stratum representing something different—where did I, mentally, fit in? With the glitz and glam of first class, the hopes and dreams of the passengers in second, or the raw determination of those lost in third? The control and precision of the captain's deck or the chaos of the laborers shoveling coal deep in the bowels? All stacked neatly and looking cohesive from the outside. Perhaps I belonged on the promenade, hurrying around the perimeter until called to enter one of the levels. From my personal attempts to balance ambition with insecurity, glamour with grit, I knew that nothing was ever as perfectly put together as it seemed.

I caught my brother, Freddie, watching me curiously, his hazel eyes a lighter shade than my dark brown. I was taller than he when we were kids, but somehow he'd soared past me, leaving me at a few inches over five feet. My little brother had become my big brother. Our mother, Ann, held his arm, the bow on the side of her green cloche hat fluttering in the wind, a slight smile on her still-young face. Which layer of the ship were they—control, chaos, hope, determination?

"Would you look at that, Delly?" Freddie used my nickname, a play on Adele, then glanced back at the steamship in awe. "Our whole future before us."

Our whole future—success or failure.

Ever since we were kids, we'd boarded trains, traversing America on the vaudeville circuit, and then spent the past six years on Broadway. Neither one of us had ever set foot on a ship. This trip represented a major shift in our show-business careers—a debut on the London stage. A chance to show the world that we were rising stars. After nearly two decades of dancing, singing, and acting together, we were at last bursting onto a scene that we'd been clamoring for, with all the glamour and influence it brought.

Hopes and dreams.

But I couldn't help asking myself—did I want it? I'd been working since I was eight years old. The sacrifices I'd made to get here—friendship, romance, rest from my constant exhaustion, a *life*—how much longer was I willing to put up with days that consisted only of rehearse-perform-sleep, on constant repeat? *I didn't ask for this . . .*

"Everyone keeps calling it the 'Ship Beautiful,' but I don't see it," I teased. "It's a massive hunk of black-and-white metal."

I was nervous as hell about trudging up that gangway and onto a miraculously floating liner that looked heavy enough to sink. I tucked a loose dark tendril beneath my camel cloche hat and prayed our ship didn't run into an iceberg like the *Titanic* had on its maiden voyage eleven years ago. The *Aquitania* had been built to emulate the *Titanic* in luxury and comfort, but at least this vessel was outfitted with enough lifeboats, should we run into similar trouble.

We weren't the first in our family to set sail. Four years before I was born, Pop—now stuck back in Omaha—had made the trip from Austria to Ellis Island, leaving his parents and siblings behind. If he could survive a transatlantic voyage, then I supposed we could, too. After all, we were living his dream a generation later. Making it big onstage, something he'd wanted to do himself.

Determination. Lost.

I think my fear of drowning was now more figurative than literal.

For the first eight years of my life, I was Adele Austerlitz of Omaha. Daughter of Fritz, an immigrant and a Catholic convert of Jewish Austrian descent, and Johanna, a first-generation American Prussian. I was sister to Freddie from the time I was three. Then, suddenly, I was Adele Astaire from New York City. A name that was less Austrian, less controversial. A name for a *star*.

I'd been Adele Astaire for so long, I didn't even know who Adele Austerlitz was anymore, or whom she might have become.

Sometimes I wanted to know. The rest of the time, I brushed it off. After all, the show must go on.

I set aside my nerves, letting my fear be overtaken by excitement about what this trip represented—a grander future. Our parents had sacrificed so much for us, practically everything; maybe even who they were. That reminder brought with it so many feelings: fear of failure; an oppressive sense of obligation. Success was the only option.

"There you are." Alex Aarons, our impresario, approached, a half-smoked cigar between his teeth. His wife was beside him, stylish in her fur-trimmed overcoat. Aarons had arranged for the show and our passage with a producer in London. "This is going to be a hoot."

With our luggage taken by the porters, the five of us clambered up the gangway. Once on deck, I didn't want to go inside. Not yet. I looked back at the pier. At New York City. The way my father had seen it when he first arrived. The view of the city of dreams. How I used to think New York embodied mine. Now I wasn't so sure.

I leaned my elbows against the rail, waiting for the ship to move, the coolness of the metal bar penetrating my coat.

"What are you doing?" Freddie paused beside me.

"Let's give them a goodbye that makes them eager to have us back," I said. The fame we'd garnered in the past few years of our acting circuit made us easily recognizable in a crowd. Part of me feared that leaving to tackle the world at the height of our success would mean starting over when we returned—working even harder. It had happened before, and I didn't think I had it in me to even try.

"All right." Freddie shrugged as if it were nothing.

I smiled, glad he was being a good sport rather than the killjoy he sometimes could be. We'd tried to stay inconspicuous dockside, not drawing the attention of the reporters, but, with a barrier between us and them, I grabbed Freddie's hand and we waved to the crowd. The cries of excitement in response seemed to melt any last hesitation on Freddie's part. He doffed his cap, waving it. The cold wind off the bay blew the ends of my hair around my face, threatening to dislodge the hairpins from my hat.

Cries of goodbye rose from the crowd on the pier—all come to bid farewell to their loved ones. *Maybe*, just *maybe*, a few had come in hopes of seeing us off, too.

"Delly, let's go inside. You're going to catch your death," Mom chided.

And where would you and Freddie be then?

When, on the cusp of womanhood, our act had been pulled from vaudeville for two years until Freddie could catch up—I realized that I was the center of everything. Or at least they wanted me to be. But why should Freddie's career depend on me? Perhaps without me he would soar. It was hard for him to shine standing in my shadow.

"Soon, but not yet." I blew the loose hair from my face and shivered, waving even more vigorously to those gathered below until the chill persuaded me to call an end to my antics. After all, Mom was right, and I couldn't imagine being ill the rest of the trip. If I thought her domineering now, it would be ten times worse if I was confined to bed. I lowered my hand.

As I was about to turn from the railing, my attention was caught by a man on the pier, scribbling away in a notebook and taking photographs. I recognized him as a newspaperman who followed me around like a pet lamb. I think he had a crush. He wrote pretty things about me, describing the way I danced as "a lilac flame," and all that. He glanced up at me now, waving, so I indulged his admiration by blowing a kiss.

"Don't do that, Delly," Freddie's voice rumbled, a near growl. "That man needs no more encouragement." He sure did hate Mr. Nathan, and anyone taking my attention away from our goal—stardom.

I cocked my shoulder and let out an impish laugh. "You're just mad because he said he only liked to watch dancers who didn't wear pants."

Freddie rolled his eyes. "Yeah, and likely he'd be happier if you weren't wearing a skirt, either."

I pretended to be shocked and outraged, poking Freddie in the chest, but the truth was my brother made me laugh harder than anyone else could.

"You're right. I'm sure that reporter, and every other man looking, would prefer I was a tart." I liked to flirt—and dance and blow a kiss or two—but I'd been reluctant to settle into anything more significant, not wanting to interfere with my obligations to the stage and to my family. My gaze wandered past the reporter to a woman nestled in a man's embrace. They were lost in each other's gaze, lips parted in a joy I couldn't even fathom. My chest twinged with a sense of loss for something I'd never had. What would adoration from someone with whom you were equally enamored feel like? Sadness nipped at my thoughts, and I pushed my attention back to my brother.

Freddie grunted disapprovingly. "Keep blowing kisses and he'll have you written up as one."

I laughed, though my heart wasn't in it. Shoving aside my melancholy, I reverted to what I knew best—teasing, good ol' Delly, always good for a laugh—winking at Mom, who was shaking her head at us, much as she did when we were younger. As often as she tsk-tsked and bossed us about, Mom was our chief supporter. She'd given up her life for us, moving from Omaha to New York City when we were kids so that we could enroll in dance school and make something of ourselves. Pop had remained behind to work and support us financially. Sometimes I wondered who wanted our success more.

From the time I was eight, Mom, Freddie, and I were an inseparable threesome. For this big trip, I'd feared our trio would be down to a duo, because our new producer in London initially refused to pay for Mom's passage. But there'd also been a modest twinge of hope for that sort of freedom. However, she and Freddie made a stink about my needing a chaperone. In the end, the producer relented. Despite my hopes for breathing room, I couldn't imagine leaving Mom behind. Our big break on British shores was as much a culmination of her hard work as it was ours—seemed only fair that she get to witness it.

Cozied up together, the three of us waved at those on the pier until the gangway was pulled up and the ship's horn blasted, vibrating in our ears and limbs.

"A dance, Freddie, for our admirers." I gave him the puppy eyes that always made him agreeable. Freddie hated doing any sort of exhibition without a million hours of practice. It was a large ask, but I made it all the same.

He stared at me, his indecision almost palpable.

"Please? A treat for our fans to remember us by until we're back?" I said.

Freddie sighed in resignation.

"Don't go breaking an ankle here," Alex warned, his gaze stern. The man was out to protect his investment.

"Oh, Alex, we're unbreakable." Freddie grabbed my hand and gave me a twirl.

We swiveled into a shortened version of our favorite dance from

"The Bust and Judy," a.k.a. *The Bunch and Judy*. If the whole show had consisted of numbers like this one, we'd have sold out every night. We tapped our feet to catch the beat, and then swayed in rhythm to a song only we could hear. *One-and-two-and-three-and-four*, we faced our audience dancing side by side. *Step, step-heel, and step. Step, step, step-heel, and step. Shuffle-step, stomp, pivot, step-heel, and heel-step.* Then we faced each other for a waltz before breaking into jazz swings.

Dancing came as easily to us as walking, and we grinned at each other with glee. Our finale was a comical exaggerated walk, ending with a pair of step-kicks. Alex put two fingers in his mouth and whistled.

"Ta-da!" I laughed, wiggling my fingers. "More of that in London, folks."

We posed for the cameras: my arm around Freddie's shoulder, his arm around my waist, and our right legs flexed midair. The gathered crowds on the pier and the ship clapped. Despite so many years of performing, the sound of applause never grew old. It still made my heart skitter across my ribs.

The steamship lurched away from the pier, the space of water between us and land slowly increasing. Our adventure was finally beginning.

When New York was a speck on the horizon, we went inside to explore. Ushering us over a black-and-white-tiled floor with a long bright-blue runner, our porter took us up a wide circular staircase under a massive oval glass dome ornamented with leaded lunettes that allowed the sun to light our path.

OUR ROOMS ON the first-class deck were adjoining—Freddie in his own, Mom and I sharing. The white walls were decorated with intricate wood trim and reproductions of paintings I'd seen hung in museums. If I hadn't felt the ship moving gently beneath the plush blue carpet, I would have thought we were back at the Plaza Hotel. A pair of polished wood bedsteads covered in silky cornflower-blue duvets greeted us. A small mahogany table was flanked by two chairs, and a marble sink was topped with a shiny mirror. Palm-leaf-shaped white porcelain sconces adorned the wall. Square windows lined the back wall, giving us a full view of the ocean.

"It's warm in here." I was surprised by the comfort of the cabin. I was always cold, and heating was important to me. I took off my fur stole and my coat, hanging them in the wardrobe. I fixed my dark hair in the mirror, pinning one of the curls back that had come loose. My cheeks were tinged pink from outside, but my red lipstick was still perfectly bright. "I think I'm going to like steamship travel. Do you think they'll let us have a glass of champagne?"

It'd been three years since Prohibition began, and we couldn't legally purchase alcohol in the States. But did the ocean count?

"I hope so," Mom said.

Once settled, we made our way to the Louis XVI restaurant, where we met Alex and his wife. The five of us were seated at a table in the center of the dining room. Marble balustrades supported a balcony that hovered over the tables, and the ceiling was a work of art: scrolls and designs that made me think of photographs I'd seen of the Palace of Versailles. The color scheme was wine-red and soft yellow, with a plush plum-colored trellis carpet over an oak floor. Through large Georgian windows, I spotted guests lounging in a garden room.

"Champagne all around," Alex announced. "Time for a toast."

Crystal and cutlery clinked against fine china. I'd never felt so spoiled in my life. We'd been living at the Plaza, but Freddie kept a tight fist on our budget. The main expenses I incurred were my daily stocking purchase and sometimes weekly shoes, necessary because I wore them out so quickly when performing.

Champagne in crystal coupes was passed round. Alex raised his glass high. "To the stars of the newly minted *Stop Flirting*. You guys are going to knock 'em dead."

"I hope we keep some of them alive; what good is a musical comedy without the laughter of live bodies?" I teased.

Alex and his wife laughed freely, but Mom's chuckle was weak, and Freddie's nervous. We clinked glasses, and then I took a sip of the effervescent bubbly. It tickled my nose and the back of my throat in the most delicious way. I wasn't much of a drinker, but champagne was more than a drink; it was an experience. One I could get used to.

"To resounding success." Mom's words, though said with a smile, sent my heart skipping a beat, and Freddie stiffened beside me. The pressure weighing on us was immense, and constantly growing.

We ordered oysters on the half shell, followed, in my case, by Surrey Chicken, which tasted as if it could have been made at the Ritz.

As we finished our meal with bowls of plum pudding in brandy sauce, an older gentleman approached, his dark ship's uniform covered in brass buttons and rows of insignia pins. He carried his cap under his arm, revealing the silver of his thinning hair.

"Good evening, ladies and gentlemen. I wanted to extend my personal welcome to the *Aquitania*." The captain's British accent was thick and an enjoyable reminder of where we were headed.

"It's a pleasure to meet you, Captain," I said.

"You are our honored guests. And, if I may, we've a request of you."

I had a hunch it was a performance request. If we whetted the appetites of the London-bound passengers, maybe they'd come see our show. On the other hand, I worried that the captain's invitation would make Freddie anxious, and that we'd spend the entire time on board practicing rather than enjoying ourselves. I'd been looking forward to a period of rest.

"There's a charity event for the Seamen's Fund after dinner tomorrow," the captain continued. "We'd be honored if you would perform a dance for the event."

"The pleasure and honor will be all ours," Freddie said.

Tomorrow. I kept my grin to myself. The timing meant Freddie wouldn't force me to get up at dawn to practice for days on end. The last time I'd had a break—a real break from daily dancing—was in 1909, when the Gerrymen pulled us off our show, declaring that child actors were exploited, comparing us to youngsters in sweatshops. I won't lie and say it didn't feel like that sometimes.

"I worry about the tilting of the floor." Freddie frowned. "And where we'd practice."

"Not to worry, Mr. Astaire, we've a gymnasium at your disposal."

"Don't worry about the floor, Freddie," I said. "Nothing can be tipsier than that stage in Nebraska."

He chortled, remembering how we'd had to redo all our footwork, purely so we didn't fall off. "What do you say, Delly? Shall we dance?"

"Yes." Was there any other answer?

"We'll need to meet with the orchestra, to arrange music," Freddie said.

"I can take care of that," Alex offered.

Captain Charles bowed slightly and moved off to greet other guests.

"I think this calls for another round of champagne," I said. "We're about to make our international-waters debut."

"I think you've had quite enough." Mom plucked my glass from my hand and set it by hers, as if I were six years old rather than twenty-six.

For a brief moment, I regretted the lack of freedom that came with this life.

THE FOLLOWING EVENING, outside the dining room, I paused, taking a deep breath. Freddie wore a warm beige linen suit, and, as always, looked made for the stage, never nervous. I, on the other hand, needed a moment to center myself before every performance. We were opposites that way.

During rehearsals was when Freddie's nerves got the better of him. He'd insist on practicing, "perfecting" choreography, to the point of driving everyone mad. While he fretted over footwork, I danced, sang, and teased the rest of our crew, with no audience to worry about. Showtime was when I grew anxious. Never wanting to disappoint. But I never let my jitters show. My nerves were a secret solely for me.

I glanced at my reflection in the mirrored dining-room doors. My dark hair was in a finger wave, my long tresses curled under, giving the effect of a bob. I had on a lavender crepe dress with a pleated skirt, adorned with a large flower at one hip on the low waistline. To complete the look, a string of pearls was twisted in a knot between my breasts.

I smiled broadly and nodded at Freddie to open the door.

"Ah, the evening's guests of honor: Fred Astaire and his sister, Adele," the captain announced to at least two hundred guests, who sat or stood around the perimeter of the room.

We walked to the center of the oak floor to the sound of applause.

Rather than doing one of the numbers from our upcoming show, we decided to keep it simple—a Viennese waltz with a few jazz moves tossed in. The orchestra started, and Freddie held out his hand. I placed mine in his, laid my other hand on his shoulder, and we began to move into the natural turn. This was one of my favorite dances, and Freddie was a superb partner. We flowed like the waves of the ocean, in perfect harmony. Something about the waltz made me feel free, and alive, as if I were floating. We moved into our first fleckerl spin, followed by a contra check—then things got interesting.

The ocean chose this shining moment of ours to turn choppy. We did an extra step to catch our balance as the vessel lurched to the left.

"Oh, dear." I made a face at Freddie.

His eyes widened, and he held on tighter.

I suppressed a laugh, pinching my lips closed as he twirled me. I spun away three steps, leaving room for each of us to do a jazz shuffle.

The ship listed enough that I wobbled on my feet, and I started to slide backward, with Freddie chasing me, trying to gain his balance as he reached for my hand. The audience gasped, but the orchestra kept playing.

"We should stop," he whispered as he pulled me close. His eyes flicked toward the audience. All his worries about being taken seriously in London were bouncing around in his brain.

"Too late now," I murmured. "Let's have fun with it." We continued the waltz, the ship steady for a few moments.

Gaining a foothold, Freddie spun me out again. His jaw tightened, and I could tell he was struggling with whether to end the dance. Well, I *was* going to have fun with it. We were here to entertain. We weren't performing a tragedy in London, but a musical comedy. I was prepared to give our audience what they wanted.

When the ship tilted in the opposite direction, I purposely dropped onto my knees, sliding fifteen feet across the dance floor.

Horror written on his face, Freddie ran after me. I had my arms outstretched, reaching for him, and the closer he got the farther I slid, until the ship rocked and rolled in the other direction, and now I was the one in pursuit.

Freddie looked appalled, but all I could do was laugh. As soon as he saw that, he said, "We're going to make this a farce, aren't we?"

"You betcha." I wiggled my brows with glee. From that moment on, we made all our movements extremely exaggerated: rolling with the ship; sliding around; even making a play of almost falling into several audience members' laps, one of us catching the other at the last minute. With every lurch of the ship, the audience called out "Oohhhhh!" or "Ahhhhh!" laughing right along with us to see what we'd do next. Encouraged by their reaction, we did the foxtrot, and even the Charleston—the risqué jazz dance. This was what we were good at, he and I. Dancing and being silly, exciting a crowd.

When at the end we collapsed onto the ground in exaggerated bows, the applause was deafening.

Freddie helped me up and we bowed again to the audience's cries of "'Core! 'Core!" for "encore," but we merely laughed and hurried off the floor for the next act.

Alex Aarons shouted to the crowd, "More performances in England! Look for *Stop Flirting*!"

"I'll be sure to attend with a large party," said one gentleman, shaking Freddie's hand. "Jolly good show. You'll be a hit."

"Thank you." Freddie gave a slight bow. I just smiled, content to let my brother do the talking for me.

"Can you teach me how to dance?" A woman gazed up at him, hand held to her bejeweled neck as she blinked rapidly, all doe-eyed.

I elbowed my brother in the ribs. "I'll leave you to it."

"Don't you dare, Delly," he warned out of the side of his mouth.

But I knew he loved the attention and was often jealous when it was directed at me.

With Freddie surrounded by a gaggle of females, I made my way over to our mother, chuckling as I went.

"You shouldn't have left him," Mom reproached me, handing me a glass of water.

Her censure sucked all the fun out of me. I clutched a chair when the ship went wonky, and watched Freddie catch three women against his chest. Other men caught women in their arms, cheeks flush with romance. And I'd never felt more alone, with only the chair and Mom for comfort. "Oh, Mom, he's in heaven right now."

"You must be as well. All that applause."

"I'm having the time of my life." I drained the water glass, mostly to avoid looking my mother in the eye, because it was a lie. On top of my sudden surge of loneliness, my knees ached, not merely from falling but with a constant, bone-deep throb that had started a few years back and never seemed to ebb. I feared that at some point my body was just going to give out on me, leaving me in a pained heap on the stage floor.

"The two of you really are hams." There was a faint hint of a frown on Mom's face, as she refilled my glass, her expression at odds with her words.

It was hard to tell if Mom was frowning at me, at this moment, or at some distant memory. But there was no point in asking. She was closemouthed about her feelings; doubtless why I overcompensated for mine with a ready answer for everyone. "You must've been a bit of a ham yourself to have raised two limelight-lovers."

"Mercifully not." She touched the side of her light hair. "You're both quite special. Your father always said his children would be stars. I wish he could see the two of you in London."

I nodded, sadness welling in my chest. Hearing the way she said *his children*, as if distancing herself from her motherly role, or per-haps that of wife. Pop had seen so few of our shows that I could count them on one hand. But he loved to get copies of the play-bills. Bragged to everyone that his kids were stars. Where Ann Astaire was all seriousness, Pop was all smiles.

When I was younger, I'd been jealous of other kids who had a whole family. Both parents, same dinner table—or even same city. For Freddie and me, Mom filled every role: mother, father, teacher, and manager. Pop was a figure we wrote to, excitedly shar-ing news. Wanting the approval and love of an abstract and absent parent. For all intents and purposes, we had it. But love was not quite the same when it wasn't there in person.

"What's wrong?" Mom said.

I must have let my face fall.

Quickly I flashed a smile, tucking my worries away and pulling Mom's Delly back to the surface. "I'm a bit queasy from the ship tossing, that's all."

But it wasn't all. My mind liked to pluck at my nerves at times like this with a question that had no answer. *Who is Delly really?*

Delly is a show girl, an actress, a comedian. A dancer who whirls like a lilac flame. Onstage I was whoever the audience de-sired. Offstage I was not much different—I was who *they* wanted me to be. Whoever *they* were at the moment. A daughter, a sister, a contract.

When I'm alone, I'm at a loss. What was a puppet without its master? Nothing but a heap of string and painted wood. But I wanted to be more. I wanted to be whole. I wanted to be loved. So, alone, I grasped at the curtains in my mind, teasing them open, hoping to reveal just who Delly was by herself—who I was and if I was happy with that. But I never seemed to be alone long enough to come to any satisfactory conclusion . . .

WHEN SOUTHAMPTON, ENGLAND, came into view, we stood on the gallery deck as the *Aquitania* closed the distance. Like the New York pier, this one was a flurry of families waiting for passengers to arrive, and porters ready to cart bags. The ship's horns pulsed through me, compounding the excitement and angst of exploring London for the first time. To see if this voyage would finally reveal who and what Delly should be.

A bubbling blonde reached the bottom of the gangplank in front of us and leapt into the arms of a uniformed gent, who swung her around. He bent to kiss her, both of them oblivious to their surroundings. Completely besotted with each other. A twinge of envy threatened my excitement but was quickly forgotten as Mom took my arm and steered me past.

Alex Aarons arranged transit for our bags and then bustled us off to the train station. Seated on the London train, I took in my fellow passengers with interest, enjoying the lilt of their various accents. I'd thought New York fashion was posh, but England seemed a step above. The women around me had fabulous hats and shoes. I looked for the couple I'd seen on the gangplank, and my eyes instead found a dozen other twosomes contentedly holding hands and chatting, or sighing and staring into each other's eyes.

I closed my eyes, shutting them out. Just as I was nodding off, the whistle blew, jolting me back awake. I gripped the side of my seat as the train came to a hard stop, dumping me onto the floor, my handbag falling from the overhead rack onto my head.

"Oh, my goodness, Adele!" Mother cried, lips puckering.

Freddie was quick to lift me up. "You all right?" Brows pinched, he examined me for signs of injury.

I laughed. "Of course. Only a smidge embarrassed." I straightened my skirt and then tried to right my hat, which seemed to have been flattened by the handbag. Outside the window, a sign said WELCOME TO LONDON. "I guess we can say we came into London with a bang."

That made everyone in our group hoot, and took their attention off me—except for Mom, who was still looking at me as if I'd sprouted horns. "Do be more careful. We can't afford for you to hurt yourself before the show even begins."

But it's all right afterward? I wanted to retort, but I bit my tongue and simply nodded, mumbling a vacant reply. Being stuck in close quarters with Mom on the ship had been a challenge. I knew she meant well, but sometimes she forgot that I was a grown woman. She managed everything, down to the last wave of my hair and the color of my stockings.

The taxi ride from Waterloo Station was, thankfully, less eventful. Our driver wove in and out of heavy traffic, everything from automobiles to buggies. The occasional pedestrian darting into the street earned a long horn blow and a shaken fist. I stared at the buildings, which all seemed shorter than in New York City, but significantly prettier. Older. More elegant. I had the strangest and grandest sensation—as if I were coming home. London was a breath of fresh—foggy—air and filled me with renewed energy.

What would happen if, when *Stop Flirting* ended, I stayed here instead of returning to New York?

The sky was hazy, though whether that haze was clouds or smoke, I couldn't tell. This "London fog" and crossing over the Thames reminded me of a nursery rhyme—"London Bridge Is Falling Down"—that suddenly switched on in my head. I tapped my foot, humming a few lines and watching fishing boats pass under us.

A few minutes later, our taxi pulled up to the Savoy, and we clambered out. Freddie yanked Mom back before she could be trampled by a pair of grays pulling a brewery truck.

"Pardon us!" I called, and one of the horses snorted back. "Do you think the horses have accents, too?"

Freddie gave a mocking shake of his head. "You're too much."

"I sure hope so. Better to be too much than not enough, Moaning Minnie." I brought out the childhood nickname I'd given Freddie for constantly worrying over everything. Despite my joshing him, I was glad for his caution and planning, because it meant I didn't have to worry.

"Whatever you say, Good-Time Charlie," Freddie replied with a roll of his eyes. He took Mom's arm, the two of them marching in front of me into the marble-filled lobby—black-and-white-tiled floors, columns.

Even the stairs looked to be marble on either side of the lush burgundy carpet running up their center. Furnishings of gilded wood and plush velvet held the rears of glamorous guests dressed to impress in their London finery. Potted palms and massive colorful floral arrangements softened the starkness of all the stone. It smelled divine, like expensive perfume—decidedly different from the street, which held a note of something sour, like exhaust and horse shit, not unlike New York, really.

A liveried groom greeted us with glasses of champagne. What a pleasant change: Nobody treated a cocktail as if it were the Devil.

I took a small sip and spun in a circle, looking up at the ornate ceiling. I could get used to this. I could be one of those shimmering Londoners, spritzed with French perfume and talking about important things.

A man in a smart suit approached us. "Ah, you must be the Astaires. Welcome to the Savoy. Allow me to show you to the Riverside Suite, which has been reserved for you."

"Rest up," Alex Aarons said as we headed into the elevator.

"Tomorrow we meet Sir Alfred Butt, your producer, and see a show. Then rehearsals start."

While rehearsals always seemed to exhilarate Freddie, they made me shudder.

"Last morning to sleep in," Freddie baited me, the pitch of his voice eager for a row.

"Wake me up with a wet towel again and I will end you." I pointed my finger at him and narrowed my eyes, recalling vividly that cold, soaked cloth slapping against my cheek.

Freddie only chuckled. We'd see who was laughing when I hid his dancing shoes. Now, that made me smile.

CHAPTER TWO

VIOLET

THE LIMELIGHT

Spotted at the Shaftesbury Theatre this week, Fred and Adele Astaire, along with a never-ending line of performers hoping to eke out a spot in the much-anticipated London debut of *Stop Flirting*. Mimi Crawford, Jack Melford, Marjorie Gordon, Henry Kendall, and a host of other major British stage celebrities are cinching on their dancing shoes. Also spied glaring at each other was none other than the feuding background pair, Bridgette Hughes and Maya Chopra. With those two the drama never stops at the stage . . .

1923
Shaftesbury Theatre, London

Violet Wood pressed a handkerchief to the back of her neck and then beneath her armpits. This was the most nerve-racking day of her life. An opportunity she'd not only visualized, but bled for.

The path to becoming a star.

She wanted to be a dancer so badly she could taste it. Arriving at this moment had involved broken toes, sprained ankles, and bruised knees.

"Get out there, Vi. Show them what you're made of." Drenched in sweat, she appraised herself in the grimy mirror. Her dark hair, neatly tucked into a bun, was too long for the current fashion. But, if she cut her hair into a bob, her mum, who already thought she was courting trouble, would throw a fit.

Violet smoothed a fresh swipe of red onto her lips, because her teeth had already worried through her first layer of lipstick. Having waited for an hour already, she felt like vomiting or fainting every other moment. They were taking the dancers in clusters, and her group had yet to be called.

All her life, Violet had been told she was reaching far beyond—beyond her station, her talent, her upbringing, her meager funds. It didn't matter what she strove for; she was constantly made to feel that whatever "it" happened to be was unattainable.

Bleedin' wankers. She'd have none of their defeatism. Every morning she woke with hope bubbling so close to the surface of her skin that she could feel it undulating beneath her flesh. Today that hope would pay off.

"This'll have to do." She practiced a few smiles and murmured, "How do you do? I'm Violet." The harshness of her unrefined inflection cut through the cultured quality she tried to affect.

Elocution lessons had been minimal on account of time, and lack of "bees and honey"—money was everything, and she'd barely a bob to buy tea. She'd managed exactly one session, in exchange for a house cleaning. Now she studied the hoity-toity talk of the nobs who came to watch the shows instead. Her confidence sagged.

What if she didn't get this chorus spot but lost her job because Mr. Cowden saw her out of her work attire and spinning onstage?

Her shift at the theatre bar, catering to the box seats of the toffs, didn't start for a couple of hours, but that didn't mean he wouldn't see her.

Don't give up.

The door to the bathroom whooshed open, revealing a petite woman, dark hair coifed in a style all the rage, whose eyes met Violet's in the mirror. "Love that shade on you. Divine."

American. One of the performers for the show? Violet glanced at the woman's T-strap dancing shoes. A green silk dress draped her petite frame, the large bow and sash slung low on her hips, looking marvelous. Her friendly smile held a hint of mischief. Violet liked her immediately.

"Thanks." Violet tucked her lipstick back into the heavy, ratty satchel on her shoulder that contained her waitressing uniform. "I'd best go before my number is called."

"Auditioning?" The woman pulled out her own lipstick, the same shade as Violet's.

"Yes." Her tongue was too twisted to say more.

"Break a leg . . ." The American paused, waiting for Violet to give her name, but she was so nervous that she bustled out of the bathroom without taking the cue.

Then it hit her, and she poked her head back in. "I'm Violet."

Once she rejoined the dancers waiting to audition, Violet realized she'd forgotten to ask the woman's name. The latest dancers onstage were finishing the song that had been on repeat all morning. Violet was happy about having a later spot. Watching the prior groups, she'd memorized the choreography and picked up what captured the attention of the producers.

Violet wiped her sweaty palms down the flowing skirt of her black silk dancing ensemble. Two more groups needed to dance, and the theatre opened in a couple of hours for a performance of *The Cat and the Canary*. They needed to pick up the pace.

Until today, she'd never had the guts to audition. But once she'd heard about auditions for the upcoming American play held at the theatre where she worked . . . it felt like a sign. Violet doubled her practice hours. This was her shot. Maybe she didn't have the talent, but how would she know without trying? Her mum rolled her eyes at the idea of Violet being a professional dancer. Even Madame Meunier, who owned a dance studio that Violet passed daily, scolded her after catching her peering through the window and copying the movements on the street.

Succeed or fail today, it was worth taking a shot, even if it was a long one. At eighteen, Violet knew what awaited her if she failed. She'd end up like her mum. Working her fingers to the bone, living in the East End with barely a bob to her name.

Even when her father had been alive, they'd been poor. He'd died near the tail end of the Great War when she was thirteen, not before getting Mum pregnant again. Violet counted herself lucky to have the job at the theatre. She had never been happier to get out of the laundry service Mum ran out of their small flat. Mum thought Violet toffee-nosed for getting dressed in a uniform and serving cocktails. But the money she made helped Mum care for Violet's younger sister, Pris.

The last note sounded, and the dancers cleared the floor. The producer stood, list in hand, and read off the next round, names running together in Violet's mind—until she heard her own.

Dancers rushed forward, and Violet did, too, trying, despite her excitement, to walk gracefully up the stairs and toward the center of the stage. Lost somewhere in the middle of the group, she cursed herself for not moving faster and snagging a place in the front row, or at least one more visible to the producers. All around her, dancers waited with bated breath for direction. Fingers fidgeting. Feet tapping.

The lights were brighter than she was used to. But Violet knew the stage by heart from the few mornings when she'd snuck into the theatre to practice before it opened. With everyone crowding around her, the stage felt warmer, too. Sweat trickled down her spine and pooled beneath her arms.

"On three," the producer called.

Violet immediately moved into first position, but before she could count to three the accompanist stabbed his fingers into the piano keys and the bodies all around shifted in a mass of choreographed movements.

You know this. Steady.

Violet tapped her feet. *Five, six, seven, eight. One, two, three, four . . .*

Some of the dancers seemed not as practiced as she, more jiggling than swaying to the tune. She tried to ignore their uncoordinated and out-of-step movements.

Arms outstretched, fingers slightly curled as she'd seen other dancers do, she spun; left kick, right kick. Shuffle, shuffle. Tap left, tap right. Arms wide, head dipped, slide.

On they went, moving increasingly quickly as the pianist upped the tempo. The music swept through her, an arpeggio from head to foot, the scales sliding up and down the keys, encouraging her to let herself be one with the refrains.

Auditioners bumped her, knocking her off balance from the back and the left. Violet held form, praying that those watching, judging, noticed that she wasn't making mistakes.

On her application she'd admitted she wasn't formally trained. Probably why she'd been added so far down on the list, and why she'd been lumped in with a bunch of wiggling, no-rhythm bodies.

I am better than this.

Jostled again, Violet made her move: shifting forward on a

graceful turn into an open space nearer to the front, picking up the moves where she'd left off. No one bumped her this time. She showed off the skills she'd perfected over endless hours for years.

Sweat dripped into Violet's eyes as they moved into the next number. Five routines total. With each her confidence increased. She was certain she outshined them all—hitting every step, keeping up with the vigorous, endlessly changing pace, shifting from ballet to tap to jazz to ballroom. When it was required, she easily swung into the arms of a partner at the front. He was as sweaty as she. He didn't spare a smile, but he didn't make a mistake, or tread on her toes—and that was what really mattered.

When the music ended, Violet bowed to the judges. They weren't looking at her—or at anyone—just conferring among themselves. A woman caught Violet's eye—the one she'd seen in the bathroom. She sat beside another woman, who looked slightly older, and a young man. They were chatting with one another, but her bathroom companion smiled up at Violet in recognition.

"That'll be all." The producer stood and waved them offstage.

Violet's smile faltered. That was it? Was it time to change and leave, or would there be another round for those who showed promise?

"Excuse me, sir?" She hoped to catch the attention of the producers. But they studiously ignored her. The woman, however—how Violet wished she knew her name!—looked in her direction, and cocked her head, studying Violet.

Heat flamed in Violet's already sweaty cheeks. She was embarrassing herself standing there waiting, being ignored while the other dancers shoved past. She bent to a pile of discarded handbags and satchels on the floor and picked hers up, then joined the others who'd auditioned and were walking away.

"When do you think they'll tell us?" She worked to keep the unrefined tones from her voice.

A tall, razor-thin dancer with severe cheekbones, her blond hair in a sharp bob, looked down her nose at Violet. "They just did, darling. It's either 'Yes' or 'That'll be all.'" The prickly blonde grinned with an unjust hint of malice.

Cut. *Already*.

Tears stung Violet's eyes and she blinked to hide her disappointment. She'd been so sure today would be the day that changed her fate. The first step toward her goal of becoming a star. Violet nodded, trying to smile, though her lips trembled a fraction.

Violet retreated quickly to the ladies' room, eager to be gone. But she waited in line nearly a quarter hour for a stall before giving up, moving into a corner, and starting to strip.

She didn't care if that offended anybody's sensibilities—passed over for the chorus, the last thing she needed was to be fired, too. Smiling and serving cocktails seemed to be her destiny, as miserable as it sounded.

Violet's dress was damp and the zipper hard to reach, but she managed, slipping out of it and folding it neatly back into her bag. She removed the dancing shoes, which pinched, being at least a size too small—but beggars couldn't be choosers, could they?

Violet washed her face in the sink, refreshed her lipstick, and slipped out, ignoring those who stared at her working-girl uniform. Must be nice to change into regular clothes, not to have to scramble, scrimp, and save for the most meager things.

By the time she reached the bar, she was on the brink of tears, but she bottled them at the sight of several patrons. The doors must have been opened early, of all the bleedin'—

"Wood!" Mr. Cowden barked her surname. "You're late."

Violet lifted her chin. "I'm an hour early."

He frowned. "Your pal is late, then. See to the customers."

The other cocktail waitress was always late, but she got away with it, because Mr. Cowden liked her a little too much.

Violet stashed her bag in the small storage room behind the bar, then plastered on a joyful, if entirely false, smile.

Theatre attendees liked cocktails before, during, and after a show. Violet made sure they got what they wanted. Even though she brought home a decent wage, her mother continued to hound her for trying to rise above her station with "fanciful notions of being a star."

She'd failed so far; maybe her mum was right. Maybe she should just give up.

Violet's heart sank even as she distributed cocktails, offering up witty quips, winks, and grins. When a few of the men got too friendly, she ignored it. Although sometimes the busboy would come out and bump the man on purpose but feign his most sincere apology for the "accident."

She regarded a leering, gray-haired man in a tux. The thought of the posh, drooling man jostled . . . it was the pick-me-up she needed.

Violet suspected that the busboy *liked* her, but she was too busy to be liked. She spent more time practicing choreography than being a friend to anyone.

As she moved to the next table the busboy gave her a smile as he mopped a spilled drink off the floor. He was a year older than Violet, his dark hair always a mess, flopping over his eyes. She wanted to bring in a pair of shears and chop it off. He whipped his head, moving the hair back into place as he scrubbed, gray eyes finding her.

Violet grinned, but then her smile faltered. A group of the dancers who'd auditioned walked past, eyeing her with recognition. The sharp-bobbed blonde was at their center and shot Violet a smirk that could have peeled paint.

Violet wished she could present the blonde with the gesture she'd seen the busboy give a rude customer's back. But she didn't want to get canned, so she gave the witch a friendly smile, then turned before she reacted. Best to send a message now that she wasn't going to be bullied. But Violet needed to avoid antagonizing the woman, because she'd obviously gotten a part in the production and would be around the theatre awhile longer.

"Why would you wan' 'o be like 'em?" The busboy's thick Cockney accent at her side surprised her.

Violet frowned. "I *don't* want to be like them."

"You wan' 'o be a dancer."

"Being a dancer doesn't mean you have to be an arsehole." Violet rolled her eyes and headed to collect another round of cocktails for the private theatre boxes.

He grinned, hurrying to keep pace with her. "I don' think dancers say things like *arse 'ole*."

She cocked a shoulder and gamboled into a two-step tap. "Like I said, I don't want to be like them. I just want to dance." *To be a star* . . .

CHAPTER THREE

ADELE

THE LIMELIGHT

Though we've yet to see them perform onstage on this side of the pond, it seems no talent is required for our two American stars to take center stage. Seen dancing at nearly every exclusive club in the city, we're not surprised at America's sweetheart gaining the title "Good-Time Charlie." We're afraid to know what they call her brother . . . Let's hope these shuffle-stepping stars get a good night's sleep before they debut. After all, we're fairly salivating to see what this "runaround" business is all about!

After a brief flirt with London and a few shows, such as *Battling Butler*, starring Jack Buchanan, Freddie got his way—the fun stopped and we strapped on our dancing shoes. Waking before the sun, we danced until my toes cried for relief and my bones ached. Then I changed from my torn silk stockings into a new pair, and we danced some more.

It'd been several weeks of nonstop practice, eat, sleep, and repeat. I felt like a marionette on a string and the only way to break loose would be to convince someone to sneak a giant pair of shears onstage and hack at the bindings. No such cuts were forthcoming. If anything, the trusses grew tighter the closer we got to our preview performance tour. I stopped wearing drawers just to make my bathroom breaks quicker. Boy, did that bring a bit of scandal as I raced after my brother one night and a gust of wind blew. "We'd better take a taxi, or all of the West End is getting a good look at the ace of spades, Freddie!" I'd called after him.

We didn't walk back to our hotel again after that. Despite Mom's insistence, I rather liked the free flow of going without covering the naughty bits. Or maybe, with so much of my life decided for me, I relished taking control where I could. Small victories.

"I want to go over the 'Stairway to Paradise' number when we get back to the hotel." Freddie refined his steps after a long day of rehearsal every night.

But I wanted to truly enjoy and experience this wonderful city. We might never get this opportunity again. I couldn't let a chance to visit London clubs pass me by.

"By all means. I won't stop you." I had plans of my own that involved a night out with Mimi Crawford, another actress in the play. Mimi promised I'd see a few aristocrats, and, being from New York, we didn't have a lot of those around. Not unless one considered the Vanderbilts and all the other stuffy surnames.

"Ciro's tonight," Mimi declared, flicking her gaze toward Freddie, who'd busied himself instructing a chorus dancer. Mimi's light hair was curled around her ears, and she smiled, an air of mischief in her blue eyes. "They have a great band, and we can dance all night."

Mimi had the most audacious friends. They called themselves the Bright Young Things, spending their nights dancing, drinking champagne, and running amok in London. Pleasure seekers, all of them. It was intoxicating. After years of stringent schedules and early morning rehearsals and the laws of Prohibition in the United States that made everything feel taboo, London brought a sense of freedom, even with Mom's strict midnight curfew. For the first time, I'd decided I would sneak out if she didn't give me permission—sad, considering I was twenty-six years old.

It wasn't that I wasn't willing to put in the hard work—but I wanted to live, too. Couldn't I do both?

"Freddie will join us." I grinned in my brother's direction, waiting for him to realize that I'd hauled him into our plans.

"Good. I'll meet you in the lobby of your hotel. My friend will drive." Mimi slunk away.

Hiding my glee, I collapsed onto the stage floor, the hard surface cool against my burning muscles. I slipped off my dancing shoes, curling and uncurling my toes. The cracks echoed in the auditorium. Euphoria tunneled through my veins at the release of the tension.

"What was that about?" Freddie sat next to me, unlacing his shoes, his gaze in the direction of where Mimi had disappeared.

"We've been invited to have fun." I kept an air of mystery, playful.

Freddie frowned, which I expected. He sure knew how to put a damper on a good time when he was in a mood about his dancing. What he really needed was an excuse to relax.

"It'll be a gas," I said, stretching my legs out and leaning over one knee, the muscles in my back, hips, and thigh stretching. I grabbed hold of my foot, the tension easing in my calf. My pinkie toe wiggled through a hole in the silk of yet another pair of worn-out stockings.

Everything hurt, and I was exhausted. Physically and mentally. It took a lot of work to put a face on for the world. To force a body that had been working for nearly two decades to keep on going.

Freddie's frown deepened, and I wasn't sure if it was because he was fighting his desire to have a good time, or if he was truly mad about my insistence. "How are drunkards and hooligans fun?"

I shook my head with a little laugh. "You take yourself too damn seriously, brother. One day you'll look back and wish you'd had more fun."

A trench formed between Freddie's brows, and I thought for sure he was about to give me a dressing-down about the importance of goals and taking our job seriously, but instead he said, "Tonight only."

I'm pretty sure my eyelashes touched my hairline, my shock ran so deep. I'd been gearing up for an argument. "So, you'll go?"

"One night."

"Excellent." I laid my head against his shoulder, patted his back. The cotton of his shirt was damp from exertion, but he smelled of soap and sweat. Familiar, like home.

"I hope I don't regret this," he muttered.

I pulled back, peered into his eyes. "What's to regret about letting loose after a hard day's work?"

Freddie sighed with embellished caution. "You sound like our father."

"I didn't say get sloppy silly, now, did I?" I grinned to lighten the stinging reminder that sometimes our father imbibed too much.

"And not too late," Freddie pushed, his expression reminiscent of a grandpa warning a child against too much pop.

I made a slashing sign of an *x* over my heart. "I'll make sure you're home before the carriage turns into a pumpkin." I didn't plan to stay out until dawn, because rehearsals would be total hell with no sleep.

"You, too, Delly." Freddie raised his brows, giving me a look that made me want to slug him.

With an exaggerated eye roll, I said, "Whatever you say, Moaning Minnie."

Freddie muttered, "Good-Time Charlie at it again," and saun-tered off to gather his things, and I headed for the dressing room, eager to peel off my torn stockings and rub at the red line where my pinkie toe had been subjected to a noose of silk. The cho-rus girls were clearing out, waving their goodbyes as I stuffed my shoes into a bag.

"Oh, shoot," I mumbled, taking note of the discarded weight of a missing bracelet on my wrist, the one Mom had given me for my birthday last year. It must have fallen off during rehearsal.

I hoped the white-gold links would sparkle under the lights. Before I pulled back the curtain onstage, sweet harmonic notes stopped me in my tracks, punctuated by the tap of heels on wood. With perfect pitch, someone was singing the Gershwin brothers' "Stairway to Paradise," originally composed for George White's *Scandals* but which we'd incorporated into *Stop Flirting*. In addi-tion to that song, we'd also added two other songs, changed the setting to Bourne Lodge near Maidenhead, and removed some of the American lingo that often didn't translate. Didn't want to have the same issue as *Anna Christie*, whose lines practically re-quired a dictionary for its British audience.

Freddie and I were going to sing "Paradise" during the first act with nearly all the cast members plus the chorus, whose voices I'd become accustomed to. But this was a soprano I'd not heard before.

"I'll build a stairway to Paradise / With a new step ev'ry day!" Shoes tapped to the corner of the stage as if walking up a flight of stairs as her voice rang out. *Tap-tap-slide*, and I imagined the twirl in the right spot as she trilled about having the blues. The taps grew in tempo, and I could envision the exact complicated choreography that Freddie had refined with the rising lyrics about building a stairway to paradise.

I peered around the thick maroon velvet curtains, curious to see who'd come on our stage to belt out the lyrics to a song that Freddie and I had perfected.

Dressed in the shadows outside the beams of the stage lights was the girl I'd met in the bathroom, who'd danced her heart out and then been cut. I would have recognized her anywhere. She was a taller version of myself. And it seemed she hadn't given up. She knew the moves and lyrics by heart. Every step was in seamless accord with the imagined notes, music only the two of us could hear pinging around in our skulls.

"Violet?" I stepped into view.

She stopped, whirling about so suddenly that she stumbled. Her limbs flashing in and out of the spotlight reminded me of a comedic act we'd seen on the vaudeville circuit.

"Oh, do be careful. We don't need you breaking a leg." I rushed forward, not that I'd reach her in time if she toppled.

Violet righted herself, a tiny smile on her lips. "Doesn't that mean good luck?"

I knew there was a reason I liked her.

"Yes. I've heard rumors it was started in ancient Greece, when the audience stomped so hard in admiration they broke their legs."

Violet widened her eyes. "Not sure I've admired anything so much I'd be willing to break my leg over it."

"Not even me and Freddie's runaround?" I teased.

Violet seemed to grow shy, remembering where she was and whom she was talking to. I tried to swallow the disappointment of losing a friend before I'd truly made one.

"Sorry about intruding." Violet rubbed her hands over her arms, looking ready to bolt. "I'd better get back to work."

"Wait." I held out a hand. "You've been watching us?"

"I'm sorry. I shouldn't have," she said nervously.

I couldn't help remembering when Freddie and I'd been chased down by the Gerrymen, intent on taking us off the circuit. Who was chasing Violet? There was something about her; I couldn't put my finger on it. I wanted not just to help her but to befriend her. Ask her how she'd memorized all our lines and dances without having practiced with the rest of the crew. Violet was a natural—which I suppose reminded me a bit of myself.

I took a small step forward, hoping my smile was disarming. "Why not? You're fantastic. You'd be great in the chorus."

Violet shrugged, her features relaxing and her hands falling to her sides. She seemed more at ease. Or at least trusting that I wasn't about to toss her out on her ear. "I did audition, but unfortunately the producers didn't seem to agree."

"I remember." Violet had tried harder than every other dancer onstage, which made her cut perplexing.

Violet's eyes lit up. "You do?"

I nodded. "You were smashing. I'll have a talk with our director to see if he can find a place for you. If he heard you sing and saw what I just did he'd be happy to add you to the crew."

Violet's hands came to her chest, palms pressed together. "Thank you so much."

"You're welcome. I hope you like hard work." No use pulling punches. This business wasn't for the faint of heart. Even those of us with heart—and talent—sometimes wanted something different.

"It's all I've ever known."

I cocked my head, studying her. "Me, too." I left out the part where I longed for something in complete contrast to where my mother, my father, and even Freddie, had led me.

Don't get me wrong, I loved to dance. My heart and soul were in dance—everything I was, expressed through creative movement. But when expression was the only thing you had, versus action . . .

Violet brought me back to the present, scrambling off the stage as if she were about to get hooked like those on vaudeville after an overly long performance.

"You'll have to be less skittish for performances," I called after her, but she'd already pushed through the doors to the lounge area, and they squeaked shut behind her.

I found my bracelet off the edge of the stage, the clasp broken. Well, if that didn't dampen my mood. I loved that bracelet. Tucking the broken jewelry into my purse, I meandered backstage, passing a chorus dancer, who gave me a tight nod. The smooth skin of her bronze brow pinched together, her lips a thin line. It was only as she breezed past that I noticed tears in her dark eyes. But she didn't respond when I called after her.

She'd come from Mr. Moore's office, the door of which was shut tight. "Mr. Moore?" I knocked.

No answer. But I heard movement on the other side. "Mr. Moore? It's Miss Astaire."

I knocked three more times before he answered, hair mussed, shirt half unbuttoned. Lying on a chaise behind him was another chorus girl, splayed out like Mom's Thanksgiving turkey. Good lord.

"Shouldn't you be at home resting?" I asked her, daring her to say otherwise.

The girl sat up and nodded, rushing around the two of us and down the hall, the scent of sweat and perfume in her wake.

"What can I do you for?" The theatre director's face was a bit red at being discovered, or maybe because I'd sent home his plaything.

"You can't do me for anything," I said with a smirk. "But you can hire another chorus girl. Name's Violet."

"No." Mr. Moore shook his head and turned away.

But I wasn't going to be deterred. "Why not?"

He crossed his arms over his chest, emphasizing the bare flesh there. I tried not to grimace.

"I'm afraid the answer's no, Miss Astaire. We have enough girls already."

Well, wasn't he being a rotten plum in the barrel? "Then maybe I should let Mr. Butt know you made an inappropriate pass at me." I raised my chin and stared down my nose.

He snorted. "As if that will make any difference."

I'd encountered a lot of jackasses in my day. Twenty years in the entertainment industry had allowed plenty of opportunity. But this guy beat the rest—including the choreographer who was a bit handsy, back in New York. "Actually, it will get you fired, Mr. Moore."

His cheeks grew redder now, and he glared so fiercely that I thought the pinched skin in the center of his forehead would crack.

"How do you figure?" he growled.

"Well, I couldn't possibly act under duress, let alone sing and dance." I batted my lashes, showing him my honed innocence.

Mr. Moore's arms dropped, his fists clenched. "Are you threatening to quit?"

I refused to back down, even at his show of anger. "Are you still refusing to hire Violet?" I didn't know the exact reason that I was going to bat for Violet, other than a wee rebellion for the younger version of myself I saw in her, disappointed whenever I was handed a no. For the women he'd lured back into his office who felt they had no choice.

"This is blackmail," he seethed.

"No more than you were blackmailing that girl just now." I peered down the empty corridor.

"I did no such thing." His cheeks were purple now.

"What do you think happens when a chorus girl is approached

by the director asking for favors?" Thank God for Freddie, keeping me safe. Not enough girls had someone looking out for them. Falling into an unwanted embrace felt like the only choice they had.

Mr. Moore frowned, not wanting to respond, clearly.

"I want Violet onstage." I clicked my heels together to punctuate my demand.

Mr. Moore stood silent for a beat. If he thought his lack of response was going to make me turn away, he was sadly mistaken.

"No."

"Your funeral. It just so happens I have dinner reservations with Mr. Butt tonight," I lied. "I'll let him know I won't be back." I turned and started to march, hoping he didn't call my bluff.

At last he called after me, "She'd better be decent for as much as you're sticking your neck out for her."

"She's better than decent." And I was confident in the words tossed over my shoulder. Violet needed to be discovered.

"I'll be the judge of that."

He could judge all he wanted, as long as he gave her a spot in the show. "Better see her tomorrow."

"I'll talk to Felix about it," he snarled.

It wasn't a direct hire yet, but it was a good sign. "Thank you."

"I won't say 'you're welcome.'" Boy, was he churlish.

I smiled sweetly at him from down the hall, the kind of smile that said *I don't care; you mean nothing to me.* "I never expected you to." Until now he'd only had to deal with Freddie when it came to direction and demands. But the man had just learned that I wasn't a simpering wallflower.

MOM WAS HAPPY to wave me off to Ciro's nightclub with Freddie chaperoning. As promised, Mimi, dressed to show off in an emerald-green silk dress cut in the latest fashion, waited in the lobby with another friend, who looked as dapper as a prince in his black top hat and tails.

Thank goodness Freddie had insisted we shop in the early days after our arrival, else we'd have looked like last season's leftovers.

"Oh, darling, you're ravishing." Mimi leaned in to kiss my cheek, her expensive perfume mingling with the floral scents in the lobby. "This is Paul Reid."

"A pleasure to meet you both." Paul gave me a kiss on the cheek and then vigorously shook Freddie's hand.

We headed out of the lobby, swishing through the brass-and-glass doors as if we were important. Parked right outside was a baby-blue Fiat with a delicious creamy leather interior, exposed to the nighttime elements because its roof was removed. We'd ridden in a lot of vehicles, but this one took the cake. Freddie let out a low whistle.

"Is that a 501S?" Freddie ran his hand along the hood the way some cowboys did their horse's flanks.

"Yes. Twenty-seven horsepower." Paul joined him, the two stroking the car as if it needed warming up to be driven.

I could barely contain myself, thinking about the way they were loving on the car about as hard as a boy with his first girl. "What I wouldn't give for a man to admire me like that," I murmured, which had Mimi in stitches.

"Want to drive her?" Paul asked.

"Oh, no, I couldn't." Freddie shook his head, even as he fingered the Fiat symbol on the hood.

"Oh, no, I insist." Paul tossed him the key.

"Don't kill us, Freddie," I said with a laugh, and climbed into the backseat with Mimi. My brother barely knew how to ride a bicycle, but he turned over the engine like a pro and we were off.

Mimi and I clutched onto our hats, shrieking and gasping as Freddie whizzed through an intersection.

Paul gave directions until at last we landed—or, rather, parked—at the club. Mimi and I climbed over each other to escape.

"I can't decide if I'm happier to be alive, or happier I didn't throw up," I said to my brother.

"Not bad for a beginner, eh?" Freddie winked.

Paul laughed so loud it turned a few heads. "You should join me for the Grand Prix in Tours this July."

"France?" I asked, feeling some glee at the prospect.

"*Oui, mademoiselle*, France." Paul wiggled his brows.

Coming to London had been a dream—but to know that France was merely a boat ride away . . . I stared, pleading, at Freddie.

"Well, if we're free," he said.

The way he said it, with the slightest inflection of doubt, as if he thought we'd be across the pond, back in New York, and dancing on Broadway by then. But I decided to have hope that *Stop Flirting* lasted longer than *The Bunch and Judy*'s sad run.

"Super." I linked my arm with Mimi's. "Now, who wants to dance?"

Paul and Mimi led us through the elegant doors of Ciro's to the grand ballroom where musicians sang onstage and ritzy people lined the dance floor. The air smelled of gin and pricey cologne, foreheads glistened with perspiration, and cheeks were rosy from exertion.

"Oh, I love the sound of jazz," Mimi gushed. "This big band is just divine." She tossed her clutch and hat onto a chair while Paul took her overcoat.

I grinned at Freddie as he took mine, and said under my breath, "Should we show these London upper crusters what real dancing is?"

Freddie smirked. "We're here to have fun."

"And *that* sounds like fun to me." I did a lively shimmy, already drunk on exhilaration alone.

"All right." Freddie took my hand, giving me a twirl, and Mimi squealed as she convinced Paul to do the same.

"Would you look at that, Freddie? It's Noël!" I called.

Freddie glanced across the dance floor where our friend Noël Coward danced with a lovely brunette in a soft blue dress with pearls studding the bodice. He'd come to our performance in New York, met us backstage, and we'd been fast friends since. Lord, was he a funny man, and partially the reason we'd entertained a stint in London, him having insisted that we'd be a hoot.

We danced our way over to Noël, who was so surprised that his shriek gave the trumpet player the slightest pause.

"My God, I'd been hoping to see the two of you." He pulled us in for a double hug.

The evening went by in a blur of champagne, dancing, and chatting a mile a minute with other theatre and literary types who'd come to Ciro's to blow off steam. I danced with one dashing flirt after another, which only made me long for something more. A deeper connection. Someone whose shoulder I could lay my head on, as Mimi did with Paul.

Before the clock struck midnight, and as the party seemed to be getting a second wind, Freddie cut our fun time short. I pouted for only a minute, because, really, the idea of collapsing into bed sent a ripple of pleasure through my tired limbs.

With a farewell kiss on Mimi's cheek, we ducked out of the club into the cool night air. While Freddie lit a cigarette for a questionable female, I turned in a circle, staring up at the charcoal sky, its film of clouds covering the stars. In the cab, Freddie was reflective, staring out the open window, his elbow on the rim, chin resting on his fist.

"What's on your mind?" I worried he might have regretted the evening.

"I need better clothes."

I laughed, having thought his worries were about something

much deeper than a pair of dress pants and a tailcoat. "Maybe one of the London chaps can point us in the right direction."

"Paul mentioned Savile Row. Might have to make a stop there before we make our debut in Liverpool in a couple weeks."

"I could use a few more things myself."

We sat in silence for a few minutes, me thinking about how it would go tomorrow when I came face-to-face with Mr. Moore again, and Freddie either dancing in his head or outfitting himself at an imaginary tailor shop. "There's something you should know," I said.

Freddie glanced at me, concern knitting his brow. I was rarely serious, and I knew the tone of my voice was worrisome to him.

"I asked Mr. Moore to talk to Felix about adding another chorus girl."

"Why would you do that?" Freddie didn't sound mad, merely perplexed. "We've plenty, and we don't want to have to redo the entire choreography. Gus is going to be beside himself."

"There's a girl whose talent was overlooked. And, like you, I want this show to go off without a hitch, and to last more than a month."

Freddie pursed his lips. "Is she a project?"

I slapped Freddie lightly on the arm with a frown. "You know I'm not one for projects."

"That's true."

"I met her during the auditions, and I watched her dance, certain she'd be chosen." I shook my head, still perplexed at how they could have cut her.

"She was cut?"

"Yeah. And, wouldn't you know it, she's still practicing and learning the dances. It won't be any trouble at all to add her in."

Freddie let out a long sigh. "Why don't you leave the handling of the show to me next time?"

Here we go again. "I'm not some shy schoolgirl, Freddie. You might be taller than me now, but I'm not your little sister."

Freddie let it go. "What did Moore say?"

"He didn't want to add her." I bit my lip, hedging about how I'd tell him the rest. "But I didn't give him much choice. Especially since I caught him canoodling with a chorus girl." I didn't mention the girl who'd come away upset, not wanting to cast judgment until I had the facts.

Freddie frowned. It was an ugly part of theatre life, we'd learned, that managers and directors often took advantage of vulnerable girls. Making promises that weren't kept. And what could the poor girls say about it? Tell everyone what happened? They'd only be shamed for their participation and loose morals—even if that was the opposite of what had happened. It was all ridiculous, and perhaps part of the reason Freddie was so sensitive about me forming any sort of male attachments. Too many times, we'd seen women like me taken advantage of.

"Anyways, I thought you should know, in case Felix asks. He's more likely to come to you with that sort of thing," I said.

"All right. Well, be careful around Moore. He strikes me as a man who can be a loose cannon if the mood is right."

I'd gotten the same impression. "I will."

We climbed out of the cab, walking into the brilliantly lit Savoy. Music came from a nearby ballroom. Another club. As we climbed the soft-carpeted marble stairs, the music faded, and by the time we reached our suite it was only a distant memory.

Mom was asleep already. Freddie waved as he went into his bedroom, and, after washing my face and changing into my nightgown, I slipped between the silken sheets of my bed, resting my head on the feather pillow.

I'd forgotten to draw the curtains and could see the lamplight from the streets outside. The distant honk of a car horn reminded me of New York. I'd not been in London long, but already I was feeling as if I'd come to a place that I didn't want to leave. One that felt like home. The people, the atmosphere, the food, the cocktails, the music—not to mention the theatre life itself. All of it felt . . . incredible.

Was there such a thing as being born in the wrong place?

I decided no. Because if I'd not been born where I was, to whom I'd been born, I'd not be where I was at that moment, snuggled in a bed at the Savoy in London. I'd not known this was where I wanted to belong from now on.

All I had to do was figure out a way to stay behind here. A way that wouldn't hurt Freddie and Mom. Yet that was a path that seemed doomed to fail. And who knew if I'd even have a place onstage after our London debut?

We could totally flop.

CHAPTER FOUR

VIOLET

THE LIMELIGHT

What happened to Maya Chopra? She was nowhere to be seen when Bridgette Hughes was bumped from the primo spot in the chorus line of *Stop Flirting* by the up-and-coming Violet Wood. This mystery showstopper appears to have emerged from the shadows of the theatre curtains to dance the stage front and center. Just who is Violet Wood? Perhaps the bigger question is, will she survive life in the West End?

M r. Cowden was waiting in the center of the lobby, bracing himself as if spoiling for a fight. The tips of his polished oxfords pressed into the burgundy carpet, and his meaty fists rested on his hips. His cheeks were flush with temper, judging from the scowl on his face.

"Wood," he said gruffly, jowls jiggling as he wagged a finger.

Violet stopped in her tracks. *Here it comes, the whole bit about who do I think I am and why am I always reaching above my station.*

"I want you to turn it down." His tone made it clear that he expected her to do as he said.

Turn it down? There was only one thing he could be talking about, and she'd yet to be offered the chorus-girl spot.

How could she refuse him? Yet to appease him would mean to betray herself.

Violet's insides curdled like milk left in the sun, and she clenched her fists, her palms growing slick. She had a sudden urge to run to the nearest waste bin to retch and retch and retch.

You're stronger than this.

That pocket-sized voice inside her, the one that made her get back up when she was too tired to rehearse, that made her carry on, spoke up. The voice of the girl inside her who wanted to shine, and was willing to sneak into the theatre after hours, came alive, helping Violet straighten her spine. Violet didn't intend to betray herself. What she desired most in the world was worth the risk of losing some things, including Mr. Cowden's approval.

Violet cleared her throat. "Pardon me, sir?"

The silence in the vestibule echoed like a battering ram.

Mr. Cowden's look suggested he knew she was fibbing. "Chorus girl. You're a cocktail waitress, and I need you to stay that way."

Wasn't that what everyone was always saying? *You're* this, *and you need to stay* that.

As if their demands, their doubts, were enough to hold Violet back, to keep her from pursuing her dreams. She lifted her chin. Why should she listen? Irritation made her heart pound, nearly drowning out the jubilation she felt as she realized that Adele Astaire had made good on her word and spoken up for her.

"I've not heard yet," Violet replied. "But if it's true, then it's only temporary, and I promise to help any way I can when I'm not onstage. I'll come in early to set up and stay late to clean."

Her offer seemed to appease Mr. Cowden. Although his brows continued to hold a deep groove, it was normal for him to appear in a perpetual state of displeasure.

He jerked his head into a nod and gave a great huff. "Fine. But you'll be working whenever you aren't onstage. I don't have time to train a new girl."

"Yes, sir, of course."

"Miss Wood?" A man she recognized from the audition approached through the auditorium doors. "I'm Felix Edwards. We have papers for you to sign before you join today's rehearsal." His words were clipped, no-nonsense, and she didn't hesitate to jump.

"Yes, sir," she said briskly. First impressions were everything, weren't they?

"You brought your dance shoes, I assume?" Mr. Edwards's gaze scoured her from head to toe. She tried to ignore the pinch of his brows and the way his lips turned down, as if she had shot a lemon peel into his mouth.

Violet nodded, patting her satchel.

"Good." He turned abruptly, giving a click of his heels as he left.

Violet hurried to follow Mr. Edwards backstage, where the other chorus dancers chattered giddily in their flashy dance getups.

Violet's gaze fell on the one person whom she dreaded seeing—the sharp blond dancer who'd snubbed her before. The woman's narrowed gaze met Violet's, practically screaming—*What are* you *doing here? You don't belong here!*

Rather than be cowed, Violet flashed a triumphant smile. Oh, what she wouldn't give to have the expression on blondie's face captured in a photograph. The woman's mouth fell open and her blue eyes bulged, reminding Violet of her landlady's pug, Moon. The few chorus girls surrounding the blonde tittered, whispering behind their hands.

Violet didn't care what they were saying, not letting them ruin this monumental moment.

In a small office, Mr. Edwards shuffled some papers toward her. "This is on a trial basis, Miss Wood, which means we're not going to pay you what we pay the more experienced dancers. Pay is distributed weekly."

Violet nodded, too ecstatic for the opportunity to worry about that; besides, it was more than she made as a waitress. She barely read the words and signed, the smile on her lips about to crack her face. Then she was shoved back toward the other girls. A woman with spectacles perched on the end of her nose and holding a pencil between her teeth marched toward Violet with a measuring tape. After taking her size and tutting, she stomped away and zipped back with a beautiful ensemble.

Flowing, gauzy yellow skirts and a bodice that sparkled when it caught the light. Violet barely had a chance to enjoy the sight before the woman was ordering her to try it on. Despite the prying eyes of the other girls, Violet stripped right where she was, knowing that doing so revealed the threadbare fabric of her underthings. She dared not look at the judgment in their eyes, the mocking joy Sharp Blondie surely showed at the way Violet's drawers no longer held their shape.

Violet closed her eyes as she slid the costume on, feeling the newness of it, the softness of the silk, the scratchiness of the tulle against her skin. All of it a wonder. Then her eyes popped open again as the costume-fitter jerked her into an abrupt about-face, buttoning up the back of the dress, which clung to Violet as if it had been made for her.

"*Voilà, c'est bon.* Go." The woman shoved her forward.

The other girls rushed past her, knocking her aside. Violet hurried to put on her shoes, fingers fumbling with the straps. Finally, she ran out onstage—the last to arrive.

Mr. Edwards glared so fiercely, a vein pulsed in the center of his forehead, threatening to explode with his sharp tongue. "We don't tolerate tardiness."

Violet could have made excuses, all of which were already obvious to Mr. Edwards. She'd only signed on the dotted line this hour and been fitted for a costume in the same breath. But that wouldn't matter. He wanted to put her in her place. Fortunately, being onstage was exactly where Violet wanted to be, anyway.

The music started almost immediately. Violet jockeyed for a place in line. Her nerves were taut, but it only took her a fraction of a second to pull herself together. She knew this music, the moves; she just had to let them happen.

Violet stepped in time with the music as it flowed through her body, and the exhilaration of being onstage—of being part of the show—hummed through her limbs like the vibrations of a tuning fork.

As she twirled, smiling toward the empty seats, she spied from the corner of her eye a petite brunette backstage, peering from behind a curtain.

Adele Astaire. The woman who had gone out on a limb for her. For *her.* The woman whose actions had given Violet the chance she'd worked toward her entire life.

Being watched by someone she owed that debt, who was also the star of the show, only made Violet dance harder. The girls beside her noticed that she was able to keep up, and some of their curious glances turned sour. Sharp Blondie even managed an elbow jab. But Violet had been prepared for blowback, and she twirled away in time with the choreography as if nothing had happened—even though her ribs smarted.

Being a late addition to the chorus-girl team meant that the director shifted her around a few times, until she was on the front line. Not center, but not behind anyone, either, and she was more than happy with that.

The hours of dancing went by in a flash. Even after so much exertion, her body sang with energy. She could have kept going but hurried offstage with the others to change. Violet peeled off her sweat-dampened costume, carefully hanging the frothy confection where it belonged. She ran her hand down the length of the dress, wondering when this dream bubble was going to pop.

As if she could hear Violet's thoughts, Sharp Blondie passed by her, hissing, "Don't get too comfortable, street rat." She gave Violet a bump in the back with her shoulder.

An inappropriate rebuke was on the tip of Violet's tongue when Adele appeared, putting a salve on the sting.

"Keep your cattiness to yourself, Bridgette. We're all replaceable," Adele said.

Bridgette's face turned the same shade of red as a pair of knickers Violet had once seen on a prostitute in an alley near Brick Lane in Hoxton. But Bridgette didn't say anything in response, merely slunk from the dressing area.

"Thank you," Violet murmured to Adele.

Adele waved her hand in Bridgette's direction. "Girls like her are a dime a dozen and they know it. Don't pay her any attention."

Violet nodded, though she was certain to remember Bridgette's mockery. Her father, before he'd passed, had told her that remembering the rebuffs from one's enemies helped to prepare for future attacks. At the time, Violet had thought her father paranoid, stuck in the brutal trenches of the Great War even when home on leave. But it all made sense now.

"I'll try not to," she managed, around a dry tongue.

"Saying you'll try is for those without true commitment. You have to *do*." With that piece of advice, Adele hurried away.

Violet looked around. The dressing room was nearly empty now, a suddenly large space scattered with discarded hole-riddled stockings, combs, and powder puffs; robes slung over benches; and racks of costumes lined up in a row.

She'd snuck backstage plenty, but never been part of this scene. Everything felt surreal. The opportunities boundless. At what moment would reality come crashing down? Because this had all happened so fast, and it didn't feel real.

Tearing herself away, Violet dashed to the ladies' to refresh herself. Her skin was slick with sweat, and she still had to run cocktails for Mr. Cowden. Her feet already hurt, and she hoped she wouldn't be hobbling by the end of the night.

One of the other chorus girls was applying fresh lipstick in the mirror. She glanced over at Violet and grinned. "Good job out there today."

"Thanks. I'm Violet."

"Caty." She turned back to the mirror, fluffing her hair.

One of the stalls opened and Sharp Blondie came out, scowling. "Marjorie, wasn't it?" she said, staring down at Violet with disgust.

"Violet," Caty corrected.

Sharp Blondie snapped her gaze toward Caty, who just went about applying her lipstick as if nothing had happened.

"Let's get one thing straight, Violet"—Bridgette said her name as if seconds ago she'd dumped a can of sardines into her mouth— "I'm the lead chorus girl for this show."

"If you say so." Violet resisted the urge to roll her eyes. She could care less if Bridgette was the lead girl. Had Adele Astaire singled Bridgette out and gotten her the job?

Bridgette sniffed. "You need to know who is in charge."

"I assume you mean Mr. Gus, the choreographer. Or were you referring to Mr. Edwards, the producer? Or perhaps—"

Bridgette let out a disgusted snort. "You're nothing and will never amount to anything."

Violet shrugged. "If you say so." Being looked down upon as if she were a pile of rubbish was nothing new. The only difference now was that Bridgette was obviously jealous. That was very interesting, and made Violet feel less like rubbish.

"Well, if you're done berating me, Bridg, I've got a job to do."

"'Bridg'?" the blonde sputtered, but Violet was already pushing past her.

Bravado flashed through her, but she clamped her mouth closed before she could tell Bridg to shove it. The show was going to last only a few months, and after that she was going to need a job. If luck would have it, she'd be picked up for the next show. But one could never bet their future on luck.

Violet had a lot of gumption. The nerve to get up and do what she needed. Despite her being born on Drysdale Street in Hoxton, a stone's throw from Shoreditch, a veritable orgy of despair, luck seemed to have touched her when she met Adele Astaire.

And she wasn't going to let someone else ruin that. Bridgette, in a whirl of perfume and hate, hurried to storm out of the bathroom before Violet.

Caty rested a palm against the sink as she turned to Violet with a sympathetic face. "Ignore Bridgette. She's a rotten nut, but if you get into it with her, she'll make you sorry. Trust me, I speak from experience."

"Thanks for the advice."

Caty winked at her. "We've got to stick together."

Violet nodded and left the bathroom. Rounding the corner, she practically ran into Adele, and stumbled backward. She'd been clumsier from nerves in the presence of the star than ever before in her life.

Adele's slim fingers wrapped gently around Violet's upper arms. "Are you all right?"

"Yes." Violet smiled. "Thank you."

"Any more run-ins with You Know Who?"

"Only one." Violet let out a nervous laugh.

Adele shook her head. "I used to deal with women like that a lot on the circuit, and a few in New York, too. Don't let her bust your chops."

"Bust my what?"

Adele laughed, her dark brown eyes dancing. "You know, give you a hard time."

"Oh, right." Violet felt naive and silly. "Well, I wasn't."

"Could have fooled me." Adele put her arm around Violet's shoulder and steered her toward the stage.

Violet should have told her that she had to work before Mr. Cowden came looking for her, but she couldn't help being led in the opposite direction.

"You remind me of myself," Adele said.

Violet was surprised, unable to spot the similarities. Adele was beautiful, charismatic, and an incredible dancer. Adele was petite and confident, and Violet was tall and less sure of herself. Adele had perfectly smooth skin, while Violet had a faint scar on her jawline from a childhood dog bite. Adele was gorgeous, the epitome of style, whereas Violet perceived herself as mousy and unimportant.

But she wasn't going to tell Adele all that. Or point out the biggest differences: that the American star hadn't grown up in the East End of London scraping for food; that Adele had a mother who supported her dancing career, enough to cross the pond with her, while Violet's mum discouraged her.

Adele guided Violet backstage, which was now empty, then sat her down at a dressing table and spun her chair away from the mirror. The cushion was soft, and the room held the lingering floral scents of the departed dancers' perfume and the underlying sting of sweat.

The famous dancer stared at Violet's face, eyes moving from one side to the other. Then she nodded perfunctorily and picked up a powder case. Violet had never worn powder before. Lipstick, yes. Much else, no.

Adele dipped the puff into the powder and smoothed the makeup over Violet's cheeks, sweeping up over her forehead and down her nose and then blotting her chin, paying particular attention to the area where the white line of the scar marred her jawline. There was a sentimental glow about Adele as she applied the cosmetics.

"How old are you, Violet?"

A flutter of nerves in Violet's belly made her hold her breath for a moment. Then she said, "I'll be nineteen this summer."

Adele put the powder down and picked up some rouge, dabbing it onto Violet's cheeks. "I remember that age. The world is so big and bright. I'll be twenty-seven this autumn. Have you always wanted to be a dancer?"

"From the time I could walk. Not sure I took a first step so much as I did a twirl."

"Same for me." She rubbed the rouge softly into Violet's cheeks. "But dancing as a profession is quite a commitment."

"I'm ready for it."

Adele uncapped a red lipstick and dabbed color onto Violet's lips. "Elizabeth Arden, Venetian Rose," she said with a wink, and doing an exaggerated press of her lips for Violet to mimic. "I thought I was, too. But sometimes I wonder what it would have been like if I was married now. Had a baby."

"Is that what you want? A family?" Violet furrowed her brow.

"Someday." Adele gave a dainty shrug.

"Why would you want to give up everything you've achieved?" Violet couldn't imagine having the opportunity to dance onstage, establishing a career doing so, and then letting it go. She couldn't imagine a world in which she stayed home to raise babies. Mum had been miserable doing that, and Violet by extension.

Adele snorted and looked around. "My achievements?" There was a teasing note in her voice. "You mean broken toes, aching bones, and hours of stress?"

"Sounds like heaven." Violet laughed.

Adele nodded. "You know, right now it feels like we're just getting started. On the cusp of something. If I even mentioned wanting a husband, Freddie would hyperventilate until he passed out." She said this last part with a humorless laugh.

Freddie. How close they were. Violet felt a different sort of envy. Her sister, Pris, was so young still . . .

"Well, what do you think?" Adele spun her back around to face the mirror.

Violet smiled—stunned. She looked like a more mature, confident version of herself. There was a glint in her eyes she'd not noticed before. Something bordering on determination, but also . . . life. *Hope.*

"It's marvelous. Thank you."

"A few of us might go dancing later; care to join us?" Adele asked, sorting the items on the dressing table.

Would Violet ever . . . but reality came crashing down with the echo of Mr. Cowden's voice in her head. "I have to work."

Adele looked confused for a minute, the differences in their situations never more apparent.

"So, he's not going to let you go, huh?" she said at last, pursing her lips. "Stubborn jackass."

"Not if I want to keep my job after *Stop Flirting* is finished."

Adele studied her with a pondering expression. "Where you go is up to you, Violet. But a word of advice: if you have the talent, and the drive, you can go anywhere." She smiled. "Look at me and Freddie. A country girl born to two people without a lot of means. My parents saw potential before I knew the meaning of the word, moved me to New York, enrolled me in a dance school, and then sent me on the circuit. I'm a lot lazier than Freddie. But with his drive, we've hopped the pond."

Hopping the pond in the other direction—now, there was a spectacular dream. America seemed like the land of possibilities. Where she wouldn't be rooted in place by class and her East End accent that sometimes slipped out. "You're very fortunate."

Adele laughed. "Fortune isn't the crux of it."

Violet shrugged in disagreement. "I think it is. Life's all about knowing the right people, and perhaps making an impression on just one who'll give you a lucky break."

"That's fair." Adele looked thoughtful. "I noticed you for your talent. It took a"—she pinched her thumb and forefinger together—"nudge to make everyone else notice, too."

"And it was my luck you did." Violet smiled, bringing Adele around to her point. "I'm grateful. Really, I am."

Adele grabbed Violet's hands and pulled her upright. "Come out dancing with me, then; it will be a gas." She leaned in close, conspiratorial-like. "And we'll show the Bridgettes of the world they can't hold you back."

What Violet wouldn't give to tell Mr. Cowden to bugger off and then spend the rest of the night in the company of stars. But the few hours of pleasure she'd gain would not be worth the repercussions that blowing off her work would bring. "Some other time."

Adele sighed. "Your boss must be an old hard-ass like my brother."

Violet was shocked—and amused—not only by Adele's vulgar tongue but by the easy way she shared a personal annoyance. An unlikely friendship seemed to be blossoming between them. Violet didn't usually have the time to commit to friends, because she was always busy working or practicing. And her ambitions set her apart from most of the women her age in her building and wider neighborhood—with many of the girls thinking she was putting on airs, with her incomprehensible ambitions.

But maybe this time, with Adele—a woman who could understand those ambitions—she could open up a bit.

"Wood!" The shout came from somewhere in the auditorium.

Violet sighed. "I have to go. The old hard-ass is calling." The words left her tongue with more ease than she'd expected.

Adele let out a long, exaggerated sigh, meant more to be funny than depressing. "Better get to it before he has a heart attack."

"Thank you again . . . for everything."

Adele squeezed her hand. "My pleasure. This run is going to be a good one, I can feel it."

Violet made up an excuse for Mr. Cowden about leaving behind her stockings and ignored his berating as she got down to business. The crowd for the evening show was already turning up, ordering drinks, and bantering about in their designer clothes purchased by special design. Clad in Schiaparelli, Chanel, Lanvin, and Vionnet, the women were a veritable sea of rainbows framed in diamonds and black coattails.

"'Ow did i' go?" the busboy asked, hours later, as they cleared a table in one of the private boxes.

"It was divine." She could think of no better way to describe her day. Even now that her feet ached.

He winked at her as he hustled off with his load of rubbish, calling back over his shoulder, "Tha's aces."

But it wasn't all aces when she arrived at home. Her mother sat at the table, a cup of tea in front of her and disappointment feeding the crease of her brow.

"Mum, I got the dance part." Violet rose onto her toes. Despite trying to keep her excitement tamped down, it came out—as it often did—in dance. As if she were onstage, she lowered her heels into first position.

A loud groan escaped her mother and she set her teacup down hard. "Are you ou' of your mind, girl? You're courtin' trouble. Nothin' good will come o' this. I won' 'ave it. Not for Pris."

Violet felt as if she'd been slapped. "You won't have it?" Confusion warred inside her. For once, why couldn't her mother just be happy for her?

Mum avoided eye contact, looking toward where Pris pretended to sleep on her bedroll. "I won' be a wi'ness to you ruining yourself. If you wan' 'o dance, then you need to leave."

"Leave?" Violet recoiled; where was this coming from?

Over the years her mother had seen how much she'd practiced dancing, knew it to be Violet's passion; told her it was a waste of time, but never had she made this kind of demand. Adele Astaire had picked her out of the crowd to join *Stop Flirting*, and Mum was . . . kicking her out? This should have been her shining moment. A chance to celebrate.

Tears threatened. "But why?" her voice cracked as she asked. "I'll be making extra money; it will help all of us."

Mum looked at her with a pinched brow, something akin to hurt in her gaze before she glanced down at the teacup. "I was your age when I go' knocked up. Ge'in' above your station, you are, and tha's wha' will happen." She shook her head. "I can' have tha' around Pris."

"Where am I supposed to go?"

Her mother dragged in a ragged breath, as if she'd hoped that by offering this ultimatum Violet would quit dancing.

Violet swallowed the words she wanted to shout. The ones that would sting and hurt her mum the way Violet was hurting. Instead she bit back the pain and disappointment of years of browbeating.

"I'd hoped you'd change your mind. See reason. But you're jus' as stubborn and ungra'ful as ever." Her mother picked the teacup up and stood. "You can stay the night, and then you're gone. I jus' hope you'll keep your legs together."

Violet watched as her mother walked away, her mouth agape, her voice hidden somewhere in the recesses of her throat. This was truly happening. Filled with sorrow, she escaped to her room—a small space behind a curtain.

She crawled onto her thin, lumpy mattress and pulled the moth-eaten blanket over herself. Where was she supposed to go?

Six-year-old Pris slipped around the curtain and curled her tiny frame against Violet's on the bedroll. Her dark hair, twisted into a bun, tickled beneath Violet's nose.

"I be' you'll be glamorous," Pris said in a tired whisper.

"Thank you," Violet whispered. But her younger sister had already fallen back to sleep.

CHAPTER FIVE

ADELE

THE LIMELIGHT

For those unfortunate souls who don't have the great blessing of living in the city of London, you're in luck! The American theatrical duo Fred and Adele Astaire are taking their show on the road before its West End debut. The Royal Court Theatre in Liverpool will host a preview of *Stop Flirting* as the cast hoofs it upstage and downstage. Catch the full performance and an early view of the costumes designed by renowned French costumer Idare et Cie!

April 30, 1923
Royal Court Theatre, Liverpool

The curtain was raised, the lights blinding, and the hushed whisper of the crowd caressed our ears the second before the orchestra started to play. We shimmied our way into place, the soft white silk of our dresses swishing around our knees, and the click of dancing heels on a dangerously angled wood floor added to the atmosphere.

Unfortunately for performers, the sloped construction of our performing ground produced better views and acoustics for our audience. Some playhouses slanted them more than others, like this one.

The music from the opening dance wound down, and the show began in earnest. Freddie and I tossed out our often comedic lines, accompanied by the occasional saucy look, hoping they'd land with the crowd. Back and forth, shuffling on- and offstage we went. Dancing, singing, and portraying the show's intertwined love stories with all their pining, flirtations, and schemes. The very "Whichness of the Whatness of the Who" that came out in vibrant, hilarious song.

Despite the tilted stage, every act went off without a hitch. Laughter echoed off the theatre walls, and the crowd egged us on. As the final curtain fell, we caught snatches of "Encore! Encore!" over the thunderous and gratifying surge of applause.

We screeched with enthusiasm behind the curtain, reclaiming the stage for a final round of bows and reminding our audience that the true encore would be their coming to see the show again—and bringing their friends.

Slick with sweat, my body still humming from the excitement, I collapsed into the chair at my dressing table. Freddie squeezed my shoulders.

"Fantastic, sis," he said.

"You were perfection." I winked at him over my shoulder.

Freddie grinned. "You stole their hearts, Delly. Can't wait to see what the papers say in the morning."

Out of the corner of my eye, I watched Violet strut through the backstage area. It'd only taken Mr. Edwards promising to fill Cowden's theatre with thirsty customers for Violet's boss to agree to let her accompany us. Her cheeks were flushed; sweat glowed on her brow. She held her head high, and her dark hair was tucked beneath a silk-and-floral headdress that was only a smidge more exaggerated than my own. Unlike many of the other dancing girls, she wasn't part of a little clique. She was still having a hard time making friends, besides Caty, her flatmate, but at least she'd gained confidence. I could see it on her face.

"My God, that was marvelous! Darling, you were glorious!" Mimi settled into a seat beside me, staring into the mirror, her blue eyes wide. She pulled off the gloves she'd been wearing for the last number and plopped them onto the makeup-littered table.

"And you were amazing," I said, running a hand over my hair to smooth some of the wayward strands, and pinning some of my curls back into place. "I couldn't have asked for a better cast. I was expecting . . ." I trailed off, not sure what to say. I'd thought the British would be stuffy compared to our American high steppers. And I'd known the audiences were tough. I'd sat in a couple over the past months, and more than once watched as Londoners booed performers off the stage. What a relief the same hadn't happened to us—that we hadn't been run out of the city.

Mimi unpinned her own costume's hat and threaded her fingers through her tamped-down blond tendrils. "That runaround was brilliant. You and Freddie put the joy back into performing and are a good reminder not to take our world so seriously."

I cocked my head, trying to figure out what precisely she meant. But, before I could sort it, Freddie said breezily, "Believe me, Mimi, my sister doesn't take anything seriously." He laughed, chucking me under the chin. I gave him an exaggerated frown in return.

"Freddie would have you believe he's never had a day of fun in his life, or indeed that the only idea of fun he's got is to work, but, trust me, I've seen him let loose"—I paused before landing the punch line—"at least once." I tapped my lip, looking ponderous. "At least, I think I have. Oh, well; maybe some other time."

Freddie groaned, with an exaggerated bow. "Bah . . . dancing, performing, what's more fun than bringing pleasure to an audience?"

Mimi snorted. "I can think of a number of things."

"There you are!" Noël Coward popped around the corner, looking dapper in long black coattails and shiny shoes. He hooted as he pulled Freddie in for a back-slapping hug. "We're going to a party."

"All of us?" I asked, glancing around the room, my eyes unwittingly seeking out Violet at a corner dressing table.

"Why not? A supper at the Adelphi Hotel, hosted by the ever-generous Lord Lathom."

Freddie raised a brow, the telltale downturn of his mouth suggesting he was about to decline on both our behalf. "A party thrown by a lord, huh?"

"Yes." Noël nodded at me with a wide smile, showing his teeth. "To congratulate you on your show. Trust me, you'll all be welcome." He glanced at Mimi and gave her a wink. Mimi pretended to be flustered, fluttering her lashes and biting her lip coyly.

The tease. But it was wasted. Apparently she hadn't picked up on what I'd caught—that Noël had more interest in my brother than in any bit of skirt backstage.

"I'm in no shape to go to a party," Freddie began, but I gave his hip a tap from where I stood beside him, interrupting before he could definitively decline the invitation.

"We would love to come," I said. "And, if you're sure, I'll let the chorus girls know, too."

"The more, the merrier." Noël flashed a handsome smile, a slight hint of mischief in his eyes.

Mom arrived at just that moment. Rather inopportunely, to my way of thinking. "You both were brilliant. I wish your father had been here to see it." Her pride was evident.

I slipped my hand over Freddie's and gave his a squeeze. "We'll write to Pop and tell him all about it in the morning."

"Are you going somewhere?" Mom asked.

Noël lifted her hand to his lips. "You look younger every time I see you, Mrs. Astaire. Do say you'll come with us to his lordship's dinner."

Mom laughed and swatted him away. "You Brits are all terrible flirts."

"Are you telling me to *Stop Flirting*?" Noël asked, working the show's title in with a chuckle. The rest of us groaned. But I also offered him a smile. He'd won Mom over and saved my evening for sure.

With Mom in tow, we exited the theatre at the head of a sizeable group. Freddie strolled ahead with Noël and a few of the other male cast members. I linked arms with Violet, while Mom and Mimi chatted behind us. A handful of cast members had decided not to come along. They were exhausted—and with good reason. But every bit of tired I'd felt as the curtain went down had disappeared with our audience. I was ready for the fun to begin.

We'd been popular in New York City, but no one wined and dined like Britain's elite—not even New York aristocracy. Applause broke out in the dining room of the Adelphi as we entered, and even the orchestra stopped playing to welcome us. Men and women stood, clapped, and clinked their glasses.

My heart did flutter kicks against my ribs as I was swept through the room meeting this person and that, their names and faces a blur of vowels and shapes. If bellies had been rubber bouncing balls, mine was being kicked down Copperas Hill outside the hotel by a bunch of rowdy hooligans. I smiled wide, putting on my best show for those who expected it.

My brother clinked his glass with the ring on his pinkie. "Thank you for inviting us. I can't tell you how pleased we are to make your acquaintance," Freddie said to the crowd in general. "Adele and I have been trying to hop the pond for some time now."

"And how!" I did a short five-step tap, ending with an exaggerated curtsey, to emphasize our excitement.

The rest of the crew followed in step, which sent the stunners watching us into giggles and applause. Down the line of actors, I saw Violet standing tall, an identical grin on her lips. When she was on display, gone was the scared girl. I was mesmerized by how much it felt as if I were looking in a mirror.

Freddie was over the moon, though whenever he caught himself smiling he quickly adopted the serious look that he felt made him seem like a man of consequence. Mom was chatting away with a woman who looked like she was probably related to the Queen, judging by the diamonds dripping from her earlobes, melting into a gem-encrusted necklace that might have weighed as much as I did. The woman's gown was a divine gold crepe, and she wore a diamond-and-gold tiara perched on the very top of her head.

Violet put on a good show—carefully hiding her reaction to it all—but when just the two of us were alone in the ladies' room she gushed. Not that I blamed her. I might not have been from the East End, but I didn't come from this milieu, either. It had taken me years to adjust.

My glass of champagne never seemed to get below half-full, which was fine by me. Although when I became slightly light-headed I only pretended to sip. I managed to give off a nonverbal signal, a slight cut with my hand, to the footman to stop serving. I was still getting used to the contrasts between America's Prohibition and Britain's blessing of booze.

After all, if I got too schnockered, it was going to be a hell of a day tomorrow. The last thing I wanted to do was disappoint Freddie and Mom, and even Pop from afar. We'd worked our asses off—*literally, where has my ass gone?*—for this moment. No way was drink going to ruin our triumph.

We had performances every day this week—twice a day—and then we'd move on to the King's Theatre in Glasgow for a couple of weeks. No break for the weary, because after Glasgow the Royal Lyceum in Edinburgh would be awaiting us. Only then, with our sketch thoroughly hashed out, would we board the train back to London to make our debut there. That debut—if we were lucky— could be the genesis of a whole new career. We'd been climbing the mountain for so long and now a sparkling pinnacle was almost within reach. Soon we'd be teetering on the edge of the slope, ready to either grasp it firmly, or fall, hard.

THE NEXT WEEKS went by in a blur and frenzy of dancing and performing. My hotel room dripped with gifts—bottles of champagne, chocolates, cards, creams, perfumes, cuff links for Freddie, and a string of pearls for me. But I had little or no time to enjoy any of the goodies. At one point there were so many flowers in my room that Mom and I pretended we couldn't find each other. I teased about opening a florist's shop and using the proceeds for shoes, then gave half the flowers to Violet, who really was my favorite.

When we weren't catering to an audience we were rehearsing, and when we weren't rehearsing we were attending to the elite bits of society that had deemed us their pets for the short term.

The funny thing about pets is that they have such a different view of things than their humans do. Lady So-and-So might think I was her petite dancing darling, but really it was she who catered to *my* sensibilities—fawning over me and filling my champagne coupe as quickly as she overflowed my social calendar. And it was all in good fun. In fact, I wouldn't change a thing, except maybe to rehearse less. At some point the play was as good as it was going to get. But, unlike me, Freddie never seemed to recognize that tipping point, and he continued to insist we devote hours and hours to lines and dances we'd already mastered.

I was barely able to snatch a few hours of sleep, let alone have any real time to myself. In the quiet mornings, before Mom and Freddie woke, when the sun was barely an orange slit on the horizon, I'd wake up and let my mind wander. What would it be like to lie in this same bed with the feel of a warm, solid body beside me? Or to be awakened by the cries of a child wishing to be comforted? To do something normal, such as stroll down to the corner market or take a dog for a walk?

I wanted a dog.

I wanted a child.

I wanted a husband.

I *wanted* . . .

But desiring something other than the achievement and success I had made me feel ungrateful. Right about the time each morning that the sting of that guilt sliced through my thin layer of fantasy and reflection, Mom would wake up, or Freddie would come knocking.

Finally, the preview performance tour was at an end. On that Saturday evening, May 26, after the curtain dropped, we boarded a sleeper train to London.

But really they should have called it the *no*-sleeper train. Mom and I had a double cabin to ourselves, with Freddie next door. But for all the gentle rocking, the soothing *chug-chug* of the wheels on the tracks, all I could do was stare at the maroon carpeting with gold medallions and try not to count the pile.

Freddie paced the corridor outside our compartment, his shadow bouncing off the window every time he trudged past. Finally I'd had enough. I pulled on my robe and flung open the door.

"What in the world are you doing, Freddie? We need to sleep. Aren't you exhausted?"

Freddie stopped in his tracks. He didn't have to answer that question: the matching dark circles beneath his eyes were evidence enough. "Don't you know what's about to happen?" He raked a hand through his wild hair, which was not in its usually neat coiffure.

What was he talking about? Had we made plans I'd forgotten about? In my exhausted state, I glanced up and down the corridor of the train car, seeing nothing. I peered out the window at the dark beyond, but only our reflections bounced off the glass. Barely visible beyond the mirroring panes, the night-covered countryside slid past.

"Well, what's supposed to happen is sleep. But it's not happening because of your endless pacing. So, how about you lie down and we both get some shut-eye before dawn breaks and we arrive in London? That is what's going to happen—we are going to pull into that station whether we sleep or not."

"Exactly." Freddie tossed up his hands. "*London*."

I frowned and reached forward, pressing a hand to his brow. It was cool to the touch, if not marginally damp from his train-car-stalking exertions. "Are you all right?"

Freddie shooed away my fever checking and laid his forehead against the window. I moved to stand beside him, my back to the outside world, my focus solely on my brother's clear distress.

"No, I'm not all right, Delly. We're about to make our London debut. London, for Pete's sake."

I crossed my arms casually over my chest and studied his profile, and the fog on the window made by his breath. "Freddie, we've been doing this musical comedy for a month. We've made the tweaks and our audience loves it. London is merely another venue. What's the deal?"

He rolled his head to the side, staring at me. "London could break us."

I raised a brow in challenge. "Or London could love us, like they did in Liverpool. Like they loved us in New York City—on Broadway, what we thought was the pinnacle. Think of London as New York."

"It's not the same."

"Oh, dear, Moaning Minnie's at it again." I scrubbed my face with my hands. "Do you ever simply believe in yourself, Freddie? In the rest of the crew?"

He frowned at me. "You can't just believe in yourself. You have to do the work."

"No one is disputing that. But we've done the work. And, really, Freddie, you work harder than anyone I know."

"Precisely."

"Which begs the question of why you won't believe in yourself, then. It's going to be fine."

He faced me, crossing his arms in a pose to match mine. "It needs to be better than fine."

"It will be spectacular." I did an embellished shuffle, trying to cheer him up.

But that only seemed to make things worse as he groaned and dropped his chin to his chest. I could tell that Freddie was in one of those moods that would be long lasting and would mean a sleepless night for us both if he didn't snap out of it.

"You know, when I was a little girl, I used to keep a diary. I wrote a whole number about a boy once." If only my younger self hadn't jinxed me with that last line she'd written about not getting married.

Freddie crinkled his nose in a frown. "So, you think I should write in a diary?"

"Or do what you normally do and write to Pop. I'm sure he

wants an update, and you can get some of your worries out. Then go to bed." I smiled at him in a mixture of goodwill and irritation.

To my utter elation, Freddie nodded in agreement. "Good idea."

By the time we arrived in London, Moaning Minnie was still scribbling, and I'd gotten only two hours of sleep. But two was better than none.

"Dress rehearsal today," Freddie started up, but I cut him off.

"We need a rest, brother. And I'm not asking, I'm telling."

He looked ready to argue, but I pointed to the swelling beneath my eyes. "I haven't seen what a fright I am, but I'm pretty sure these puffy eyes resembling mouse bellies won't go away without a good rest."

Freddie gave a mock shudder, and I slugged him in the arm. We stumbled off the train to join the rest of our party. As soon as we reached our new digs, I was going to sleep for the rest of the day.

"Would you look at that, Freddie?" I shimmied with excitement as we stood outside the Shaftesbury Theatre. Overhead atop the marquee, our likenesses, from head to toe, were blown up to nearly three times life size in one of our famous dance poses, the one where I popped my heel. Parallel to our colossal bodies was another sign that practically shouted our names in bold. And in between, in looming cursive, *STOP FLIRTING*. "Not bad for two vaudeville kids from Omaha," I said.

"Looks like New York City, only older," Freddie teased back, referring to the low-rise buildings adorned with scrollwork, which dated back ages and ages. Certainly, no royals had trolled the streets of Broadway, at least not on the regular.

I laughed and gave him a bump with my hip. Then I stared up at our names again. The long hours of rehearsing, doing nothing but eating, sleeping, and breathing dance and performance—and now our London opening was here at last. A thrilling rush went through my limbs then, making my hands tremble.

"Fred and Adele Astaire?" a woman said beside us, her gaze directed at the larger-than-life cutouts of us strapped onto the building.

I turned to address her but then realized she wasn't looking at me.

"*Stop Flirting*?" her friend beside her said with a snobbish lilt in her voice, as if even the title of our play were rubbish.

"Sounds cheap, doesn't it?" I said, unable to help myself. "Only Americans would be so crass."

They gaped at me, their gazes flicking to the cutouts and back, and obviously taking note that Freddie and I were one and the same. One of them had the decency to blush at her gaffe. I grinned with a wink, then danced my way through the shiny glass-and-brass doors with Freddie groaning behind me.

"Do you think they'll come to the show?" I teased, putting my thumb on my nose and wiggling my fingers toward the door, though they'd already moved on.

"I'd rather Charleston," Freddie said dryly.

"Hey, that's my line."

"It's nobody's line, yet," he reminded me, because it was a song he'd been working on with George Gershwin for us to use in a future bit.

"Well, it *will* be mine."

Fred nodded toward the door, with that worrying crease between his brows. "Not if you keep up those shenanigans. We'll be tossed onto the nearest barge and shipped out to sea."

"Oh, I'm just having some fun. Besides, if they see the show, they can tell all their friends they got to talk to the lead dancers."

Freddie shook his head with a serious expression, which only made me want to tease him more, but I reined myself in.

We were the first to arrive, as usual. It would be a good hour at least before we were joined by the rest of the crew, which would give Freddie time to get comfortable. He liked to do all the blocking—the path of our movements—himself. He played around with the choreography and any changes he wanted to make.

"Want to check the stage?" I glanced at my brother, who seemed even more nervous than usual. He bit at the corner of a fingernail, and I batted his arm down.

"Yeah, let's." He shoved his hands in his pockets.

We walked down the center aisle of the theatre, stopping right in the middle to take it all in: the red carpet; the plush red velvet seats in neat rows rising up three levels; the grand cupola with its massive chandelier; imposing columns of marble with gold beading and carvings of miniature angels playing instruments. All of it carried me back into the Renaissance age. The richness of the place, and the fact that we'd be performing here, had me tingling all over with pride.

We climbed the side stairs to the stage. The sound of our shoes clacking against the wooden floor echoed in the vast domed space. Freddie shuffled from one end to the other, as if he could feel the boards through his soles.

I slipped my shoes off, stretching my toes against the cold planks. I closed my eyes, sliding along the boards, doing a few pirouettes as I felt for wear in the wood. My body leaned as I moved, becoming one with the stage. When I twirled into Freddie, I opened my eyes and smiled.

"Not as bad as the Royal Court," I said with a shrug as I hiked upstage. "And not nearly the same incline as the last theatre."

"Agreed." Freddie did a five-second tap number, then a shuffle tap forward and a perfect slide downstage to the edge, his arms outstretched.

I mimicked his moves, facing him with a teasing grin. We went on for a quarter hour, making the stage our own, letting our feet and limbs grow accustomed to the vagaries of the structure.

"Our show is going to be great," I said.

Freddie nodded, but I knew he didn't agree. He was too superstitious for that—and too relentlessly certain we were underprepared. After rehearsal, as the other actors and I changed and the crew left, my brother remained in the theatre. As I put on my street clothes I could see him in my mind's eye—worrying, surrounded by the ghosts of the show. Too nervous to leave the stage, fearing it would jinx opening night. I wondered: Had he slept on the stage after rehearsals earlier in the week? I hadn't seen him at our hotel at all.

"Is he going to be all right?" Violet asked, as she followed me out of the theatre and onto the sidewalk. She was dressed in the uniform for her other job as a cocktail waitress, the job Cowden had miraculously held for her. Serving champagne to those in the boxes before the show and trying to avoid a pinched bottom, then rushing to change for our performance.

I cocked my head. Violet looked truly concerned, and it warmed my heart. "Depends on how you mean?"

She shifted nervously, shoving a hand into the front pocket of her apron. "I'm not sure what I mean. In general, I suppose."

I laughed and reached forward, giving her arm a squeeze. "You really are swell, Violet. He'll live. Now, whether or not the rest of us will is another story."

<hr />

May 30, 1923
Opening Day

The few bites of scone I'd managed that morning to take the edge off my hunger felt like lead in my stomach as we waited for the curtain to rise on the first show of the day, a 2:30 p.m. matinee.

We'd have another show tonight, taking note of what was a hit or a miss with the audience this afternoon.

As usual, Freddie's nerves were on fire, blazing outward from his body to burn mine, but he'd refined every move, every word, until there was nothing left to perfect.

I, on the other hand, was always afraid I'd walk out onstage and stumble into the orchestra pit, landing on the tuning pins in the baby grand piano, with the lid slamming down on my head. *That's all, folks! Show's over*, I could practically hear the producer saying.

Of course, this was a ridiculous fear, given I'd yet to do it in the decades we'd been performing together, but still—that's what fears were all about, right? The unknown. The chance that something won't go the way you want.

I flashed a smile at Mimi, squeezed Freddie's hand, and turned to nod at the rest of the crew, catching Violet's eye, and she looked about as nervous as I felt.

"Break a leg," I said with a chuckle to the whole gaggle.

The chorus girls shouted back in unison a clever cheer they'd taught me at our first preview performance: *"Merde!"* The word was French for "shit," and allegedly stemmed from the Paris Opera Ballet, at which, the better the show, the bigger the audience. The bigger the audience, the greater the number of carriages. The more carriages, the more horses—and, hence, more shit. *Merde!*

Our laughter was cut short by the snap of Edwards's fingers, as the lights went down and the overture sounded. That brief inhalation as the musical score began, right before the lights came back on and the curtain went up. The opening chorus was off and running as the orchestra struck up the first tune and the curtain rose.

Freddie and I charged onstage for the next scene, singing "All to Myself" before reciting our comedic lines. The audience was less than enthusiastic—barely a laugh, and rarely a cheer—and my stomach started to tighten. This was certainly not the reception we'd received in the earlier opening shows north of London.

By midway through Act 2, the crew was starting to feel their nerves at the lack of audience interest in our performance. One night in London, and surely we were going back to America.

I stared up at my brother as we waited for our cue to go on for the "Oh Gee! Oh Gosh!" number.

"Let's give 'em hell, Freddie." I tried to smile.

He grinned down at me, as if some of his jitters were ebbing for a minute, making me feel better. "That's all we know how to do, right?"

"Yeah. They don't know what they're missing. We could be popping out of cakes," I said, referring to our first vaudeville act when we were children.

Freddie chuckled. "They have no idea."

We frolicked onto the lit stage, ready to make the most of the rest of the second half. Four more numbers to go, and then we could tuck tail and return to New York.

Our lines cued and Freddie gave an exaggerated character scowl over my shoulder. "Well, I'm surprised you were flirting with that fortune hunter . . ."

I put my hands on my hips and stuck my tongue out. "Well, it's none of your business who I flirt with."

"It is, too! It's every man's business to protect foolish women."

"Oh, I'm foolish, am I?"

After some light bickering with a humorous edge, Freddie, my supposed love interest, leaned in close and started to sing about a reluctant lover needing to express himself to his desired partner.

There was a decided shift in the audience then, and we could both feel it. An energy that started somewhere in the middle and fanned outward. I lifted my shoulder, extra quirky-like, gazing coyly at Freddie as he continued through his lyrics, pulling out the funny lines about being mad about me, sad about me.

If this was going to be my last night in London, the audience better bet their asses I was going to blow them away. I batted my lashes, did a hasty twirl away and then leaned back, hands clasped over my heart, and sang about my beating heart.

There was a collective whoosh of air in the house as several people laughed and even more applauded. We were finally winning them over. Freddie and I kept singing, our energy growing with the audience's excitement. And it continued that way through our next number, "It's Great to Be in Love," and then when we sang "The Whichness of the Whatness" and broke into our runaround move, circling the stage as if we were on bikes, going faster and faster, making one face after another at each other. The audience lost it—thank God!—and I knew in that instant that we were going to be a success.

The entire company joined us onstage in the limelight to shouts from the crowd for an encore. The blood in my veins zinged with excitement.

What had started out looking like it would be our last overseas performance had quickly turned around. I beamed at Freddie and he looked back at me with equal delight.

"You did it," Mimi murmured beside me as we took our bows. "You saved us."

"Oh, I don't know about that. I think it was 'The Whichness of the Whatness,' which is all of us." I gave an exaggerated cluck-cluck of my tongue.

Mimi laughed at my subtle play on words.

I peeked behind me to see Violet grinning radiantly out at the crowd. I remembered my first audience, the exhilaration of their approval, the desire to keep going, to give them everything they wanted and more. When I caught her eye, I winked, and she blushed, mouthing, "Thank you."

We bowed again and again, until the audience quieted down, and Sir Alfred Butt and Alex Aarons came out to join us onstage, thanking the audience for attending our London debut. Then the two men pointed at each of us in turn and we waved to the crowd with more enthusiasm than I'd ever waggled before.

A few hours later, we did it all over again, and this time the audience was even more excited. A few flowers were tossed onto the stage, daisies, roses, and tulips resting at our feet. And I couldn't be too certain, but I was pretty sure I recognized some of the faces from our matinee.

"Thank you so much!" I called out to the audience, and in my exuberance, with a bit of teasing to boot, I said, "I'd invite you all to tea, if I could."

Cheers and laughter went up at that, and then we stayed in place as the heavy velvet curtain dropped with a whoosh, separating the players from the watchers. We all let out a collective sigh amid congratulations and jokes about tea and scones.

The dressing rooms were abuzz with chatter as we peeled off our sweaty costumes and stockings, rubbed our aching feet. But nothing felt as good as having had a successful show.

Freddie was waiting outside my dressing room, and I threaded my arm through his, exhausted but energized all at the same time. That was the way it was after a successful show, and to have had two in one day . . . all the pent-up worries Freddie'd had, which I'd internalized, drifted away.

As we approached the stage door, it sounded like a horde was on the other side. Freddie and I exchanged concerned glances.

I was unnerved, to say the least. "Jeepers . . ."

On the other side of the door were at least two dozen people, dressed in their finest and calling out our names. Actors, literary phenoms, and aristocrats, all wanting us to come out to the clubs, to not let the night be over.

"Well, I'm starved," I said with a shrug, completely ignoring the chaos only a few feet away.

"Who's up for dinner first?"

A series of chuckles and notes of "*How charming she is*" went up through the crowd.

"You don't know my sister," Freddie said. "She's completely serious."

That only made them laugh harder. Then a handsome fellow stepped forward and the crowd seemed to show him deference. I recognized him instantly from his pictures in the papers, but I had to be wrong. There was no way on earth a prince would be here.

Another man beside him cleared his throat. "His Royal Highness, the Prince of Wales."

I nearly lost my breath at that. It *was* him. Jeepers!

"Major Metcalf," Freddie said beside me, then whispered, "I thought it was a joke."

I didn't have time to reply before the major reiterated an earlier invitation that my brother had not taken seriously. "The prince would like to invite you to dine with him at the Riviera Club."

"We adored the show." The prince spoke to us as if he were a regular Joe and not a royal born. "You must all be in excellent shape to move around so adroitly."

"Thank you."

"So, shall we?" the prince asked.

I tried to lift my jaw from the floor to answer, but Freddie beat me to it. "We'll need to change first."

"Oh, there's no need for that." The prince waved away the idea, as if he couldn't see we were drenched in sweat and smelling as though we'd come out of the royal slosh pits.

"I think we'd rather," Freddie hedged, and I couldn't help adding, "Trust me, you'd rather we did."

The prince laughed, his blue eyes dancing merrily. "As you wish. I'll have my driver pick you up at your hotel and bring you to the Riviera."

Freddie thanked him, and the prince acted as if it were no big deal. I could barely feel my toes.

Was this some kind of jest? A test to see if we could be easily fooled? Perhaps it wasn't even the prince, but another actor putting us on. I stared at the handsome fellow, trying to assess if it was serious or not, but the way the crowd stood in awe and the ladies drooled, I had a feeling he was exactly who he said he was.

The prince departed and we made a push through the galleryites and out the door toward our hotel. An hour later, we were in a car, the prince's own driver taking us through town to Grosvenor Road in Westminster.

I barely looked at whatever supper I forked into my mouth, too enthralled at our luck. When our meal was cleared away and a big band struck up a tune, the Prince of Wales leaned toward me. "Miss Astaire, please tell me you aren't too tired to dance with me."

"I may be exhausted, Your Highness," I teased, leaping up and holding out my hand, hoping he didn't notice how it trembled. "But never too tired to hoof it with a royal."

"Delly, do call me David."

That night, I had the extreme pleasure of teaching the prince to tap-dance at a nightclub, and we posed, with smiles wide on our faces, as the flashes of photographers caught it on camera.

When it was nearing midnight, Freddie signaled it was time to go. As we settled into the prince's car on the way back to our hotel, I whispered to my brother, "Oh, gee, oh, gosh, I think I'm going to like it here."

CHAPTER SIX

VIOLET

THE LIMELIGHT

This just in, a certain playboy Prince has been dancing until the wee hours with a noteworthy starlet nearly every night this week. Does our current drama Queen hope to make a play for a crown jewel on her finger? Perhaps she's better at making her curtsey onstage instead of before the throne. Experts encourage sticking with what you know, and one thing has been proven—the Astaires can dance.

December 1923

Violet huddled close to Adele, whose thick fur coat collar was tucked around her chin, as snow floated down onto their heads. Violet wished she had more than her decades-old, threadbare coat to keep her warm. She'd sewn a faux-fur liner around the collar and hem to make it look more fashionable, but that kept her about as warm as a pair of stockings in an ice bath.

Beggars couldn't be choosers. The low salary she made dancing onstage was enough to pay her half of the rent with Caty—whom she'd been fortunate enough to confide in before being forced to spend nights sleeping backstage—and send some money back home for Pris. Her mother never acknowledged the letters with the money, but Violet tried not to be hurt by that, knowing that she was at least helping her sister.

She and Adele had continued to grow close, much to the dismay of certain people, such as Bridgette, whom Violet unfortunately still had to see daily for their performances and rehearsals. Their show continued to run, selling out daily for both the matinee and night shows. There seemed to be no end to the amount of flirting London folks wished to see.

"There he is," Adele whispered, her cheeks pink with excitement. Anyone else would think her flush was simply from the cold. But Violet knew that sensation, that stirring in the belly that made one feel as if they had a deep itch that needed to be scratched.

The fancy Rolls pulled to a stop outside the Savoy, where they'd gotten ready.

The Prince of Wales—the *prince*!—leapt out of the car and Adele executed a flawless curtsey. The prince made a show of dipping into a low bow toward Adele. He'd been courting her for months now. All the papers were going nuts for it: Adele, the star of *Stop Flirting*, the gorgeous and exotic American actress who'd captured the prince's attention. Everyone knew he loved all things American.

But he wasn't the only one to have been captivated by Adele. The papers were flying out of the newsboys' hands and off the carts faster than they could be printed.

Most of the London elite, with their fancy shoes and dazzling jewels, adored Adele Astaire. Clamored for her. If one had an *Hon.* in front of their name, or was addressed as "Your Grace," it was almost guaranteed that they'd seen Adele onstage *and* invited her to dine.

Luckily, or not, Violet was there to witness it all. To be a part of something greater than any goals she had envisioned for herself. Violet pinched herself every night, waiting to wake up. In the morning when she woke, she found that she was still living two lives: the tossed-out daughter of an East Ender, working her arse off from before dawn until after sunset just to survive, and also the close friend of a megastar who dated a prince.

"Gosh, he is so handsome," Adele whispered, leaning so close that Violet could smell the Amami shampoo in her hair, the Ponds cream on her skin, the Chanel perfume that surrounded her. Violet had her own bottle of Chanel No. 5, which Adele had given her on her birthday.

"He is." Violet wouldn't begrudge the prince his good looks, but the royals lived luxuriously, lapping up clotted cream–covered scones and caviar while their people got by on cabbage soup or a crust of bread. She tried not to be bitter about it, but sometimes it got the better of her.

"And his brother is so charming."

The statements about their looks and charm were given so casually about the princes. As if they were everyday people. Violet adored Adele, but in this instance she believed her friend's eyes had become quite hazy in the glare of a glittering crown.

"They sure do make a very striking duo." Violet wished she'd not agreed to come tonight. A pint with Caty over a game of checkers sounded so much better than trite conversation with uppity blue bloods. But schmoozing was necessary if she wanted to gain a sponsor for a future performance.

"Oh, this is going to be fun." Adele slid a glance toward her brother. "Don't tell Freddie *how* much fun."

Adele took the prince's arm as he led her toward the inviting white-leather interior of the vehicle.

"Get in!" Adele called as she slid across the seat, beckoning to Violet.

For a second, time seemed to stand still, and Violet stared at the grinning faces of the glittering, beautiful people in their expensive car, asking her to join them. She'd accompanied Adele for dancing before, but never when royalty was involved. This seemed an altogether different bridge to cross.

Violet thought of her mother, could hear Mum reminding her of where she belonged, forcing her to see that Adele's world wasn't hers. Try as she might, she couldn't make it stop.

"I really ought to get home." Violet flashed an apologetic smile that she'd perfected over the past few months, as she gave one excuse after another for having to bow out of invitations, mostly because she couldn't afford to accept them.

The guilt of disappointing Adele would be nothing compared to the guilt of telling Caty she couldn't make rent. Or the regret she'd feel in the morning when she woke too early after not nearly enough sleep.

"Oh, come on, Violet, you're always running home." Adele pouted, but it wasn't she who'd spoken.

Violet turned with surprise to see Fred Astaire grinning in her direction.

"Now, as one who prefers the comforts of home, and the hours of sleep necessary to keep this show going, I can appreciate your reluctance. But"—he nodded toward the Rolls—"how often do commoners like us get to go dancing with royals?"

Fred had a point. One that made no sense to refute. She'd just limit her drinks and subsist on porridge for the rest of the week to pay for it. At least she could say she'd sacrificed for a prince. And who could say no to His Royal Highness?

With a weary grin that matched Fred's, Violet nodded and joined Adele in the back of the Rolls. Glasses of champagne in hand, they toasted the show and friendship, bubbly dribbles slipping down the sides of the glasses as the Rolls maneuvered through traffic.

They arrived at the Riviera Club a few minutes later. Violet was not much for drinking alcohol, and the champagne made her legs wobbly as she climbed out of the car. The first sip had gone straight to her head and made her cheeks flame with heat. Fred helped her stay upright when she momentarily lost her balance.

The club was crowded with the upper crust of British society, their jewels flashing in the low light. Clouds of their various expensive French perfumes mixed with peals of laughter and saucy tones.

Violet was out of place, and the valet who took her threadbare coat knew it as he passed her a strange look, seeing her with the princes and other aristos. *What are* you *doing here?* his expression questioned. Violet looked away. She couldn't even offer him a smile of apology because it would feel too forced. She'd once heard one of the snotty Mayfair types say it was terribly American of Adele to befriend a young dancer from the slums.

But Violet wasn't sorry. Not in the least.

She followed the line of gods and goddesses deeper into the club and slid into the seat beside Adele, placing on the table her small purse that she'd embroidered herself for her fourteenth birthday. What was another passing of a year in this life if one couldn't give oneself a gift?

At least she felt more comfortable in the dress she was wearing. It was the first thing she'd splurged on for herself since taking the chorus girl position. Not exactly a fancy, famous designer, but, if anyone looking squinted just so, they would never notice. Besides, Violet felt beautiful in the dress, with its silver sequins sparkling and the fringe swishing below her knees. Dressed like this, she blended right in with the rest of the flapper crowd.

"Cocktail?" Prince George, the younger brother of Adele's beau—also known as Bertie to his good friends—gestured at her. "My treat."

Violet nodded, promising herself she'd only sip it, and not drink more than half. Adele leaned closer to the Prince of Wales, who was paying her particular attention.

Freddie glowered in their direction until the band struck an upbeat tune, trumpets humming and drums thumping. Without a backward glance, he two-stepped his way to the parquet dance floor.

Violet tapped her feet to the beat under the table, watching a ring of dancers form around Freddie to observe. She twirled her untouched cocktail.

"This is a great song, isn't it? Let's go dance, Violet," Adele's singsong voice called out, over the din.

Violet glanced up from the swirling curl of lemon peel in her glass to find Adele wiggling her brows.

When it came to fun, Adele's energy was boundless. Even when exhausted during rehearsal, if someone suggested they go out dancing instead the American dancer would be the first in line. Her sore toes were miraculously healed, or too numb to notice.

Violet admired her energy and enthusiasm for life and often tried to mimic it, because it seemed like so much fun to be Adele Astaire.

"Of course." Violet hopped up.

"You going to dance?" a gentleman asked, his light-blue, intelligent eyes meeting hers.

"Yes." She flicked her gaze toward Adele, who'd already started to make her way through the crowd.

"Do you have a partner?"

Oh, my . . . what would Adele say? If Violet admitted she didn't have anyone to dance with, would he think her not worthy, or would that get her an ask? Navigating the wilds of the upper-class life wasn't exactly her forte. She knew how to dance, she could serve them a drink, and that's about where her talents ended. With a flick of her tongue across her lower lip, she said the first Adele-like thing that came to mind. "Depends."

"On what?" He cocked his head.

Suddenly she felt bolder. "On whether or not you're going to ask me."

His brows raised, nearly touching his forehead, and then he broke out into a wide grin. "You bet I am."

He held out his arm and, with a grin right back at him, Violet took it.

As they joined those on the dance floor, Adele caught her eye and winked. Violet winked back.

"I'm Paul Reid, by the way." He twirled her around, and then into his arms.

Ah, the infamous owner of a fancy sportscar who'd been court-ing Mimi at the beginning of the show. They'd since broken up, from what Violet had read in the papers. "Nice to meet you, Paul. I'm Violet."

"You dance wonderfully."

The compliment sent a thrill through her. After dancing pro-fessionally day after day, her confidence had grown exponentially. Even music had a new tenor for her, now that she'd danced center stage. The past months had been incredible, to put it mildly.

"A good thing," she teased. "Else Adele would kick me off the stage."

"Oh, no, I think that'd be Freddie."

Violet laughed. Fred Astaire couldn't stand anyone not up to snuff. And she made it her daily goal *not* to be on his radar.

They danced to one slow song, and then an upbeat one, swinging over the parquet floor as if their feet had wings. Sweat trickled down her spine, and her limbs felt vibrantly alive.

❖

February 1924
Paris

Violet and Caty barely slept as their excitement for a trip abroad kept them awake most of the night. They'd tried on everything in their closets, swapping dresses, blouses, and skirts, until their small bags were bursting with fabric. They'd then ridden the Tube as far as they could before hailing a taxi to the airport, and hopped a clipper to Paris with Adele and the others. Violet was grateful she'd taken their producer's advice early on to get a passport, should she need to go abroad.

Now, standing beneath the Eiffel Tower, its iron bars perfectly crisscrossed at precise angles as it jutted sharply toward the starry sky, she was grateful for a whirlwind holiday. A chance to see a piece of the world. And once again, she was grateful Mr. Cowden had let her go. The number of people coming in to see the show had softened his hardness toward her.

Midnight in Paris was different than in London. The streetlamps emitted a soft yellow glow, and people still walked arm in arm as if it were just past dinner. The clubs were abuzz with instruments and singing.

Even if her dancing career didn't take off, even if *Stop Flirting* was the last show she ever did, Violet would still have this moment in time to look back on with a delighted shiver.

"Incredible, isn't it?" Paul asked.

Violet cocked her head, deciding how to answer. The truth was, she'd found it more incredible in the daylight when she could see the tip at the top, whereas now it blended in with the sky.

"I can't see the top."

Paul moved to stand behind her, his hands on her shoulders as he shifted her position. "Now look."

There it was, the triangular pinnacle with the moon as its backdrop. She let out a breath. What a magical year this was turning out to be. But, as with all dreams, she had that angsty feeling in the back of her mind that everything was going to burst and she'd come tumbling down from the clouds.

"Now you understand," he said with a chuckle.

And she did. Strangely mesmerized by that point. Paul's hand slid down her arm before it fell away, as he stood behind her staring up.

He was one of the entourage that had followed the Astaires to Paris, which included a few swanky literary types whose names all began with *Honorable*. Then there was the prince, who'd taken to calling Adele "Delly," as Freddie did.

"I would kill for some ice cream right now," Adele announced to the group.

"Should we find a shop and warn its owner?" Caty teased.

At this hour, was it even likely that anything would be open?

Violet yawned. They'd arrived in Paris that morning and barely taken a break since. Her mind reeled from the show at the Moulin Rouge and the cocktails she'd become accustomed to accepting—and drinking.

Freddie was lagging like Violet, while Caty seemed as energetic as Adele. Violet wished it wouldn't be inappropriate to beg Paul to escort her back to the hotel, but she didn't want to give him the wrong message because he was obviously interested.

Mimi grabbed hold of Adele's and Caty's arms and they romped around in a circle, doing the runaround dance that had caused a stir across London. Several other shows had copied the Astaires' signature move. In fact, Violet had jokingly suggested that Adele go to one of the shows on April Fools' Day and greet the dancers at the end, congratulating them on their "original" work. So far, the plan had taken root, and they were expecting to do that in just over a month's time with a large group, whose members were excited for the coup of the season.

"I know an ice cream shop," Paul piped up.

Violet looked at him, surprised, because he often didn't like to play midnight shenanigans when they'd gone out with the group before.

"Just up the road, actually."

He offered Violet his arm with a wink. She'd really grown to like him quite a bit over the past few months that she'd gotten to know him. But she needed to keep him at arm's length. Allowing anything or anyone to derail her from her goal was out of the question. When her mum gave her the ultimatum to either stay behind and have a roof over her head or seek her place onstage, Violet had promised herself she'd never let another person get in the way of her dreams. And right now those dreams were looking like they'd become a reality.

"Do you like ice cream?" he asked.

Violet nodded, too embarrassed to admit she'd never had it before. Ice cream was one of those treats that seemed as far away from her possession as a diamond tiara.

"Then you will simply keel over from La Crème," he said.

"I'll have to eat it sitting down," she teased back, hoping he didn't notice how much of an imposter she really was.

Paul shrugged. "Or I could hold you up."

Her face flamed with heat, and she smiled but didn't want to encourage him with a reply.

Paul was not wrong—the parlor was open for business. The cold, sweet, creamy confection melted on her tongue and Violet closed her eyes in sheer pleasure, swaying on her feet. Paul, true to his word, pressed his hand to her elbow, then the small of her back, leaning close to whisper against her ear, "I knew you'd like it."

A shiver snaked its way dangerously down her spine. Rather than believe it was from Paul's whispered words, she decided it was the pleasure of the ice cream. Denial was a skill she'd had all her life.

How Violet could ever go back to a world of boiled cabbage and crusts of bread was beyond her. Impossible, really. Already it had been nearly a year since their first show, and there seemed to be no end in sight. The audience was still raving mad, with some people claiming to have seen them perform fifty times. She was starting to understand that bone-deep ache Adele talked about, but she wasn't going to let that stop her from getting to the top.

CHAPTER SEVEN

ADELE

THE LIMELIGHT

Soon all of Great Britain will be in mourning. Rumor has it the best long courtship between London's darling and the West End is coming to as abrupt an end as the American star's romance with our beloved Prince. Time to bring out your black veils, and join us in our sorrow.

August 1924
Strand Theatre, London

Agust of late-summer wind pushed against my chest as if it could delay the very last performance of *Stop Flirting*. This moment was bittersweet as I stood outside the Strand, Freddie at my side, likely wondering why my feet had stopped moving. We'd toured all over Great Britain, from London up to Scotland and back. Multiple theatres across the West End.

I was exhausted. And I knew that Freddie was, too, even if he didn't want to admit it.

The endless rehearsals and getting used to new stages, followed by hundreds of performances, were grueling. *Stop Flirting* had run longer than any of us had ever expected—more than five hundred showings.

The cast had started to mimic me, calling the show "Nonstop Flirting," because we were on an endless loop. The bottoms of my feet were so calloused that I could have walked on a bed of nails with nary a puncture, and there wasn't a night that went by when I didn't toss and turn, trying to find a comfortable position that didn't put pressure on my hips and shoulders, which seemed eternally agitated.

Everyone was beyond exhausted. So much so that one night in Glasgow when Freddie, midshow, had gone back to his dressing room to disrobe, utter chaos ensued as everyone tried to find out where he'd gone before his next scene. My poor brother had been so bushed from performing 144 dances a week for more than a year that he'd simply forgotten to finish the show. I found him, purple smudges beneath his eyes, with his shirt half undone, ready to call it a night.

In true Astaire fashion, we'd cooked up a scheme right quick. Freddie improvised, with his character claiming to have been assaulted and forced into a fistfight just outside, which explained his disrobed and disheveled appearance.

I winged it and cooed over his rumpled shirt, and the audience went wild. But that had been the beginning of the end for this run. Much to everyone's dismay—well, not *everyone's*. I was damned excited at the possibility of a break and a return to our own shores. I loved London, had thought I wanted to stay, but I also found myself missing New York terribly.

We were London's darlings, but this wasn't our hometown. After the longest run of our lives, we needed a reprieve. Just standing outside the theatre now, I wondered if my knees would give out the moment I stepped onstage, and all of me would just crumple to the floor. My body done, even if my mind begged for one last dance.

I was equal parts excitement and trepidation. What was next for us?

We'd been gone from home for a long time. Those in show business were often forgotten in weeks, let alone in the year we'd been out of New York's limelight. Our success in London had been prolific, netting Freddie and me advertising deals for things like face cream and top hats. Even those who didn't visit the theatres knew who we were because the papers printed articles about us nearly weekly. We also wrote pieces ourselves on dancing, performing, and, really, anything they asked, because it kept people buying tickets.

Our faces were just as recognizable as the Prince of Wales's—my one regret maybe leaving him behind. But, as much as I thought myself in love with David, there was no future for us. He was a prince, after all, first in line to the throne. And men who were going to be kings didn't marry American stars. That was a comical idea: an American married to a royal. I shook my head. *Never going to happen.*

Oh, but the stories I'd have to share about our courtship would last me a lifetime.

"Delly?" The worried expression on Freddie's face begged to know if I was about to run off.

"Just taking it all in," I said.

What was next for our crew? I wouldn't deny feeling some guilt at leaving all the good friends and dancers behind. Especially Violet. Even though she no longer lived at home, she still sent most of her wages to her mother, hoping they helped to support her sister. The East End of London wasn't all that different from some of the poor areas of America, where kids worked to help feed the family. Hell, that was what the Gerrymen had been invented for. I could understand completely Violet's angst about that.

Being friends with Freddie and me, Violet had managed to stay away from the grabby hands of the stage manager, and I hoped it stayed that way. She'd yet to tell me which show was next for her, but I knew she'd been on a few auditions. Violet was on the rise, and I wished her nothing but the best.

"You okay?" Freddie asked, not pushing me to go inside, as I knew he wanted to.

I nodded slowly. "Just thinking about this long run, and the crew."

"We'll keep in touch," Freddie said. "And we'll be back."

"One can only hope." I grinned, though inside I kind of hoped that the only reason to make the ocean-liner journey back would be to visit our friends, rather than put on another epic performance.

"Ready?" Freddie nodded toward the door, his voice a little anxious.

"As I'll ever be."

We made our way inside and backstage to start getting ready for the show. The scent of gardenias hit me with a blast of sweetness as I entered my dressing room. Every day, dozens of bouquets were delivered, and it felt as if I prepared for each show in a veritable greenhouse. Everyone kept saying I was London's darling, but if they'd only known me well they might have changed their mind.

As I sat at my dressing table, looking at my reflection, to think this was the last show was surreal. We'd been going at it for so long, it felt strange to realize that tomorrow we wouldn't.

I dabbed some makeup beneath my eyes, hiding from the audience the toll a run like this one took. A scratch sounded at the door.

"Come in," I sang out, the way Violet always said sounded as if I had a permanent smile in my throat.

But Violet knew better. We all wore masks here, tucked up tight around our faces; no one could see the parts of us we kept hidden. The longing part. A darker piece of myself that huddled somewhere behind my ribs, wishing for things that weren't. It had grown since I'd broken things off with the prince, not wanting our goodbyes to languish over the impossible.

I recognized something similar in Violet, a mirrored fragment within her, though we longed for different things.

And, speak of the devil, Violet stepped into the small room, shutting the door behind her.

"The face I'll miss the most when I go back to New York." I pointed a smile her way, then pulled on a pair of stockings, my toe poking out the end. With a groan I pulled them off and riffled through the drawer until I found a new pair. "Why don't you come with me, Vi? You'd make a stunning star there, and I'm not sure how I'm going to make it without you."

"You've made it this far," Violet said, leaning over to sniff a fresh bouquet.

"Fair enough. But what about you? What are you planning to do?"

Violet shrugged, moving on to another bouquet and giving me the impression she was avoiding the question.

"We'd get you plenty of gigs; you might even get a chance to be one of Ziegfeld's Follies." I wiggled my brows, suggesting it would be a scandal.

Violet gave me a curious glance. "Ziegfeld's Follies? What's that?"

"Only the most popular dance show on Broadway." I curled my lip in the mirror and scrubbed the line of lipstick off my teeth.

"Oh. That does sound like heaven. Is that what you'll be doing?"

"No." I smiled, not wanting to voice the murmurs of a new show, because what I really wanted to do was lie in bed for a year. "Think about it?"

"All right." Violet nodded. "I'll think it over. But I'd hate to leave Pris . . ."

"It wouldn't be permanent, just long enough for a run." Seeing that Violet was uncomfortable, I decided to change the subject. I could tell by the way she was looking at me that she was going to say no. Even with her mother having kicked her to the curb, Violet held on to the unfair guilt. "Break a leg out there today, Vi. Are you going to join us for the party afterward? It's our last show; we'd best make a toast." I started the process of pinning my curls up, making it look as if I had one of the short, fashionable bobs, when in fact my hair was down to my waist.

Violet nodded in the mirror. "I wanted to give you something." She reached into her satchel and pulled out a small envelope. The card was a lavender color and covered in adorable blue birds with golden feathers.

I stopped pinning for a moment to accept the beautiful card, which had to have cost Violet a small fortune. "What's this?"

"A note to say thank you so much for all you've done for me." Tears gathered in Violet's eyes, and my throat did that funny tickling thing it did when I cried.

I flew out of my chair and wrapped my arms around her. "I'm going to miss you so much, Vi. London, this show, wouldn't have been the same without your friendship. Promise you'll stay in touch?"

"Of course." Violet attempted a smile, but the wariness of it prickled at my ribs. "Find me when you're back in London."

"If only I could be so lucky."

"You're an international star now. You'll be back."

"Freddie said almost the same thing. So, if the two of you believe it, then it must be true."

We put on our best show to date, all of us feeling the emotions ten times more than at any other performance, knowing this was the last. At the end of the night, when the crowd cheered and called for an encore, we sang "Auld Lang Syne." I let the tears fall then, in unison with the rest of the cast. Although we were crying for the end of a show, all of us had new adventures to go on to. New dreams to fulfill.

We blew out of the theatre with laughter and sobs and hugs, everyone planning to attend one last party. But as we finalized our plans Violet edged away, making me pause my steps.

"Where are you going?" I asked.

"Goodbyes are hard enough, made worse by a few drinks." She shrugged. "I think I'll head off now before I'm crying into a cocktail."

"Oh, please come. It's our last night together."

"You have to come," Caty, her roommate, chimed in. "We're going to shake the whole club down."

Violet shook her head slowly, the set of her mouth firm. "I'm no good at goodbyes."

Caty pouted and tried to tug on Violet's arm, but the young dancer remained rooted in place.

"Can I at least offer you a ride home?" I knitted my brows, wishing I could change her mind, but I understood Violet well enough to know when she was in a mood like this there was no turning it around. She'd made up her mind, and the best thing I could do was support her. "I hate for us to part like this."

"I'll be fine." Violet smiled, and then hugged me so tightly that I could barely breathe. I hugged her right back. "And we're not parting forever."

"I expect to see you on our next London leg, if we're so lucky."

"I will be in the front row."

"Rubbish, darling, you'll be onstage with me." I embraced her one more time, giving her a kiss on the cheek.

Violet stepped away from the group, walking in the opposite

direction without turning back. The space behind my ribs was suddenly tight with regret at not having begged her harder. My dearest friend in London, not someone any of the upper classes would have expected. But it always came down to the roots, didn't it? And maybe that's what I found so enchanting about Violet. Born to nothing, like me, and we were showing the world up.

Cars, taxis, and trucks whizzed by, oblivious to my heartbreak. A lady with her dog jostled past, her husband hot on her heels. And the world went on. As if I'd not just said goodbye to a show, and a dear friend, scarcely moments before. As if it didn't matter what the world held in store for us.

PART TWO

SHALL WE TANGO OR JAZZ?

"The Astaires were like automatons. They were magic, covering the stage with this terribly smooth, gorgeous rhythm bringing the best of American choreography together—we couldn't believe they were quite human."
—HERMIONE BADDELEY,
REFERENCING *LADY BE GOOD!*

CHAPTER EIGHT

ADELE

THE LIMELIGHT

There's trouble in paradise for the famous brother-and-sister duo Fred and Adele Astaire. The slap heard round the world! Arriving late to a show, after tippling too much on the arm of her new beau, Adele Astaire was allegedly slapped by her brother for her irresponsible behavior. It begs the question, did he also shout "Lady be good!" as he did it? Perhaps a stunt for their show with the same name?

Late 1924
New York City

We'd no sooner walked down the gangplank to find our pile of luggage than Alex Aarons was waving a contract in our faces, which we signed on top of the trunk stack. I suppose we should have been grateful for the employment, but, sheesh, he could have let us settle into our digs first.

With a little time left before our next show's rehearsals started, Freddie and I took in all the hottest numbers on Broadway, both for the fun of it and to check out our competition. A year and a half is a long time to be away from home, and, after all those months away, there were some new up-and-comers.

"Tonight we're going to El Fey Club," Freddie whispered as we left Dillingham's new musical, *Stepping Stones*. One actress stood out to me, Dorothy Stone, a debut who was going to hit it big.

I pressed my hand to my chest in mock shock, the sounds of New York filling our ears as we waited for a taxi. "Why, Freddie, you want to go to a speakeasy? But what about our rest? What about rehearsal? It's already nearing midnight."

He rolled his eyes and gave my ribs a light jab. "If there's one thing I know about you, sis, it's that you were planning to go already."

I shrugged coyly as Freddie waved his hand for a cab. "Anyone who is everyone will be there."

"And we'd best get it out of your system before rehearsals for *Lady Be Good* start."

I grinned as we climbed into a taxi.

"West Forty-Fifth, Mac," Freddie said.

We whizzed through the familiar New York streets toward El Fey Club. We'd heard so much about this joint, owned and managed by Texas Guinan, an actress whom we'd met on the vaudeville circuit. Although El Fey was often raided, it was a sight to behold and the place to be for theatrical celebrities, the rich and famous, and a sprinkling of underworld mobsters.

As we entered the speakeasy, through cigarette smoke made blue by the lights, Texas's voice rang out over the crowd. "Hello, suckers! Don't dawdle, come on in. And while you're at it, leave your wallet on the bar."

"Oh, boy," Freddie murmured, but all I could do was laugh as we were swept up into the dimly lit club, its music's beat thrumming through our veins.

It sure did feel good to be back in New York.

We claimed a table, quickly surrounded by friends we'd long missed—George Gershwin among them—but as the drinks were being served, Freddie's eyes were on the dance floor, watching a man hoof a Charleston like I'd never seen. His footwork was quick, executed with a precision and flair that made us look like amateurs.

"Who's that?" Freddie asked, waving off the offer of a cocktail from a smartly dressed waiter.

"George Raft," George Gershwin called out over the music as he lit a cigarette.

In an instant, Freddie was up from the table, parting the crowds as he approached the dance floor. He took the man's hand in two of his, shaking vigorously as he spoke. Although Freddie might have been enthralled by this bloke's fancy feet, it seemed there was a high volume of mutual appreciation going on.

Not a second later, the two of them were facing off, their feet flying, and those on the dance floor had backed up to form a circle around them to watch—and blocked my view. I didn't want to miss out on what felt like a monumental moment. I leapt up from the table—not too upset to leave my bootleg gin behind; it wasn't my bag—and joined the boys.

The three of us danced until sweat dripped from our brows, and even Texas joined us, egging the crowd on as we shuffled.

We closed down the house, bleary-eyed, at five o'clock in the morning when the doors shut, with Texas begging us to come back.

"Thank God rehearsals don't start until next week," I said, rubbing my temples, which hurt from exhaustion and dehydration more than anything else.

Freddie chuckled, wiping his hands over his face and then loosening his collar. "I'll be honest, Delly, the plot of this one seems pretty stupid."

"At least we're cast as brother and sister instead of lovers."

"Good point."

We linked arms and then hopped into one of the waiting cabs.

FREDDIE WAS RIGHT—*the* plot *was* stupid. But the numbers were good; magical, even. The lyrics and beat allowed Freddie and me to capitalize on what we did best, which was showcasing our talents with comedic highlights. Naturally the crowd loved us, calling the show witty, playful, and full of the Astaire spark. We even added a new bit of fun to our stage exits, which was to continue our dance steps, traveling offstage without stopping. *Lady Be Good* got such rave reviews that by April 1925 Alex Aarons asked if we'd be willing to perform in London at the year's end, to which we heartily agreed.

"I think it's time we got a Rolls-Royce," Freddie said one afternoon after rehearsals, while we were changing out of our dance shoes.

"I'm surprised it took you so long to say so," I answered, with a waggle of my fingers and my thumb on my nose. Freddie had been eyeing a pamphlet on Rolls-Royces for months.

"They are pricey," he hedged.

"How do you propose we pay for it?" We'd been getting a good salary and had plenty of money in the bank, especially with Freddie doing the accounting. But he was rather frugal when it came to our keeping it that way, so I knew he'd not want to spend the funds outright. We'd learned more than once as kids that in showbiz the money could dry up just as easily as it flowed.

"Funny you should ask," he said. "We've been offered a gig at the Trocadero Club."

I wrinkled my nose; hadn't we just turned down Texas? "Performing at a nightclub?" I enjoyed dancing at clubs, and I liked watching others do the entertaining. But there was a big difference between dancing for fun and dancing for money. "It'd have to be after midnight, with *Lady Be Good* going on, and you'd hate that. We'll be totally wasted—and not in the sense of being drunk."

"But I'd love to drive a Rolls." Freddie's head rolled on his shoulders the way a toddler's would when he wanted something.

I laughed and held out my hand for Freddie to pull me up. As he did, everything cracked, and I spent a few breaths stretching out the kinks in my spine. "For how long?"

Freddie's head snapped back into place and he locked eyes with me. "Six weeks. And they've agreed to pay us five thousand a week to do it."

My eyes nearly bulged from their sockets at that sum. "You're kidding."

"Nope."

"That's thirty thousand dollars!" The sum was so large for so puny a job that I practically choked on it. "Just to dance a couple hours a night?"

Freddie nodded and wiggled his eyebrows, as if we'd gotten away with highway robbery. "We'll have enough for a nice flat in London even after we buy the baby Rolls. Besides, it's a bit of friendly competition, and I know how much you like that. The Trocadero is trying to mirror the success of Club Mirador, where Marjorie and Georges are dancing."

Freddie knew just the right way to send me spinning off the edge. "Oh, we're better than those two Brits."

"Exactly." He pointed at me and winked.

For three weeks Freddie and I danced nightly starting at 12:45 a.m., after having performed *Lady Be Good* once or twice that day already. We had a whole slew of new routines, and then some old ones that we rechoreographed. Then, one night, after we'd finished dancing and were sitting at a table with a few friends, shouts came from the entrance to the club, followed by a waiter rushing past us with a tray full of cocktails.

"Everybody stay put and this will go easy!" shouted a police officer, backed by nearly a dozen others in uniform, their pistols raised. The man doing the talking had a good sheen of sweat on his upper lip as he surveyed the crowd, taking in the odd mix. "Get back here, son," he called to the escaping waiter with a tray full of contraband.

But in his haste to make it to the kitchen to dump the illegal alcohol, the poor sap tripped over his own feet and the tray went flying. Everything moved in slow motion at that point. Glasses flying up in the air, champagne shooting upward from the coupes like golden, sparkly fountains and then slamming into the thick red carpet, obliterated.

"Damnit!" the officer shouted just as he reached the waiter and all the evidence of what he'd carried soaked into the floor.

Didn't take long for everyone else to follow suit, either tossing their drinks back or spilling them—and then there were the runners. It was all rather fascinating.

Freddie grabbed my hand and pulled me backstage, where we hoofed it out the back door and down the street. Neither of us had been imbibing, but we weren't willing to risk our necks for a Rolls. After the raid, business at the club slowed during the next week, and we agreed to take a pay cut for the last two weeks of the deal. We danced our hearts out every night, eager to please the crowd, even though we both knew we'd only done it for a lark.

When we weren't dancing, Freddie was back into horse racing with his friends Jock and Sandy, and I was going along for the ride sometimes, but mostly to avoid all the boys who were chasing me down. When you've been courted by a prince, everyone else seems so boring.

I fired off a letter to Violet, hoping she'd audition for the show, but for the past several months all the correspondence I'd sent her had been met with silence. Even the *Tatler* and the *Limelight* magazines were reporting that she'd basically disappeared from the stage. I was worried for her and had sent another letter to Caty, asking where she was, but Caty's reply had been vague, saying that Vi had gone on "holiday." When I arrived in England I would get to the bottom of it.

In the end, we decided that, with our upcoming run in London, we'd hold off on buying the Rolls until we got there. No sense in buying it now, only to ship it with us and then ship it back. Better to have to do that only once.

We performed *Lady Be Good* for an astonishing 330 shows in New York, with the final engagement in late September 1925, followed by a slew of performances on the road.

Although we'd kept in touch with most of our friends through letters, I'd hoped when returning to New York that the pull of London wouldn't be so strong, that my love for Europe was simply a phase. However, when the January morning came to board the *Majestic*, Freddie and I were both eager for it. The journey was swift, the air frigid when we walked on deck to get some exercise. But when you're cooped up on a ship for two weeks, the last thing you want to do is hide out in your cabin.

At last we stepped off the train in London, and I drew in a long gulp of cold city air. The sky was overcast, but that did nothing to dampen my bright mood. We had several weeks lined up to enjoy the West End shows and London clubs, and visit with friends before rehearsals started in March and we opened at the Empire in mid-April.

I searched the playbills for Violet's name but found it nowhere. When my telegrams went unanswered, I ventured to the little flat she shared with Caty and knocked on the door.

A muffled voice called something from within, and then hurried footsteps followed before the door swung open.

"Caty, darling," I said to the wide-eyed gal staring back at me, wearing a silk robe as if she'd only just been summoned from bed.

"Why, if it isn't Adele Astaire!" She smoothed her mussed hair.

"In the flesh."

"Do come in." Caty opened the door wider, beckoning me into the cozy flat. There was a small sofa and two matching chairs. A cellarette with a few bottles of liquor, some plain crystal, and a gramophone. It smelled of women's perfume and gin.

"I'm so sorry to tell you that Violet isn't here." Caty frowned, tightening the knot on her robe. "She's on holiday."

"You mentioned that in your letter. But that was months ago."

"Yes." Caty drew in a deep breath, the pinched look on her face disappearing into one of *I have an idea*, which meant she was probably going to lie. "How about a drink? I've gin or tea . . ."

I set my purse down on the sofa and stared right into the other dancer's face. "Caty. I didn't come for gin. Or tea. What is going on? Where is Vi?"

Caty straightened her shoulders and looked as if she was going to fight or lie her way out of answering, but then her shoulders sagged. "Well, she's gone up to Scotland to help an aunt."

"And given up the stage?"

"Her aunt needed a lot of help." Caty nodded, more as if she were trying to convince herself, rather than me.

I narrowed my eyes, seeing right through her antics. "She got knocked up?"

"The aunt?" Caty pursed her lips, then nodded empathically. "Yes. And Vi's gone to help. She had enough money to pay her part of the rent, though, so that was incredibly good of her."

"Caty, you're a brilliant dancer, but you're not a very good liar."

Caty's face fell, and for the first time I felt as if she was being genuine. "She swore me to secrecy. You can't tell her I told you."

"She's in trouble."

Caty nodded.

"Do you know who did it?"

"Some producer; she wouldn't tell me who."

"Damn. I was hoping she was just ignoring me." My heart ached for the friend who'd worked so damn hard to not be in this situation. She'd come up from the slums of London, been kicked out of her home by her mother, and now this?

"I've sent everything you posted up to Perth," Caty rushed. "She's grateful for it all. And I'm sure when she's back, she'll find you."

"When will that be?"

"Should be only a month or two more. She's due to pop any day, and then needs a few weeks to snap back into shape."

I let out a long sigh, wishing my friend had reached out to me, felt confident in confiding in me, but I understood. One of the earliest things I'd told Vi was to be careful of the pawing producers. To know she'd succumbed when I'd warned her off of that must have made her feel embarrassed.

"Thanks for telling me, Caty." I pulled a little note from my purse with our address on Park Lane, in hopes that Violet would come see me when she returned. "Now, you'll come to the audition for chorus dancers, won't you?"

"I would, you know I would, but I'm already cast in *Scotch Mist* with Tallulah Bankhead."

I grinned at the mention of the rising starlet. "We're going to see that show tonight. I'm sure you're smashing."

"I'm something." Caty laughed.

"It was good to see you, Caty. Don't be a stranger."

"It was lovely to see you, too, Miss Astaire. I'll be sure to catch *Lady Be Good* when you open."

"I'll send tickets."

"Thank you."

As spring pushed some of the winter chill away, and *Lady Be*

Good wowed our London audiences, Violet continued to remain absent. I looked for her, thinking a few times that I'd seen her in my peripheral vision, but it always seemed to be just a ghost of my imagination. As if Vi had never truly existed.

———◆———

August 1926

Our chauffeur pulled our black baby Rolls up to 17 Bruton Street.

"I don't even know why I'm here," I said to Freddie, who was straightening the lapels of his suit jacket and admiring his new diamond-and-ruby cuff links.

"Because when a royal invites you, you go."

"It's just a baby." I was pouting something fierce.

Freddie grinned at me. "Right, a harmless baby. Just the granddaughter of the king and queen, who made a point to come to our show last night. Would you snub Their Majesties?"

"No," I said begrudgingly. But the thing was, seeing our good friend Bertie and his duchess settled down with a baby after we'd danced together in dozens of clubs on our last tour, was a little depressing, and only a reminder that I'd yet to do the same. I was also a little nervous that David might be there.

"Out you go."

Our chauffeur came around, opened the door, and we stepped out into the London summer heat. We were ushered by the royal staff of the Duke and Duchess of York's residence into a drawing room, where Elizabeth stood beside Bertie, with a proud grin. Her short dark hair was parted in the middle, with a fringe of trimmed bangs on her forehead, which was all the rage. Elizabeth wasn't beautiful, and when Bertie had asked her to be his wife there'd been plenty of pretty ladies put out by it. But she had an elegance about her and a commanding demeanor that seemed to keep her husband at attention beside her, and which I'd come to respect.

David was nowhere in sight, and I let out a sigh of both relief and disappointment.

"Welcome, welcome." The usual stutter of the Prince of Wales's younger brother was momentarily restrained.

"Your Graces." I dipped into a curtsey, which I'd perfected on our last tour, and Freddie bowed.

"We're so glad you accepted our invitation," Elizabeth said. "Bertie told me your show is delightful, and I do so wish I'd been able to join last night when the King and Queen were present."

"It w . . . wa . . . was brilliant," Bertie said.

"We're so glad you enjoyed the show." I felt restrained in too formal a setting. I was used to dancing the Charleston with the princes, not feeling oppressed by the grand portraits hanging on the walls, and the forced stiffness of a proper state tea.

"Do sit down." Elizabeth indicated the gilded wood and upholstered armchairs and then went to the bell pull.

A moment later, tea service arrived, followed by a nanny, who brought with her an infant dressed in white. The baby was quiet, reflective, and, though she was almost four months old, still to me seemed so small.

"Would you care to hold her?" Elizabeth asked me.

I glanced at Freddie, afraid to say no, and desperately wanting to. But my brother nodded, reminding me that if I shunned the offer it would offend not only our friends but the King and Queen as well.

"Of course."

I held out my arms, feeling awkward. Had I ever held a baby before? Certainly I'd tried to hold Freddie, but I'd been so young, practically a baby myself. And I didn't even remember that.

The nanny pressed Princess Elizabeth into my arms, her wide, blue eyes staring up at me as if she knew my trepidation and dared me to drop her. She was light, but surprisingly solid, with a tuft of light curls on her head.

"Well, hello, Princess," I cooed softly, feeling as if I couldn't move an inch for fear of dropping her onto the thick carpet.

Princess Elizabeth burbled up at me, wiggling her arms, with a smile of delight that reached a place deep inside of me and squeezed.

"You're a . . . a . . . natural," Bertie said.

I glanced up at him and smiled. "I never would have thought so, but she is such a pleasant baby. Certainly it is because of that."

Elizabeth grinned with pride at her infant, and there was a little answering twinge in my belly. Apparently I, too, wanted to grin with pride at an infant I'd grown in my womb.

Before I started to panic, the nanny stepped in and took the baby from my arms, perhaps sensing my sudden change. She brought her to the duchess, who kissed her on the forehead, and then the baby princess was swept away.

"So, what's next for you two?" Elizabeth asked as she poured us tea, a swift recovery from mother to hostess. Royals certainly did fascinate me.

"Delly is sitting for a portrait painted by the Austrian Expressionist Oskar Kokoschka." Freddie smirked. "But he won't let her see his progress."

"Is that s . . . s . . . so?" Bertie asked.

"Twice a week, with Wassie." I made an exaggerated anxious face. "I am a bit worried he's painting me to look more like Wassie than myself, though, the way he's being so secretive."

"That darling Scottie of yours." Elizabeth grinned and I sipped the perfectly prepared tea. "He'd give you a handsome face. I do so love dogs."

I chuckled at that, surprised that Elizabeth had a sense of humor. From all her airs I would have expected her to be stuffy.

"What about a new sh . . . show?" Bertie lit a cigarette, the smoke curling around his face as he sipped his tea. Elizabeth cast him a look that said she didn't like him smoking, but he ignored her.

"*Lady Be Good* is supposed to run for another few months, but Alex Aarons is already floating a new idea our way for the States, called *Smarty*."

"Another comedy?" Elizabeth asked.

"Yes," Freddie replied.

"And will you be brother and sister again?" Elizabeth asked.

Freddie shook his head. "We wanted something different— and no more lovers, either." He chuckled. "This time I'm going to be a guardian to three girls, and Adele happens to be one of them."

"Oh, I can't wait for it to debut in the West End." Elizabeth daintily bit into a cucumber sandwich.

"The way our last couple of shows have gone, hopefully London will have us back again after the New York run," Freddie said.

Having spent the better part of 1926 in London, and knowing it would be well into 1927 before we were back in the States, this side of the Atlantic was starting to feel like home again. Was it possible to have a home in both places?

"Your baby will be a toddler by then," I jested.

Elizabeth chuckled. "Oh, my! I can't even imagine it."

"We've still a good few months of the show here in London before we tour in Glasgow. You haven't gotten rid of us yet," Freddie said.

Bertie drew in a long drag of his cigarette. "I'll p . . . p . . . pester my brother to host a farewell party for the both of you at S . . . St. James's Palace when the time c . . . comes."

"We'd be honored." Freddie took a scone from the platter. "The parties at St. James's Palace are one of a kind."

"Your family has been so good to us," I said. "We're very lucky to count you as friends." I bit my lip, hoping that referring to a prince and his wife as friends wasn't a "common" gaffe. "Is that okay to say?"

Bertie laughed and flicked his cigarette ash. "Even royals need friends."

And I was glad we'd remained so; even though the courtship between myself and David hadn't lasted, we'd remained on friendly terms, and he'd even been to see *Lady Be Good* at least half a dozen times, bringing an entourage with him each time.

"Well, you can certainly count on us," Freddie said, nodding in Bertie's direction.

<hr />

August 1927
Philadelphia, PA

"Freddie, this is an epic disaster." I dropped to the stage floor, stretching out my legs. It was nearing one o'clock in the morning, and we'd been rehearsing for what felt like days on end at the Shubert Theatre in Philadelphia.

"A total turkey," Freddie agreed, taking off his hat and tossing it out into the auditorium. "If we never get it right here, New York will jeer us off the stage."

"Tomato is certainly not my color," I added, hoping the joke would crack a smile onto Freddie's face.

"Especially rotten ones." He grinned, but it didn't reach his eyes.

"I don't want to be here all night." I lay all the way down on the floor, stretching out my sore muscles, especially my calves, which felt particularly tight tonight. What would it be like to wake up and not be in pain?

"At this point we'll have to be here the rest of the year to get it right."

It wasn't that the musical numbers weren't good, and the choreography wasn't bad either, but nothing seemed to be hitting the mark. The comedic punch lines fell flat, the timing in the script awkward; everything just felt skewed. And, after two fantastic shows that blew the critics' hats off, this felt wrong.

"Let's call it a day?" I suggested, my arm flopping over my eyes. I could fall asleep right here. Disappointment made exhaustion all the more potent.

The other members of the cast and the theatre crew had stilled, listening intently. Freddie was the unofficial referee for us when it came to calling the shots.

"All right, but we'll be back here first thing."

The auditorium echoed with the whoops and hollers of everyone's excitement. Even I sat up with a bit more oomph than I'd had for the past couple of hours.

Outside the theatre, our shiny black baby Rolls, which we'd shipped back from London, waited with our chauffeur to take us to our hotel. It was one of the only ones in New York, and probably Philadelphia, too. We'd been back in the States barely a month before rehearsals had started at the Shubert, and, boy, did I have some major regrets, one of which was not being in New York.

The following morning, not as refreshed as we would have liked, Freddie and I returned to the theatre to try to rehearse this performance into shape. Freddie told me to go on ahead while he spoke to the chauffeur about washing the Rolls, which had a few white blotches of bird poop on the hood.

I meandered into the auditorium to find Alex Aarons talking

to a handsome gentleman with a distinguished mustache and dressed in a three-piece suit that looked as dapper as the ones Freddie had bought on Savile Row. The two of them turned their gazes toward me and I couldn't help but smile.

"Ah, the lady of the hour," Aarons said. "Sir William Gaunt, this is Miss Adele Astaire."

"A pleasure." William Gaunt's British accent sent a thrill through me, as did the warmth in his brown eyes.

He took my hand in his and brushed my knuckles with his lips, his mustache tickling my skin. I knew I missed England, but in that moment I missed it even more.

"Mr. Gaunt owns a theatre in London and is interested in expanding his financial backing in the States."

"I saw your performance of *Lady Be Good* in the West End," William said. "I'd like to support you and your brother here as well."

Freddie took that moment to walk through the doors, and judging by the way his shoulders stiffened he wasn't too pleased to see possibly another suitor taking a shine to me. Freddie had been offering to fight them off for years, but there was something different about William from all the other beaus.

Maybe it was my nostalgia for London, or maybe the fact that I was hating this play so much, but the idea of settling down was creeping closer to the surface. Whatever it was, Mr. Gaunt's charm was utterly enticing.

"Fred Astaire." My brother stuck out his hand, breaking the spell.

"Sir William Gaunt." They shook, perhaps a little harder than necessary.

"A Brit," Freddie said with a not-so-friendly grin. "Welcome to the States."

William either didn't notice Freddie's brusque behavior, or he brushed it off.

"I'd love to take the two of you to dinner tonight." He glanced toward Aarons. "Of course, with your producer here as well. To discuss bringing *Smarty* to London."

Freddie and I looked at each other, a little bit of panic in us both perhaps, given that the show was a total wreck.

"Dinner it is." Freddie's tone might have sounded cordial to everyone else, but I'd known him since the day he was born, and, boy, was my brother feeling the opposite right now. "We've got to rehearse. If you'll excuse us."

Freddie took my elbow, and I let myself be led away. "You're being unfriendly," I said under my breath.

"That guy's a total cad."

"You think anyone who shows a romantic interest in me is a cad." I folded my arms over my chest.

"Did you see the way he was looking at you?"

"Clearly not the way you did."

Freddie humphed. "Mark my words, Delly, that Sir Cads-a-lot is up to no good."

I chuckled. "Oh, Freddie. It's not like I'm going to marry him. We're going out to dinner. For business."

"Ha! That's how it all starts."

And Freddie was right. William charmed me right into his arms, and within a few months, I'd said yes to *the* magic question.

———⋙◈⋘———

FREDDIE WAS GOING to kill me.

My vision was a little crooked as I gazed at the watch I'd slipped from William's pocket.

Funny Face—renamed from *Smarty*, and epically better than when we'd first started—would have already had the curtain call by now. And I wasn't at the theatre. *Jeepers*! Instead I was definitely a bit sozzled at a cocktail party I didn't even want to attend.

"I need to go." I faced William, trying to swallow around a thick tongue. I rarely drank liquor, and especially not before a show.

"Oh, come on, that's what Sugar's for," he said, referring to my understudy.

I shook my head, but it felt slow, and as if my brain were sloshing around my skull. How much had I drunk? Too much . . . it was because I didn't want to be at this party, and had been strongarmed into it by William, whom I'd agreed to marry in a moment when he was being sweet.

"No, William. I need to go." I dropped his pocket watch and turned around, stumbling a bit to the right.

William grasped my elbow, steadying me. "All right, but you're not going to be any good onstage."

"I shouldn't have come here with you." Already my head was starting to pound with the beginnings of a hangover.

"Why?" William frowned, then switched to a smile, the one he used to try to convince me that he was right. "You're allowed a little fun. And you want to retire when we get married, anyway."

I scowled. "That doesn't mean I want to disappoint my brother and the cast."

William shrugged, as if my responsibilities were unimportant. "They might as well get used to it."

That didn't sit right, but I ignored him, and the wrong feeling in my belly, because it was hard enough to concentrate on walking, let alone the strange things he was saying.

We made it to the theatre, and I found my way backstage, tripping only twice, on who knows what.

"What the devil?" Freddie shouted when he caught sight of me. "You're twenty-five minutes late! The curtain's already gone up and we're supposed to go on right now."

"I just need to put on my costume," I said, but it came out sounding slurred and it took me forever to form the words.

"You're drunk. How can you be drunk?" he said accusingly, arms flung wide in exasperation.

I rubbed my forehead and closed my eyes. "I don't know."

Freddie cursed under his breath and practically dragged me back to the dressing room, where I fell gratefully onto the chair. A sharp tang in my nose made my eyes water, and I coughed as Freddie wafted smelling salts in front of my face. I waved him away.

"Get ready," he ordered. "I'll ask them to hold the curtain for five minutes. But that's all you've got. I can't believe you've done this." He mumbled on his way out, and a maid rushed in, helping me dress. There wasn't time for makeup, and my hair would have to be what it was. I was mortified—and dismayed. My brother had had to pull me out of a number of scrapes throughout our lives together, but never had I disappointed him more than I had tonight.

I made it onstage and climbed into the toy wagon, trying my best to pull the necessary faces as Freddie sang. Fortunately, I barely had any lines in this number, but when it was time for me to stand and dance I nearly went over the edge of the stage. Freddie grabbed hold of me and we played it off, but those who'd seen the show before would know.

Freddie dragged me offstage at the end of the number, and before I knew what was happening he slapped me hard across one cheek and then the other.

The shocking sting on both sides of my face brought tears to my eyes, but all the fuzziness in my head went away in a flash. "You hit me," I accused him, touching the hot places on each cheek.

"I'm sorry about that, but something had to be done! You nearly fell into the audience out there. You could have broken your neck."

"I can't believe you hit me." My brother had never laid a hand on me in my life.

"We'll talk about this later. Now's the time for you to sober up.

Our next number is coming up, and I can't be wondering if you're going to fall off the stage."

"Freddie, you hit me!" I was practically hysterical.

"Delly, don't. You are drunk and a danger to everyone on that stage. I needed to do something to sober you up. Now, I'm sorry, but you need to get it together." As an afterthought he tossed out, "I'll give you twenty bucks later."

I could have argued some more, but we had a show to put on. With one last glower in his direction, I rushed back to my dressing room and stared in the mirror at the twin cheery handprints. What had I been thinking, showing up to a performance drunk? In all our years together, this had never happened before. Not until William had come into my life. I took out the powder puff and did my makeup, covering up the slaps.

By the time I was done, and our number was cueing up, I felt a heck of a lot better than when I'd first gotten there. We finished out the show—not our best, by any means—but I didn't fall into the audience, either.

I vowed to never drink before a show again, and Freddie handed me twenty dollars.

"I know who was behind that," Freddie said, as he slipped his wallet back into his pocket. "And while I blame you for imbibing, I blame him for encouraging you."

"You hate him anyways."

"He's no good for you, Delly. No good at all. He's controlling, opinionated, and a real jerk." Freddie shook his head, and I felt the weight of his judgment and was embarrassed by it.

I sucked on my lower lip, nodding. I knew William and I weren't perfect. There were a lot of quarrels between us, and we didn't always see eye to eye. But I did love him, and when we weren't at odds he could be rather jolly.

William was my ticket to something new, and I was awfully tired. My bones ached something fierce. I just wanted to get married and have babies. And William wanted that, too. With him being in the thick of the theatre world, it wasn't as if I'd be completely out of it, just offstage. "He's not so bad."

Freddie snorted as if I'd made a crass joke.

Holding on to William was about more than just the man. It was the dream that William represented. The life I wanted.

A life that was very nearly about to go up in flames.

CHAPTER NINE

VIOLET

THE LIMELIGHT

Where in the world is Violet Wood? After upstaging Bridgette Hughes in *The Princess and the Pea*, Miss Wood seems to have slipped back into whatever shadow from which she'd first emerged. Whatever hopes for a comeback Miss Hughes sought to make with Miss Wood out of the way were dashed when she broke a leg during her performance in *MacBeth* following a slip which also tossed Maya Chopra into the front row of the audience. Miss Chopra was said to have injured her hip. With our three favorite drama queens hiding, who will be next to make her debut as the favorite stunning starlet?

July 1927
London

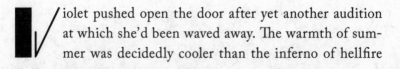

Violet pushed open the door after yet another audition at which she'd been waved away. The warmth of summer was decidedly cooler than the inferno of hellfire inside the theatre—brought on by the humiliation of another rejection.

"Bollocks," she muttered, and despite herself cast her gaze back toward the theatre, catching one last haughty look from her nemesis. Bridgette was a constant nag. A reminder of what Violet had and lost. It was *her* voice whispering in Violet's head, *You're not good enough. Worthless, East End rat.*

Violet doubted the bitter bitch had ever been through the trouble she'd found herself in since the final show of *Stop Flirting*. The only thing that made Violet feel slightly better about her current danceless situation was the support of her roommate, Caty.

Violet sucked her tongue against her teeth as she resisted the tremendous urge to show Bridgette what she really thought. Somewhere deep, very deep, inside, she summoned the will to mosey on her way.

"There you are. I thought I'd find you here." Violet looked up to see Caty, smiling at her in that conspiratorial way she had. "I've found something."

"Tell me it's a wad of cash we can use to pay off a year's rent."

Caty laughed. "I wish. No, it's an audition."

"I've just left one. No luck."

"We'll get this one, both of us. It's no *Stop Flirting*, but it'll pay well, and the cocktails are free."

"I do like free cocktails." Violet looped her arm through Caty's. "Lead the way."

It'd been nearly three years since Violet had last seen the Astaires, though they'd been in London for a year up until a few months ago, with their latest show, *Lady Be Good*.

When Adele had first arrived in London, she'd sent Violet a telegram at her tenement house. But when this invitation to audition for *Lady Be Good* was delivered, Violet was already ensconced in Scotland with her aunt Dahlia.

Due to unexpected events, Violet hadn't kept her promise to Adele of staying in touch. For good reasons, she told herself. Violet read the articles about *Lady Be Good* and wanted desperately to sneak into the theatre to watch. But then Adele would ask where she'd been and why she hadn't auditioned. Even if Violet tried to lie, Adele would see the truth.

Ultimately it was her fear of rejection, of being judged unworthy and stupid for the mistakes she'd made, that kept her away.

After *Stop Flirting*, Violet had been keen on getting a new part in a show. She was offered a position by a producer who'd said her eyes reminded him of an Italian canal, whatever that meant. It was only after taking her place onstage during rehearsal that Violet discovered that payment was expected. She couldn't do anything but relent to the producer's pawing hands and other roving parts. When her period didn't arrive for a second month, she knew she was in the pudding club.

That was last spring. Violet had quietly gone to Dahlia's in Perth. She'd had enough in savings to pay Caty her share of the rent, with a promise to return. It wasn't as if she was the first girl to bear a bastard, but even so she didn't tell her mother.

Aunt Dahlia was barren, and all too happy to accept a "wee miracle." Following hours of hard labor, Violet's eyes met the blue-eyed gaze of her son and she felt a flicker of hesitation. But the moment he'd wailed, rejecting her in his sorrow and then quieted in Dahlia's arms, Violet knew she'd made the right decision.

Violet wasn't the mothering type. Even deemed so by her own son. Any emotions about what had happened she kept tucked deep inside, hidden in a place she couldn't reach.

Although no one in London knew about her predicament, plenty guessed. Fortunately her young body had snapped right back into shape. But the time away caused her career to suffer. Finding any sort of part was nearly impossible.

If she didn't get a gig soon, she was going to be homeless. Her savings were nearly depleted, and Caty wasn't well-off enough to pay Violet's share of the rent, not that she'd ever ask her to. Worst-case scenario, she was back in Hoxton, doing laundry like her mother.

There seemed to be no end in sight to the fate that she refused to resign herself to.

They rounded a corner and Caty stopped, waving her arm dramatically. "We're here!"

A poster caught Violet's eye, advertising the Café de Paris, a new swanky club in the city that boasted nightly live bands, singers, and dancers. The ad depicted a curtained window behind a table set with white linen, red chairs, and a maître d' with a tray of champagne flutes. At the table were ladies dressed in the latest fashions, their caps poised jauntily over one eye, and gentlemen beside them.

The name of the café itself tunneled back to those wonderful moments when she'd gone to France with Adele and . . . Paul. Lord, it'd been an age since she'd thought about him. Mostly she kept those memories buried deep, for her own sanity.

Club dancing felt like such a step down from theatre but beggars shouldn't be too choosy, should they?

A man walked through the brass-and-wood doors, lighting a cigarette.

"Well, are you coming in or not? We're only taking a few more girls!" he snapped toward them, looking them up and down, eyes settling on their calves. He was dressed smartly in a herringbone suit with a striped shirt. His oxfords were recently polished, and his homburg was pulled precisely to the center of his forehead. "You're dancers, I can tell. But we don't want anyone with stage fright."

Violet straightened her spine, and Caty popped her hip.

"We're not afraid," Caty said. "Just sizing up the club."

"Then go inside and get warmed up." He rolled his eyes as if they'd given him a hard time.

Without hesitating another second, the two of them hurried in, taking note of the glorious dining room and ballroom a whole level below. Wrought-iron rails lined a balcony that encircled the entire room, and, in front of them, not one but two L-shaped stair-cases led down to it. A massive crystal chandelier dangled from the burgundy-curtained ceiling, lending to the opulence.

Being a chorus girl at a club wasn't exactly Violet's dream job, but it beat doing laundry, especially in a place as glamorous as this. If she wanted to get back into the dancing and theatre world, she needed to start somewhere. Adele had climbed from the bottom up. If Violet was going to take inspiration from her, now was the time.

Trembling, Violet descended the stairs. Caty was decidedly more quiet than usual, and the chatter from the women below grew louder the closer they got. There was a thump of someone practicing on the drums, a blare of trumpeters warming up, the trill of a piano, and the familiar tapping of shoes. Although some might consider the ca-cophony an assault to a normal person's ears, to hers it was glorious.

The ballroom was filled with a myriad of performers, and a smile practically split Violet's face as she squeezed Caty's arm.

"This is so exciting."

"It is!" Caty agreed.

No, she didn't want to dance in a nightclub, but she missed performing so much that merely hearing the music and buzz of excitement sent delight through her. They put down their things and pulled on their dancing shoes over their stockinged feet.

"Name," the same man said, his pencil poised over a clipboard, his hat now tossed on a nearby table, revealing his slightly sweat-dampened hair.

"Violet Wood."

"Caty Marks."

He nodded perfunctorily toward the women who were starting to assemble. "They'll show you the routine once, and then you'll have a chance to show us what you've got."

Violet and Caty stood in line with the other girls. Tried to feel the confidence that had taken a beating. Fake it until you make it, Adele had said once with a laugh, and, boy, was Violet faking it right now.

A man walked up and down the length of the line, eyeing them from the tops of their heads to the points of their shoes, lingering in places that made Violet want to squirm. This was all part of the job, checking measurements for costumes, but, if she'd gotten unwanted attention in the theatre, it would be naive to think that she wouldn't also get it in a club.

Focusing her gaze straight ahead, Violet assumed the various positions that the other dancers demanded. Hand on the hip, knee popped, other hand on the shoulder of the gal beside her. Then they kicked their right foot forward, all their legs extended in a line. When they were through with that, the choreographer signaled to the band.

"You'll march forward in a line, hands on each other's shoulders, kick and kick, and then turn to face the audience, and this." He tapped in rhythm, pretending to swish skirts with his hands, and then bent with his knees together, first to the right, then to the left.

Violet paid attention, memorizing his movements, and when the music started she replayed it all in her mind in the seconds before demanding that her limbs follow suit.

"Smile, ladies, smile!" someone called from the audience. And Violet's face split with a smile so wide it practically screamed, "Pick me!"

The choreographer continued to walk down the line, telling the dancers to repeat moves, adding in steps, and culling the herd until the number of hopefuls dwindled to just four.

"Report back at three p.m. for rehearsals. First show's tonight at eight o'clock."

Violet stood there, stunned, exchanging a nervous glance with Caty, who beamed. Five hours to rehearse before a show? That was absurd. All she could think about was how Freddie would have had a heart attack and Adele would have likely rejoiced.

"Excuse me, sir," she asked. "What about costumes?"

He glowered at her, lips pursed, and she had the sudden fear that he was going to dismiss her simply for having asked.

"They'll be in the back dressing room when you get here. Don't give me any more trouble with your questions." With that, he stomped away.

Violet smiled at Caty, who was now clapping her hands and introducing herself to the other dancers. There was none of the snobbery among them that she'd experienced with Bridgette and the other girls from Shaftesbury Theatre.

"I'm Violet." She cast her gaze on the others.

"Maya," the dancer on her right answered, sweeping a lock of her glossy black hair away from her face. There was something familiar in her dark almond-shaped eyes, her caramel-colored skin, the faint hint of an accent that Violet couldn't place.

A blonde with a short, curly bob waved. "Eleanor."

"Well, this is going to be fun," Caty said, her chestnut hair swishing in excitement.

"You're really good." Eleanor's eyes lingered on Violet's shoes—a stunning pair bought for her by Fred Astaire during their last week of *Stop Flirting*. The shoes were the only part of her that looked out of place right now. "Have you danced here before?"

"Not here, no." Violet sat down to remove her dance shoes, not wanting to scuff them up outside. Slipping into her old shoes, she completed the look of an East Ender trying to blend in.

"Where?" Eleanor asked, toeing off her ballet slippers, not exactly shoes to audition for a chorus-girl spot in, but that hadn't seemed to bother their suit-wearing keeper.

"Here and there," Violet said. "I suspect all of us have."

"She's being modest," Caty said, flipping her hair over one shoulder. "We danced with the Astaires in *Stop Flirting*."

Eleanor narrowed her eyes, the friendly air she'd had a moment ago gone. "Poppycock. People who've danced with the stars don't stop, and considering how your timing was off for the first number, I'm guessing you're new to the business. If you danced with Adele Astaire, why are you here now instead of up on a stage with your poncy friends?"

"That's none of your business," Violet said, before Caty could answer. It wasn't Caty's fault she'd not gotten another theatre part, nor that Violet had gotten knocked up. "But the four of us, we're a team. And if we're not fluid with each other, the audience will know."

Caty nodded but didn't say anything. Eleanor looked at her curiously, eyes full of questions Violet didn't want to answer.

"I'm sorry, then," Eleanor said. "You're right."

"Apology accepted." Violet stuck out her hand, and Eleanor shook it.

While Caty busied herself in the bathroom, Violet headed outside. Maya was lighting a cigarette, the smoke curling into the air before evaporating into what had become a gray late-afternoon London sky.

"Those'll make it harder for you to dance," Violet said.

Maya held out the pack of Chesterfields. "If Adele Astaire can smoke them, so can I."

Violet shook her head, unsure if she was referring to the advertisement that Adele and Freddie had done for the cigarette company or whether she recognized Violet as being friends with the sibling pair.

"You don't remember me," Maya said, all but confirming Violet's earlier sense of familiarity.

Violet studied Maya. Her short dark hair, the soft brown of her eyes. Although there'd been far too few Indian dancers, Violet had been to so many auditions over the years that she could barely remember even the producers. She was still drawing a blank.

Maya grinned and sucked in a lungful of smoke. "I quit the *Stop Flirting* production. The producer was a bit handsy and threatened to fire me if I didn't sleep with him. You were my replacement."

Violet's chest tightened.

"Is that why you're here?" Maya asked. "Did he finish with you where I left off?"

The extremely personal question took Violet aback. Though it had been a different show, the producer was the same. She'd never confessed to anyone what had happened with her and the producer. Never told a soul, because it wasn't as if he'd attacked her, though she'd never really agreed, either.

Maya shook her head, taking Violet's refusal to answer as an answer all the same. "Well, that explains a lot."

Violet swallowed, trying to make her tongue form words.

"You don't have to say anything." Maya nodded toward the café. "And I won't tell anyone. I wasn't the first and you won't be the last. Probably those two in there have a few bastards themselves somewhere." She let out a bitter chuckle and tossed her cigarette. "Well, I'll see you in a few."

Maya sauntered away, leaving Violet a touch more exposed than she had ever felt in her life. How had this girl been able to strip away all the lies she'd insulated herself with and reduced her to little more than a naked, brittle shell?

CHAPTER TEN

ADELE

THE LIMELIGHT

London is rejoicing once more with the news that the dynamic brother-and-sister duo Fred and Adele Astaire will soon Charleston in the city. And not a moment too soon; after seeing the grotesque Kokoschka portrait that was supposed to resemble our favorite starlet, we're left wondering if she's changed. In other news, we have found Violet Wood and Maya Chopra. They've teamed up to entertain the prestigious crowds at Café de Paris. We're glad Miss Chopra has recovered from the disaster of her last performance. But where was Violet and what secrets are behind her nearly yearlong disappearance from London? Why they chose that venue to exhibit their talents is anyone's guess. Their sets are overfilled with footwork and vocals that should be celebrated with a wider audience. We've heard it whispered more than once that we might still see them audition for a part in the new "Astairical" musical. One can only hope!

July 1928
New York City

There were a lot of things I'd done so far in my short life, and now I could say that one of them was surviving a fiery boat explosion.

Dressed in a hospital gown, rear end exposed, I stood in the bathroom of my assigned room. The woman who stared back at me from the mirror resembled Kokoschka's painting of me more now than she did two years prior, when his cross-eyed, smudged version of me had been released to the world. Even my blue velvet Madame Jenny dress with the pleated skirt had come out painted like a sack in that hack's rendition of me. And my Scottie, Wassie, looked like a Sasquatch.

I rubbed the sleep from my eyes, trying to wipe away the bleary look of myself in the glass.

"Damned fire," I muttered.

It'd been two weeks since that sunny July 8 when I'd gone out with my fiancé, as well as Billy Leeds and his wife, Princess Xenia Georgievna Romanov, for a boat ride. Everything happened so fast. One minute we were getting ready to cast off for a day on the water, and the next, a massive fire erupted on deck. Flames engulfed me. If not for Billy's quick thinking, more than my legs would now be covered in bandages. Hell, I'd probably be six feet under. My friend had dragged me off the boat, shoved the *Fan Tail* out into the water, and we watched it explode, right before I passed out.

And my fiancé . . . well, he proved his worthlessness by standing there and watching in horror, rather than trying to help.

"Adele?"

Snapped back to the present, I turned away from the glass, the door to my room fuzzy as it cracked open, and Mom peered in. She was staring at the bed, an anguished pinch in her forehead.

I wondered if she was remembering what it had been like when she'd cared for my father a few years back until he passed away. My chest seized to contemplate what was going through her mind.

"I'm right here," I said. "They haven't carted me off to the morgue yet."

Relief flooded visibly through Mom, her body sagging as the tension ebbed. I felt it clear in the center of my chest.

I shuffled forward in my New York Hospital–issued medical socks that protected my burns from air, and my mother grabbed hold of my arm, helping me back toward the bed.

"You're not supposed to do that on your own," she admonished, tucking me in as she had when I was a child.

"Oh, really? I thought you taught me how to use the toilet as a toddler for that reason."

Mom clucked her tongue and sat on the edge of the bed. "You know what I mean."

I ignored her. "I'm not getting out of here by lying in bed."

"You'll be staying in longer if you don't let yourself heal."

"Humph." I crossed my arms, feeling more like myself now that the drugs they had given me for pain had worn off, and all I wanted was to get out of here. I didn't have time for this. Already we'd had to postpone rehearsals for our next show. The longer we waited, the more chance there was of us becoming irrelevant. And I wanted to end my career on an upswing. "Where's Freddie?"

"He's home. He's fine." Mom's tone was dismissive, evasive. She stood up abruptly, pretending to be interested in the ugly, lackluster painting of a garden on the wall.

"Oh, Mom. What's going on with Freddie?" I raised myself up on my elbows, cringing as my legs scraped against the sheets. A flash of fear for the future rushed through me, and I tried to ignore it, but in the back of my mind was the never-ending drumbeat: *Will I dance again?*

Mom glanced toward the door, as if she'd rather run out than tell me whatever it was that she'd just let slip.

"Just say it, Mom. Nothing can be worse for a dancer than having her legs burned in a fire."

"Oh, dear. They said you'll heal just fine. You have to believe them." Mom rushed back to my side, in a wave of rarely shown emotion. She sat down on the edge of the bed again and reached for my hand, her thumb brushing over my knuckles.

Mom was always so beautiful, so young-looking, that even now her hands were smooth and free of any signs of aging. She'd started lightening her hair recently. Gone were the dark tendrils I'd known in my youth, replaced by a blond bob that matched the sophistication of her clothes. She looked like she belonged to the elite social class of New Yorkers, people who were descended from the robber barons of the Gilded Age.

"Freddie and Mary were in a car accident," Mom said, using the low, quiet pitch she often did with stage managers and reporters.

Meanwhile, all the air was escaping from my lungs.

"They rolled over on their way to a house party on Long Island," Mom said.

I pressed my hand to my chest, trying to quell the rapid pounding behind my sternum. "Is he all right? And the tart?"

Mom ignored my jibe at Freddie's current girlfriend. *The tart.* "Just fine. So odd it was the same day as your accident."

That sent a cold shot of dread through me. If that wasn't a sign, what was?

A sign of what, though? That I hadn't retired soon enough?

Mom and Freddie were already conducting a smear campaign against my fiancé, William, calling him a cad and arrogant and bossy. They blamed him for my decision to retire from the stage as soon as we were wed, whenever that might be.

I'd yet to decide.

We'd become engaged ages ago, but something held me back from setting a date. Every time I asked Mom to pull out her date book so that we could flip through the pages and settle on a day, I pulled back. A muscle cramp, a sudden need to run to the shop, a headache; I was tired, or in desperate need of a sandwich.

I wanted to get married. Truly, I did. But when I did, it would be the end of one life and the start of a new one. Me, Mom, and Freddie were all I knew. I barely remembered Pop being with us. Rest his poor soul. We'd been a trio from the time I was eight, and we'd breathed, slept, and eaten dance. Funny thing was, I'd always thought when I got married I'd quit dancing to be a wife, and, I hoped, a mother. So what kept me from pinning down a specific stopping point?

All I could picture was William's nod of inevitability when I'd suggested I retire that first time. A choice I was making on my own. But somehow, in that look, he made me feel as if it were the obvious course, and that he'd made that decision for me. As if any wife of his would be too good for work. Or wouldn't be allowed to work. Perhaps that had been the way of it. I felt as if my agency had been ripped way. All the independence that I'd sought from a new life squashed before it even began.

William had grown up in a family where, generation after generation, the men were responsible for all the finances and heavy decision-making. It was how they'd built their wool manufacturing company to such a degree that William had been able to buy the London theatres I performed in.

I wasn't that unused to being managed—after all, Freddie handled our finances, and Mom had before him. But still, it gave me a moment's pause. Did I want to be managed?

Part of me said, *Yes, of course!* Life was easier that way. The other part paused a beat too long. That part that hesitated to set a date with William, because maybe I didn't want to be bossed around anymore.

Just when I'd thought no one could sweep me off my feet like the Prince of Wales had—I mean, I'd had dinner at St. James's Palace!—William Gaunt Jr. had swaggered backstage on our last tour in London for *Lady Be Good* and struck me right in the heart. He'd made me forget completely about convincing a prince that it was all right to marry an American. William was a charming, rich British fellow, and he metaphorically knocked me out of my dancing shoes. Yet here we were, a year later, engaged with no date, and me in the hospital and him nowhere to be seen.

When I could finally find my voice, I sucked in a lungful of air. "I'm glad Freddie's not badly injured."

"No, he'll be fine." Mom patted my hand. "The both of you will. They've postponed your show in London until the fall, of course, so you have some time to recover."

Funny Face. Our third tour of London. As much as I'd clamored to get back to New York when we'd been in London on our first go-around, now I found myself feeling quite the opposite. Maybe that was why I'd agreed to marry William—that, and the way he waxed on about my dancing. Because he was British, and I wanted a reason to put down roots there. To start a family. To be loved.

"Mom . . ." I hedged, staring down at my bandaged legs, feeling prickles of pain through the gauze.

Mom stood, her spine snapping into place, and she fussed with some pink carnations in a vase on the table beside me. She hated heavy conversations.

"I'm going to be scarred," I said. "Aren't I?"

Mom blew out a breath, turned the vase one more time, then clasped her hands in front of her, avoiding looking at my bandages. "Well, darling, what do you think stockings are for?"

I couldn't help but laugh. Because she was right. Stockings would cover up the scars of my injuries just as laughter hid the scars of loneliness and regret. I was nearly thirty-two years old, and what did I have to show for it, other than a bit of fame, and a fiancé whom my family hated? All the heated embraces in the world wouldn't make a rift with Mom and Freddie worth it.

I touched my cheek, which still stung sometimes from the night of the performance of *Funny Face* in New York City, when Freddie had slapped me hard. I should have known then what I knew now: that William didn't care enough about me or my reputation to make sure that I didn't show up to a performance sozzled.

Freddie had been forced to lead me through the numbers, holding me upright when my balance was off. And his slap to wake me up . . . not only had that been mortifying to my soul, but it'd sobered me up quick enough to finish the play. I never wanted to disappoint my brother like that again. William had said that this was a good enough reason to quit acting, quit being a star. Because why should my brother manage my social life?

But the question really should have been, Why did my fiancé insist on my going to a cocktail party and filling my glass over and over when he knew that I had a performance that night? Perhaps a better question was, Why hadn't I the guts to tell him no?

Love wasn't all it was cracked up to be, really. It wasn't fairy tales. Or the grandly sweeping plot of a novel. Love was work. It was a partnership. And, if I was being honest, it wasn't what I had with William.

"Mom, you can take those pink carnations with you. Or toss them in the garbage. They're giving me a headache." But really what I was doing was pushing those flowers away, and the one who had given them—William.

———×◊×———

I SHIFTED THIS way and that in the sunlight streaming through my hospital window, trying to see if the scars were visible through my thick silk stockings; either my eyes were playing tricks on me or they really weren't noticeable. But, boy, were the stockings irritating against my freshly healed skin.

"Knock, knock." Freddie peeked around the corner of the hospital-room door. "Oh, good, you're dressed. Ready to scram out of here?"

"Boy, am I ever."

William had offered to fetch me, but he didn't know yet that I planned to call things off. It had taken a freak accident to show me that life was precious. Freddie was planning to break things off with his girl, too. Don't let it be said we didn't do things together at the right time.

"London's calling." Freddie grinned widely, anticipation in his lilt.

"You're just looking forward to going back because you need another suit and hat, and they've the best tailors and haberdashers this side of the planet."

"Hey, don't tell anyone I'm that much into my style," Freddie said.

I rolled my eyes, picked up my light-blue hat, and pinned it into place, shifting the satin bow trim a degree. The hat was a gift from Mimi and came all the way from a Paris shop. "Well, I won't tell about you, if you don't tell about me."

"What's there to tell?" He pinched his lips closed.

We'd had our ups and downs, certainly, but I didn't know how to exist without my brother. Without the bond we'd formed. It was part of the reason I was so lonely—at least, I thought it was.

"The doc says you're well enough to travel, but how do you feel?" Freddie stared down at me, concern etched on his face. "Really?"

"I feel like I need to get the hell out of here. I've had enough mushy, bland food to last me a lifetime. And I've had enough with the poking and prodding. Do I look like an invalid to you?"

"You look like Delly to me." Freddie chucked me on the chin.

I grinned up at him, and then gave him a pinch on the cheek, like some of our producers used to do when we were younger. "Good, because I feel more like Delly today than I did yesterday."

Mom had seen to packing my bags earlier that morning, planning to meet us at the dock, so the only thing I had to grab on the way out of the hospital was my purse.

Freddie's shiny Rolls waited at the curb.

"You going to miss her while we're gone?" I nodded toward the car.

He laughed. "I wish I could drive her right onto that ship and take her with me."

"Why can't you?"

"Don't tempt me, it cost a mint last time."

I slid onto the creamy leather seat, breathing in the New York City air, which always had a specific scent: a mix of food, engine exhaust, horse manure, boiled peanuts, subway fumes, garbage. Which, taken individually, weren't appealing smells, but when they were all put together smelled rather like home. I waved goodbye to the hospital, hoping the next time I graced its doorstep was only to give birth or to die—preferably as an old woman for the latter—then turned my gaze toward the skyline. There really was nothing like New York City.

Freddie climbed behind the wheel, his hands at ten and two as he stared out into the traffic.

"You all right?" I asked, wondering if he was still trepidatious about driving after his accident.

He turned to face me, all serious in his expression. "You scared the shit out of me, Delly."

My mouth fell open, and all that came out was a whoosh of air, shocked at his language, because he tended not to curse. But also at the emotion laced through his outburst. My brother usually kept his emotions bottled up like cola.

"The *shit*." He took off his hat, tossing it into the backseat, and ran his hands through his hair. "When we flipped the car on that curve, my first thought wasn't, 'Oh, Jesus, my gal is going to get hurt'; it was, 'Oh, dear God, don't let me die, Delly needs me.' And then when I came to in the hospital, to hear people thought I'd been in a boat explosion . . . I was trying to tell them, no, I wasn't. What the hell were they talking about? Only to then find out it was because *you* were. My God, I thought I was dying all over again."

I scooted close and wrapped my arms around my brother. My chest felt tight, and all I wanted to do was hold Freddie until we both realized it would all be okay. "I'm not going to die until I'm an old lady, Freddie. Don't you worry. Besides, if I died now, there'd be no one here who could calm the Moaning Minnie out of you, and Mom might strangle you in your sleep."

He laughed at that, squeezing me back with one arm before quickly grabbing the wheel again. "Good. And I promise I won't die on you, either."

"Good. Besides, those who already have Astairia will go raving mad." *Astairia* was a term the tabloids had coined, a combination of our surname with *hysteria*.

Freddie laughed at that, and I gave him a quick kiss on the cheek before pushing back to my seat.

"Astairia, I love it. We should put that on a postcard."

"It'd make for good propaganda. Now all we have to hope is that we make our run in London as successful as before."

"I don't have any doubt, sis." When a cabbie drove too close to us, Freddie laid on the horn.

"Is Mom meeting us at the dock?" A pang of sadness pinched

then. If only Pop had seen us make it this far. "And does she have Tilly and Wassie?"

It'd been a torment not to have my sweet dachshund and Scottish terrier with me in the hospital. I was convinced that having their warm, soft bodies curled in the crook of my elbow and against my hip would have helped me heal faster.

"Yes, pups in tow, she's on her way there with the porters who came to collect our trunks and bags. I tried to get her to come to the hospital, but you know how she is when it comes to organizing everything to the letter."

"I do." I huffed a laugh. I plucked Freddie's hat from the backseat and teasingly crammed it onto his head, patting the top. "Onward, then; the haberdasher doesn't wait for anyone."

We made the rest of the drive to the harbor in reverent silence. I tried to memorize the city, admiring the Statue of Liberty as she jutted from the Hudson, and wondering how long it would be this time before I saw her again—if ever.

My gaze was riveted on the black-and-white smokestacks of the ship as I stepped out of the Rolls onto the docks. Suddenly I was gripped by as much anxiety as I'd experienced on our first journey to London. But gone now was some of the naivete of that time. The nervousness wasn't for something new that I'd never experienced before, but rather about cutting ties with a future that I'd agreed to. Although I'd made the choice when I thought I wanted it.

William was going to be in London. It was likely he would greet us at the docks and maybe insist I stay at his London flat rather than the Savoy with my brother, with Mom. And I'd have to say no. I'd have to say it wasn't about propriety, but that I didn't see a future with us together. That the family we'd talked about, the boys who'd ride on the moors and go hunting with him in the fall, the girls who'd dance and learn piano—all those dreams we'd talked about in hushed whispers would disintegrate into thin air, vanishing like dreams often did upon waking.

I was dreading it.

———— ❦ ————

WILLIAM DID NOT meet us at the dock. Nor at the hotel. And no one, especially me, was very surprised by it.

That first night in London, unable to sleep, I climbed out of bed, intent on shutting the curtains to block an irritating light that streamed through the window. But I paused, an idyllic scene in the street making me lean forward for a better view, my elbows resting on the windowsill. Below, leaning back against a lamppost, was a woman. Her lover moved in close, captivating her with whatever he was saying. She laughed, and I wanted desperately to know what he'd said. The longing I kept under lock and key banged hard against my chest, demanding to be one half of a romantic couple. I'd had a lot of dates. A fiancé, for goodness' sake. But nothing like what was happening under the midnight London sky right now outside the Savoy.

I wanted it. Wanted it as much as I wanted our London show to be a success.

But there was one thing I knew to be the truest fact of them all, and that was that I couldn't have both.

With a sigh that felt heavier than the stones that formed the foundation of the hotel, I fell back onto the bed, and my arm flopped over my eyes. "Stop being an idiot," I muttered.

How could I even think about ruining the good life that I had for something that might never be?

CHAPTER ELEVEN

VIOLET

THE LIMELIGHT

The East End cleans up nicely, or at least some of it does—Violet Wood was spotted leaving the Café de Paris and riding the Tube all the way to the less-than-illustrious side of London. But the real question is, while Miss Wood has been enchanting the midnight club dancers—at the detriment to the more sophisticated theatre crowd—Adele Astaire has yet to make an appearance at Café de Paris and is rarely seen with her alleged fiancé. Is trouble brewing in paradise for our American starlet?

With Maya leading the line, and Violet's hands on Eleanor's hips in front of her, and Caty holding on behind her, Violet tapped her way forward until they all parted in an arcing swish, grasping the feather fans from inside the tops of their massive hats. They finished the complicated number to a rumbling of drums and trumpet fanfare.

From the crowd, a woman screeched in a distinctly American accent, "Violet! Oh, my God, Violet, is that you?"

Violet tried to peer through the stage lights and the blue haze of cigarette smoke to see who was calling her name. The voice was familiar enough to make her skin prickle with excitement.

And then she spotted her: Adele Astaire, as glamorous as ever, in the center of the dance floor, waving madly. Freddie was beside her, and their usual entourage surrounded them.

Beneath the flush of exerted blood in Violet's cheeks, a new shade graced her skin—one of embarrassment at her old friend seeing her on this stage, dancing at a place she'd once frequented.

"Encore! Encore!" Adele shouted, and the band, who wouldn't deny the starlet her desire, struck up the same song again. Violet, Caty, Eleanor, and Maya whirled back into their initial formation.

By the end of the number, Violet was laughing as Adele pulled Freddie and her other friends into a line on the dance floor, mimicking their moves, all the way down to waving their fingers in front of their faces as imaginary fans. Oh, how Violet had missed them. The fun, effortless way they led their carefree lives.

"Come down from there," Adele called, signaling to someone out of the corner of Violet's eye.

She caught sight of her stage manager, who nodded, giving her permission. Violet walked to the edge of the platform, and Freddie lifted her down, smiling.

"Been a long time, kiddo." He winked, looking as dapper and debonaire as she remembered.

Violet smiled, shy at first, but a second later gave him a full show of all her teeth.

"Where have you been?" Adele pulled her in for a hug, the beading on Violet's costume snagging on the ecru lace trim at Adele's bosom.

As they disentangled themselves, Violet tried to think of an answer that would make sense. One that would assuage any hurt feelings at having completely ignored their last tour. For not reaching out.

Violet swallowed. It was too hard to say aloud.

"Well." Adele's large brown eyes met hers fondly. "We don't need to talk about whatever it is if you don't want to. I'm just glad to see you now! You were positively smashing up there. Do say you'll sit and chat for a minute?"

Violet glanced toward her manager, who she could tell wanted to call her backstage from the way he'd focused in on her with a narrowed gaze. But the man was smart enough not to dare contradict Adele Astaire and risk upsetting an important patron.

"A few minutes, but then I'd best get back to change. We've another number coming up," Violet said, her pitch an octave higher in her excitement.

"Of course, of course." Adele grabbed Violet's hand and dragged her toward a table in the corner.

"Club soda, please; two of them," Adele called to a waiter. "Not saying you can't have a cocktail, but you look a bit parched."

Violet grinned. "I wouldn't want a cocktail midperformance anyhow."

"I've done that before and it wasn't a good idea." Adele giggled.

The drinks were delivered and Violet sipped hers, having forgotten how fancy it felt to drink water that fizzed.

"So, now that we've gotten pleasantries out of the way, I'll get right to the point, and you know me, I don't hesitate to say what's on my mind." Adele pinned her with a knowing stare. "Why didn't you come to the audition for *Funny Face*? And why did you avoid me on my last tour for *Lady Be Good*? I was heartsick over it. And avoiding me again this time. Why?"

Violet didn't want to talk about last time. Or this time, really. She took a sip of her club soda, trying to decide exactly what she'd say.

"Didn't you get my letters?" Adele asked.

Violet stilled, the bubbles from the club soda popping on her tongue. She decided on the safe route and shook her head.

"Oh, well, fiddle-dee-dee," Adele said. "I sent you a letter before I left New York telling you that I simply had to have you in the show. And then another when I arrived in London a few weeks back. When you didn't show I figured you weren't interested. I had no idea you were dancing here."

A personal invitation to dance onstage with Adele Astaire, and she'd not even bothered to open it.

"I would have loved to dance with you." Violet skirted the disappearing act she'd pulled two years prior when Adele and Freddie had come back to London to take the theatre world by storm in *Lady Be Good*. She'd wanted so badly to see them perform when she'd returned from the country. But, if she had, they'd have asked where she'd been, and she was still too raw then to have to explain herself or think of any better excuse.

"Well, what about now?" Adele drummed her fingers on the table. "I simply loathe my understudy, Bridgette; I think you remember her?"

"Bridgette?" *Hell's bells.* "You want me to take her place."

Adele rolled her eyes and leaned forward, plucking the lime from her club soda and giving it a little suck followed by a squeal. "She is driving me mad. And, to be honest, she's a very skilled dancer, but she's got no fire in her. No passion. Pretty sure she got the spot because of who her daddy is, anyway. I'm exhausted. If I collapse, I need to know Freddie will be dancing with someone I trust."

"Who's her daddy?" Violet shook her head. "Doesn't matter. Never mind." She stared back at the stage, seeing her manager tap his watch in her direction.

"Say you'll come." Adele's eyes were pleading. "Be my understudy. It'll be grand."

Violet wanted to shout *Yes!* She wanted to rip off the feathered headdress bending her neck with its weight and continue the rest of the night out with the friends she'd missed.

"I have to at least finish here tonight." Violet chewed her lip, imagining what she'd tell her manager and the other girls. What she'd tell Caty. That flicker of hope burned brighter inside her, and she realized in that instant how very much she'd longed to be back in the theatre world.

"Of course, of course," Adele said in a rush. "But then tomorrow—eight o'clock sharp; say you'll be at rehearsals!"

Violet grinned. Life seemed to be turning around for her again. The dreams that had drifted toward unreachable, that felt smashed to pieces and handed back a bit at a time, were finally within her grasp again. The proverbial dangling carrot. And here was Adele, swinging it back and forth before Violet's eyes.

"All right. I'll be there." A thrill surged in Violet's chest.

Adele clutched her own. "Thank God! I've missed your face, your wit. Oh, how much you kept me grounded. I'm so glad you'll be back." She leapt up from her chair and came around the table to give Violet a squeeze, the scent of her familiar musky perfume arresting. "And one of these days, you'll tell me what happened. But it doesn't have to be today."

Violet nodded. One of these days she'd have to confide in someone.

CHAPTER TWELVE

ADELE

THE LIMELIGHT

At last, our prayers over the last five years have been answered. The Astaires are being joined onstage by everyone's favorite East Ender, Violet Wood. Tickets are sold out for the musical comedy *Funny Face* this week. Perhaps you'll be lucky enough to have a friend who is willing to part with a stub for the night, for this show is guaranteed to be the bee's knees.

September 24, 1928
Empire Theatre, Liverpool

The trill from the orchestra indicated the first act was starting, and the curtain rose, footlights beaming.

Before the show, Mom had materialized in the dressing room, her worried gaze mirrored in Freddie's, who stood behind her. I'd shooed them away, looking over their shoulders for any sign of my fiancé, William, but there'd been none. From the way Mom kept opening her mouth, squinting, and then pausing, it was obvious she wanted to tell me something. Perhaps "Oh, he'll be here soon" or maybe even "We told you he was bad news," but I shook my head, silencing any articulations.

There was no use in worrying about whether William would show up—because *not* showing up was his particular talent. No sense in making myself crazy wondering if he'd be a part of the crowd on opening night. Tamping down disappointment when it came to William—whom I'd not broken things off with yet—had been a skill I'd perfected nearly as much as my chaîné turns and relevé.

Instead I threw myself into the act, making sure my resident "funny face"—the namesake of the show—was on in full force.

I gazed up at Freddie as he pulled me on a wagon, the over-the-top silk-and-wire bow bouncing on the crown of my head just out of my peripheral view.

Freddie winked at me as he started to sing about how he loved my "funny face" and that beyond beauty I had a lot of personality.

I cocked my head this way and that, making eyes at the audience. I often found a few members to lock my gaze on, giving them that personal effect. Really connecting with them. Then when Freddie turned his back, still singing, I put my thumb on my nose and wiggled my fingers at the crowd.

The audience roared with each additional comedic act. Then they grew silent, in awe as Freddie and I did our dance numbers, until the signature runaround, which of course we had to toss in. The masses howled with laughter.

The cries of "Encore, encore!" filled the theatre, even as we took our bows in the finale and the curtains closed.

Any worries I might have had about a flop were a distant memory.

Backstage, I wiped at my brow with a towel and grinned at the cast as I stretched out my hips, which had been sore for weeks.

"You all were magnificent." I was thrilled to be back in England. Despite its fog, London always felt like a breath of fresh air compared to New York.

"You stole the show like usual." Alex Aarons, our producer, clapped loudly, slipping his cigar from one side of his mouth to the other. "You and Freddie both."

Freddie grinned, and I elbowed him playfully in the ribs. "Freddie keeps me in check. If he hadn't pushed us, rehearsing for thirty hours a day, I might have made a complete fool of myself out there."

"Impossible," Aarons said. "There are only twenty-four."

"Tell Freddie that." I let out a mocking groan and slumped over as if I might crumple to the floor, which actually sounded like a good idea.

"No one would know I worked you to the bone," Freddie added. "You are the most brilliant comedienne. Honestly, Delly, I don't think you realize how much the audience roars just for you. One minute you're dancing like a feather, and the next your comedic genius punches them in the face."

I started to blush, feeling his words all the way down to the tips of my tender toes.

"Oh, stop, Freddie." I glanced at the rest of our crew, who were nodding in agreement. My breath hitched as my chest swelled with overwhelming emotion.

"Take a bow, sis; you're unquestionably inimitable, even though we've seen people try. They are no match for you. And I doubt there will ever be another as bedazzling."

Tears stung my eyes then and I tossed myself into Freddie's arms, my spine cracking as he hugged me fiercely. "Do stop; I can't take it."

Freddie laughed and then tapped me on the nose. "Can't stop, won't stop."

The spell broken, our crew all started to talk at once. I joined the girls in the dressing area, tugging the pins that held my large bow in my hair, tucking an errant curl back into place, and then reapplying my lipstick. I changed into a new dress that my mother had bought me in Paris, the light-blue silk smooth against my skin, then double-looped my pearls around my neck.

I took an extra minute with my stockings and shoes, waiting for William to find me—willing him to have been in the audience, even though I knew better. At last I was forced to admit to myself—*again*—that the man I'd agreed to marry was a total jackass. I needed to find the gumption to kick him to the curb. But it was harder said than done. I wasn't getting any younger, and I didn't have any other offers.

A commotion at the back door had my hopes swirling anew.

I turned, my smile bright, ready for my fiancé to finally prove to everyone that he did in fact care about me and my career, only to see it was the royal entourage making their way through the door. My heart skipped a beat.

"Your Highness," I gushed, as the Prince of Wales—David—grinned at us all. I'd only dared to hope he'd want us in his circle on our third tour in Europe. The last time we'd been in England, the prince and I had flirted outrageously, though we'd both agreed not to pursue a romance again. I worried that he'd grown tired of me. But here he was.

"You are a sight for sore eyes." David took my hand in his, brushing his lips over my knuckles.

"And you are a glorious beam of sunlight for us peasants," I jested, wishing I could hug him outright.

David introduced me to a few of his friends, but my eyes cast on one alone, his blond hair neatly arranged, and blue eyes staring. He looked much like the prince, perhaps a cousin. He gave me a shy smile, his eyes jolly behind his spectacles.

"May I present to you Lord Charles Cavendish." David waved the handsome stranger closer.

"My lord, a pleasure." I was mesmerized by his gaze. He surrounded my dangling fingers in his larger, warmer grasp, sending an unexpected thrill up my arm.

"Cavendish, please. The pleasure is all mine, Miss Astaire." He, too, bent over my hand, brushing the air above my skin with his lips, and I shamefully wished that he'd made contact.

"Well." I cleared my throat, a sudden influx of strange emotions swirling in my chest. I was an engaged woman. Although no one would know it, given that my fiancé was never present. "Adele, then."

"You were brilliant tonight, Adele." Cavendish's gaze skated over my face, my hair, leaving me breathless.

"We were hoping you'd join us." The prince momentarily broke the spell, addressing me and Freddie.

There was no other option but to say yes. One simply did not turn down a royal. Besides, I was infinitely intrigued by this Cavendish fellow. How had we only just met?

Still, I glanced toward Freddie, who nodded subtly. "As long as we're back in our hotel by midnight, all's fine by me."

"Mom, I'm sure, would wish to join us as well," I said, probably for the first time ever, when it came to late dinners and clubs. But I knew I needed her tonight, to make sure I didn't flirt too ostentatiously with the man whose gaze kept drawing mine. A flush fanned its way over my chest.

"Oh, you dears go on ahead," Mom said. "I'm exhausted, and I've an early breakfast planned."

"Are you certain?" I asked.

Mom cocked her head at me as if trying to discern my thoughts, because they were distinctly different than on any other occasion. "I am, dear." She smiled and squeezed my fingers. "Have a wonderful time."

And then I understood her reasoning. She despised William, and any chance I might have to flirt with a prince and his peers she wanted me to take. Guilt mixed with irritation churned in my belly.

"All right." I searched the rest of the crew for Violet. At least if she was there, I could make my excuses should they try to stay out too late.

Needing a keeper was one of my biggest flaws. But I couldn't help it. When fun was being had, I never wanted it to end. I was Good-Time Charlie, after all.

Violet grinned as she hurried to join us, and I threaded my arm through hers as Freddie moseyed ahead to talk to the men about their favorite haberdasher.

"Great job tonight." A soft smile filled Violet's pretty face. Although she was my understudy, when Aarons found out she'd joined the crew he insisted she also dance a chorus-girl part, because she was the best dancer he'd seen, after me. I wondered why Violet had settled for a gig at the Café de Paris instead of auditioning for bigger shows. But it felt like prying to ask, and she wasn't offering up any answers on her own.

"And you as well, Vi."

"I'm thrilled to be working with you again." There was a wistfulness in her voice that hinted at secrets she'd not yet divulged. I knew there was more to her avoiding me than she'd let on. When she was ready, I was all ears. Friends didn't judge each other. They were there when needed.

"As am I." I leaned close, teasing. "And those bathing-suit costumes, my goodness; I think you nearly gave a few of the older ladies in the audience a fit of the vapors."

Violet chuckled. "I did half expect to have the indecency police storming the theatre and demanding we put on wrappers."

The bathing suits were worn by all the chorus girls during one of the acts. They were the Bathing Beauties of Lake Wapatog and danced a rather evocative number in their navy-blue suits with sailboats and waves embroidered on their chests, their hair tucked up beneath bathing caps. Their legs went on for days.

"I'll say it once, just as I've said it before. You've got great legs, Vi. You'd make a perfect Follies girl, and one of these days I'm going to get you to New York and introduce you to Flo Ziegfeld. He's a Broadway impresario and has his own theatre. You could be the star of his Follies."

I sat beside David at dinner, and, before Cavendish could take the chair on the other side of me, I tugged Violet into it. But that didn't matter so much, because he circled the table and took the seat opposite me, grinning with a knowing wink at how I'd tried to avoid him.

Oh, Lord, I think I'm in trouble.

Dinner was a boisterous affair, with one course after another paired with one drink after another. I still didn't imbibe much, but every time I turned around my glass was freshly filled. And I swear Cavendish must have had a hole at the bottom of his glass, because it didn't seem to matter how many times he called for a refill—his gaze never wavered, his speech never slurred. Not like mine.

I glanced at Violet. "I think we'd best leave after dessert," I murmured. "No club for me tonight. Is that all right? I honestly don't think my body would forgive me if I worked it any more tonight."

She nodded vigorously. "I need to get home soon, too. I promised Caty a chat after she gets off work," she said. "And Freddie wants us at the theatre at the crack of dawn."

As she said it, I looked over her head to where Freddie sat, on her other side. "Have no doubt, Delly," he said, "the crack of dawn it will be. Don't you go making plans to go to a club past midnight. Not tonight. There's nothing doing after the clock strikes."

I rolled my eyes at my brother's warning, which Cavendish

caught, and he chuckled. "You're as funny offstage as you are on," he mused.

"I suppose that's what makes me so good at my job." Heat came to my cheeks at how much attention he was paying me. "I am the face of *Funny Face*."

He chuckled. "You're a doll."

"Not quite. I assure you. I've got a not-so-sweet side."

"Oh, is that so?" Cavendish said.

"I can cuss like a sailor." I gave a perfunctory nod, unsure of why the hell I'd said that.

He laughed. "Well, as a soldier, I challenge you to that."

"A soldier? I thought you were a lord?"

He grinned at me and took a long sip of his drink, eyeing me over the rim. "I'm a lieutenant, and, yes, I am noble born, though a lowly second son."

"Is a second son so lowly?" All the title stuff with these aristocrats confused the hell out of me. "You look better than low to me. You are bloody fetching." *Now I've done it . . .*

Cavendish's grin widened. "I'll take that as a compliment. In the eyes of the peerage, however, yes. My father is the Duke of Devonshire, and my elder brother the Marquess of Hartington, and I am merely Lord Charles Cavendish."

I cocked my head to the side, trying to understand. I might have hung out with princes but that didn't make me a peerage expert. "I'll take your word for it. But I bet you live in a castle."

"Sometimes." He winked. "My other houses are merely manses."

I laughed and pointed at him. "You're a tease."

"So say my servants." He shrugged, his eyes twinkling with humor.

That made me laugh harder. "Do stop."

"It's true, I'm filthy rich and I've only ever known privilege. Will you forgive me?"

"Yes. But only because you're funny."

He chuckled. "So, shall we give your vulgar tongue another whirl?"

Dash it! My eyes widened, and I nearly choked on said tongue. "Pardon me?"

Cavendish let out a roar of laughter. "That did not come out the way I intended. I meant your claiming to possess a sailor's vernacular, beyond a mere *bloody*."

Heat flushed my face. My God, I hope he didn't find me to be dopey. "Ah, Cavendish, you're quite the jester. I've not had nearly enough gin for that here."

"Shall I escort you back to your hotel, then, for a nightcap?"

Oh, I wanted to say yes. Because the idea of a scandalous chat with this handsome lord was oh too delicious. But it would also be in all the papers, and have William, traitor that he was for not coming to my opening night, flying off the handle. Not that he deserved his ire. If he ever showed up I'd break things off. Didn't seem right to do it in a letter.

"I don't think my fiancé would like that." It'd been hard to say the words, and I was certain it would squash any future conversation between us. Disappointment made my belly do a dive.

Lord Cavendish lowered his specs on his nose and looked back and forth down the table and then straight into my soul when he said, "I don't see a fiancé here."

Oh, yes, indeed, I was going to be in trouble. Deep trouble.

"That's because he's a rat, but you didn't hear me say that," Freddie interjected, leaning across the table.

"Dear Freddie, do be kind," I said, but my heart wasn't in the admonishment. Because I was feeling an awful lot like my brother was right.

Lord Cavendish had aptly pointed out that my fiancé was nowhere in sight on my opening night. That cut deep. I'd known William was a bit dismissive of my career, though he liked asking me to pay often enough, considering. And because I wanted to get married, to start a family, to finally stop working and start living, I'd let his lack of consideration go. Had been lazy in letting him go, too.

At thirty-two years old, I was practically ancient for not having married yet. If I waited any longer, whatever was left of my womb would dry up and crumble into dust.

Nearly being blown up on Billy Leeds's *Fan Tail*, lying there in pain and staring up at the sky, I'd realized it was about dang time I got moving on all that. Did I really want to die, having only a career to show for myself? Did I want to dance until my legs gave out, refusing to move another inch?

I thought perhaps no. That I should be content to die once I'd had a family of my own. Something more than dancing and working.

William was heir to a vast fortune. I could retire from dancing easily when the time came to start a family. Maybe in a year or two. By then he'd be out from under his father's purse strings—and not perpetually broke—or, at least, that's what he promised.

But even the thought of quitting the theatre and leaving Freddie at the height of our popularity caused a spasm of guilt, and fear, too. I didn't want to disappoint my brother. Or Mom, who had sacrificed everything so I could succeed.

I also didn't want a sham of a marriage. If only I'd met Lord Charles Cavendish *before* William. The man sitting in front of me only reinforced that my fiancé didn't deserve me.

———◆———

December 20, 1928
Shaftesbury Theatre, London

"No use getting up this morning, Delly," Freddie called through my bedroom door.

"What?" I pulled my arm from beneath Wassie's warm body and moved the blanket that Tilly was lying on to free myself. I rose quickly, pulling on my robe and opening the door a crack. "Why not?"

Rehearsal was in an hour, and I'd never known my brother to miss even a minute. In his mind, if you weren't early, you were late.

Freddie held out a cup of coffee, the steam rising from the nectar of the gods. "If I'd known that was the fastest way to get you out of bed, I'd have started using that line a long time ago."

I rolled my eyes and took the offered coffee, sipping the too-strong cup. "What's going on?"

"All the streets around the theatre have blown up."

I nearly spit out my coffee as I followed Freddie down the hall to the breakfast nook. "Blown up? How?" My skin itched from where I'd been burned, phantom pains for the men who'd just suffered.

"Some poor city-worker chap was looking for a gas leak with a lit match."

I wrinkled my nose as his words sank in. I set down my coffee on the round breakfast table and slipped onto a chair. "Oh, dear . . . is he . . . ?"

"From the sounds of it, he's still alive."

I let out a breath and rubbed absently at the faint burn scars on my ankles. "That's a shock, and a relief."

"Yeah. But the streets are all a mess." Freddie shook his head and sat down opposite me, opening a copy of the morning newspaper, my face staring back at me from one of the columns we'd started to contribute to on dancing.

"So much so, they are closing down the show?" I asked.

"Only for a few days." Freddie folded the paper and slid it across the table toward me. "Want to go and see the damage for ourselves?"

"I do." Flashes of my own explosion danced before my eyes. But it was necessary to face our fears, wasn't it? To grow stronger?

"Go and get ready," Freddie said, pushing away from the table. "I'll take your hounds for a quick walk."

"Thank you." Taking the paper with me so I could cut out our article for a scrapbook, I hurried to get dressed. Bundled up against the winter chill, we headed down to the Shaftesbury Theatre but were stopped a couple of blocks away.

The streets were barricaded and lined with dozens of workers. On the perimeter were masses more people trying to get a peep like us, their breath puffing in white clouds of steam.

"Can't get you farther than this, sir," the cabbie said.

"We'll hoof it from here." Freddie paid the tab and opened the door. We climbed out, waved through by the policemen who recognized us, and picked our way across the road that looked as if it had burst open from below.

The streets themselves were rubble, large portions disrupted, completely impassable—even swaths of sidewalk. A lamppost right outside the theatre was leaning over, hanging on by some invisible thread from underground, the glass dome at the top crooked. Looked a lot like a drunken dancer to me. But the smell was the worst. The acrid scent of smoke and something burning, and I shuddered, remembering that smell from the boat explosion.

My breathing grew a little heavier, and Freddie took my elbow. "Are you all right?" he asked.

I nodded absently. "Well, I can see now why they won't be opening."

Secretly I was happy for the reprieve. William had called the day before, begging me to take the train to Edinburgh and spend Christmas with him. He'd been so apologetic about missing my shows and told me how awful he felt. Business had been tough recently, and he'd been buried up to his eyeballs in it. He begged me to forgive him, promised to make it right. It seemed like the right thing to give him another chance; after all, I'd fallen in love with him for a reason, hadn't I? But forgiveness required an energy I just didn't have.

Of course Mom balked at the idea of me going, for more reasons than one, the primary being the show. I'd casually said there was an understudy. Not because I wanted to make it work with William, but because I longed for a break to rest my aching bones—and I knew Violet would do the job perfectly. I'd seen Cavendish plenty and flirted with him enough to be half in love with the bloke. He danced like a dream and wowed me with his family lineage and tales.

I was ready to break off my engagement and not just so I wouldn't feel so guilty—but because a part of me was clamoring to see if there was anything more with Cavendish. But I knew myself, too, which was the only reason I was holding back. I'd had plenty of flirtations and flings; fancied myself marrying a prince a few short years ago. Nothing ever stuck. That was probably why I was being so stubborn about remaining engaged to a man I couldn't even find the nerve to set a date with.

William, for his part, was trying harder. He'd even come a few weeks ago and apologized to Mom for his rudeness; brought her a dozen roses, too. How could I not see the merit in that? Then again, why was I still bothering?

I sat on a pile of rubble next to Freddie, staring into a gaping hole in the road, wondering if this was a sign, and what sort of message it could be. And I decided *not* to go to Scotland.

CHAPTER THIRTEEN

ADELE

THE LIMELIGHT

Break out the hankies! Word in the West End is that Adele Astaire has managed to steal our star from the East End. Violet Wood will be making her debut on Broadway. New York City had better take care of our darling, because they can't keep her, else risk the threat of another revolution! But we've high hopes we'll see both enchanting twinkle toes back on this side of the pond considering Miss Astaire has once again attached herself to a handsome noble bachelor.

December 31, 1928
St. James's Palace

Our car was waved through the gates of St. James's Palace in a long, meandering line of taxis and chauffeured Rolls-Royces. We were lucky to have been sent a driver by the Prince of Wales himself, who'd invited us to dinner at the palace. It'd been a gas when we were invited on our last leg in London.

Of course William was busy tonight. By now I was used to it and didn't care too much, anyway.

Freddie was dressed to the nines in a new suit from Savile Row, and the gown I'd sent for from our apartment in New York—a Mariano Fortuny—had arrived just in time. A minute-pleated, apricot silk confection that hugged my frame. A matching apricot belt with silver double-vine embroidery encircled my waist, with hand-painted glass beads sewn onto the silk cord along the seams. I wore a brand-new pair of silver shoes, and a white fur-lined wool coat.

The Rolls came to a stop in the lighted courtyard of the palace and the door was opened by a royal servant with a bow. We were escorted with the other guests to the reception hall, where our coats and hats were collected. A soft murmur of voices filled the air.

The palace was as elegant as ever, with gold and marble and crystal gracing nearly every surface. We followed the crowd past the liveried footmen and the stoic butler and through the double doors to the dining room. The grand hall was lit up by an impressive crystal chandelier that sent rainbows dancing among the guests.

"The Astaires!" David gushed as we approached. "Most delighted you could come. My goodness, it would have been stuffy without you, but do not tell anyone I said such."

I curtseyed and Freddie bowed as we gave our thanks for the invitation. His brother Bertie, with his wife, Elizabeth, greeted us next.

"You're both to sit by me," David called to us. "Don't let anyone take your place cards."

"Not even your brother?" I teased, with a grin at the Duke of York, whom I'd grown so fond of over the years.

"Especially not him." David winked, and we were whisked away so that he might greet his other guests.

We were seated at the long table, impressively laid out with crystal, china, and gold utensils. Silk napkins were snapped into our laps by footmen, and champagne poured into our flutes.

The table was filled mostly with aristocrats. Freddie and I were the only Americans. The moment I thought the seat across from me wouldn't be filled, Lord Charles Cavendish was ushered into the dining hall by the butler and hurried over.

"Apologies for my delay," he said to the princes.

"Charlie, I've seen you dive naked into the Thames on a dare; never apologize for something so mundane as time." David laughed heartily.

Cavendish took his seat, glanced across the table at me with a shy, boyish smile, and raised his champagne glass in my direction. "Apologies to you, then, Miss Astaire, for the image my friend here has just placed in your mind."

I grinned saucily. "Who says I minded?"

Freddie hid his smile, and Cavendish gave me an appreciative nod. Oyster soup was served, followed by lobster, and a half dozen other delectable dishes. But I could hardly process the taste of anything I put in my mouth, because my attention was fully on the handsome lord who sat across from me, continually making me laugh.

After supper, Freddie hung back long enough for Cavendish to take my arm and escort me up the grand stairs to the drawing room. A small band started playing music as we entered. Although half the guests were immediately drawn to cocktails and chairs, Cavendish raised his brow in my direction.

"I know your feet must be tired after weeks of performing, but could I convince you to dance with me?"

I was impressed that he even thought about how endless dancing might affect my body. Most people just wanted me to entertain them. Cavendish was different. "My feet could have fallen off and I'd still say yes."

A small dimple appeared in his cheek. "Considering you float like a fairy when you dance, then I suppose you don't need your feet."

Cavendish held out his hand and I slipped my fingers over his palm. "I should say no," I said softly as he pulled me into his arms.

"Pesky fiancé?"

I laughed. "Yes."

"The daft fellow doesn't know what he's missing. Does he truly exist?"

"I think so." I shrugged as he twirled me. "But I'm starting to believe I might have been mistaken."

May 10, 1929

"You're never going to believe this, Delly." Freddie rubbed his hands together the way he did when he was very excited.

I skewered the olive in my cocktail and smiled sunnily at our guests, who'd come to celebrate Freddie's birthday. Dozens of them loitered about our living room, leaning against the white wood-paneled walls and lounging in our clamshell silk chairs and on sofas. Several admired a new painting that hung in a gilded frame above the brick fireplace, a countryside horse-racing scene, which Freddie had bought at an auction in London because he'd become such a fan of the sport. "Well, don't keep me in suspense."

"We've had a telegram from Flo Ziegfeld."

My God, was this going to be about a new performance? The idea of a show back in New York did hold some appeal, and an artist was never happier than when they knew they had another gig in the pipeline. Then again, I wasn't certain I really wanted to leave London and the possibilities the city held—namely, personal ones. "What could he want?"

"He wants us to costar with Marilyn Miller. It's going to be huge. I need to know. Are you willing to go back to New York?"

I knew what he was talking about—William. Whenever I thought of my fiancé another man's face flashed in my mind's eye. I was avoiding the situation entirely. I told myself it was because I was so busy with the show. But part of it was because I was scared to lose the one man who'd asked me to marry him. Scared to lose the dream of a family. It was stupid, yes, but I really had no other excuse.

"Yes," I said without hesitation.

Freddie narrowed his eyes at me. "What about William?"

I shrugged and bent to pick up Tilly, who was wearing the most adorable lace collar for the festivities. I kissed her sweet face, right between the eyes. "What about him?"

"Won't he balk? He expects you to stop working as soon as you say 'I do.'"

I bit my lip, finding it hard to express exactly the hesitation I'd been feeling lately. We'd been engaged for well over a year, and still I couldn't make myself set a date. Whenever William asked, I kept saying, "When the show ends," because I was too much of a coward to say "never." And now here was the end.

The strain of yet another show, ignoring my body's demands for a break, the stress of more work and more press—all of it seemed like a breeze compared to committing to William.

"You're not wrong," I settled with, letting the squirming Tilly down to go mingle with the guests.

"Delly, sister, dear," Freddie drawled. "Give me the lowdown on the two of you. Are you going to marry him or not? You've postponed the wedding more than once already. Doing the show for Ziegfeld is going to postpone it again."

"It should probably be postponed indefinitely," I murmured, picking at the red polish on my nails as I finally admitted to my brother what I'd been admitting to myself for a while.

Freddie's eyes widened. He exhaled so long, I wondered if he'd been holding his breath for the past year. "I see. Are you sure?"

I squared my shoulders, meeting my brother's gaze, and nodded. One more time. "Tell Ziegfeld we're in."

Freddie let out a whoop, clasped my hands in his, and then twirled me about, much to the delight of our guests. The Mayfair flat we resided in for the remainder of the show—transferred to the Winter Garden Theatre after the accident near the Shaftesbury—came back into focus. The tinny music playing on the gramophone entwined with the chatter of the actors, literary people, and aristocrats draped over our furniture or standing in circles, cocktails in hand.

"Now, get back to our guests, before they ask us what our good news is," I said.

I liked our flat better than hotel living on one hand, but not the inconvenience of no room service on the other. Although I'm certain the waiters at the Dorchester were relieved to see me gone after I'd cried over their lack of tapioca pudding. I tried to explain, after apologizing profusely, that it wasn't exactly the tapioca pudding I was having a fit over.

William had been there, dining with us, and the more I looked at him, the more I heard him talk, the more I wanted him to go away. Whenever I thought about walking down the aisle and seeing him at the end of it, my heart seized strangely in my chest.

So when the waiters offered only chocolate mousse—which happened to be William's favorite—I asked for tapioca.

Being denied the tapioca felt so much more like being denied a future I wanted, a delicious dessert—or, rather, a life—that would make me happy.

"Are you all right?" Violet's soft voice interrupted my thoughts and brought me back to Freddie's birthday party.

I glanced up, pulled from my reverie. "Yes, sorry, I was just . . . lost."

Violet smiled in that way that said she was all ears. "When I get lost, I have to sit down and look at a map to put myself back on track."

I laughed. "Is there a map of life?"

"There's a map for everything." Violet winked.

"What if I told you I wanted to retire?" I leaned close. "What if I told you I didn't want to marry You Know Who?"

"You've always encouraged me to follow my dreams, and I wouldn't be a good friend if I didn't tell you the same thing. Besides"—Violet glanced around the room—"I don't see the man you're attached to here."

"You'd not be the first one to point that out." Once again, William was absent from something meaningful to me.

"Does that mean something, then?" Violet asked.

"I think it does." I ate the olive off the tip of the toothpick, letting the briny juice burst over my tongue.

"What would you do if you retired?" Violet sipped her soda water. She didn't tend to partake too much of cocktails at parties anymore.

"I have no idea when that will be. But I suppose maybe travel to Paris? Maybe lounge at one of the German clinics in Freiburg that I've heard about." I leaned closer. "They soak nude in the springs."

Violet grinned. "Ooh la la. Would a certain lord be in attendance?"

I smiled, then ducked my head, pretending interest in my glass. It wasn't as if I'd kept my interest a secret from everyone. Cavendish and I were often seen together at clubs. Of course, we were with a big group when we went. But to Violet I had confessed the way my heart was turning. "If only I could be so lucky."

"A wise woman once told me that we make our own luck." There was a flash of sadness in Violet's eyes. I wondered if she regretted doing what she'd finally told me about, her secret. That she'd had a child and left him in Scotland. That the sacrifice she'd made had afforded her the chance to be onstage once more.

"Why don't you come with me to New York? We've a great show coming up, and it would be your opportunity to show yourself to Ziegfeld onstage. I know you'll wow him in an audition; he'd be bonkers to say no."

"I'm not sure . . ."

"Think about it, at least?"

A small, wistful smile lifted Violet's lips. "I will."

"Adele, darling." I turned at the sound of William's voice.

He'd sent his regrets, having had some business matter to attend to, and yet here he was. Perhaps jealousy had made him come. After all, photos of me dancing with princes and lords were often splashed across the gossip rags. Tonight, of course, Cavendish had sent his regrets, too, already previously occupied with his good friend Prince Aly Khan.

"William." I leaned in as he kissed me on the cheek, not getting a single thrill from the touch of his lips on my skin.

Violet nodded and said a soft hello before ducking away, and I wanted to chase after her, to run away from his presence. He wasn't supposed to be here. The times I wanted him, he didn't show, and the times I didn't want him, there he was.

"I thought you weren't coming." I led him toward the bar to get him a drink.

William's face darkened, that frown more often on his face than any smile, reminding me exactly why I preferred tapioca. "Are you not happy to see me?"

I patted his chest, giving a reassuring nod I didn't feel. I couldn't do this anymore. The realization was both a relief and nerve-racking at the same time. Too long I'd pretended, and ignored myself. My hand shook as I took a glass, plopping an ice cube into it. By the time I'd finished making his gin and tonic, however, the trembling had ceased. I hoped he would gulp it down and then take his leave. "Of course I am. You surprised me, is all."

William grunted. "Well, after the chat I had with Mrs. Astaire, I thought it prudent to show my face. After all, we are to be married."

I took a sip of my drink so I didn't have to respond. Mom had let William have it recently for not being there or acting like a fiancé in the slightest. I shouldn't encourage him. Not when I planned to break things off. But now, in the middle of my brother's birthday party, was not exactly the right time for a breakup.

"And when exactly will that be?" He drew out the syllables. "You've already postponed it twice now."

"The show is doing quite well, and I just can't leave Freddie with an understudy. We've still a bit of time left." This, I knew, was a lie.

"But you've trained her yourself."

"True enough, but it wouldn't be fair." Of course, with Violet as my understudy Freddie would be fine. My dear friend was a fantastic dancer, and there was a spark in her that would sizzle onstage if she were to take my place.

For so long my dream had been to settle down, to start a family. That was what William offered. He hadn't promised warmth, or love, so where had I gotten the notion that they were part of the deal? But I needed those things.

With William, I didn't see that happening.

Away from the stage. Grounded. A husband whom I could lean on and who would take care of me in a way that no one ever had. A lover who would press my back to a wall and kiss me senseless beneath the stars. Someone else to do the work, while I dripped in children.

The thought of marriage, of motherhood, used to make me smile. But when I saw William in place of the shadowy face in my dreams, it only made me anxious. In fact, my heart started to speed up right then and there, and not in a good way.

William took my drink and passed both of ours to a waiter, then held my hands in his. I stared longingly after the half-drunk martini making its way toward the kitchen. I wasn't finished.

"Pet," he said, "it's time."

I cocked my head, trying to appear pleased rather than bristling, as I was on the inside. I hated being called a *pet*, as if I'd not a thought of my own, and no voice to be heard. Where was the spine I'd once had?

"Darling." I tugged one hand away to brush at an errant piece of hair on my cheek. "When my show concludes I will be happy to entertain a date, but until then I can't." And I hoped that before then I'd have the nerve to say what needed saying. Or else I'd be sneaking onto a ship back to New York without a word.

"Can't? Or won't?" He dropped my hand, snatching a glass from a passing waiter and not offering to get one for me to replace the one he'd taken.

I glanced around and saw a few of the guests taking notice of his peevish attitude. Jeepers, but he was going to make a scene.

"William, this is neither the time nor the place for this conversation. Why don't we enjoy the party, and then in the morning over brunch we can chat?"

"Chat?" William let out an obnoxious snort. "As if it were nothing more than mundane chatter about the weather?" His voice was getting louder now.

I laughed nervously, hating how I was trying to hide his anger from the rest of the crowd. I was used to it by now. I'd been out and about with him in New York and London long enough to notice when he was climbing onto his pedestal and staring down at the peasants below.

"I wasn't jesting, Adele," he said. "I mean to marry you, and I mean for it to happen sooner than later."

Boy . . . wasn't he being a complete jackass?

I opened my mouth to appease him with softer words, but my gaze caught Lord Charles Cavendish entering the party with Prince Aly Khan. Another man who'd sent his regrets and then shown up—but this time I wasn't disappointed.

The duo were seen in the London clubs quite often. Cavendish smiled at me, his gaze settling on William with a noticeable frown. And suddenly I had more of a backbone than I'd had a moment ago. When I looked at Cavendish, I felt my stomach flutter, not tighten with the anxiety like I felt with William.

Lord Charles Cavendish was tapioca.

I straightened my spine and met William's glare. This wasn't the place, and it was not a good idea to break off our engagement here in the middle of my London flat, the gramophone playing Ruth Etting's "Love Me or Leave Me" and surrounded by friends, but what else could I do?

William seemed to sense the change. He glanced behind him, but, fortunately for me, Cavendish and Prince Aly had moved on. There was no one for him to see. Still, when he turned back to me, there was a hardened edge to his mouth.

"I'm not letting you go." His voice came out in a possessive growl, as if he knew what was coming.

"That's not really up to you," I replied, more steel in my voice than I'd ever managed before. "I no longer wish to marry you."

William shook his head. "You need some time to think on this. You're making a mistake."

"Maybe I am, but right now it feels right."

William gripped my wrist tightly, and bared his teeth for half a second before he remembered himself. And, thankfully, Freddie sidled close.

"William." Freddie glanced purposefully at where my fiancé gripped my wrist, his expression filled with warning.

William let go.

"Mr. Gaunt was just leaving," I said, refusing to use his given name.

Freddie's eyes widened a fraction of an inch with dawning understanding. "I'll walk you out, sir." He tucked his arm around William's shoulders and winked at me as they walked away, giving my former fiancé a bit more of a nudge than he should have. "Thanks for stopping by, Mr. Gaunt."

———◆———

July 1929

There's nothing like summertime in Paris.

The way the sun rises, flashing like diamonds on the Seine, and glistening on the soft, light-pink petals of freshly blooming cherry blossoms. Splashes of color in the shapes of tulips, daffodils, and peonies dollop the parks in various vibrant shades that made me feel as if I were walking through one of the landscape paintings that hung so proudly in the Louvre.

And the nights . . . they were magical. Streetlamps lit and Parisians dining and sipping wine at outdoor cafés until past midnight. The Moulin Rouge filled with music, laughter, and fun as Black American stars Adelaide Hall and Bojangles lit up the stage with their song-and-dance numbers in *Blackbirds*.

But best of all that I'd discovered on this spring trip was Charlie. Lord Charles Cavendish, and what a *dish* he was.

On the last performing night of *Funny Face*, on a whim I'd invited everyone at our table to go to Paris for a long weekend before I sailed back to New York City. Of course Freddie said no, because he had some things to tie up in London, but, surprisingly, he'd told me I should go. Mom agreed to join me, as did Violet, Mimi, who'd come to see us off, a few of the other castmates and aristocrats, Prince Aly Khan, too—but, most important, Lord Charles Cavendish.

Charlie and I maintained boundaries the whole weekend. We danced a few times at the clubs, shared smiles, and walked arm in arm through the parks. I'd made a point to do the same with Prince Aly so no one would talk. But it wasn't Prince Aly or any of the others whom I thought about kissing. That was all Charlie, and we'd nearly done it, too, on one of our walks back from a club in the wee hours of the morning.

The streets had been quiet, the sun blinking on the horizon. I dropped my hat, which I'd not put back on, and the wind started to blow it down the street. We chased after it together, and when we turned around our party was a quarter mile away, none the wiser. I stared up into Charlie's eyes, the laughter slowly fading from our throats as something more intense took over. He'd brushed at a long tendril of my hair that had come loose, curling it around his finger.

"Paris will never be the same for me," he'd said, and I think my knees nearly gave out then, because I started to wobble. For a girl with legs as strong as mine, and grace on the stage, it was an awkward moment.

Charlie slid closer, his hand gliding down my arm and then falling to my hip. I tipped my head up to look at him. When he started to lean in, one of our group noticed we were behind and shouted our names.

The moment was spoiled, but the spell wasn't broken. From that moment on, there seemed to be a charge between us that never fizzled.

Even now.

Oh, how disappointed I was that that afternoon I'd hop a train to Cherbourg, where I'd join Freddie on the SS *Homeric*, bound for New York. The flirtation with Charlie was coming to a complete and utter halt before we'd had a chance to see where it would truly take us. A kiss I'd longed for taken away too soon.

Church bells rang out the hour for lunch as we walked from our hotel through the Jardin des Tuileries to Café Runard. The streets were scented strongly of chocolate as the chocolatiers showed off their ornately decorated and impressive brown sculptures for a festival. Chocolate Eiffel Towers, a chocolate Notre-Dame, and eggs that were painted delicately to resemble Fabergé handiwork. Even a chocolate cherry blossom tree, with pink petals of hardened sugar.

Our small group was seated at a table outside beneath the eggshell canopy, each of us tired from the whirlwind weekend.

Across from me, Charlie stared, a small, sad smile on his face that I was certain mirrored my own.

"I hope you've enjoyed your short holiday," he said.

"Made all the better by good company." I felt my cheeks flush as his smile widened.

"If only I could join you on the ship. I've been hankering to get to New York," he said.

"You should come for the New York opening of *Smiles* this winter," Mom interjected.

I tried not to choke on my champagne—in Paris it was never too early for a bit of bubbly. "Oh, Charlie, you don't have to do that."

"No, I think that's a great idea." He refilled his champagne coupe and took a sip, studying me over the rim. "New York in winter is one of my favorite times. Besides, I'd not be a very good fan if I didn't come see your show."

"You'll have to dine with us." Mom gave a short dip of her chin in my direction, a subtle indication that she approved of Charlie.

"It would be an honor and a pleasure." Charlie winked at me.

As we ate our meal, me mostly picking at my poached salmon in lemon beurre sauce, I kept stealing glances at the handsome man who'd stolen my heart. He had charm and humor, was handsome to boot, and had a joie de vivre that I could relate to. Charlie was someone I could be myself with. He didn't mind when I acted silly or wanted to stay up all night talking, as we'd done on a walk back from the clubs until three a.m.—much to Mom's chagrin.

He never asked me to pay his bill, and he always showed up.

I'd learned from him that he didn't get along so well with his mother and father, but he delighted in the relationship that I had with my mother. He found Mum Astaire—as he called her—to be quite delightful. When I told him that she wasn't so delightful when trying to pin my hair under my cloche, he only laughed.

He had five sisters, along with an older brother, which explained why he seemed to understand me as a woman so well.

There was something easy about Charlie that I'd never found with any other man. He made me feel . . . safe. With my feelings, my desires, my dreams. I could tell him anything, and perhaps sometimes I told him too much.

I was going to miss him when I boarded the train and eventually the ship. An ocean to cross was too much, and this winter, when he promised to visit me in New York, so very far away.

Yet I didn't want to give up *Smiles*. Performing at Ziegfeld's was the icing on the cake when it came to my career. And if things happened to head in the direction I was hoping, then the show might be my last, and I'd be back in London before I knew it, having gone out with a bang. If dreams came true, that is.

"I would like that," I said to Charlie, and I genuinely meant it. "I'll show you around the city."

"Then I won't disappoint you."

No words more magical could have been uttered to a girl who'd just dumped a man who disappointed her left and right.

Paris took on a whole new meaning for me then. Paris meant falling in love.

CHAPTER FOURTEEN

VIOLET

THE LIMELIGHT

Looks like Miss Violet Wood is moving up in the world. Spotted in Mayfair coming and going from a recently rented flat, Wood appears to be the newest resident of the swanky address, along with her roommate, Miss Caty Mirren. But fresh digs aren't the only thing the West End's current favorite has that's new; she's also been sporting designer clothing courtesy of the designers themselves . . .

Late July 1929

There were those in life who seemed to have all the luck. Who flashed a smile, waved a hand, tapped a toe, and all the gifts the world had to offer fell in neat little rows at their feet.

That had not been the case for Violet.

Good luck for her always felt like a glass of water after inhaling a mouthful of ash, or finding a shilling in a crack in the sidewalk, only to trip and break a finger. Good luck was usually paired with bad, canceling each other out most of the time.

But today was different. She'd decided while in Paris that she would join Adele in New York City for the new show. In her new Hermès bag, she had gifts for Pris and her mum, hoping the treats would make up for the disappointment they'd surely feel at her going to America, not that Mum wanted anything to do with her. Caty would be doubly disappointed, and likely have to find a new flatmate, which was bittersweet given all they'd been through to-gether.

The journey from Paris to London had been easy, and though they were all exhausted from their whirlwind holiday on the heels of hundreds of performances, they'd spent the hours on the boat and train carousing. The sun had barely risen as they pulled into London. Violet stumbled onto the platform, grateful for the early hour, which meant it wasn't crowded. She made her way toward the Tube station for the train to Hoxton. She'd splurged on gifts of macarons and French perfume for Mum. For Pris, she had a new Sunday dress, wrapped in tissue. It'd been so long since she'd seen her family, and despite her mum, she'd found she missed them, and was determined to see them this morning. Mum couldn't turn her away, not this time.

By the time she turned onto Drysdale Street, her shoulder ached from the weight of her bag, making her wish she'd dropped the extra coin for a cab. She'd been able to save a lot while on the circuit, opting to remain in the flat thus far with Caty so that they could both set aside sizeable nest eggs. One that would now help her set up residence in America.

Violet knew all too well the consequences of being poor, and she didn't want to ever be in that situation again.

The sun was fully up now, beaming down through the usual London haze to illuminate the filth on the East End street, a cue that she was no longer on the good side of the city. Strangely, there seemed to be fewer people rushing about, as if the city had yet to awaken. Extremely odd for a workday. Puzzled, she picked up her pace.

The first sign of something gone wrong was the old man missing from his post on the stoop of her building. Not even a stray mug or blanket to show he'd gotten up only for a minute to go relieve himself somewhere. Just gone. She bent and touched the place where he usually sat, still chilly from a night without the sun's warmth.

She straightened up and looked around. Maybe after twenty-odd years he'd decided to find another stoop to sit on. But he was nowhere in sight, and it made her throat tight to think that he might have departed for good.

With a frown, she turned back to her old building and glanced up, for a second wondering if in her exhaustion she'd gone down the wrong street. But there, at the top of the ancient boarding-house, was the shingle hanging by a thread. It had been that way before she'd left, clinging with everything it had to stay in place.

Like most of the people here. Clinging to life, one small gust from ruination. What a surprise to see it still held on.

Violet hurried up the stairs and into the building, the familiar scents stinging her nose, along with something else. A new sour-ness that was sharp and unnerving. As she reached the first floor, a door below closed quietly and footsteps hurried up behind her. Violet turned to see the boardinghouse's landlady, Mrs. Beech, her brows drawn as usual, but there was something else in the usual twist of her lips. Sadness mixed with her unfailing disappointment.

"Good morning, Mrs. Beech." Violet tried not to let her exhaustion and irritation shine through. The last thing she wanted when she'd had too little sleep was a confrontation with the busy-body landlady.

"You've been gone a long time," the woman said, pointing out the obvious.

"Yes, ma'am." Violet stopped short of explaining herself; it was none of this woman's business.

"Well." Mrs. Beech twisted her hands in front of her in a clear sign of nerves, which Violet in all her years had never seen. "There was a sickness tha' passed through while you were away."

Violet drew in a slow breath, shifting her satchel on her shoulder from the painful place where it pinched. Was that what had happened to the old man? "What sickness?"

"Another flu." Mrs. Beech kept flicking her eyes back and forth between Violet's gaze and the wall, unable to make steady eye contact.

Violet's mind whirled back to the Spanish flu that had struck after the Great War. Her father, who'd made it home from battle, had caught the illness and passed. Mum had lost one of her babies. The whole of the East End—in fact, the world—had been struck by the raging pandemic. Now anytime anyone had a sniffle Violet panicked.

"Were you ill?" Violet reached for the collar of her dress to tug it over her mouth, afraid that the disease was still in the building.

Mrs. Beech shook her head, and Violet couldn't help the ugly thought that went through her head: *Of course, not even a viral epidemic would get the old goat down.*

"Bu' your mum . . ."

"Oh, my God." The words barely edged past her quickly closing throat. Not bothering to hear more of what Mrs. Beech had to say, Violet turned on her heel and ran the rest of the way up the stairs to her family's rented rooms.

She burst through the closed door, slapped first by the stench and then by the utter silence. *God, no.* The small flat was empty of life.

Mrs. Beech was right behind her, panting from having run to keep up.

"Where are they?" Violet asked, whirling around, her heart in her throat, her vision blurring.

"Priscilla is downstairs, in my fla'."

"Where is my mum?" Violet faced Mrs. Beech fully then, willing the older woman to stop her dallying and give her an answer. Violet grabbed hold of her landlady's shoulders, prepared to shake her if she didn't respond.

Mrs. Beech gently removed Violet's hands from her shoulders and clutched them in her surprisingly strong grasp, conveying in her touch how sorry she was. "As I said, Priscilla is in my fla'. She's doing fine. Sleeping s'ill."

"You're no' answering the question. Why?" Violet's voice had gone shrill with panic, some of the Cockney she'd banished from her tongue sneaking back.

Mrs. Beech's iron rod of a spine seemed to snap then, the way metal did when too great a weight had been resting on one end. "Your mum's gone to the Lord."

All the air left Violet in a whoosh. Her grip on the old woman's hands dropped and her body felt as though she'd been struck by a lorry. Her bag dropped to the floor, and she dully registered the sound.

The news was too much for Violet. Her knees crumpled, and she sank to the floor, stunned. All this time away, they'd never reconciled, and now her mum was gone. *Died*. And she'd never get the chance . . .

"Oh, dear." Mrs. Beech knelt in front of her. "I'm so sorry this is the news you 'ad to come 'ome to." The older woman made a clucking noise with her tongue and patted Violet on the shoulder. "I'll pu' a ke'le on downstairs. Come when you're ready."

Violet nodded absently as the landlady disappeared. She shifted onto her knees, staring into the small space that had been her home for so long. Once bustling with Pris's boisterous behavior. Now all was quiet.

The flat echoed now only in distant memory, which was fading faster than she could grasp it. Laundry still hung on ropes tied from one wall to the other. The teakettle was on the small stove, and a cup and saucer waited on the table to be filled. A few plates with crusts of toast and decayed apples littered the table.

A tremble started in her hands and great stabs of guilt shredded her insides. If only she'd been able to convince her mother to let her back into their lives. Violet had tried. She'd sent money, even came knocking once, but her mother wasn't home. Violet had written letters, said they could find a better place to live, together, now that she'd been making a better salary. But all her inquiries went unanswered.

If she'd been here instead of flitting about Paris like the upstart her mum said she was, she might have been able to take them out of the tenement building to a safer place, a hotel, where they could avoid the germs. Every scenario that ended in her saving her mum played in her mind, followed by the crushing defeat of knowing that her selfishness had not even afforded her the opportunity.

Violet was a failure. And now there was no way to make up the loss.

A scraping sound in the hallway pulled her momentarily from her torment, reminding her that she wasn't alone. There was someone who still needed her. The least she could do was be there for Pris. Never again would Violet let her sister down, let selfishness stand in the way of caring for those who needed her.

And Pris needed her now more than ever.

Violet pulled herself together, searching for a strength she wasn't certain she had, and headed downstairs to retrieve her sister. Today would be the first day of their new lives. Pris had only Violet to look after her. There would be no going to New York now. She couldn't leave Pris behind, and she certainly couldn't take her sister to a new city in a new country. There would be no one there to look after her, and Pris wasn't quite old enough to do the looking herself.

Violet lifted her hand to knock on Mrs. Beech's door, but the landlady swung it open before Violet could get in the first thump, presumably having heard her approach.

Beside Mrs. Beech, Pris stood, shoulders squared, chin thrust out. At twelve years old, she already looked ready to fight battles. Her face mirrored the one that Violet herself had worn so often. They would figure this out together.

"Pris." Violet was proud her voice hadn't cracked, even though her throat felt ready to collapse.

"I'm glad you weren' 'ere." There was a quiver in Pris's chin, but her lips were pressed into a thin line.

"I wish I had been." Violet wanted to tug her small sister into her arms.

"If you'd 'ave been 'ere then you'd be dead, too," Pris said. "So, I'm glad you weren'. And you can' make me change my mind."

"I wouldn't dare try." Violet did reach for her then, pulling Pris into her embrace. How could her young sister ever understand that the vehemence and sentiment of her words were exactly what Violet needed to hear?

Pris clung tight, squeezing the breath from Violet, arms looped around her waist, face pressed to her chest. "I don' want to be alone!" she cried.

Violet's heart shattered then, and she choked on a sob.

"I won't leave you alone." Violet stared at Mrs. Beech over her sister's head, and the woman, for once, had the sensitivity to look

away, to step back into her flat and leave the two of them alone
to grieve in private. "Why don't you gather your things, and we'll
go back upstairs?"

"You talk funny. I don' wan' to go back there."

Violet smiled into her sister's hair. "I don't want to either, Pris,
but we ought to. The sooner we do, the sooner we can get back to
normal."

Pris's head was bowed, and Violet had the impression she was
trying to bury their family along with her gaze. "Wha' is normal?
There is no normal withou' Mum. Why couldn' I 'ave died, too?"

Violet throttled the sobs launching an attack on her aching
throat. In a voice that was tight, and oddly distant, Violet managed
to say, "It wasn't your time. Nor mine."

Pris jerked her head up then, eyes red, glistening, and angry. So
much fury firing from a child's eyes, as if she were ready to burn
down the world.

"Who ge's to decide those things?" Pris demanded in a crack-
ling voice, slightly higher in pitch.

Violet was almost afraid to answer, but there was no use in hiding from the conversation her sister wanted to have. "You know
it's up to God."

Pris humphed. "Well, I'm mad at 'im."

The same anger churned in Violet's gut. "Perhaps we should go
and have a chat with him, then?"

Pris let go, chin jutting forward and deep divots replacing the
smooth skin between her brows. "I don' want to."

Violet shrugged. "Neither do I, really. But it might help."

Pris swiped angrily at her tears. "Fine." Then she turned on her
heel to gather her things. "But I'm no' promising I'll behave."

Violet laughed softly, feeling like the obstinance in her sister
was a step in the right direction. Pris had always been forthright

with her feelings. "I suspect your impudence is one reason you're still alive," she murmured.

"I don' know wha' you mean." Pris stuck out her lower lip.

"Come on, then." Violet started to call out for their landlady to let her know they were retreating, when the woman appeared. In her hand she held a small satchel of Pris's things, proof that she'd left them alone for a minute out of sight, but that she'd been listening in the entire time. "Thank you."

"You're welcome." Mrs. Beech bobbed her head. "And also, dear, your mother did pay up the ren' for the next month, so you'll no' need to worry about tha' ye'."

"Thank you, but we won't be staying." She hoped Caty wouldn't mind Pris bunking with them. She'd figure out a new job soon now that she wasn't going to New York; in the meantime her savings would suffice. When that ran out she'd pawn her Hermès and the sapphire brooch that one of her admirers had given her. But there was no way they were coming back here.

Silently they descended the stairs to the street, Pris taking Violet's hand in hers. Violet glanced down at her younger sister, but Pris stared straight ahead. The determined set of her jaw relaying the effort to remain that way.

They walked down the street, past those bustling off to work or the market. A few children played jacks on the sidewalk and a dog rushed by chasing a cat.

Shoreditch Church wasn't too far. Just down Kingsland, and then there it was, looming, its white steeple pushing up into the sky always looking too fancy for the neighborhood.

They headed up the stairs and through the great heavy doors, the quiet of the nave inside more shocking than the sounds outside the church. There were a few people inside, kneeling in pews, palms pressed together in prayer. Pris squeezed Violet's hand harder as the reverend approached. They'd once been good about going to church on Sundays, but sometimes work and life got in the way. Mum always said that God understood if someone had to work rather than visit his house, and Violet truly believed that. As long as they said their prayers each night, and followed in his footsteps, they'd be forgiven for missing a sermon.

"My dears," the reverend said, searching their faces and clearly trying to figure out their names.

"Violet and Priscilla Wood," Violet said.

"Ah, yes. The Wood girls. I'm so sorry for your recent loss. Have you come to pay your respects?"

Violet nodded.

"Out this way." He led them through the church and out to a neighboring burial ground. "Mrs. Beech made a donation, so you needn't worry about that."

Violet nodded gratefully, though she'd not even thought about a donation, let alone worried over it.

He led them to a grave, the turned earth with shoots of green grass sprouting signs of new life. There was no grave marker. Merely a wooden cross.

As Violet and Pris stood there, the reverend offered them a prayer before disappearing back into the church. The two of them stared at the grave so long that he eventually returned to see if they were all right.

Violet assured him they were, and when he'd disappeared once more she tapped Pris on the nose. "How about some fish and chips?"

Pris cocked her head, a slight, hungry lick of her lips showing that she liked that idea a lot. "From a pub or the chipper?"

Violet smiled. "Hmm. How about a pub? We'll not make a habit of it."

"I've never been to a pub," Pris said.

"Well, it beats cabbage soup."

"Everything bea's cabbage soup."

Violet smiled at her sister's ornery tone. "That's a fact."

As they made their way to the Red Lion pub, a small sliver of hope slipped into Violet's belly. They were devastated beyond consolation, no doubt, but standing there with Pris's warm hand in hers she had a feeling that not all was lost. It couldn't be. They would make this work.

They had to. Violet was a survivor. A planner. A doer. She made things happen. Or, rather, she tried to make things happen. And she couldn't face another failure staring into her soul.

There was no looking back, no wondering about the future. Only forward motion and survival. She'd adapted before, when her mother had kicked her out. And she would do so again. She would show Pris, too, that not all was lost, even if it felt that way right now.

CHAPTER FIFTEEN

ADELE

THE LIMELIGHT

In a recent interview, Miss Violet Wood stated that she had no intention of returning to the theatre at present, and that her priority remains the raising of her younger sister after the tragic death of their mother. Letters have been pouring into our office since the announcement of her turning down a lead role in *Wake Up and Dream*, as well as offers to sponsor a governess for the young Priscilla Wood, which Miss Wood has rejected. We were prompted to speak with the absent star after her repeated refusals and she had this to say: "My sister is all I have left in this world, and though performing onstage had been a lifetime dream of mine, it is not worth losing the most precious part of my life that remains."

September 1930
New York City

My mother once told me I'd regret wishing to grow up faster, because once I was her age I'd wish the days were longer. There's a reason Freddie and I always said Mom knows best.

Exhausted after rehearsal, I made my way back to our apartment at 875 Park Avenue, two blocks east of Central Park. My brother, in usual Freddie fashion, had chosen to stay behind to work on a few things. It almost felt like things were normalizing.

The past twelve months seemed like the forgotten year. Where days passed in blinding numbness. Seasons changed and melancholia took over pretty much everyone. Money was at the root of it all. Wasn't it always?

The end of 1929 had not been good to the world. The market crashed—Black Tuesday—and, although we weren't bankrupted, we weren't rich, either. Our bank accounts went from an excess of $100,000 to less than $27,000. And Flo Ziegfeld, who'd been nearly bankrupted himself, had been forced to postpone our show *Smiles* for almost a year. Our promised weekly performance salary of $4,000 disappeared in the sudden shift in the wind.

A few times I'd found Freddie staring blankly out the window, and it was only when I enticed him to rehearse dancing with me that he realized there was something wrong—because I was never the initiator of such activity.

Charlie's promise to come to New York was pushed off with the world's doom. Desperate for connection, we wrote to each other nearly daily. Perhaps my most lavish expense was postage, because besides my letters to Charlie I was also still trying to keep up with Vi, though her letters had dwindled down to none, the two of us losing touch as sometimes happens with friends who go their separate ways.

Like the rest of the world suffering from the Depression, we'd decreased our spending to practically nothing. More than once Freddie thought he might soon be standing among the men in the breadlines waiting for a hot meal or a cup of coffee if things didn't turn around. Children begged outside restaurants so often I started carrying a couple of sandwiches in my purse so I could feed them. And, once a week, Mom, Freddie, and I volunteered to serve food at the local kitchens. In comparison to others, we were extremely fortunate.

Then fall had turned the leaves of the trees filling Central Park to beautiful shades of gold and red, the only sign the world still turned. And after a year of wading through endless days we got a sign of our own. Ziegfeld finally received enough financial backing that he promised us an opening in Boston at the end of October, and in New York City by November. All we could do was pray nothing else catastrophic happened.

As depressing as the last year had been, I harbored no regrets about my decision to break off my engagement with William. I'd rather have lived in New York eating toast and beans, writing to Charlie for a decade, than be living with William as lavishly as he had promised.

Turning onto Park Avenue, I felt fortunate to be where I was. I loved living so close to the place where as children we'd ridden a trolley car from our apartment to Central Park on Sundays to play or row a boat on the Lake. It was a shame they'd dropped the trolley service last year; I rather liked the nostalgia of it.

Before the Crash, we'd taken long strolls in the park and rowed a boat now and then. A few times Freddie had even convinced me to roller-skate along the pathways, swerving around the secret dips and valleys.

But, after the Crash, we'd learned the hard way that taking a picnic to the park wasn't such a good idea right now, when we were accosted by a band of displaced children in search of food. It was incredibly heartbreaking. Now if we ever ventured there it was by auto to the club, or a stroll in the right parts, and never alone.

I ducked beneath the green canopy of my apartment building, with the white numbers of its address painted boldly on the flap, as I fished in my purse for my keys.

"Miss Astaire." The bellboy's voice sounded off. Almost British.

As he held open the door, I jerked my head up from where I'd been rummaging to meet the blue eyes of Lord Charles Cavendish.

"Charlie!" I exclaimed, my keys flinging from my hand to land somewhere behind me. Not caring for propriety or manners or any of that, I tossed myself into his arms.

He hugged me tight, and I clung to him, not realizing until that moment how much I'd feared never seeing him again. I breathed in his spicy cologne, my cheek itching with the familiar scratch of his wool coat.

"What are you doing here?" A smile split my face so wide that it hurt.

Charlie bent over and picked up my keys, dangling them from a long finger. "I'm working at J.P. Morgan in the city, and I couldn't pass up an opportunity to find you and ask you to dinner."

"Well, that's grand." I took the keys, the metal warm from his grasp. "And I would love to."

"Brilliant. I'll bring my car around tonight." He tipped his hat and started to depart.

"Wait," I said, not wanting him to leave just yet. "How about a walk before you go? I'll get my dogs. It's been so long since . . . Paris."

Charlie flashed a grin that said he'd hoped I'd ask. "I'd love a chance to stretch my legs and see your sweet Tilly and Wassie again."

"Swell." I could hardly find words to say how happy I was. And he'd remembered my dogs' names. *Adorable.* Normally so talkative, I felt like my brain was moving faster than my tongue and leaving me speechless. In that moment I regretted so much not having found the courage to share my feelings in my letters. "Would you like to come up with me?"

We rode the elevator to my floor, both of us nervous in such a small space together. Bits of chatter about the weather and such. I gathered the pups, and then on the way down Charlie crouched to rub their heads and let them lick him on the nose.

He held out his arm to me, and I slid my hand over the expensive wool of his overcoat. He took one leash in hand and I held the other as we walked down Park Avenue like a comfortable couple out for a stroll. I loved it.

"You look well." He glanced down at me, a vibrancy behind his sky-blue eyes.

"Looks can be deceiving." We turned left on Seventy-Eighth and walked the two blocks toward the park, dodging children who ran this way and that, mothers with prams, and other couples walking arm in arm.

"Do tell me, then, darling, what are my eyes not seeing?" He peered inquisitively at me.

I laughed, feeling a heaviness lift from my chest that seemed to have settled there during the past year. "I might have been suffering from a bit of gloominess. But that's all over now."

"Because you've a show starting soon?"

"Yes." *And because you are here.*

Charlie patted my hand where it rested in a familiar fashion. "I'd love to join you in Boston for the opening if my calendar allows."

"The New York opening would be better," I said.

"Why's that?"

"Boston is really a practice round. We usually do an opening somewhere different from where the show will take place for the long haul to work out all of the kinks."

A child's ball came careening down the sidewalk, and Charlie leapt effortlessly over it, quickly recovering Tilly, who'd gone in pursuit. "Then it would be special for me to see both. A one-of-a-kind show."

I laughed, calming Wassie, who was intent on hunting two squirrels that chased each other over a fallen acorn, not unlike the men on Wall Street whom Charlie was going to be working with. That nut being everybody's lost fortunes.

We headed to the right, toward the Metropolitan Museum of Art, rather than going straight ahead to Belvedere Castle, where the homeless who hadn't been run off by the police were camping by the drained reservoir. I thanked my stars every morning that we were fortunate enough to not be among them.

"How is your city faring in light of the recent Crash?" he asked.

"They say in the papers that the 'Haves' who live on Park Avenue get to look down from their lofty, comfortable windows at the 'Have Nots' in the park," I murmured. "It breaks my heart. We do as much as we can for them."

"You have a kind soul."

"I don't know about kind, but certainly I am feeling guilty whenever I sit down to a full meal and then worry about dancing again so that we've a steady income, when there are others out there suffering so much more."

"You needn't feel guilty about that."

"All the same, I do. I've started calling it my 'champagne problem.'" I rolled my eyes and paused for a minute as the dogs inspected a patch of grass. "Essentially, while I'm sitting in my designer chair with my steak, some mother is trying to figure out how to stop her toddler from crying because they haven't enough to eat."

"You inspire me to be a better man." He tilted his head to the side, looking so at ease in my world that it felt as if the year since we'd last seen each other had never happened. "Say, isn't this where the Central Park Casino is? I hear the dining and music are incredible."

"Oh, boy, that's a touchy subject." I grimaced, my mood dampening as I recalled the details. "My brother was a fan. Freddie's a lucky duck. A few months ago, the place was raided for serving liquor and nine patrons were arrested. Freddie doesn't imbibe too much and was fine. But Mom has begged him not to go there again."

"Maybe she'll change her mind if I promise to watch over him." He winked.

"I think you forget we're not in London anymore. Drinking is illegal in the States." We continued down the path, Tilly and Wassie leading the way.

"So antiquated. Banishing spirits only makes it more desirable."

"I agree, and has only bred a whole line of new criminals. But, alas, our country was founded by Puritans, and it seems every now and then we settle back on our old roots."

"Well, hopefully that doesn't mean witch hunts are going to make a comeback."

I laughed. "Don't start calling me Goody Astaire yet."

That night, when Charlie picked me up in his limo, he took me to the St. Regis to dine in the rooftop restaurant. The spacious dining-room walls were brushed a deep blue, with painted blossoming apple trees curling up from their roots near the floorboards to entwine above our heads. Brightly rendered roosters and macaws in oranges, reds, blues, and greens perched on the branches, lit by crystal chandeliers as they watched over the patrons who settled into blue velvet chairs around pristine, white-clothed tables.

"Did you know this room was designed by Joseph Urban?" I asked, playfully pulling out a bit of trivia.

"I did not." Charlie brightened beside me. "Pray tell, who is this famous architect?"

"Well, he also happened to design the set of a musical that Freddie and I did in 1919 on Broadway. Guess which one!"

The maître d' escorted us to a table near the arched windows that looked out onto the brilliantly lit cityscape. There was some-

thing about New York that I didn't think would ever leave me.
The city of promise, of hope and self-discovery. It was here I'd
had my start, and I wondered if it would be here I'd have my end.

Once we were seated in our chairs, Charlie tapped the table as
he looked at me. "Give me a clue, but don't tell me the answer."

"The name of the musical is right here, on display."

"Oh, that is a good clue." He glanced about the room, studying it for several moments, his lips slightly upturned as if he were
truly trying to discover a secret. "Hmm, a quandary of the first
order. Perhaps a parody on gardens? *The Macaw*?"

I laughed and took a sip of the lemon-flavored mocktail the hotel touted on its menu. Charlie pulled a small flask from the inside
pocket of his jacket and tipped the contents into his tumbler, with
a conspiratorial smile. "Got this from a bootlegger contact. Want
a dribble?"

I declined with a shake of my head, taking note that Charlie's
drinking hadn't ebbed a bit in the year since I'd last seen him. "Oh,
yes, you have rehearsal in the morning. I would never interfere."

Charlie rubbed at the condensation on his glass as he continued
his perusal of the dining room. "All right, so, about the clue," he
said.

"I'll give you a hint." I leaned forward. "It's not the birds."

Charlie leaned over the table, too, the tips of his fingers touching mine, and he winked at me. "And you think I don't remember
you telling me about *Apple Blossoms*?"

"Ha! So you do remember." I was so pleased I'm pretty sure my
smile was what powered the lights in the room.

"I could never forget." He clinked his glass to mine. "Here's to
a wonderful night."

"Here's to more than just one," I said.

After dinner, Charlie helped me with my wrap, his palms
brushing my shoulders, and my skin tingled. We'd come so close

to a kiss in Paris, and it had been stolen away in the second before it could become a reality.

On the drive back to Park Avenue, we sat together in the back of the car, our knees bumping, the heat of him so close, yet an inch away. Every now and then our fingers brushed, until he took my hand in his and brought it to his lips.

"I never want this night to end," he said softly.

"Me, either." But the car pulled to a stop outside the building. If I didn't get inside and was late to rehearsal in the morning, Freddie would have my head.

Charlie climbed out and opened my door, taking my hand as he helped me alight. He walked me to the building's front door, where in the past I would have bid a man courting me goodnight.

"Walk me to my other door?"

Charlie nodded. "Of course."

As the elevator slowly cranked up the levels to my floor, Charlie leaned close, edging my back against the wall, one of his hands braced above my shoulder. His heated gaze slid over my face, warming me all over.

"I've been wanting to kiss you since Paris," he said.

"We've no friends in here to stop you this time."

Charlie chuckled, the sound a thrill as he leaned down, the pad of his thumb stroking the slope of my cheek down to my chin, and finally he captured my lips with his. I sighed into his kiss, relishing the gentle way his mouth nudged mine, igniting every nerve as if he'd been a spark.

I hoped no one wanted to get on this elevator, for I certainly never wanted to get off. I'd never been kissed by a man the way Charlie kissed me. Subtle possession, alluring and intoxicating. When he started to pull away, I gripped the lapels of his coat and pulled him back.

"Not yet," I murmured.

But the elevator dinged, and the door on the other side of the crisscrossed iron grate whooshed open. Still entwined in our embrace, eyes locked, I half expected to hear a gasp from someone waiting on the other side, but there was no one there.

"Good night, darling Delly." Charlie took my hands from his lapels, kissing the knuckles on each one.

"Thank you for a wonderful evening." I pushed open the grate, one of my hands still in his. For some reason, walking away was the hardest thing I'd ever done.

Charlie grinned at me as if he knew something I didn't. Then he gave my hand another gentle squeeze and swooped forward one more time to brush my lips with his—this time much too quickly. "The pleasure was all mine, doll."

Two days later, Charlie was at our apartment, both dogs managing to curl onto his lap as he regaled Mom and Freddie with stories of a horse race he'd been to before leaving England, of course enthralling my brother, who'd become quite obsessed with horses and racing when we were abroad. He even had plans to buy his own racers at some point. Charlie fit in so well with my family, and the joy I received from that realization nearly split my ribs, my chest puffed so wide. Pop would have loved him. For all his title and riches, Charlie was a regular guy, and funny to boot.

No one would ever know his family had castles in England, Scotland, and Ireland. That his father was a wealthy duke, or that his family line went so far back that they were probably mentioned in the Bible. Everyone in Great Britain knew who Charlie was, and yet he sat there petting my dogs as if life in a New York apartment were completely normal for him.

He was the perfect match for my Good-Time Charlie moniker—and how funny that Freddie would name me that, now that I'd found my own good-time Charlie. It seemed we were fated to meet.

From that moment on, we were out together most days after Charlie left work and I finished rehearsals. We played hours of backgammon at 875 Park Avenue and danced at every nightclub in the city, making appearances at speakeasies often, despite Mom's displeasure at the idea. Freddie took us to one of his favorites, the Cotton Club, where Duke Ellington's band knocked our socks off, and Adelaide Hall, looking as gorgeous as she had in Paris, crooned wordless vocals in "Creole Love Song," her unique jazz style of scat singing, until the audience roared.

I'd been stressed to the max with everything for so many years, and Charlie was the breath of fresh air I needed. I was always surrounded by pressure, but with him weights were lifted.

I got the feeling Charlie was having a lot more fun in the city than he was spending any time working. But for right now that seemed just the type of person I needed. One who wasn't so stressed. He was oblivious to the economic and emotional depression that had taken over not only the city but the entire country and other parts of the world. Charlie's wealth and privilege allowed him to enjoy life to the fullest, and he was whisking me along for the ride. But that didn't stop me from asking him to join me more than once to ladle soup at the kitchens.

On the eighteenth of November, when we were back in New York City for our opening night after our preview in Boston, Charlie brought his winning smile backstage with a bouquet of white roses and lilies.

"Why, if it isn't my biggest fan," I teased, jumping up from my makeup table to accept the offered gift, and to lean in for a kiss on the cheek.

"I made a promise, and from what I've heard, a man never backs down from a promise to the woman who dances like a lilac flame."

My goodness, the man was simply sweeping me off my feet. The things I'd longed for in a connection with William and every other past lover, Charlie had in spades. I laid the flowers on my dressing-room table, put my hand on my hip, and cocked my head.

"Have you read my old reviews, you scoundrel?" I made a funny face at his reference to the newspaperman's comments about my dancing.

"How I've missed your funny face," he said with a laugh, putting his thumb up to his nose and wiggling his fingers.

"And I have truly missed yours." My voice had taken on a serious edge that I wasn't used to. The charming lord caused everything in me to tighten and exhale all at once. Just the mention of his name had my teeth flashing and my eyes crinkling.

I think I'm falling in love.

Charlie reached for me, sliding his fingers down the length of my forearm to tap the bones on the back of my hand before threading his fingers with mine. He, too, grew serious, pupils dilating as he tugged me closer. "Then let's make sure we have enough time to ingrain these memories forever in our minds before I depart."

I glanced away, toying with the pearls at my neck with my free hand. "And when is that?"

Charlie touched the side of my face. "A month or more."

"Then it will be a memorable month or more."

"I'll be here every night," he said.

I was about to protest, like I had in Paris, but instead I popped one shoulder forward and said, "So will I."

Charlie chuckled, squeezed my fingers, and opened his mouth to say something else, but a shout from my director had us both pulling apart.

"You'd best get to your seat," I said. "And I'd best put on a damn good show, now that you've come all the way across the ocean to see it."

"You could stand on your head for three hours, and I'd be entertained," Charlie said.

"Don't tempt me, you might see me do it." I shooed him out of the dressing room.

"Who was that?" Marilyn Miller asked. "He looked like the Prince of Wales."

"Hands off." I laughed. "I may have entertained a courtship with a prince, but that wasn't him. That was Lord Charles Cavendish."

"Lord of what?" Marilyn bent to peer into the mirror, patting the side of her hair.

My heart. My dreams.

I shrugged. I still found the titling of British nobles confusing. From what I understood, Charlie wasn't necessarily lord of anything, though he did have responsibilities. "His father's a duke."

Marilyn wiggled her brows. "Ah, so he's the lord of an inheritance."

I laughed but my heart wasn't in it. Explaining titles and inheritance and second-son business to a fellow American would be like trying to teach a fish how to run on land. At some point, between dumping tea overboard and now, we'd forgotten how it all worked.

"He sure is handsome." Marilyn eyed the doorway through which Charlie had just disappeared.

"Don't you even think about it, Marilyn." I poked her in the shoulder.

Marilyn brought her finger to the center of her lower lip. "Freddie, then?"

I rolled my eyes and laughed. "If he'll have you."

"I'm not sure Freddie's having anyone." Marilyn pouted and peered out of the dressing room, either in search of my brother or to make sure he wasn't listening.

"Oh, don't you worry, he's having plenty." Freddie was handsome, wealthier than most in such low times, and had dance moves that seemed to make more knickers drop than rain fell in London.

"Plenty of what?" Freddie bounced into the dressing room, oblivious to what Marilyn had said, but overhearing my response.

"Plenty of fun." I ruffled his hair and he ducked away.

"Now I know you're lying." Freddie wagged his finger at me, then the orchestra struck the first note, our cue it was time to get back to work.

Marilyn took Freddie's left arm and I the right, and we danced our way out onto the stage, ready for *Smiles* all around.

I'd thought our shows had been hits before, but *Smiles* was even more of a crowd pleaser. The laughter was a deafening roar, and the applause at the end nearly made my ears ring. People needed something good with all the bad going on.

Reporters and fans thronged the stage door, so many that we were trapped in the building. They were shouting our names, calling out questions, and every time we opened the door flashes of light blinded us as they took pictures. They blocked all the entrances, as in a comical farce, running from one door to the other in anticipation of which one we'd open. This part of celebrity life I would not miss at all.

"Come on." Charlie grasped my hand, tugged me close, and led me through the crowd, Freddie following suit with Mom at his side, and a host of our crew behind them.

"My car is over here," Charlie said, and true to his word there was a Rolls waiting at the curb and a driver standing there ready to open the door. There was a line of other cars and taxis behind it.

"Thanks, Mac, you're a life saver," I said to the driver as I climbed into the back, and Charlie came in beside me, his warm thigh pressing against mine.

Freddie, Mom, and Marilyn climbed in, too, with the rest of the crew dispersing down the sidewalk or into waiting cars, as the cameras flashed wildly.

"Where to?" Charlie smiled down at me with mischief in his eyes as we slammed the car door shut, cutting off the blinding lights and muffling the bellowing reporters.

"Why, what other place is there than the 21 Club?" I grinned.

The speakeasy had been our favorite place to go and dance and laugh, and Charlie availed himself of all the bathtub vodka he could get his hands on.

"Brilliant, I'm up for it. How about the three of you?" Charlie asked.

"It'll be a gas." Marilyn grinned at Freddie in a way that made me think she might just take a bite out of him later.

"I'm zonked, maybe I ought to go back to the apartment." Freddie ran his hands down his legs, a move he'd done more than once to show he was nervous.

"Oh, come on, Freddie," I said. "One day we'll be too old for this and then you can sleep all day if you want, napping in a chair like the old men at the chess pavilion."

Freddie laughed and leaned forward to pinch me, but I scooted out of the way. "All right, but only for a little while."

True to history, Charlie ordered a tall bathtub cocktail when we arrived. "That stuff will rot your gut," I told him later as he ordered another between frolics on the floor. I stuck to soda water.

"Negative, sweetheart, I'm invincible." And then he whirled me around, my body pressed to his, and all I could think about was the euphoria of having him all to myself.

I was half in love with him. No—*fully* in love with him.

Charlie was everything a girl could want, all wrapped up in a neat, rich, aristocratic package. He was handsome and funny, and when he kissed me I truly did see stars.

With Charlie, I wouldn't have to worry about money. Not like I had with William, who'd sworn he was well-off with a straight face. Charlie would not leave me with his bills and promise that one day he'd come into his inheritance and pay it all back. If anything, he was spoiling me already. I touched my finger to my ear, where one of the pearl-and-diamond earrings he'd gifted me as an early Christmas present was clipped.

A thought returned to me then, a question I'd posed to myself before. Did I want to be managed? I certainly wouldn't mind if it was Charlie doing the managing . . .

I laced my fingers behind his neck, fiddling with the soft hair trimmed neatly at its nape. "Charlie, darling . . ." I bit my lip, the exhilaration of the night fueling my words. "You and I, we get along so well."

"That we do, darling dancer." He dipped me low, and I swung my leg up, toe pointed.

"Well, do you think we ought to get hitched?"

Charlie might have been British, but my American slang wasn't lost on him. He lifted me slowly until we were both upright, ceasing his movements altogether in the middle of the dance floor. At first his color faded and he appeared stricken, but then his eyes widened and a wild excitement flared there. "Are you proposing to me, Delly?"

I nudged him back into a waltz. "I suppose I am."

A grin wider than the Seine, which we'd nearly kissed beside over a year ago, filled his too-handsome face. "How could I refuse such an offer from such a brilliant woman?"

I shrugged. "Easy, if you wanted to."

Charlie pressed his forehead to mine. "But I don't want to."

"Then say yes." I spun away, doing several shuffles on my way back to his arms.

"Yes." Charlie picked me up, twirling me around, my legs flying out behind me. The rest of the night soared by in a whirl, ending with a long kiss in a too-short elevator ride.

The following morning, Mom woke me with a gentle shake of

my shoulder. "Delly, dear. Charlie is on the telephone. It's awfully early." Disapproval laced her voice, but all I could think about was, *What has happened? Is something wrong?*

Why was he calling me at the crack of dawn?

I raced to the telephone in the foyer of our apartment, Tilly and Wassie at my heels, likely hoping for a walk. "Charlie, what's wrong?"

The charming sound of his laughter filtered through the earpiece. "Oh, Delly, now you sound like your brother. I was only calling because you proposed to me last night."

I chewed my lip, glancing toward where Mom hovered in the corridor nearby and hoping she couldn't hear what he was saying. Part of me had wondered if he was going to forget it had ever happened, having imbibed too much bootlegged spirits for the memories to last. Or "forget" out of respect for my feelings, because he wished he'd declined. But never had I expected him to call when sleep still filled my eyes and sound so jovial. "I did," I admitted.

"And I accepted."

Heedful of Mom peering around the corner, my lips quivered. I managed to swallow the laugh that reached from the back of my throat. "You did."

"Well, I was calling to let you know that if you don't marry me, I'll sue you for breach of promise."

That did it. I let out a roar of a laugh, relief flooding my body, because I'd still half expected him to call the whole thing off.

"One day, in the morning, when I call, you won't have to race to the telephone, you'll only have to roll over." The words were sweetly whispered and conjured the image of a mussed Charlie lying in bed.

"I can't wait." And, oh, boy, could I not wait. To be able to bring those kisses into my bedroom instead of keeping them in the elevator.

"There's something else, Delly."

"What's that?" I couldn't imagine there could be any more wonderful news than this. I was going to get married. To a man I was well and truly in love with. A man who made my toes curl when he kissed me, a man who made me laugh.

"I'm going back to England. Sooner than I thought." There was a long pause on the other end, and I sensed there was something he wanted to say but wasn't sure how to.

I, too, couldn't form words. I thought we'd have more time. A month or more, like he promised. A moment ago, my head had been a bubble floating up from a bath, only to be popped by an annoying finger.

"J.P. Morgan and I have decided to part ways," he finally said.

"Oh?" I tightened my grip on the receiver.

Charlie let out a long sigh that sounded at least as disappointed as I felt. "Seems they like the more boring types in this city rather than a man like me."

"How could anyone not love my own charming good-time Charlie?"

He chuckled. "And I've got my own Park Avenue party girl. But from what I understand, these bankers would have preferred a teetotaler."

"Lots of self-righteous types out there," I said, hoping to soothe what had to be a bruised ego. "Abstaining from drink doesn't make you a saint, just as imbibing doesn't make you a criminal."

From the corner of my eye I watched Mom cock an eyebrow. I shifted so I didn't have to see.

"Have I told you lately how right you are for me?" Charlie said.

"I'll never grow tired of hearing it." I chewed my lip and then asked the question that was really on my mind. "When do you have to leave?" *What does this mean for us?*

"Unfortunately, soon. I'll try to aim for a couple of weeks, but not much longer after that."

I brightened. At least he wasn't leaving tomorrow. "You'll be here for Thanksgiving, then." The irony of me, an American, inviting my British fiancé to celebrate a feast of English exiles was not lost.

"I wouldn't miss it. The lot of you colonists have been filling my head with visions of stuffed turkeys and cranberry sauce. I do enjoy dining out on the town, but I'd be lying if I didn't admit to missing a home-cooked meal."

I stifled a laugh so Mom wouldn't come around asking what he'd said. "Good. Then we will have our feast together."

"And then, when your show finishes, you'll come to England? Meet my family? Marry me?"

Meeting his family hadn't yet crossed my mind. I prevaricated for a moment, wondering if it would be out of the question to request a stay of introduction? "Well, I've got *The Band Wagon* next."

"We can still get married. I'll come back to the States when it's time for your show to start."

"What will your mother say?"

Charlie made a sound on the other end of the line as if he were scared and worried, followed by a chuckle. "She'll likely breathe fire, darling. But we won't let her ruin our fun. She'll come around. I'll have a chat with her about the most enchanting woman I've ever met, who's asked me to spend the rest of my life with her."

"Well, if you were able to charm my mom, then I suppose I should trust you with your own." I hazarded a peek at Mom over my shoulder, who was grinning as if she'd just won at the horse races. "Best to hold off on any announcements until then, just in case she says she's already signed a marriage contract between you and a Greek princess." I was teasing but also completely serious. The papers had been going nuts lately over the two of us out on the town together. The last thing we needed was for an engagement to take away from the show.

Now I needed to figure out how to tell Freddie when the time was right.

But, as it turned out, that decision was made for me several months later.

Charlie and I had been writing to each other daily, comparing the dangers of snow- and ice-slicked roads in London and New York, and then the blooms in Hyde Park versus Central. He told me his mother was warming to the idea and his sisters couldn't wait to meet me.

Our overseas courtship even included a few short telegrams that said things such as . . .

I MISS YOU.

PARTIES AREN'T THE SAME WITHOUT MY PARK AVENUE PARTY GIRL.

CAN'T WAIT UNTIL YOU HOP THE POND.

THE CLUBS ARE DULL WITHOUT MY FAVORITE DANCE PARTNER.

Not one of those sweet letters or telegrams, however, told me that he'd already started announcing to his friends that we'd agreed to tie the knot, and that the news had leaked to the press. I was in my dressing room at Ziegfeld's, completely oblivious, taking some preshow interviews on the last night of our *Smiles* run. And the end couldn't come a minute too soon. *Smiles* had not been the epic show we'd hoped for. Working with Marilyn Miller had been irritating, to say the least, with her glomming on to Freddie like pollen on the windowsill in spring, and Ziegfeld was out of his mind with his demands.

"Miss Astaire, are the rumors true that you are engaged to be married?" the reporter asked, bringing me back to the present.

I managed to peel my lips away from my teeth in some semblance of what I hoped was a smile. "Well, you know I ask my former producer Charles Dillingham to get hitched once a quarter, but he keeps refusing. Alas, I am unattached."

"What about the rumors that you'll be moving to London this summer to marry Lord Charles Cavendish, and that your brother will serve as the best man?"

"What?" I blanched, then had to quickly recover. "The only plans I have for the summer are performing in *The Band Wagon*. We'll be at the New Amsterdam Theatre." I'd told not a soul about the proposal. And it threw me quite out of sorts to hear of it. After all, I'd thought he was asking about my constant, half-a-decade-long tease with Dillingham.

"Can you confirm your engagement to Lord Charles Cavendish?" the reporter asked.

I shook my head, then brushed one of my falling curls back into place, pinning it so it didn't fall again. "Why, that's simply . . ."

"Could you clarify what you mean, Miss Astaire?"

"I'm not ready to announce . . . anything." My gaze flicked toward the door, where Freddie lurked, a crease in his brow. "Why would Charlie . . ." I was glad for my stage makeup, or he'd have seen just how beet-red my face had become.

I looked away from my brother, from the secrets I'd kept. Too late I remembered that I was in front of a reporter and that anything I said would end up in the gossip columns. I was an actress, after all, a comedienne. If anyone could pull off a funny face at a moment like this, it was me.

"So are you or are you not engaged, then?" The reporter's gaze bored into mine, his pencil poised above a well-worn notebook.

"Of course I adore him, more than any suitor, Mr. Dillingham aside." I huffed a teasing laugh, tossing my head, and with it the shock that I'd had a moment ago. I crossed my legs, giving one a casual swing. "He's a charming and kind man, and very important to me. But I'm a working actress, and I have contracts to fulfill. The only other thing I'll say is the lot of you know me well enough, don't you? There are a dozen's worth of British nobles who've tried to put a ring on this finger." I waved my ringless left hand at the man. "And yet it remains empty."

The reporter grunted. "Well, if it ends up getting filled, you be sure to let us know."

"I assume I won't have to," I said. "After all, isn't it your job to find out the dirt on us celebrities before even we know about it?" This last part was a dig at the man for ambushing me with Charlie's premature announcement.

As peeved as I was that he'd done it, I was also elated. Because the reporter was right. This summer, I *was* going to England and I *was* going to marry Lord Charles Cavendish. And we were going to live happily ever after in a castle in the countryside with all our children surrounding us. Paradise found.

———⟨⟩———

AFTER MY NIGHTTIME bath, I padded down the hall in our apartment to find Freddie at the dining-room table going over the books. A task he did most nights, especially after our recent losses.

"Don't hunch so much or you'll be dancing with a view of your toes," I teased.

He glanced up as I came in, nodding at the teakettle, an extra cup and saucer placed in front of him.

"You were expecting me," I said.

There was a sad look in his eyes as he nodded, closing the ledger and setting down his pencil. We hadn't talked since he'd overheard the reporter in my dressing room, and I'd put it off even longer after coming home and claiming to need a bath. But I'd been procrastinating long enough. Freddie deserved to know the truth about me and Charlie, my future plans. My brother had been nothing if not patient over the past few months.

"I'm sorry I didn't tell you sooner," I began.

"Lucky for you, Charlie did, months ago. I was merely waiting to hear it from the horse's mouth." Freddie smiled wanly. "What took you so long?"

I sank into the chair, my teeth scraping the balm from my lower lip, my mind gnawing at his loaded question and trying to find a suitable answer.

"Fear, I guess?"

I poured us each a cup of the tea that was still steaming hot; my brother must have timed it precisely. Tilly and Wassie begged for some sugar, and I indulged them each with a cube. They settled contentedly under the table, by my feet.

"What are you afraid of?" Freddie asked.

I let out a long sigh, adding the milk and then the lumps of sugar. We drank it the same way in New York that we did in London.

"I didn't want to worry you." I stirred the tea.

"I don't think Charlie is another William. Do you?" Freddie murmured his thanks for the tea and took a sip.

I shook my head, droplets of water from my wet hair flicking my face. "Definitely not."

Freddie wiped a sprinkle from his forehead. And I made a silly face at him. "Sorry about that."

"Better than the sweat that sometimes gets flung on me during rehearsal. You love him?"

I nodded without hesitation, confident in my feelings for Charlie. "I do."

What was it going to be like not to have Mom and Freddie around? Not to hear my brother practicing some new choreography in the middle of the night when he had an idea at three a.m.? Or not to hear Mom humming in the kitchen as she made us toast and tea in the morning?

What would it be like to live without the only two people I'd spent my life with—thirty-four years with Mom and thirty-one with Freddie? To get used to the different habits of another person—a man? A husband?

"And what about *The Band Wagon*?" he asked. "We start rehearsals soon."

I bit my lip, finding it harder to say the words now than when I'd rehearsed them. "I think *The Band Wagon* will be my last show, Freddie."

We'd been in talks about it around the time Charlie had agreed to marry me, and, now that the show was officially booked to start in just a few months, I didn't want to leave my brother and the entire company in the lurch. "I want to finish out the run with you in New York, and maybe even a few performances on the road. But I want to get married, Freddie. Start a family of my own. I'm not getting any younger." I reached across the table and squeezed his hand where it rested. "Soon I'll be as gray as Mom."

"My hair is more of a silver," Mom called from where she was reading my friend Anita Loos's *Gentlemen Prefer Blondes* for the third time.

Freddie and I laughed, and he called over his shoulder, "You're gorgeous, Mom!"

I topped off our tea. "I don't want my kids to look up and ask me if I'm Grandma."

Freddie leaned closer, looking behind him to make sure Mom wasn't coming, and then whispered, "I know. I'm starting to feel the itch, too."

I'm pretty sure my eyes almost popped out of my head then, giving me the look of a French bulldog. "To get married?"

Freddie grinned, glancing back again, the paranoia coming off him in waves at the idea that our mother might hear her thirty-something-year-old children discussing marriage, as if we weren't old enough to consent. "Both of us getting hitched at once might be too much for Mom."

"And not Marilyn Miller, please God." I crossed my fingers.

Freddie snorted and swatted my fingers. "She was fun for a few nights on the town, but I don't intend to put a ring on her finger."

"Ginger, then?"

"No, but she's a hell of a lot more fun than Marilyn."

"And Tilly Losch, she's married."

"Is she, though?" Freddie asked with a wiggle of his brows.

I tossed a lump of sugar at his head, and the dogs darted to grab it when it fell to the floor. "Do be serious."

"You're being serious enough for both of us," he said.

"And isn't that a wicked turn of events?" I jerked forward, spine straight, my hand slapping the table. "Someone, hurry up and take me to the sanatorium!"

Freddie chuckled, the sound of his humor slowly fading as he looked at me with sad eyes again. "What am I going to do without you?"

"What you were meant to do, brother. You need to take the Freddie show on the road. Join the pictures, like people have been begging you to do for years."

"Us, Delly. They've been begging *us*."

Beneath the table I gave his knee a nudge with my foot. "You were made for this life, Freddie. I wasn't. I love to dance, to have fun, but all the rehearsals, the discipline—you know that's not me. Could you imagine me spending hours and hours on a boring set?" I shuddered in mock horror. "I'm holding you back, and it's time you left your cocoon and showed the world what you really have to offer. Spread those gorgeous wings."

"I suppose I knew this day was going to arrive, I just didn't realize it was going to be so soon." Poor Freddie looked so crestfallen, like a child whose lollipop had been stolen.

"I'll be out in the audience, cheering you on." I waved exaggeratedly, my mouth wide, teeth flashing in mock excitement. "Like this. And then I'll tell everyone around me that you're my brother and I'm your biggest fan."

Tilly and Wassie leapt up at my antics and started to yip, tails wagging, as if to say that they, too, would be in the audience, making a scene.

"Goodness, don't." Freddie pressed his palm to his face with a great sigh. "They might not let you back in the theatre if you make a big show of it."

I waggled my fingers to the dogs to calm them and they rushed over for a few pats before lying down again. "They better. I'll be Lady Charles Cavendish, and you know how those theatre types like aristocrats." I held up my teacup and clinked it with his.

Freddie chuckled, and it was his turn to throw some sugar, except that I caught it in my mouth—much to the chagrin of my dogs—the sweetness of it melting on my tongue.

"I love you, Freddie. This is going to be a new beginning for us both, even if it is scary."

Serious again, Freddie grabbed my hand and squeezed it. "I love you, too, sis. And if we've made it this far, I guess the sky really is the limit."

CHAPTER SIXTEEN

ADELE

THE LIMELIGHT

Our American darling is back on British soil. But don't pull out your wallets just yet. Miss Astaire, soon to be Lady Charles Cavendish, isn't going to be in the West End unless it's a box at the theatre. The beloved star has hopped the pond this time to get married, and the only performing she'll be doing now is in lavish noble drawing rooms. A tragic loss to every fan of the lilac flame.

Spring 1931
New York City

don't know whether it was because we all knew I was soon to retire, or because our shoes had wings, but *The Band Wagon* felt like the beginning and the end of a new era all at once.

The show was popular among the critics, and, unlike Marilyn Miller, with whom I'd squabbled, Tilly Losch was my favorite in the cast, and we became inseparable.

Tilly was a statuesque brunette who hailed from a Jewish family in Austria. In addition to our similar cultural background, she'd also studied ballet since childhood, performed in London with our good friend Noël Coward, and made the rounds with all the honorables there whom we'd partied with. It was a wonder we'd never met before. Even Freddie had a hard time telling us apart from the back.

She teased Freddie in her Austrian accent, calling him a "silly ham" nearly every hour, and we tore up the New York speakeasies as if I were trying to imprint every dance floor, barhop, and stool on my brain. Freddie introduced Tilly to the Cotton Club in Harlem, where he loved to watch the young Black American Nicholas Brothers, Fayard and Harold, tap-dance until sparks ignited from their shoes. At only eighteen and eleven, their talent surpassed Freddie's and mine, and we were double their age.

Setting sail for London, I didn't know when I'd be back in New York. A part of me was unquestionably sad about that, but the other part was so elated to start a life that I'd dreamt about since I was a young girl. Marriage, motherhood. Freedom from the strains of dancing and showbiz. No longer wearing what my mother wanted me to wear, or doing my hair the way she said. No longer asking Freddie to give me some money for new shoes.

I was going to be a married woman. A lady.

I'd at first been a little upset that Charlie had let the cat out of the bag, but then I realized that his doing so had forced me to tell my brother. Something I'd already put off for months. I wanted to marry Charlie. And I needed a man like him, who would take the lead.

True to his word, Charlie had been there for the opening night of *The Band Wagon*, looking as dapper as ever. And he'd brought with him his younger sister Anne, whom I found to be completely delightful.

We'd cut it up at 21 and every other club, grinning for the cameras. When he'd headed back to London without me, I'd longed to stow away with him. But Charlie had smiled at me as he kissed me goodbye, and told me to cherish these moments, because he was certain that I would miss the stage.

I didn't believe him. By now my ankles cracked every time I moved them. My knees clicked when I stood or sat or walked up the stairs. When I reached for a teacup in the cupboard my right shoulder gave a little pang. Daily life hurt from having spent so many damn years abusing my body. And what really sounded good was a long nap. Being able to sleep uninterrupted. No one to wake me in the morning except the sun itself.

So although my darling Charlie thought I'd grow weepy over retirement, in fact, I felt quite the opposite. A whole new world was opening up for me.

I sat down with Freddie and Mom, and I told them that I was ready to be done. My understudy was not nearly as talented as Vi had been, and there wasn't a day that went by that I didn't regret her not coming with us to New York. But the understudy was good enough. And whatever Freddie didn't like he could make her do better. I'd done two or three new productions after deciding I was ready to be done. And it had just gotten to the point where I knew if I didn't go now I wouldn't go at all.

Surprisingly, Freddie and Mom agreed, though my brother wouldn't be able to attend the wedding due to the show. Freddie assured me he'd come and see us when we were settled and celebrate in London style.

Before they—or I—changed their minds, I boarded the RMS *Majestic* and headed to London. The journey was memorable, filled with anxiety at leaving Freddie behind with an understudy. I distracted myself with a fierce backgammon battle with Winston Churchill, and song-and-dance numbers after dinner with Paul Robeson.

By the time we dropped anchor across the pond, I was ready to hurtle myself headlong into my new life. However, the reporters swarmed the dock at Plymouth, equal to their fervor at the theatres, making it impossible for Mom and me to disembark. My backgammon opponent hid us in the lounge behind some potted palms. Then, pulling on his metaphorical armor, he told the assembled mob that we'd already disembarked and they'd missed us. Given that he was *the* Winston Churchill, well known for his political service—though for the past few years he'd been on hiatus—the crowd listened and dispersed. I was elated to escape their questions, wanting privacy rather than answering, "Are you really going to get married this time?" and "Did you really retire from performing?" We hurried on our way to the country, where I stood, stunned, outside Chatsworth House, staring up at the massive edifice.

Although it was considered a manor home or grand estate, to me it looked like a palace, with its dozens of Palladian windows and carved figures that graced the top of the house in evenly spaced rows, like stone sentries. The inside was even more overwhelming. I'd never seen anything so grand, not even at the Ritz, unless you counted St. James's Palace. Gilt, and marble, and artwork that belonged in a museum.

A nervous heat prickled my skin, and my fingers trembled slightly. I tucked one arm through Charlie's and clasped my other hand there, too, practically clutching him for balance.

I'd known his family was rich, but this was beyond even what I'd imagined.

"They are all going to love you," Charlie was saying. "Anne has been singing nothing but your praises."

"Bless your sister's heart," I murmured. He led me up a flight of wide marble stairs, our footfalls softened by the velvet carpeting beneath our shoes, down a series of hallways, and up another flight of stairs, until I was certain that I would never find my way out again.

Mom, behind me, oohed and aahed over various artifacts that I swore I'd never touch for fear of being the one person to destroy something held on to by the family for hundreds of years.

What was a girl born dirt-poor in Nebraska doing in a place like this and about to call it home?

I cleared my throat and glanced up at Charlie, who appeared perfectly calm, his blue eyes twinkling at me.

"Just be yourself," he said.

I nodded, feeling a little tongue-tied. "Wait just a second," I said, right outside a door that a footman—an actual servant!—was about to open.

I drew in a deep breath, centering myself the way I did backstage before a show. I could do this. I would do this. These people, Charlie's family, were about to be my family.

"Ready?" Charlie murmured.

"As I'll ever be."

The doors opened, like the curtain rising, and in that second, when the drawing room full of Cavendishes was revealed to me, I did the first thing that came to mind.

I let go of Charlie's arm and cartwheeled my way across the drawing room, ignoring the sharp gasps, until I came to a stop in front of his mother, the Duchess of Devonshire.

"I'm Adele," I said, holding out my hand.

The duchess stared at me, her lips pressed together, as if she'd been too dignified to be surprised at my entry.

Charlie laughed behind me, and Anne, my soon-to-be sister-in-law, clapped.

"Marvelous, Adele, marvelous. Mother, I told you she was a doll, didn't I?" Anne said.

"Your Graces," Charlie said, a bit more formally, addressing both his parents. "I'm honored to present my fiancée, Miss Adele Astaire, and her mother, Mrs. Ann Astaire, to you."

I dipped into a curtsey, as did my mother, half expecting the duchess to say it wasn't necessary, as our friends the princes did. But she didn't. Nor did she smile. I started to rethink my entry, which had been meant to produce laughs and break the ice.

I feared now that they thought me rather gauche, and Anne's pleasure, or Charlie's, didn't matter if their parents hated me.

"A pleasure to make your acquaintance," the duke said. He was just as distinguished-looking as Charlie; rather, an older version, handsome and stoic.

I smiled. "Likewise, Your Grace. You have a beautiful home."

"Well," said the duchess, her eyes roving over me from head to toe. "You are exactly as we expected."

I wasn't sure how to take what she'd said. Her tone was snobbish, and given her flat affect it was hard to tell if she simply hated me or was just too busy looking down her nose.

"Thank you," I said, keeping my voice cheerful, my smile sunny. Because, despite my soon-to-be mother-in-law's tart attitude, that was exactly how I planned to take each day of this new chapter as a married woman, as Lady Charles Cavendish—with sheer joy and exuberance. There was absolutely nothing that could bring me down now.

Or so I thought. Several days before our wedding, Charlie was rushed to the hospital with acute appendicitis, which the doctor lamented was only exacerbated by his heavy drinking. His mother was quick to point out to me Charlie's wild ways—though she'd said "defiant," as if having a few too many cocktails was a crime. Where his mother lacked empathy and even concern, Charlie's sister Anne made up for it in spades, comforting me in my fear for his health.

True to Charlie form, he snapped back, springing from his

hospital bed with a new pep in his step. Despite his mother never having warmed to me, and with such an attitude depriving us of a lavish London wedding with all the pomp due a duke's son, we were wed in a small, private ceremony on the grounds at Chatsworth.

The only disappointment—besides Freddie not coming—was that my dear Violet wasn't allowed to attend the wedding, though she promised to take a break from working to have tea with me when I was next in London.

The chapel was filled with the scents of daffodils and acacia, scarlet camellias and arum lilies. With an orange carnation bouquet to bring out the splash of orange at the waist of my beige satin Mainbocher gown, I walked down the aisle. The diamond bracelet Charlie had gifted me twinkled in the light of all the candles. As sour as my new mother-in-law was, I didn't care. For the love of my life had swept me off my feet.

After a short luncheon, the duke surprised us with the most magnificent gift—Lismore Castle in Ireland, which was to be our new home. We didn't even stay the night in England, setting sail immediately for Ireland.

The servants stood in a line outside the castle to greet us, but I was so overwhelmed by it all that Charlie ordered our dinner be brought to our bedroom. One might have thought I'd be shy, sitting across from my new husband in an old castle in a foreign country, but all I could think about were the possibilities.

When we finished eating, I turned on the gramophone in the corner, playing an old record. As the soft trills of strings and brass filled the room, Charlie unbuttoned my dress, kissing each inch of exposed skin. We stood bare in front of each other and did the most natural thing that came to me—we danced. Waltzing naked, music filling our souls, the light of the moon filtering in through the large windows. We twirled and dipped, touched and tasted. Our legs entwining, the heat of his warm body joining with mine. It was the most sensual thing I'd ever done.

Then Charlie laid me on the bed, and we made our own kind of music in a new dance that had me certain I'd died and gone to heaven.

PART THREE

SHOES WITH WINGS

To Adele Astaire
Stars danced when she was born—
Twin sunbeams at her feet,
Which touch the earth I scorn—
The stage to them is sweet.
—WALTER KINGSLEY

CHAPTER SEVENTEEN

ADELE

THE LIMELIGHT

Miss Violet Wood may no longer perform onstage, but you can find her serving cocktails to box seats during the matinee shows at the Winder Garden theatre. We hear for a sizeable tip, she'll dance with the patrons before the show. In fact, last week, a young gentleman reportedly brought with him two musicians who struck up a song for Miss Wood to teach him the Charleston before the start of *Follow a Star*. We're left wondering who has the true spotlight of the show, the actual cast, or the cocktail waitress?

October 8, 1933

There are moments throughout our lives when we look back in reflection and think, "Oh, that was certainly a most painful time." Or how we laughed, or cried, or rejoiced. What happened on this day was arguably my greatest triumph, and my darkest hour.

The tiny, perfectly molded, still-warm fingers of my baby girl rested in my palm. A hand made in the image of mine. Delicate fingernails that looked as if they'd been manicured by an angel. Dark, soft curls on her apple-sized head. Large watery blue eyes the color of Charlie's that stared into mine for the few tragic hours that she lived. Those precious few hours that felt like only seconds, when I snuggled her tiny, sweet-smelling body to my breast, and she grasped my finger weakly in her hand.

I'd spent so many years of my life in training for every stage. Hours of practice. Hours of perfection. But there was no rehearsal for loss. No way to prepare myself for the gut-wrenching sorrow and ache of the doctor saying, "She's gone. I'm so sorry."

Even the solid heat of Charlie's embrace as he tugged me to his chest while I sobbed violent tears was hardly a comfort. I wanted my baby. The sweet innocent being that I'd grown in my body, that I'd struggled to push out. The wee thing I'd come to tease when no one was around, and who kicked at my tummy with exuberance. She was going to be a dancer.

She was going to be alive.

And now she wasn't. The nursery I'd decorated with the help of our genuinely excited staff would remain empty.

What should I say? What should I do?

Where was my mother? Freddie . . . Where were the people whom I needed around me now? The ones who could provide comfort. I had Charlie, but he, too, was mourning the loss of our much-wanted daughter. We had all the lovely people at Lismore who kept the place running, who helped me be lady of the manor, but none of them could help with this.

At first I'd been dubious about being a mother. Nauseated all the time, dizzy, and even the slightest whiff of booze made me queasy—much to Charlie's chagrin. But as the days passed, and the sickness subsided, and I started to imagine . . . oh, how I imagined . . .

She was going to be sweet Annie Evelyn—named for both our mothers. I suppose she still was. Annie Evelyn Cavendish. Born and died the same day after struggling to survive for three hours.

Perhaps it was my fault. I went into labor before my time. We weren't ready. The doctor wasn't ready. Annie wasn't ready.

"Eat something," Charlie said, placing a tray prepared by our wonderful cook on the table beside the bed, and flicking on the lamp there.

The curtains were drawn tight. My sheets freshly changed. The lamp gave off a soft glow. Tilly and Wassie curled against my back, a constant comfort, knowing there was a loss, knowing I needed them. The scent of the Irish fare would have normally delighted me. But without the baby inside me, without her in my arms, there was nothing for me but despair. And certainly no hunger.

"I can't." Fresh tears stung my already swollen eyes.

Charlie didn't look surprised, but, rather, resigned. He'd not been able to eat either. "A drink, then." He pulled the ever-present flask from a pocket, unscrewed the cap, and waved its whiskey scent beneath my nose.

I turned away. He shrugged and took a long swig himself, closing his eyes before he settled into a silk upholstered chair by the shuttered window. The place where he'd taken up vigil.

"I called Freddie," he said. "And your mom should be informed on the ship."

I nodded, numb, my tongue unable to form words about this particular subject. I was grateful that Charlie had been the one to tell them of my latest failure, my tragedy. But, really, how was I going to ever get out of this bed and face the world? Freddie was in London for a show, and Mom on her way here to welcome a child who had already died.

Tears ceaselessly leaked from my eyes. It was a wonder there were any left. My eyes burned. My body ached. Even the pills they'd given me for the pain did nothing to alleviate the agonizing pulse in my chest. At some point Mom arrived, and I was happy to let her take care of everything.

Maybe sleep would help. At least I wouldn't be conscious.

Except it was hard to fall asleep, and when I finally did my dreams were worse. Darling Annie's face every time I closed my eyes, and I woke up sobbing, screaming more than once, and finding Charlie sobbing on his knees on the floor beside me, begging me not to go. He was deeper in his cups than usual, and perhaps that was the thing that brought me back, knowing that Charlie's tipples were leading to tumbles, and he needed me to get up out of this bed.

If I couldn't do it for myself, at least I needed to do it for him.

"Let's go to London," I said one morning, unsure of how much time had passed.

Charlie, startled from where he'd been reading in the chair, likely all night, peered at me over his spectacles.

"I need to get out of this room. Away from this castle." I needed to be away from the freshly dug tiny grave outside in the family cemetery with a tiny marker that said simply BABY GIRL. Without a christening, she'd not been officially named.

"All right." Charlie perked up. He closed the book, not bothering to mark his place, and set it on the side table, causing me to wonder if he'd been reading at all.

"I'll have our things packed." I tossed the blankets back, standing on wobbly legs that didn't feel like my own. I'd always had strong legs. It didn't make sense to me how quickly they'd tired.

"I'll tell your mom." He stood to leave, to find my mother, who was probably already down in the dining room having her morning tea.

Tilly and Wassie swarmed around me, between and around my legs, as if they wanted to provide the support that my muscles refused to.

Charlie paused, watching me uneasily.

Even pregnant, I'd tried to keep up the strength I'd built as a dancer. I took long walks, I ran up and down the stairs (when no one was paying attention), and I danced every morning for at least an hour or two. Reviving the choreography of all the characters I'd lived onstage.

But now my muscles didn't hold me upright. They were weak, a stranger's legs. Even my toes felt numb as I curled them into the carpet.

I straightened my back, bent myself at the knees. The cramps in my belly had ceased, at least, but the blood still trickled, as if it would never, ever stop. My body was reminding me of the loss. Of the very humanness of myself.

I lay back down in bed and the moment of surety vanished. "Maybe tomorrow."

"It's been two weeks," Charlie said, a note of despair in his voice.

"How long did the doctor say?" I pulled the blanket up over my body, sure that the doctor would agree that remaining in bed was best. Tilly and Wassie joined me, licking my elbow and chin.

"I think ten days. It's been fourteen."

"Oh." That was disappointing. I had truly hoped I'd be forced to stay there forever.

"You don't have to worry about a thing, Delly darling," Charlie rushed to say. "Your mom and I will take care of everything."

I looked over at the man I'd married. The one who'd made me

swoon. The one who'd tried so desperately in the past two weeks when he was sober to make me happy, and when he was sauced to make me laugh.

"I love you, Charlie," I said, swiping at the small tears gathering in the corners of my eyes. "I don't know what I'd have done without you."

"Well, likely you'd be dancing onstage with Freddie." He edged closer, a hopeful look in his eyes, as if he thought I might come back around.

"Let's go to London. I want to see my brother's show." After all, I had promised to be in the audience, his biggest fan. Although I could do without his new wife. *Phyllis.* A money-hungry, jealous tramp, if ever there was one. She was possessive of my brother. Too opinionated. Well, that's how it felt most days. Other times I found her sweet as apple pie, just as the rest of the world found her charming. And she made Freddie happier than a bee in a field full of freshly blooming flowers. I'd never seen him so infatuated. So I guess I'd forgive her any of the tart comments she'd made in my direction, because they were likely deserved.

They were doing a European tour for a few months, and already I'd missed some of their time here. I didn't want to miss all of it.

"There's to be a party at Chatsworth, too, darling girl. It will be a nice distraction." Charlie looked like he was ready to drop to his knees and beg, so I made the choice then to acquiesce, even if my legs didn't seem capable of holding up a feather, let alone my body.

"And Cecil's . . ." I mused. I'd declined his house-party invitation before because we'd assumed I'd be at home with a newborn strapped to the tit. A stark reminder that we were so far from where we'd thought we'd be right now. How would I be able to confront all the faces drawn in sympathy? "We can go to that as well."

"Smashing." Charlie made a fist in the air, rocking on his heels, and I realized then how very much he, too, needed to get out of this house.

For Charlie, I reminded myself.

"And Christmas in London will be nice," I added, knowing that I'd much rather be away from here, where I'd already embroidered a red stocking in white thread with BABY.

"Whatever you want, Delly. Always."

I tried again a week later. More than once I'd lain back down in bed, but between Mom and Charlie I'd managed to get dressed and onto the boat that would take us across the Irish Sea to Liverpool, and then a train ride to London, arriving at our house in Carlton Gardens.

We went to see Freddie and Phyllis, who were nothing but kindness and empathy, and I told them not to mention it again, because every time I thought of Annie Evelyn I wanted to cry. Freddie was brilliant onstage. Watching him whirl and tap and grin, I was so proud of him. And it only affirmed all the more that I was happy in my retirement.

After that night out, calling cards came flooding in from all our friends, and even some who weren't. We were invited to dinner parties, theatre performances, clubs, garden parties, musicals, operas, teas, and dinners. True to British nature and propriety, no one mentioned the loss of our baby, even if the papers were reporting it left and right—all of which Charlie had ordered our staff to keep away from me.

The first tea was a miserable affair, but that was mostly because of the company. I loathed Kitty Winn and her obnoxious, snobby mouth. I'd thought that I might like her, given that she was born in New York, and an American married to an aristocrat could use as many allies as possible, but she made me want to run out into traffic. Married to the Honorable Charles Winn, the second son of a baron, Kitty acted like she was higher on the priority list than even the Duchess of Devonshire.

Within the week, I was feeling more like myself in the social whirl. Or at least I could forget about the self I'd almost become. The self that was a mother. The self that had a tiny person relying on her.

Now it was solely me, and I was relying on Charlie and Mom. Oh, sure, anyone could say that Charlie relied on me, but really he relied most on my mother—who seemed to keep him in line when I couldn't—and on the flask in his pocket that kept him from throwing his anger at the world.

That anger was one of the many secrets he'd shared late at night as we'd lain in bed during those first few weeks of joyous marital bliss. The honeymoon, where all the secrets are spilled onto the pillow when darkness falls and all you can see is the flashing white of the moon glinting off teeth and eyes.

Charlie and his mother didn't see eye to eye on most things, which was his polite way of saying that he didn't like her at all. His father, however, was much more jovial, and Charlie enjoyed hunting with the duke. A diversion he planned to teach me when we were at Chatsworth for the house party in the coming weeks.

Hunting was not a sport I would say I intended to pursue, but, rather, I liked the idea of riding a horse at breakneck speed. I wondered if the jockeys on the racehorses that my brother and Charlie adored felt as superhuman as they looked. Mother had always made me ride so carefully when we'd visited the horse farms and camps on vacation. Oh, to be chasing through the woods on a quest for something other than my nightmares. Of course, I didn't want to be the one shooting. That part didn't interest me, but the rest, yes.

The freedom to ride and feel the intensity in the roots of my hair, the baying of the dogs as they fell in line with one another seeking their prey.

It was all rather morbid, I knew, but it beat thinking of the death of my child. The death of my dreams. It beat wondering if I was too old. If I'd waited too long. My insides shriveled up and decayed, and unable to support a growing baby.

The doctor I'd seen upon arriving in London had said that all would be well and that my body would be able to implant an egg with Charlie's seed in my womb, but only time would tell. And I wasn't ready, besides. I wondered if I'd ever be. To go through all that work, to have had such hope, again, only for it to end in tragedy.

It was a cold, rainy day in mid-November when we arrived at the grand house that Chatsworth was. A relic of the days of old and filled with history that seemed as if it belonged in storybooks rather than on the pages of an ancestral tome.

The stone edifice darkened from the damp weather, droplets coursing down the iridescent glass windows like maps. Even the carved figures that lined the roof looked somber.

Aside from the married folks, the house was rife with virgins and randy bucks who were there for a lark and a good flirt. Knowing myself how young folks acted, I wondered who was sneaking off to the butler's pantry and who would be more clandestine by hiding in the thickets of the garden that dated back to Elizabethan times. My favorite part of the castle gardens was Queen Mary's Bower, allegedly constructed when Mary, Queen of Scots, was held captive in the house, as a place for her to exercise. I'd done cartwheels there when we were first married and the future seemed so bright.

The drawing rooms and parlors and dining hall were all dripping in pine boughs and cranberries, red and gold bows, and carved wooden reindeer. The duchess did have an eye for decorations, and her Christmas tree was perhaps the most startlingly gorgeous thing I'd ever seen. Even the pine needles felt softer than the usual prick-your-skin kind.

Golden tinsel glimmered in the light from the chandelier, and the crystal ornaments let off rainbow prisms. Hand-painted bulbs of red, green, and gold were perfectly placed on every limb, and there were even several charming, gilded ornaments fashioned in the likeness of Chatsworth, Buckingham Palace, Windsor Castle, and several other great houses and castles of the realm that I couldn't name.

Charlie's older brother, Edward, was fairly dripping in young ladies, while his wife averted her gaze. Their sisters Maud, Blanche, Dorothy, Rachel, and Anne were all tittering around, sipping cocktails that made their cheeks flush, until their mother gave them a stern look. Their husbands didn't seem to care, smoking cigars and playing billiards with the other men. Dozens of society misses had come with their parents and brothers and were making a fine house party that reminded me so much of the ones I'd joined in the early '20s with those who called themselves the Bright Young Things. But their cheer was too much for me, and I felt more like Ebenezer Scrooge than Darling Delly.

I sipped the same cocktails. Charlie sipped more, adding fresh drams from his own flask to a cup that was already toxic. He was tight more often than he was sober, and, though he was still charming in his way, it was exhausting pretending he wasn't. Especially with the critical glances from his mother, the duchess. His sisters, however, were perfectly charming, and I loved Anne the most, as she was the least judgmental.

"Dance for us, just once," the lot of them would call out, as music played softly in the drawing room while we sipped our after-dinner port.

I declined.

In the quiet and privacy of our room, Charlie kicked off his shoes, tugged off his jacket, loosened his tie, and unbuttoned the top of his shirt. He flopped onto the chaise by the banked hearth and let out a long breath, his head falling back to rest on the rolled cushion.

"Are you well?" I asked, worried he was dizzy from drink.

"I think better than you," he murmured, then blinked his eyes open and beckoned me forward.

I padded across the thick carpet of our bedroom to the chaise, my own feet wobbly from the one too many cocktails I'd had to numb my pain. He took my hand in his and pulled me down to his lap. His eyes were clearer than I expected, and he stroked a path on my cheek.

"Where is my Park Avenue party girl?"

Lost.

"You don't like the dour-faced dud I've become?" I teased, trying to inject humor into a melancholy conversation.

"Seriously, darling. I could tell you weren't having a good time down there. What can I do to make it better?"

I laid my head on his shoulder, breathing in the scent of his shaving cream, watching the pulse beat in his neck. "Well, for one thing, you could tell all the virgins to calm down."

Charlie laughed. "So, you are jealous of their spritely ways?"

"Maybe a little."

"Do you wish you were still a virgin?" His fingers trailed down my arm to my hand, which he lifted to his lips, taking me back to our spine-tingling first kiss in the elevator.

"Certainly not." I laughed, very glad indeed to have put virginity behind me.

"Good. Because I don't want to be married to a virgin."

I laughed again and kissed him, my lips lingering on his until neither of us remembered the conversation at hand. Or the pain we'd tried to block, or, really, anything else, other than each other, our love, and the pleasure we could give one another.

In the morning, Charlie woke me before dawn. "Are you ready for the hunt, my petite huntress?"

"I am ready to ride," I offered, with an impish shrug and an apologetic face. "Truly, that is the thing I look forward to most."

He chuckled. "Tea first?"

"Yes, please."

"I'll have one brought up." Charlie leapt from bed and rang the bell pull. A servant returned a short time later while I was brushing my hair, with a tray full of tea and toast.

"Thank you, darling." I kissed his cheek as he poured me a cup.

Charlie had gifted me with a brand-new riding ensemble, made by the Savile Row tailors Huntsman. Breeches the color of oats, a white button-down dress shirt, and a starched white cravat I pinned in place with a diamond-and-sapphire brooch; just because one was hunting didn't mean one couldn't be fashionable. I topped the shirt with a yellow-and-blue-plaid vest, a matching neutral-colored tweed jacket, coffee-colored leather boots, and, to top it off, a black riding hat to keep my hair in place.

"There she is." Charlie wandered in from his dressing room, looking dapper and charming in his own riding getup, which matched mine.

"There *he* is," I said with a wink. "You look dashing."

Charlie glanced over me with a rakish nod. "My God, you're stunning. I never thought riding attire was so . . . enticing. We may not make it to the hunt."

"Oh, but we must; you'll have to chase me through the woods." I breezed past him, putting an extra twitch in my step.

It had been nearly six weeks since . . . well, it was the magic number, apparently, after which the doctor had given us permission to resume making love. Last night had been the first time we'd made love since the birth and death of our baby, Annie Evelyn. I'd never realized how much I could forget when in his arms, when pleasure was the first order of business, forcing thoughts aside.

I wanted more of that. Someone had once told me that a woman could be judged by the depth and quality of her passion and her capacity for pleasure. I'd loved the line so much that I wrote it down on a piece of notepaper at the Ritz Hotel in London.

We made our way down to the stable, where the rest of the party gathered and mounted their horses. Charlie helped me onto mine, a dapple-gray mare, before straddling his own. The dogs were brought out by their trainers, already baying with anticipation. I wondered if Tilly and Wassie were up in our rooms baying themselves, sad they were missing out on the excitement of the hunt. I'd asked if they could come, but had been very sternly told no. Without the proper training, my silly doggies would likely be trampled by the horses in pursuit.

"What exactly are we hunting?" I asked.

"Stag." Charlie adjusted his riding helmet.

"Ah." Those majestic creatures that stood in the center of a field, ears pricked for sound, antlers winding up through the air like horned branches, tails twitching.

We rode out, spotting a creature some distance away. The stag's muscles braced as the beast took in the scene, and then he was bounding away, with the dogs howling and giving chase. The riders rode behind them, horses leaping over ditches and fallen branches.

The men whooped and hollered, even the ladies joined in. I paused for a moment, taking it all in, and then I, too, was urging my horse forward. Thighs pinned to the sides of the mount, urging her this way and that over difficult terrain, clinging to her back. My hat blew off, floating and flying like a blackbird on the wintry air.

"Whoaaa . . ." I stilled the mare as those around me rode on. When they'd safely passed, I leapt off to retrieve my hat and pin it back in place. Wearing it was useless if it was only going to fly off again. So instead I tucked it into the satchel belted to my saddle and climbed back up. I'd not realized how cold my legs were until the warmth of the horse's body settled back into mine.

There was not a soul in sight. The baying of the dogs and the hollering of the hunters was a distant sound. I closed my eyes, drawing the country air in deeply through my nose, and letting it back out slowly. When was the last time I'd felt so at peace? So unconstrained? The heaviness of my sorrows ebbed a fraction. Still thick and heavy in my veins, but at least every breath wasn't a deep, scorching ache.

The mount stomped beneath me, puffs of steam shooting from her nostrils; irritated, maybe, that I'd not urged her back into pursuit.

"Shall we go, then?" I asked her, leaning forward and running my gloved hand over her neck, feeling the heat of her muscles even through the leather. The mare's ears flicked back, listening.

I clucked my tongue and squeezed my legs until she was galloping across the moors again, chasing the sound of the hunt, the wind at our back.

———⋈———

THE DEBUTANTES FOLLOWED us to Cecil Beaton's house party a week later. But fortunately they did not tag along to our mutual acquaintance Winn's house, though I wished they had in the end. Winn was not as much of a bore as his wife, Kitty, whom I was coming to dislike quite a bit. At least the debs would have given me some entertainment.

Kitty had a spiteful soul, glaring at everyone over the rim of her cup, without a nice word for anyone. Not only was she melancholic, putting a sour damper on the whole party's mood, but quite stupid to boot, and her husband was a pompous jackass if I'd ever seen one. Every moment spent absent their company felt as if a dark cloud had lifted overhead.

Nostell Priory, which was their home for now, borrowed from a brother, was as frigid and gloomy as its mistress.

"If I had balls, I'd have frozen them off by now," I murmured during dinner to Cecil, who laughed uproariously. I wish I could say I'd had a cocktail too many, but by that point I was so miserable in the house and with its hosts that I would have stood on the table and shouted my comment to the entire guest list.

"Oh, you do say the most unabashed things." His cadence was melodic, drawing me in. "You might be my favorite American."

I grinned. I was in somewhat of a competition with myself to say the most outrageous things to Cecil, who never blushed like the rest of London society. Uttering funny phrases kept me from the horror threatening to take over when I'd learned that a maid had been killed outside our guest-bedroom door the day before we arrived and was likely haunting the house as we spoke. The creaks and rattles of the old place were for certain desperate souls in search of their next victim.

Thank God, the servant who'd done the murdering had been arrested.

Following one unpleasant situation after another, I was ready for the socializing to be done. Kitty wouldn't quit being an obnoxious braggart. Portia—who thought she was going to be the next Lady Derby—was rudely, and deservedly, told off by Noël Coward for interrupting as if she were more important than everyone else. Because I was American, and had married a lord, I was doubly disliked. And the icing on that disappointing cake was that I lost my diamond-and-sapphire brooch—a wedding gift—which we'd not had time to insure.

The only interesting thing that happened was learning that one of my friends lived with both her husband and her lover. The situation was reminiscent of Georgianna, the eighteenth-century Duchess of Devonshire, my husband's great-times-something-grandmother, who'd lived with her husband and his lover at Chatsworth a couple of centuries ago.

Anyone who said that British society was boring compared to the lights of New York City had not been stuck in an endless loop of house parties with the likes of these Bright Young Things–turned–middle-aged.

The one soothing balm for all of it was that I was getting to spend more time with Anne, Charlie's sister, whom I adored.

"Will you be at Chatsworth over Christmas?" Anne asked.

I glanced at Charlie, who pretended not to listen. I'd initially agreed to remain in England, but now I was beyond finished with socializing and longed for the quiet of our Irish countryside. "I don't think so. We've had the castle outfitted with bathrooms, and I believe my brother, Freddie, is going to join us there with his wife."

As I said it, I realized how much I really did long for the wide-open moors of the Waterford countryside, dotted with sheep. The lazy strolls, the wee goats. It wasn't purely the need to distance myself from these pretentious idiots, but also the need for the peace I found there. That peace that was missing here, except when I was on a hunt, not forced into mundane conversation.

"Perhaps I'll have to join you." Anne angled closer, and I caught only a hint of her sweet perfume. She didn't douse herself in it as did some of the other ladies present. "To be at Lismore Castle and have real luxurious plumbing sounds like a dream."

"You and Henry and the children would be welcome anytime." And I meant it. Surprisingly, thinking about Timmy and Pippa,

Anne's children, only made me smile, rather than weep for my own lost daughter.

Anne grasped my hand in hers, our gold rings clicking together, and I squeezed back. "I'm so glad Charlie found you, Delly. You really are a gem."

"I'm the lucky one." I glanced back at my husband, seeing the corner of his lip turn up at hearing me say that. "He makes me happy."

And it was true. Despite our great loss, there was no one else I'd want by my side. No one else I trusted like I trusted Charlie.

We were going to get through this. We were going to be okay. And there would be other babies.

CHAPTER EIGHTEEN

VIOLET

THE LIMELIGHT

Spotted out of mourning and rejoining the London social circuit was Lady Charles Cavendish, along with her handsome, willowy husband. Despite her time away from the stage, it would appear that Lady Charles, formerly Adele Astaire, has not lost her flair for dance, or her enthusiasm for a good club. Neither would it seem has Lord Charles, who was spied stumbling from Ciro's after a night on the town with Prince George and Princess Marina of Greece.

July 9, 1934

Violet closed her eyes and turned her face up to the sun, leaning back, her fingers spread in the warm blades of grass. Between shifts, she came to the park to lounge. To breathe. Today was no different. Well, maybe slightly different. Set on the ground beside her was a luxury she'd splurged on for this auspicious occasion—her thirtieth birthday—a cake.

She was alone, the small tin of butter cake untouched.

Thirty had always seemed so far away. Especially when she'd told herself that if she wasn't a wildly successful stage actress by thirty she'd settle down and marry. Of course, there was no one to choose from.

Every man she'd made a connection with she'd pushed away. And now she was the sole caretaker of her sister, a position she wouldn't give up for the world, and she had no regrets. But it did mean she'd likely not make good on her promise to herself. At least her mother wasn't around to see her complete failure.

Five years had passed in a flash. Like turning the first page in a novel, only to find "The End." For the past five years, she'd been living on that empty last page.

There'd been no shows onstage. No performing. In fact, she'd gone back to serving cocktails in the theatre boxes during the shows at the Winter Garden. She was a has-been, a failure. Relegated to watching as the world turned, rather than being an active part of it. Violet loved her sister fiercely, but that didn't mean she didn't sometimes wonder what might have been.

In the decade since she'd left home, much had changed, just as much had stayed the same.

At nearly eighteen, Pris was grown-up enough to have a job at Foyles Bookshop.

Like a lot of things in her life, Violet had Adele to thank for Pris's love of books. Having spent so much time over the past decade with Adele and her literary friends, Violet had received more than one book, which she'd then gifted to Pris. To pass the time and reconnect after the loss of their mother, Violet and Pris had spent many evenings reading together, by the light of a slowly burning candle to save on electricity.

Living their lives in the pages of these books had been as much of an escape for Violet as it had been for Pris.

And, it turned out, one that led her sister to employment other than in a factory or washing clothes for strangers. A blessing it was, when books saved lives.

"There you are." Pris flounced down to the grassy patch that Violet had commandeered, a bottle in her hand.

"What's that?" Violet asked, pointing at the glass that shimmered in the summer sun.

"Coca-Cola."

Violet grinned. If her sister had a vice, it was cola. Violet was glad it wasn't something worse, like liquor. Most of the eighteen-year-olds in the East End were imbibing. After all, they said that spirits were only raised by consuming spirits.

"Well, shall we share the cola with the cake?" Violet tapped the tin.

Pris broke out into a wide grin, the kind that peeled back the years and brought out all sorts of happy memories. "Yes. But first I shall sing for you. No birthday is complete without."

Violet dropped back, lying in the grass with her hands covering her face. "Please don't."

Pris laughed, then grew silent for a minute.

"What is it?" Violet uncovered her eyes as she sat up, worried at the serious countenance of her sister, who was often quite silly.

Pris's celebratory smile waned, her eyes misty. "Just missing those who should be here with us celebrating."

Violet touched her sister's arm, then tugged her in for a hug. Hugs had been given out in abundance over the years, the best comfort they could provide each other. Only now they were the same height, and Pris didn't fold in so easily. "Me, too."

Pris tucked her head against Violet's shoulder with a sigh. She smelled like sunshine and hope.

Swiping at her tears, Pris shifted away, a smile of apology on her lips. "I'm sorry to be so blubbery on your birthday."

"For good reason. I'll not hold your grief against you." The truth was that the pain of losing people never faded; people merely learned to handle it better, made a conscious choice to seize the day. Violet held the glass bottle of cola in the air. "To those we've loved and lost. May we meet them again one day."

"But not too soon," Pris added, bumping her shoulder into Violet's.

"No, definitely not too soon." They each took a sip of the cola, and then Violet opened the tin, breaking off a piece of the cake and handing it to her sister.

They chewed in silence, Violet lost in her thoughts.

"You've grown awfully quiet," Pris said.

Violet smiled. "Thinking about how old I am."

"You're not as old as Mum when she had me."

"Fair point."

"This cake is delicious. So, what did you wish for?" Pris dusted crumbs from her hands and skirt, tucking her feet beneath her.

"Wish?" Violet leaned back in the grass on her elbows, enjoying the last few minutes of the sun on her face before she'd have to head back to work.

"Everyone wishes for something on their birthday." Pris took a swig of cola. "And I know it wasn't this."

Violet swiped the Coca-Cola, the sweet bubbles overwhelming her tongue. She much preferred tea, but she wasn't going to tell Pris that.

"I wished for this right here. The two of us joshing with each other on a sunny day in the park, where everything feels as though it will be perfect, and we've nothing to worry about for at least another ten minutes."

"That is all you wished for?" Pris sounded shocked by this. She shook her head, the dark tips of her short hair slashing across her cheeks. "Well, if you haven't wished for more, then I suppose you ought to see this." Pris pulled out a folded newspaper clipping from her sleeve and passed it to Violet.

Carefully, Violet unfolded the paper and read the headline: AUDITIONS OPEN FOR *MERRIE ENGLAND* AT THE SHAFTESBURY THEATRE. The show would be opening in the fall. Violet's eyebrows pinched together, her mouth screwed up in confusion.

"What is this?" Violet waggled the paper, eyes locked on her sister.

But Pris held a perfectly practiced no-nonsense expression, the kind a mother wears watching her offspring clean up a mess they created. "You've been waiting long enough, Vi, to get back onstage."

Violet shook her head, shoving the clipping against Pris's hand. "I can't."

Pris refused to take the paper, clasping her hands behind her back. "More like you won't."

"You need me at home." The excuse came quickly, water splashed on a spark before it could grow into a flame.

Pris groaned and rolled her eyes. "I'm perfectly capable of handling myself until you get home. I'm almost eighteen, not twelve."

"Shows go on the road. Look at Caty, she's always gone." Violet shook her head, but she still held on to the clipping, no longer forcing it back into her sister's grasp. "I can't."

"Then I'll stay with Frances; you know we need no excuse for a sleepover." Frances was Pris's dearest friend from the bookshop. As soon as the two had met they'd become thick as thieves.

Violet stared down at the paper, a tingling making her want to leap up and claim what she wanted. "The auditions are tomorrow. I'll never be ready in time."

"Sure you will. I know you haven't stopped dancing, even if you've stopped performing. We do live in the same small flat, and Caty has roped you into practicing with her a thousand times."

That was true. Violet shuffle-stepped her way through the flat every morning. No supper was complete unless she'd step-ball-changed her way to the table. At the end of the night, she twirled her way into her nightgown and fell with a dramatic knee drop. Not to mention the hour or two that she took for herself midday to keep up with the complicated steps that she'd learned over the years.

"Have you heard of *Merrie England* before?" Pris asked.

There wasn't a play that Violet hadn't heard of. "Yes, it's a comic opera about a love letter between two of Elizabeth the First's courtiers that mistakenly ends up in the queen's hands."

"That sounds like fun." Pris wiggled her eyebrows.

"It is." Violet's voice was soft, not allowing herself to put too much enthusiasm into her words.

"Then do it." Pris grabbed her hands, squeezing them and giving them a slight shake as if she were trying to rattle some sense into Violet. "On this, your thirtieth birthday, make a new vow—one to yourself. A wish for your dreams to come true."

"Maybe one last time." Violet pinched her lower lip between her teeth, as if to stop herself from voicing her desires out loud.

"Oh, for the love of . . . Vi, stop being a martyr, for heaven's sake, literally. What's in the blood is hard to remove—stop trying."

"You're right."

"Of course I am." Pris danced her shoulders back and forth. "You've spent years taking care of me. And now you need to take care of you."

———◆———

VIOLET ARRIVED AT the Shaftesbury Theatre the following morning, wearing one of the dresses she'd worn while in the shows with the Astaires, slightly altered to match the current fashion. Fortunately for her, it still fit, though her dancing shoes were a mite worn.

The front of the house looked much the same, and even though more than a decade had passed since she'd first worked there, Mr. Cowden still prowled the hallowed halls. Coming to a standstill in front of the auditorium doors, his eyebrows grayer and bushier than she remembered, he narrowed his gaze at her.

"Why, if it isn't Violet Wood," he mused, swiveling his rounded belly toward her, eyebrows shot to his hairline as if he couldn't believe it. "It's been an age."

Violet was surprised he was being polite. She'd heard him swear and stomp more than anything when she'd worked for him. She took a step back, toward the doors, contemplating escape. "Nice to see you, Mr. Cowden."

"If you've come back for your old job, I can stop you now. We've a full house." His meaty fists clenched against his hips, accenting the sour pout of his wrinkly white lips. There was the old goat she remembered.

"Then it's a good thing I haven't." She contemplated stalking past him.

"Spiky as ever," he grumbled.

Violet laughed, letting go of the tension of their reunion. "A good thing to see neither of us has changed much. I'm here to audition."

"Best get back there." He hooked his thumb behind him. "If you're not early you're late."

That kicked her nerves into gear, and she rushed to find that the auditorium was indeed quite crowded. In the cacophony, her body was sucked back in time to the first audition in which Adele Astaire had been in the audience. Violet glanced toward the empty row where Adele had first spotted her and felt a pang of sadness that she'd not seen her good friend in so long.

She recognized a few of the people—Bridgette, in particular, who shot her a nasty glare. Seemed that woman hadn't risen in the theatre world, either. At least Violet wasn't alone. What tragedy had befallen Bridg to put her in the same position? None of those in charge were familiar to Violet, and likely wouldn't recognize her name.

The director snapped his fingers and called, "Places." There was no more time to ponder, not if she was going to knock this audition out of the park, surpassing the much younger dancers on the stage.

The choreographer showed them the dance number that he wanted them to perform, and Violet did her best to memorize the steps. When it was her turn, she let her body soar, the familiarity of the stage beneath her feet, the music in her head, the tingle through her arms, recognizable and welcome. When they were asked to sing, she opened her throat and belted the lyrics. She wasn't dancing and singing solely for the audition, but for herself and all the years lost on the trek to stardom. The loss of her dreams, her friends. But also the triumphs of Pris becoming a woman, of the two of them surviving and thriving despite the obstacles.

She danced for herself and hoped it would be enough.

After everyone had had a chance to show off their talents, they milled in the back while the director, producer, and other theatre people talked in hushed whispers, crossing off names and making lists. Violet worried the cuticles of her nails until there was nothing left to pluck and scrape.

"Violet Wood." Her name, the first to be called, echoed off the walls of the grand theatre. Singled out, she was certain that it was because she was about to be cut. The other dancers stared, some sympathetic, some relieved, and others—like Bridgette—downright self-righteous. It had been too long since Violet had last been onstage, and she was going to be sent home with her head down, tail tucked. At least she'd tried.

Violet stepped forward, wishing her humiliation would end before she started crying.

"We'd like you to play Queen Elizabeth." The director's voice was austere, and he managed to look down his nose at her, though she was onstage several feet above him.

Violet couldn't have heard right. "But that's the lead."

"Indeed, it is." The man glanced at the others who'd judged her, his expression asking, *Have we made a mistake?*

"But the lead sings." Violet licked her dry lips while her brain tried to process the fact that instead of being sent home she'd been asked to be the star of the show.

"Yes." He sounded annoyed that she was questioning him.

I'm not that *good of a singer.* Her tongue had twisted too much to voice her doubts, and though all she'd had was tea that morning it was winding its way up her throat right now.

"You have an excellent contralto voice," he continued, "and that is exactly what we need."

"Contralto." The deepest of female voices. Well, she supposed that was likely why she'd had some issues singing in Adele's high-pitched tones, even though Adele had been successful. Violet thought it was because she couldn't sing. Turns out it was simply the wrong range.

"Yes," he practically hissed.

"Y-ye-yes, I'll do it," Violet stammered, nerves getting the best of her.

"We start rehearsals in four hours."

"Great." Violet didn't even bother to glance at Bridgette as she ran out of the theatre and all the way to Foyles.

Bursting into the bookshop, the silver bell above the door made a frantic ding. "Pris? Pris, where are you?" She paced the stacks on the various floors of the bookshop in search of her sister.

"Violet, is that you?" A familiar head popped out from between two stacks. Dark brown eyes shone, and a smile that could have parted the shelves themselves graced the familiar face.

"Adele." Surprise knocked the wind from Violet. Years had passed since they'd seen each other.

"You're positively beaming." Adele's smile widened as she rushed to embrace her, juggling a pile of books on one arm. She smelled of Dior, and her blue-and-white-checked tweed skirt and jacket matched her hat, at a jaunty angle over her recently bobbed dark hair. "Do tell."

"I got a lead part." Energy buzzed through Violet's body. The two women gushed over each other, wishing they'd not let so much time lapse. What were the odds that Violet would get the part and see her long-lost friend all in the space of an hour?

"The lead?" Pris dashed up from wherever she'd been, with a wide grin on her face that all but bragged that she'd told her so.

"I'm to be Queen Elizabeth. Imagine me, poor Violet Wood from Shoreditch, to be a queen." Violet straightened her shoulders, striking a regal pose.

Pris couldn't help her guffaw at that.

"You'll do an amazing job, Your Majesty," Adele teased. "And I will certainly be there for opening night."

"Oh, I would dearly love it if you were. It won't be the same without you."

Adele rummaged in her purse and pulled out a small calendar and pencil. "When is it?"

"This fall."

"Perfect. Be sure to let me know when you have the opening-night date, and I'll be there." Adele made a note and then tucked her calendar back into her purse.

"It is so good to see you." Violet couldn't stop smiling. "And you're married now."

"I am." A flash of sadness passed over Adele's face, worrying Violet about what had happened to her old friend's life and making her feel more guilty for not keeping in touch. The sadness was quickly gone, though, replaced by the funny face that Adele was known for. "But enough about me; tell me what you've been up to."

"She's been avoiding her dreams." Pris crossed her arms and stared at her sister with a now-you're-gonna-get-it look. "While I've been living mine."

"Is that so?" Adele grinned at Pris and touched her arm, expressing genuine pleasure.

"I've lived a hundred lives." Pris pressed her hand to her chest and heaved a dramatic sigh.

"Is that all?" Adele teased. "You'd better step up, then."

Pris giggled, then took Adele's mound of books from her hands, but not before Violet caught the titles: Nancy Mitford's *Christmas Pudding*, Milne's *Four Days of Wonder*, Travers's *Mary Poppins*, and Agatha Christie's latest, *Murder on the Orient Express*.

"I'll ring these up when you're ready." Pris sauntered away, leaving them alone.

"I'm so proud of you, Violet." Adele leaned a shoulder casually against one of the bookshelves, but despite her relaxed stance her posture was tight, as if she was only pretending not to be wound up. "You've worked so hard for this and it's about time someone recognized you."

"Thank you. And what of you?" Violet softened her voice, mirroring Adele's casual demeanor. "Are you living your dream?"

Adele let out a laugh that sounded more like a sniff. "As best I can. I don't have regrets, and I suppose that's better than anything else. And Charlie is a dear."

"Do you have time for tea?" Violet didn't want to press, but it seemed as if Adele needed to get something off her chest.

"That would be lovely." Adele purchased her books, and they went to a café across the street, ordering tea and scones.

They talked about the weather in London, Freddie's new wife, Phyllis, and Ireland, until the tea service was set on the table. Adele stirred two lumps of sugar into her cup, the only sound between them the clinking of their spoons, until Adele said, "I'm assuming you saw the papers about my loss last fall?"

Violet bit her lip. "I apologize but I didn't . . . I've been avoiding the papers." They cost money she didn't want to waste, and any news of the theatre only made her sad, anyway.

"Ah, well." Adele smiled sadly, looking off into the distance for a minute as if reliving her experience. "I was pregnant. A girl. We lost her after she was born."

She said the words in a monotone, and Violet could tell that her friend didn't want to expound on them.

"I'm so sorry, Delly." Violet reached across the table and held her friend's hand, trying to impart a comfort that she knew would barely assuage the hurt.

"Do you think I waited too long to become a mother?" Adele cocked her head, slipping her hand from beneath Violet's to take a small bite of scone.

The shift felt like an evasion, and Violet wasn't sure what to make of it.

"No, I don't," Violet answered, without preamble, lifting her teacup to appear busy, and unoffended that her friend had pulled back. "My mum was thirty-five when she had Pris."

"I'm so sorry about your mom." Adele's voice hitched on the last word, and for a split second her façade slipped, showing a wealth of hurt that made Violet want to leap up and grab her friend in a bear hug. But she held back, because Adele had subtly shown her before that physical comfort wasn't welcome.

Working around the knot in her throat, Violet pushed out the words, "I suppose we're both becoming accustomed to that."

"Say, wasn't yesterday your birthday?" Adele asked breezily, her entire countenance changing, a swift shift of subject from the loss of life to life continued.

"Yes. And this has been the perfect treat. I've missed you."

"So have I, darling, so have I. After your opening night, we should go out on the town like we used to, for old times' sake. It'll be a gas."

"Count me in."

"It's a plan, then. And bring Pris, too."

"She's not quite old enough for that."

"Really? She looks old enough to me." Adele raised a brow at her, with that one expression demanding that Violet admit the truth.

"I suppose she is, actually, but I've just . . ."

"You've been sheltering her. And understandably so. After what happened, I bet it was the only thing to keep you going. But you can't shelter her forever."

"You're right." Violet shrugged, ready to admit to herself that everything Adele said was true. And what was the harm? It wasn't as if she was sending Pris off alone.

"She'll fit right in, and we can all make sure she's not imbibing cocktails if you don't want. But a dance or two with a handsome fellow, maybe."

Violet blew out a long breath, knowing that the day would come when her sister would be dancing with lads, but still not ready for it. "That'd be a dream for her."

"And for you." Adele grinned over her teacup, tapping a manicured nail against the porcelain as if to bolster her point.

Violet's laugh was short and sharp, packed with the doubt that she felt. "You know settling down has never been something on my list of things to do before I kick the bucket."

"That's right." Adele shook her head. "We were often lurching in the opposite direction."

"And one half of us has made it." She picked at a currant in her scone, popping the small morsel of dried fruit into her mouth.

"No, Vi, we both have. You're a lead now in a major production. That counts."

"Oh! What time is it?" Violet glanced at the small watch on her wrist and then leapt up from the table. "I nearly forgot. The director said to be back for rehearsals."

"Oh, dear, then you'd better run! I'll see you in a couple months, if not before."

Violet fumbled in her purse for money to pay her share, but Adele stopped her with a gentle hand on her wrist. "My treat, friend. Go! Before someone calls for the queen's execution."

Violet laughed as she waved and trotted away, skating into the theatre with only a minute to spare.

Things were really looking up for her now. And it would seem being thirty wasn't the hell she'd thought it was going to be. In fact, it looked like it was going to be the best year of her life yet.

———————⋈———————

ON OPENING NIGHT in London, confidence strained against the confines of Violet's body. She was ready.

The orchestra tuned its cue and the curtain lifted, the footlights blinding the cast from seeing the audience at first. A few blinks and the outlines of their rounded heads came into view.

Sitting in the front row was Adele, with Pris on her right and Charlie on her left, wide smiles on their faces that fairly shouted their pride. Violet decided to look no farther than that. Her beloved sister and her dearest friend and idol were there. Violet gave the role everything she had, and at the end of the performance the audience cheered, "'Core, 'core!" Their applause rang triumphantly in her ears.

Happy tears stung as she beamed through the footlights at those who'd enjoyed the show. She and the cast took their bows and then were swept back to the dressing rooms to change and wipe off their makeup. As she peered into the mirror, barely recognizing the woman she'd become, a series of familiar voices rang out beyond the door.

Adele, Pris, and several other notable society folks.

She hugged Pris first, trying not to cry, and then Adele, followed by her old theatre friends, whom she'd not seen in years. Everyone congratulated her on a job well done, impressed with how far she'd come.

They made their way to the Café de Paris, and as she whirled in the crowd, certain that her feet were about to take flight, she came face-to-face with a handsome, memorable man, and her knees nearly buckled.

"Paul Reid," she breathed out. "My goodness, it's been an age, hasn't it?"

"Since Paris." His eyes twinkled, and suddenly she was back beneath the Eiffel Tower, staring up at its point illuminated by the moon.

That had been a dream. The first time she'd had ice cream, and the first time she'd thought about falling in love, and then regrettably decided against it.

"You look beautiful, Violet." Taking her hand in his, he brought it to his lips for a chivalric kiss, as if she truly were Queen Elizabeth and he one of her devoted courtiers.

"And you look as dapper as ever." She glanced around him, feeling decidedly bold. "Is there a Mrs. Reid with you tonight?"

"There isn't a Mrs. Reid." A knowing smile touched his lips, and a ball of heat coiled in her belly.

"Then there is no one to be offended if I ask you to dance." My goodness, what had gotten into her? Perhaps it was the memories of Paris, how his hands had felt on her shoulders, the smile and twinkle in his eyes under the stars as they lapped up the sweet, cold confections. He'd tried to contact her after she'd come back and found her mother dead, but Violet had brushed him off, intending to focus solely on Pris.

"No one at all. Will I need to fend off a jealous mate?" He also glanced around, striking a mock combat stance as if prepared to battle a bitter rival.

"Not at all."

Paul held out his hand again and she slipped her fingers over his palm, delighting in the warmth and sizzle of human connection. He twirled her around and then settled a hand at her waist. When before she'd run from every romantic inclination, for some reason this time she sank into it.

"Have dinner with me tomorrow," he said.

"I'm in a show." This would be where he lost interest, she was certain, since she'd essentially confessed her career was more important than a date.

Undeterred, Paul said, "Breakfast, then."

Violet worked hard to suppress the excited smile on her face as she said very stoically, "I love breakfast."

"It's a date, then." Paul winked, clearly aware that he'd made her happy.

She thought about correcting him. Telling him it was not a date but merely a meal between two friends, but she didn't want to hurt his feelings.

"I wonder, Mr. Reid, if tomorrow I'll be tasting something I've never had before."

His eyebrows shot up and then settled. "Ah, yes, I remember, you'd never had ice cream when we were in Paris."

She let out a snort that was less than ladylike. "I hate to ask what you thought I meant."

Paul groaned, his head falling back. "You don't want to know."

"Now I do. You've piqued my curiosity."

"Is Paul scandalizing you?" Adele teased as she whirled past in the arms of her handsome husband. "I couldn't help but notice both of your facial expressions."

"I believe it is Violet who is scandalizing me," Paul teased. "She's asked me to let her taste something she's never had before."

Adele exhaled a laugh, nearly falling over from the force of it. "Oh, Vi, you didn't."

"I meant breakfast," Violet insisted through a fit of giggles.

That only made Adele laugh harder. "Paul here does love to share his sausage."

Charlie, getting in on the lark, elbowed Paul.

Violet's jaw unhinged, as if she were a toy nutcracker whose lever had been wrenched at the same moment Paul pressed his lips together, sputtering as he tried not to laugh. Adele was always one to surprise them with a crass joke.

"Charlie, how I've missed your wife. Adele's humor never fails," Paul said.

"Oh, it fails plenty," Adele piped up, "but this was just too easy to resist."

"I'll be ordering bacon, I think," Violet announced, though she couldn't keep a straight face. "Do say the place you had in mind serves bacon?"

Paul chuckled. "And toast."

CHAPTER NINETEEN

ADELE

THE LIMELIGHT

Our shining starlet has returned! Miss Violet Wood knocks the socks off her audience as Queen Elizabeth in *Merrie England*. An added treat for those who attended the London premiere, Lady Charles Cavendish along with her husband sat front and center for the performance. Seen afterward at the Café de Paris, Miss Wood on the arm of the Honorable Paul Reid. The two have been spotted around Mayfair on numerous occasions sparking our interest in their burgeoning romance. Our only hope is that Miss Wood doesn't decide being married to an Hon is more important than her commitment to entertainment . . .

November 1935

'd a closet full of Schiaparelli dresses, the latest in fashionable shoes and accessories. I was a former star. My in-laws were a duke and duchess, and my husband was still irresistibly handsome. On the outside looking in, one might think I had everything. I lived in a castle, after all.

But peel back the layers, and find the bleeding, broken parts of me on the inside.

My babies were gone. Sweet Annie Evelyn, and the twin boys that came next.

The fact that I was even standing now, staring into the closet full of beautiful clothes, was both a miracle and a mystery. Most days my heart pounded so hard against my ribs I feared they'd splinter.

But I'd promised Charlie I'd go to this party, that we'd do one final swing through society before making our way to New York. My salvation. There was nothing like the swift tonic of an American city to drown my misery in until it succumbed, and I could be reborn.

Perhaps I'd made a mistake in choosing this life. To be so full of everything and empty all at once.

At least with acting and dancing I always knew what I was going to get. I could go onstage and see the result. Hear the booming laughter, the deafening applause, see the paycheck, and know that at the end of the day I'd held up my end of the bargain and been rewarded.

There were no rewards here. Even if I did wear designer clothes.

Three babies gone—I was not a successful mother.

A drunk husband—I was not a successful wife.

Zero interest in socializing—I was not a successful socialite.

I'd given up the one thing I knew I could succeed at. Freddie was doing phenomenally for himself. And Violet had risen to the top, starring in one show after another. But me? I was a puddle in designer fabrics. Brittle to the touch, I had to be careful not to be tapped too hard lest I shatter. How could anyone expect anything when, instead of standing here, I should be running after three impish Cavendishes?

"Are you ready?" Charlie asked from behind me.

Startled out of my melancholy, I turned in my black cocktail dress with the white fringe collar. My hair was done perfectly in its new shortened coif, the edges curled just so. No longer did I toil with long tresses; even that seemed like too much work. "Yes."

"You look stunning, darling." He studied my face, eyes lingering on the sleep-marred blue smudges beneath my own, an eyebrow raised as if to say, *Are you all right?*

I hijacked a smile from muscle memory and straightened his tie. "Not nearly as stunning as you. One moment; I need to don a final powder." I puffed my face and spread on a new layer of red lipstick, putting on a mask to hide . . . *everything*.

The party was packed by the time we got there. Our entire social set was present, including Emerald Cunard—that false cow couldn't help but suck herself dry in Wallis Simpson's wake, trying to prove her loyalty. One glowing and irritating viewpoint after another concerning the American leech who had miraculously landed the attention of our future King Edward VIII— previously my David. It was hard to imagine that the same prince I'd danced with a decade earlier had fallen head over heels for that American divorcée.

David was willing to give up everything for Wallis Simpson. The talk of him abdicating his place in line for the throne had grown to near-serious volume. And here was Emerald, a smear of red lipstick on her teeth, stinking up this pretty party with her blathering. One more exaggerated hand gesture and she might toss her martini over her shoulder—in fact, I hoped she would, just for the laugh.

In disgust, I marched away in search of Charlie. If only to feel the warmth of his hand on mine in the hope of calming me down. Through all our difficulties, he was still my anchor. I spotted him near the bar, drinking what I was certain was not his first, second, or third whiskey on the rocks.

"Charlie," I whispered, and he stared down at me with reddened eyes.

"A-*dele*," he overenunciated, clearly sozzled.

"You might have tightened the bridle for my first appearance," I hissed, irritated now that the one person I'd sought comfort from was in no shape to provide it. "I want to leave."

"Sho shoon?" he slurred, swirling his ice with a finger.

My God . . . I might be handling our devastations better than Charlie. "Yes."

He started to protest, but I walked away, tired of everyone and everything. I craved an escape back to America, and once I was there, besides relaxing in the presence of my old friends and old life, maybe I'd try to get some of it back. I couldn't wait to see Tilly Losch again, disappointed we'd be missing her premiere of *The Garden of Allah*. Like everyone else, Tilly kept pushing me to try out acting on film rather than the stage.

I'd had numerous offers to star in a picture. Perhaps it was time to renew my career aspirations if being a mother wasn't in the cards. There had to be something in this world left for me.

We arrived in New York two days before Christmas, to a horde of photographers and journalists who were thrilled to welcome me back to the city. I couldn't believe how many people remembered me or were actually interested in my arrival. It was quite surreal, made more so by the amount of flowers waiting for me at the hotel. A rainbow symphony that dotted every surface in pinks, reds, yellows, and purples. We spent Christmas with our friends Jock and Liz Whitney. Jock regaled us with stories of his affair with Tallulah Bankhead, whose antics were in all the gossip rags. Liz didn't seem to care as long as she had a cocktail in hand.

For New Year's Eve we were invited to Arden, a country estate owned by our friends Marie and Averell Harriman. While there, Charlie tipped his elbow one too many times and made me worry about whether he was going to overstay his welcome, with his appetite for alcohol. And whether I'd be given even a single day of the peace that this trip was supposed to provide.

On the bright side, I was offered a broadcast interview for a thousand dollars, which was too much to turn down, so I wore a pretty lemon-yellow dress with gray music bars printed on the fabric, and a smart black suede belt with a treble-clef fastener, to show that I was still a dancer, a star. On my hat, I wore a diamond-and-ruby Cavendish snake crest, for I was also now a lady.

I made nice with smiles and jokes as I talked about going from dancing to the life of the Lady Charles—and then to my surprise I found myself saying that yes, I was entertaining the idea of returning to acting.

By the time the interview aired, I already had an offer to do a screen test in Hollywood the following month. California was hot, but Freddie, Phyllis, and their brand-new baby, Freddie Jr., were a balm. I still wasn't a Phyllis fan, but she did look so pretty and upbeat with the baby, and she didn't try to gloat at all that she'd succeeded where I'd failed. Surprisingly, I didn't feel that way, either. Freddie was happy, and that in turn made me happy.

Freddie introduced me to a round of stars, and I was able to see some familiar faces such as Clark Gable, Marlene Dietrich, and my dear friend Tilly, who looked as if she'd not aged a minute.

When the day arrived for my audition, I donned a purple-blue satin dress and a new pair of shiny black pumps and made my way to Fox Studios. My hands shook as I fixed my hair.

The moment I set one foot out of the cab, with the warmth of the California sun on my stockinged ankle, I almost pulled back. We'd been on such a whirlwind since our arrival, and I'd been so intent on forgetting everything that I'd lost, that I'd not stopped to think about whether this was what I really wanted, or if this was merely what I thought I was supposed to do.

"Lady Charles." Several men in suits, flanked by women in dresses, greeted me. All smiles and Hollywood cheese. Weren't they hot out here in the sun? Not a drop of sweat on any brow.

"Call me Adele." My smile was tight, and the funny face I was known for seemed to have been left behind at Lismore in my trunk full of theatre costumes.

"I'm Mr. Kent." Dressed in a light-gray pinstripe to match his salt-and-pepper hair was a gentleman perhaps in his midfifties. "We've got someone who wants to meet you."

I should have been flattered to be greeted by the president of the studio, but it only made me more nervous. Was I doing the right thing, here?

"By all means." I followed the horde of smiling suits into the studio building, where a cherubic child with golden curls danced her way toward me in shiny patent-leather tap shoes.

My heart triple-flipped, and I gasped. My God, she was adorable.

"Shirley Temple." My smile brightened at the innocence and talent. "I adored you in *Bright Eyes*." We'd taken the staff at Lismore to see the film at Christmas the previous year, and it had been a true delight.

"They told me you're one of the greatest dancers ever." Shirley made a perfect curtsey.

I laughed, waving away the compliment that I'd always found ridiculous. There were dancers out there with triple my talent. "I doubt that."

"They said you were." Shirley pointed to Mr. Kent and his entourage.

"Well, I'm flattered." But really I wondered if they'd put the kid up to it.

"Would you dance with me?" Shirley batted her eyelashes.

"I would love to." If she'd been anyone else, I'd have denied her, not having practiced in ages. But her innocent and eager smile was irresistible, reminding me of myself at her age, performing in local gigs. How times had changed, with film seeming to take precedence over theatre.

Shirley glanced at a ready band, which must have been waiting for this, and said, "Hit it, boys."

A shocked laugh escaped me. Shirley Temple conveyed a command that some women ten times her age hadn't yet grasped. The band struck up an impromptu melody, and she showed me a few tap steps. I mirrored her and then added a twist, which only made her smile as she mimicked me. For nearly ten minutes we danced in tandem. Years of tension melted away in those few moments of escape.

"Well, Shirley, darling," I said, "it has been a pleasure. Maybe one day we can dance in a picture together."

"Oh, I would really like that," Shirley said, with her signature curtsey and giggle.

I curtseyed back, smiling wistfully at her retreating form as she was ushered off.

Taking a deep breath, I entered the room where Mr. Kent presided over several executives at a table. They passed me a script. "Feel free to take a moment to read and then give it a whirl."

I pulled the thick stack of paper toward me, reading a few lines of dialogue and action. There were a lot of similarities between this and theatre. Lines, actions, choreography. Acting was acting, after all. I cleared my throat, flashed a confident smile that I didn't quite feel, and stood as I read the lines, adding my own flair.

"That was excellent," Kent said, while the others nodded in agreement.

"And what about dancing? Think you can still dance?" someone asked.

I raised a brow and laughed. "Were you out there a half hour ago?"

A round of claps followed, as they all buzzed about my duet with Shirley Temple. "We look forward to working with you."

I left the studio with an offer in hand, saying I'd consider it. But by the time Charlie and I boarded a ship back to Britain, I'd already decided against becoming a Hollywood star. For one thing, the double-taxation situation was quite unfair. Being required to pay tax in both countries was highway robbery. To top it off, when the producer shared the rehearsal and filming schedule, I was reminded of what bothered me the most in showbiz—how time-consuming it all was.

I didn't want to work that hard. Yes, I wanted to perform, but not at the price of exhaustion. After an arduous sea voyage, which included fending off Jock's newest mistress—a married woman, and none other than the annoying Baba, Lady Curzon, whom I'd had to shoo away from Prince George back in the day—we returned to London only to find a country suffering from "Simpsonitis."

David had succeeded his late father as King Edward VIII, and his mistress, Wallis Simpson, was acting as if it were her head upon which the crown rested. Quite disgusting behavior. If I'd had a minute to sit down with David, I would have told him to let the mistress go—or keep her in the closet, for all anyone cared—to put her aside long enough to find a proper wife befitting a king.

Unless you asked Jock, who was irritated with me for voicing my opinion regarding mistresses at all. Honestly, though, Baba was a vampire, who'd eat her young and murder her own mother if they stood in her way.

Of course, a lot of people thought my opinion was hypocritical. I was, after all, an American who'd married a nobleman. But at least I wasn't an unfaithful bitch. And a second son was no monarch. Unkind of me, I know. But sometimes the truth hurt.

"What do you think about returning to Ireland?" Charlie asked me once more over tea and toast.

I stared out the window of our London house, at the busy, gloomy city beyond, longing for the peace and quiet of Lismore. "I think it's a good idea."

Just the thought of Ireland seemed to soothe some of my raw insides, which were starting to show on the outside. The longer we waited to return, the more likely it was I'd do or say something I couldn't come back from. Mom was planning to make a trip to Ireland this summer after tending to Phyllis and Freddie Jr. in California, and I needed some time to recharge before her arrival.

I welcomed Ireland's calm after all the society drama. Funny how America was supposed to do that for me and failed. Charlie and I took long walks along the River Blackwater with Tilly and Wassie, and wild rides with our horses over the moors. Our dinners were quiet, and we declined invitations, preferring to keep to ourselves for the time being. To dance naked beneath moonlight and stars.

By the time Mom arrived, my mood had improved greatly. She was on her best behavior, too, not voicing opinions about my decorating style, clothes, or Charlie's drinking. But when we returned from a country walk to find an envelope stamped with the English Film Co. address, she scrunched up her nose.

I decided to ignore the mail, not wanting to hear what she might say.

"Open it," Mom said, in her typical style as she removed her gloves.

Unable to avoid it, I took the letter into Charlie's study and pulled out the long metal letter opener I'd gifted him the year before.

With Mom practically breathing down my neck, I released the contents, skimming the pages. "My God." This was unbelievable.

"Tell me, Delly. Don't leave me in suspense."

"They are offering me ten thousand pounds to do a film with them." It was a vast sum for a part that I'd not even auditioned for.

"Well, darling, it's obviously your decision, but you'd be a fool if you didn't at least try." Mom's uttered opinion was surprisingly welcome.

"It's more than Fox," I mused.

Mom tapped the studio letterhead. "And there isn't the tax issue since it's a British company."

"And there's not an entire country plus the Atlantic Ocean between my home and the studio, just the Irish Sea, which is a day trip." This might actually be doable.

"Well, are you going to say yes?"

My heart seemed to have lost its place, falling into the pit of my stomach. "I'll have to think on it."

Did I want this? Part of the reason for turning down Hollywood had been the tax and distance issues, but the other part had been not wanting to spend twelve or sixteen hours on set. That wasn't the life I wanted. Although I'd like the extra money, I didn't need it to survive.

As July flourished into August, I was still thinking about it. Even as we joined friends in Germany at our yearly summer restorative at a health resort. I intended to take the relaxing time to think it over. Really make plans for my future.

However, when we arrived in Freiburg, the temperate climate seemed chilly. The attitude of the medieval town was tense, the smiles tighter, as if the inhabitants were one bad storm away from disaster. Plenty of people whispered, but I knew a pittance of German. One of my favorite bookshops, owned by an older Jewish couple whose grandchildren worked the register, was locked and dark. Peering inside, I could see that the place had been burned, scattered ashes and remnants of books on the floor. My heart broke at the sight, and to think of the good people who'd put their heart and soul into this place being so sorely abused.

The chancellor, Adolf Hitler, had waved his unbending iron wand across this beautiful country, and ordered books considered "un-German" to be burned and Jewish-run businesses to be boycotted, and then established the Nuremburg Race Laws, filled with ridiculous racial theories and orders. Given my ancestry and the struggle my father's family had with anti-Semitism, which forced them to convert to Catholicism, we couldn't get out of Germany fast enough.

What I'd hoped would be a healing voyage for Charlie turned into a years-long spiral that I'd rather not remember.

So I took the contract, just to distract myself.

———◆———

May 12, 1938

Once upon a time I would have found social gatherings like this one—Queen Charlotte's Ball, the annual debutante coming-out event of the season—to be mesmerizing. I would have clinked champagne glasses with my handsome husband and then dazzled him on the dance floor beneath the resplendent crystal chandeliers. I would have admired the yards and yards of gossamer silks, satin, and tulle, the iridescent diamond tiaras, and the magnificently designed three-tiered cake that was a head taller than me and had to be cut with a sword.

Instead this was the first time I'd left Lismore in a year, if not longer.

And I was alone.

I was the stand-in for the Lord and Lady Charles Cavendish,

while Charlie convalesced from his latest bout of grievances with his liver. I didn't want to be here, but Charlie had insisted. Or, rather, his mother had demanded.

I'd only managed to leave with repeated assurances from Mom that she'd telephone at the first sign of an issue, and from Charlie's doctor, who was confident he would be fine. Of course, I had serious doubts, and with good reason.

Over the past summer Mom had taken care of Charlie at Lismore while I worked on the film at Pinewood Studios. I didn't necessarily want the job, and hadn't enjoyed it at all, but I'd needed to get out of the castle, and away from the ominous, depressing gloom that seemed to encapsulate every facet of every day.

But, several months into filming, I got a telegram from my mother that rocked me to my core. Charlie had experienced a crippling attack of the liver. Guilt hit like a bullet to the gut. What had I been doing working on a picture when my husband was at home suffering? Over lunch one day my mother-in-law had glibly stated, "What good was vowing in sickness and in health, when in sickness you ran away?"

The duchess had a point, as vile as it made me feel. And yet she'd guilted me into abandoning my husband to go to this ball.

I had taken leave at the studio and rushed back to Ireland, finding the shell of a man confined to his bed. Charlie smiled at me as if he'd woken fresh from the best night's sleep, though his cheeks were sunken, and his skin had a yellow pallor.

Thankfully, he'd managed to recover enough to leave his bed. Even now, when I begged him to give up spirits, he pretended it was no big deal. Rebellious—mutinous, even—he would sneak out of bed and find the whiskey that I'd hidden. So I'd dumped it down the drain. I forbade the servants to restock, but they didn't listen. Someone was always willing to run an errand when a few extra pounds were pressed into their hand by their charming employer whom they so admired. None would confess to doing Charlie's dirty work, even when I warned that they were killing him with what they perceived as kindness.

Those times he was feeling better, Charlie would nip down to a local pub, cap pulled low over his eyes in the hope that no one would recognize him. Or we'd be out on the town with friends, and, though he'd promised otherwise, he was never without a bent elbow, crystal at his lips.

Charlie thought he was invincible. He was blind to what the rest of the world could see. That he'd let alcohol become his vice, his self-destructive weapon of choice.

How was I going to leave him again to finish a film I didn't even like? The role proved to be nothing more than a female menace, with no comedy, singing, or dancing. I needed joy, and the three things that would have made it worth it were absent—which made quitting all the easier.

About as preposterous as *this* ostentatious and glitzy debutante ball. While Hitler had frighteningly marched his army through Austria, taking full possession of the country, we were dancing and cutting cake. A godless, ruthless dictator had taken complete control over people in another country, and we were telling virgins dressed in white that the world was full of possibilities.

Why hadn't the dictator met an untimely end? Which country would be next?

I shouldn't have come to the ball. My head and heart weren't in it, and I felt like a dowdy, sour biddy on the sidelines.

"Aunt Delly." Billy and Andrew Cavendish, my two darling nephews by way of marriage, approached, yanking me from my contemplations. Twenty and eighteen respectively, they were handsome, with a youthful vigor about their eyes. "We wanted to introduce you to our debs."

I carved a smile into the stone of my face, ever the dutiful aunt, and turned my gaze on the young ladies bedecked in layers of white effervescence.

"This is Kathleen Kennedy, daughter of the American ambassador." Andrew indicated a bubbly girl beside him, her brown hair styled beneath a fashionable hat.

"You can call me Kick." She stuck out her hand, brown eyes unpretentious.

"Delighted," I said, and I genuinely was. There was something light and airy about Kick, and the way Billy was gazing at her he was obviously charmed out of his mind.

"And this is Miss Deborah Mitford." Andrew beamed at a beautiful blonde with blue eyes a tad sharper than one might expect in a slip of a thing so young.

"A pleasure," I murmured, surprised at the small inner circle of aristocrats.

I'd met Deborah's eldest sister, Nancy, years ago upon my first entry to London society. I found her funny, a bit tart in some respects, but otherwise quite affable. There were six sisters in all, and one brother—Tom, a charmer, who'd dated my darling Tilly Losch some years back. In fact, she'd even brought Tom along on one of her visits to Lismore. Of the other four sisters, I could say with good authority the eldest and the youngest were the best of them, especially when it was rumored that Unity Mitford was a Hitlerite, and that Diana had secretly wed the leader of the British Union of Fascists a couple of years before. Those two scared the daylights out of me.

Everyone claimed Diana was so classically beautiful, but all I ever thought when I saw her was that she was soulless and that something sinister was lurking behind her icy blue eyes. I suppose to make up for the two extreme fascists in the family, there was Jessica, who'd fled to America with her communist husband, a nephew of Winston Churchill, my talented backgammon opponent. Then there was Pam; no one ever saw her, so what was one to think?

Even as charming as this pretty debutante was, I couldn't help but hope Andrew tired of her soon. It wouldn't do for the Mitford name to be mixed with Cavendish, and I could only imagine the horror my mother-in-law must have felt at finding herself linked to that family, especially when she thought that I, a miserable American heiress and star, was bad for their reputation.

"We're going to see *Cinderella* at the Shaftesbury tomorrow, and we'd love for you to join us," Billy was saying.

"My new favorite actress—after you, of course," Kick added with a giggle, "is playing in the show. Perhaps you've heard of her—Violet Wood?"

I perked up at my old friend's name. "I would very much enjoy that." I smiled, remembering Violet's joy at having landed the role of Queen Elizabeth a few years before. She'd become quite a star, and I'd been so proud to watch her grow. "Violet is a dear friend of mine, actually."

"Oh, that is *wondair*," Deborah said, using her infamous Mitford idiom that most people in society found irritating. "You simply must tell us what it's like being a star."

My nostalgic smile constricted, and I found it hard to unearth the exact right answer. *It was a dream that now feels as if I see it through a haze.* "It was divine, my dear," I said instead. "Like champagne and caviar, and the love of a new beau."

Both girls sighed, their cheeks pinkening, and my nephews, nearly simultaneously, puffed out their chests. My goodness, the naivete of youth. It was almost nauseating. And yet I remembered the days when I'd been like that. When had I become so bitter?

"I heard she was engaged to a minor Scottish nobleman," Deborah said. "Have you met him yet?"

"Paul?" I asked, taken by surprise. It'd been more than three years since I'd seen Violet, preferring to let our friendship live in the happy past rather than in the gloomy present that was consuming me. And part of what prevented me from keeping in touch was selfishness. She was living the life I'd once had.

"I hear he's dreamy," Kick added, only for Billy to make an exaggeratedly crestfallen face.

"Yes, he is quite charming." A sudden wave of sadness seized me. The last time I'd seen Violet and Paul had been when we'd gone dancing. Charlie had been so full of life then. I missed her. I should have reached out. *Maybe I will.*

The girls chattered on, their voices high-pitched with excitement while the lads hung on every word. Oh, to be young again and full of hope and joie de vivre. I excused myself, unable to take their display of youthful elation any longer.

A few days later, that smoldering spark of joy was extinguished from the entire Cavendish family when the duke passed away. We all mourned, especially my Charlie. He rallied only for a short time, the old Charlie back, before his grief turned him to the bottle.

PART FOUR

ASTAIRICAL

"They are a sort of champagne cup of motion, those Astaires. They live, laugh and leap in a world that is all bubbles. They are sleek, long-shanked, blissfully graceful, both of them. Their dance steps flash and quiver with an intricacy which declines to be taken seriously but which is none the less a maker of marvels."

—*NEW YORK SUN*, NOVEMBER 23, 1927

CHAPTER TWENTY

ADELE

THE LIMELIGHT

This just in, Miss Violet Wood has broken off her engagement to the Honorable Paul Reid following a feud with her future in-laws. While we are saddened the darling of the East End is not going to get her happily ever after, it has proven marvelous for her audience, as she immediately accepted the lead role in *Under Your Hat*. Every theatregoer had been on tenterhooks wondering if Miss Wood was going to abdicate her stage throne in favor of making house. It is safe to say London has breathed a collective sigh of relief. Losing one stage darling to a noble house was enough ...

September 1938

My footsteps across the newly installed white carpet in my bedroom were silenced by the plush pile. I turned on the small portable radio to listen to the nightly news, my glass of Horlicks malted milk sitting like a stone in my belly. Even the tranquility of the blue satin curtains that covered the darkened window, a shade meant to calm, did nothing to alleviate the knots forming in my middle.

Our new puppy, Horace, put his front paws on my calf for a lift. I settled his soft body in my lap. Tilly, crotchety in her old age, found him to be a bit irritating. So much so that we'd been considering getting another Scottish terrier puppy for Horace to play with, but, having recently lost Wassie to old age, I wasn't yet ready.

Anxiety was in the air, even all the way out here on the Irish moors. Hitler and his horde had only escalated their threats and war antics. I hated the idea of our boys having to fight the bloodthirsty hoodlums.

Chamberlain's voice crackled over the radio, and Charlie joined me, sitting in the opposite yellow damask chair. His skin was sallow from his latest bout of drinking, and his eyes had a haunted, sunken look behind his glasses. It was hard to see him like this and not dissolve in a puddle of tears, so I tried to focus on the news report.

But it was harder to do than imagine, and while my ears filled with news of Hitler and Germany, my eyes followed familiar paths over my husband's face, his shoulders, his hands.

Germany would never be satisfied until it ruled every part of Europe and beyond, hammering those it didn't deem to fit the mold into work camps. And Charlie . . .

Charlie wouldn't be satisfied until he'd blotted himself from this world. He was physically better, it seemed, but mentally . . . there was a reason he'd gone to the clinic for a nice long overhaul of the body and mind. The thermal baths were supposed to have rejuvenated him. And they seemed to have done so, but there was still a darkness lurking beneath the surface, and I was terrified I'd not be able to yank him out.

Chamberlain's voice rose and fell in a familiar cadence. I pictured him as he'd looked when we'd met him at St. James's Palace. The arch of his eyebrow, the way his thick mustache twitched as he spoke. Tonight, he droned on, more of the same message he reiterated daily. Hitler had gone further than anyone ever believed he would. That vile dictator craved war. But with the Munich Agreement that Great Britain had signed, along with Germany, Italy, and France, there could be peace—at a price. Czechoslovakia had to surrender some of its territory to German forces. How could we require the subjugation of others for our own liberty?

And *voilà*, giving away whole parts of a country in the hope of peace. It felt like a double negative, canceling itself out. It was madness. Like the older children in a schoolyard agreeing to play with the younger ones, but only if they agreed to use one of their heads as the ball.

My nerves felt like they'd crack at any moment, between my husband's internal battle, our country's external battle, and the thoughts running rampant through my mind—Should I have quit dancing? If I hadn't turned down Tilly earlier this summer, would I now be preparing for a role onstage with her again? Would I be dancing with Vi?

"The PM can sign all the agreements he wants"—Charlie sounded agitated as he pulled off his glasses to rub his red and weary eyes—"but that bastard Hitler isn't going to let a thing like a signature stand in his way."

"Maybe there won't be bloodshed." My words lacked conviction, for if there was one thing we'd learned so far it was that Hitler wanted nothing more.

Charlie shook his head miserably, settling his glasses back on the bridge of his nose. "It is inevitable. We have given him the blood of the Czech people."

I swallowed hard, hating talk of politics and war. Hating how the fun had been sucked out of evenings that used to be full of romance, when we'd come upstairs after dinner, turn on the radio, and dance until we collapsed onto the bed to make love. Those happier days before the joy had been sucked from me, one loss after another.

The clock struck and the radio announcer returned, rambling on about something else. The malted milk in my belly curdled, and I hurried to the bathroom to be sick.

A week or so later, the papers shouted about Hitler's speech, in which he insulted those who'd made an accord with him, especially the British. Contemptuous cracks about how the rest of the world ought to mind its own business and leave the problems of more powerful and knowledgeable leaders to themselves.

I supposed Charlie was right. War was inevitable.

———◆◆◆———

April 1939

"I shouldn't!" I exclaimed at Freddie's offer to teach me his newest choreography, though the way my hand reached for him to pull me from the chair said otherwise.

"Oh, come on, it'll be a breeze, and I'll be gentle."

I was knocked up again. Third time's the charm, at least that was what I told myself. I glanced at Charlie, who'd been a hard nut to crack these days. There must have been something in my expression, though, because he perked up.

"I've never seen you happier than when you dance. And, boy or girl, that baby inside you will feel your joy." Charlie grinned, and for the briefest second the man I'd fallen in love with slipped from beneath the jaundiced man I was married to.

One could only hope.

Mom jumped up to change the record on the gramophone. A second later, swing music trilled, followed by the crooning of Ella

Fitzgerald through the horn. She was a big hit in the States, and my sister-in-law, Phyllis, had brought the record as a gift.

Freddie's wife, who'd been an absolute gem on this trip of theirs to Lismore, surprised me hour by hour with her kindness. She'd never been so nice in her life. Well, wonders never ceased. There was a genuineness to the crinkle around her eyes, and in the smile that said she truly wanted to be friends.

"I suppose dancing couldn't hurt." There was a flutter in my belly. Hard to decipher if it was nerves or the tiny baking Cavendish.

I grabbed hold of Freddie's hand and let him twirl me into a modified Charleston with a Fred Astaire flair.

"Now, we'll swing out, holding hands, and do a shuffle step, then tip up on your toes."

Freddie showed me first, and then I followed suit, grasping the choreography but wavering at the last second on my toes. Freddie caught me around the middle as I tipped too far to the left.

"Whoa, there, Delly. Not too much. Keep your hips pushed back so you don't topple."

I laughed and tried again, nailing it on the third attempt. A sign?

It didn't take me long to get the hang of the moves, and by the time we were called to dinner we were both sweating. My face hurt from smiling so much. My goodness, it had been exciting.

"You all go ahead into the dining room. I'll be down in a second, I need to freshen up," I said.

"Will you be all right?" Charlie asked.

I laughed and gave him a cockeyed look, which made my darling husband break into a chuckle, the sound raw, because it had been too long since he'd had so much fun.

"Of course. Going to splash cold water on my face."

I hoofed it up the stairs, Horace and our new Scottish terrier, Patience, fighting for space between my ankles. Feeling winded, I paused at the top to steady my heaving lungs and bent over to give them each a pat while I caught my breath. Then I made my way to one of the bathrooms that I'd had installed in the ancient place.

The water was cool as I splashed it on my face, wetting a plush towel to wipe the back of my neck. I brushed my short hair back into place and spritzed on some Chanel before returning downstairs. As my foot hit the wood planks of the grand foyer, I felt a tender twinge in my belly, pulsing into an ache.

I paused for a minute, swallowing my fear when it disappeared a second later. The butler had passed the mocktails I'd requested around the table—the same ones Charlie and I had shared on our first dinner at the Ritz all those years before. Mom, Freddie, and Phyllis never said a word about the lack of spirits in the castle, and I couldn't have been more grateful.

Drinks were followed by leek soup, and then the main course of spiced beef, and the apple cake with custard sauce finale.

"You'd better hold on to your cook," Freddie said, "or I'm going to end up putting her in my suitcase when we leave. There is nothing like good Irish fare." My brother leaned back in his chair and patted his middle the way Pop used to after eating. He was normally wound up about something, but I'd not seen Freddie so relaxed. "I've not eaten so well in an age."

"Thank you." I dabbed the corner of my mouth with my napkin, as prim as Mom on my right. Her judgment of my choice of napkins was enough for tonight. "She really is the heart of Lismore. It's a wonder I've kept my figure since arriving."

"All the stairs help, I'm sure." Phyllis gave an exaggerated sigh and swiped her brow. "I might have to crawl to bed."

After dinner, when Freddie asked about dancing some more, I challenged him to a game of backgammon instead, afraid of exerting myself further. There hadn't been any more painful stitches, but I'd not danced, or really moved, like that in years. I didn't want to chance losing another precious child. And, honestly, it didn't seem, given Charlie's health, as if there would be another chance.

But no matter how many rounds of backgammon or cards we played, or the number of times that I declined to dance, what had become inevitable, besides war with Germany, materialized.

I lost the baby—exactly one year to the day after the duke's death, the sixth of May. Charlie spent the anniversary of his father's passing in a drunken haze, while I curled in a ball in excruciating pain.

Never had there been so much gore. Never had there been so much pain.

"This is worse than the premature births," I sobbed to Charlie, referring to the mess, when he tried his best to help. It was so heinous that I banished him from the room. I wanted my mother. Needed her now. But she'd left with Freddie and Phyllis.

When the days and weeks of my suffering bled into a month, I received an out-of-the-blue telephone call from Deborah Mitford.

"I know this is quite strange of me to say," she said quickly, as if she was afraid I'd hang up the telephone, "but I heard of your . . . condition, and . . . well, we proper ladies don't usually discuss these things, but since we're likely to be family, I think it's all right."

"I don't think anyone has ever called me a proper lady." I tried to lace the seriousness of her hurried words with some humor.

A nervous laugh sounded on the other end. "Well, in that case, I'll just spit it out. My sister Nancy . . . well, she had to have a curettage by her doctor after . . . being in a delicate state, to . . . um . . . to . . ."

"Clean her out?" I offered.

"Yes, indeed, that is what I was trying to say."

"Thank you, Debo," I said, genuinely grateful that the sweet girl had thought to call.

I telephoned the doctor in London that afternoon, and then, with what felt like eight dozen linen rags packed in my underwear, made the journey from Ireland to our house in Carlton Gardens.

Charlie paced anxiously in the waiting room as they stuck a needle in my vein, and I fell into delicious delirium. When I woke, I felt refreshed—and the hollow in my belly, meant to be. My hopes of making Charlie well, giving him a reason to get better, by bringing into the world a child we could love and dote on, were dashed completely. The doctor advised I would likely not be able to get pregnant again. In fact, doing so might be harmful, even deadly to me.

Quite fitting, really, considering my once-vibrant husband was worse off than ever before, and the country was on the brink of war.

"I will never do this again," I said to no one in the room; the truth of the words spoken aloud was harsher than hearing it from the doctor.

On the drive back to Carlton Gardens I asked Charlie if he could acquire some French letters, to make sure we didn't conceive. At first he looked surprised, but when I explained the risks he agreed to use the contraceptives.

"I don't want to lose you." He reached for my hand and squeezed, telling me in that small gesture that he was on my side.

"I don't want to lose you, either." I clutched his hand in mine, desperate to hold on. "And I can't lose another baby. Four is enough to last me a lifetime."

"I'm so sorry, Delly." The usual stoic framework of his face fell.

"It's not your fault." I ducked my head, hiding the truth in my eyes, that this last time, I was certain, had been my fault. Dancing with Freddie had been a mistake.

"But it could be mine. Lately I've been . . ." Charlie choked on his words.

"It isn't. It was mine. I shouldn't have danced."

Charlie glanced at me, stricken. "My God, Delly, is that what you think? That your dancing did this?" He shook his head. "Your body was made for movement. It was your worry for me that made your womb toxic."

I scooted closer to him and laid my head on his shoulder as we both silently wept, neither of us understanding why our children had been taken from this world before they'd had a chance to live.

We decided to remain in London for the summer, enjoying the festivities and clubs, and our rediscovered togetherness. The new pact to keep our family solely the two of us.

September 1, 1939

"I'm so glad you agreed to meet me for lunch." I slung my purse and gas mask over my chair, the same as my longtime friend had done, then grabbed Violet in a hug. Now that we were spending more time in London, I'd made a point to connect with her.

"I'm thrilled you asked." Violet looked as lovely as ever, a natural color in her cheeks that I wished I could achieve without the help of powders.

"It's vile they've ordered us to carry around gas masks," I said, settling in at the table.

"At least they are making somewhat fashionable bags for them," Violet offered with a skeptical smile.

I laughed. "Indeed."

We engaged in small talk at first, about the theatre and the clubs, but the conversation came back around eventually to the impending war. We'd yet to see the impact on our own soil of Hitler's rampage, other than the masks and the blackout at night, which left us all blind.

"Do you believe what they are saying about the Jewish people in Germany and in other conquered countries?" Violet's mouth was a worried line.

Across the pond Hitler was gunning for Danzig, baiting Poland so he'd have an excuse to invade. Nazi propaganda papers did what they did best—incited outrage against the Poles. Precisely as they had the Jews. Hitler seemed to adhere to a strategy of allowing defenses to be weakened by hate before sending in his army.

I nodded. "Yes. And it's not the first time. There's a deep-seated distrust for some reason." I'd never told her about my father's origins, but now seemed as good a time as any. "My father's family was Jewish, and they suffered greatly at the hands of anti-Semites in Austria in the late 1800s, feeling forced to convert to Catholicism in order to be accepted in society and granted full rights as citizens."

"Outrageous! I had no idea."

I shook my head sadly. "I don't think most people understand that the foundation was there; Hitler merely needed to build the framework on top. Crazy as it is, my father's brothers, I guess in an attempt to prove their worth, were Austrian soldiers and allies with the Germans during the Great War. My father had already come over to America years before that. But still the stigma of his brothers' actions stuck with our family."

"How so?" Violet, concerned, tucked her hair behind her ear.

"One time, right after the sinking of the *Lusitania* by the Germans, Freddie and I were coming back into the States from Canada, on our way to another show. We were detained on our train, identified as being related to enemy soldiers. Of all the ridiculous notions, they deemed that Freddie and I were spies. German spies!" I scoffed, remembering those moments vividly as I shared them, the fear of imprisonment.

Violet's whole head jutted forward in shock. "That is preposterous."

"Can you imagine?" I rolled my eyes. "They eventually cleared us, but held us for questioning long enough that we missed our show. Back then we needed to perform as much as we could to put food on the table, but also to build our name. I hated that the prejudices my father suffered in Austria had followed us, made worse by his brothers supporting the anti-Semitic policies. And I'm fairly certain the rift between my father and his brothers only grew when he found out what happened."

"How awful. And scary."

"It really was." I waved away the memories, the darkness of those moments, and tapped my gas mask.

"The prime minister is a fool right now, trusting such a dishonorable government," Violet said.

"But as much as it seems a fright, I don't think the Germans will ever be able to set foot on British soil."

Violet shook her head. "They don't have to set foot. All they have to do is drop bombs. You know, Paul's joined the RAF."

"A pilot?"

"Yes." Violet gave a measured shudder, and I glanced down at where her finger was still absent a wedding ring. Apparently his family was up in arms about his choice of a wife. A stage star who performed dozens of times a week wasn't exactly wife material, in their minds. Violet had broken things off with him thrice now, only for him to come begging. I wasn't sure how she put up with it. "I hope he never has to fly."

"I hope so, too." With the new agreement between Moscow and Germany, it was only a matter of time before our lads would have to fight the Germans in the sky, but I didn't want to say that out loud. Violet had to be a mess inside at the thought of Paul joining the RAF. "Maybe Paul will have a bit of added luck if he ends up flying one of our Spitfire airplanes we're having commissioned." With Charlie's health prohibiting him from joining active-duty service, we'd funded the purchase of two fighter planes for the Royal Air Force, naming them the *Cavendish* and the *Adele Astaire.*

"God help us," she murmured. "But maybe, just maybe, this will all die down before war is declared."

But no amount of praying was going to help any of us, it would seem. Two days later, Britain declared war on Germany and London went dark, putting into full effect nightly blackouts. Never in my life had I seen a city without light. Drivers couldn't use their headlights—which created a whole slew of accidents! The streetlamps were doused. All windows were covered with blackout fabrics or newspapers or painted over with tar. Even smoking a cigarette outside had been deemed dangerous, because that tiny ember might attract the German *Luftwaffe* to drop a bomb.

The day after Chamberlain declared war on Germany, the bastards bombed a sloop off Scotland, the *Athenia*, filled with American passengers. But only harsh words came from the United States president, no swift action.

By Thanksgiving 1939, while my American counterparts were joining hands around a table laden with turkey and sweet potatoes, the war on my side of the Atlantic had become idiotic. The Brits were using lads like Paul to drop propagandist pamphlets over Germany to sow seeds of unrest, as if that was going to do anything to stop Hitler and his forces. How I prayed that there would be one big surge to end it all, and that they weren't using the *Cavendish* and the *Adele Astaire* to do it.

"How many is that?" Charlie asked, as I tossed yet another pair of socks into a basket.

"Thirty-nine." Horace jumped up onto the rim and fetched it. Patience, the exact opposite of her moniker, grabbed hold, the two of them making a game of tug-of-war out of my carefully knitted endeavor. "Make that thirty-eight."

I was knitting myself blue in the face, hoping to keep our men at war from cold or bloodied feet from all the marching.

"You're an angel." Charlie opened T. H. White's *The Witch in the Wood* at his bookmark, his finger skimming the page until he found the right spot.

I stilled my knitting needles and shifted in my chair to face him. "What do you think about me volunteering at St. George's Hospital? Seems the thing to do as a lady. I got in touch with the woman in charge, and she said there is a night shift available I could work. With your sisters joining up, I figure I should help, too."

Each of Charlie's sisters had enrolled in one service or another. It was high time I did as well.

"You nearly cracked your teeth on the curb last night, it was so dark on the street outside the Café de Paris." Charlie closed the book, his thumb holding his place. "I don't want you out so late, Delly. It's dangerous."

"Very true." I pursed my lips. "Not to mention I also have an inferiority complex about doing good deeds, given I'm so bloody lousy at them."

Charlie chuckled and wagged his fingers toward the basket of socks. "One would never know, given that pile. There are plenty of other women out there to do the jobs at the hospitals. You keep on knitting."

Maybe he was right. After all, they did need socks, and I was getting proficient at knitting, even if it was damned boring.

"Besides, the doctor has advised me to go back to Lismore. Says the fresh air will do me some good." Charlie's voice was full of a nostalgia I felt all the way to my bones, for the days when his energy had seemed boundless. "And the time away from the constant reminder of Nazi swine would be good for us."

"I'd like that." Somehow the winters were always milder at Lismore than in London.

We left the next morning, just in time to plan the Christmas party for the children of the employees of Lismore, which had become a yearly tradition. We took them ice-skating on the pond, and I whirled in Charlie's arms—and laughed at the expletives that came out of his mouth each time he fell. We lost count of the number of times he lost his footing, and by the end he seemed to be doing it on purpose.

Life felt almost normal in those moments.

Almost.

The ensuing winter was bitter in both temperature and mood. The British navy rescued some wretched seaman prisoners from a Nazi hell ship—the living conditions so inhumane that their chances of survival were slim; hence the naming of the vessels. Three hundred poor souls had been locked away in misery. Try as they might, the German navy was no match for us on the seas. Already we'd sunk several of their ships, which would hopefully save more British lives.

Letters from Freddie and friends in the States talked of life as usual. It was madness what a simple ocean could mean between countries—nonchalance and terror. Despite my misgivings, I missed America for the luxuries it still provided. While we had a ration on clothes here, my friends in the States seemed to be living the life of Riley. Of course, thoughts like that only made me feel guilty. People were suffering and I was worried about fashion.

By the summer of 1940, as I watched the goats roaming our Irish fields, I realized how utterly unimportant my life had become. I'd been hiding in Ireland while the rest of the world went war-mad. My beautiful Paris was taken by beastly Nazis, who were stomping their foul-smelling feet all over the ancient pavements. Rumors of the Nazis turning guns on women and children in other parts of the world and torturing people had spread far within our inner circle. Hitler appeared hell-bent on exterminating an entire band of humanity, as if those of Jewish descent were nothing more than rubbish. If I came face-to-face with a Nazi, would they see through my celebrity past, the "Lady" before my name, to the layers of history buried within my bones that proclaimed my Jewish descent? Would that determine my fate?

Not yet on British shores, German boots marched across Europe, guns cracking in cities and mountain passes alike. Destruction seemed the order of the day. We returned to our house in London, with wide silver balloons the size of boats floating in the skies above, meant to distract the Germans when dropping their bombs. But they didn't.

Just days later, the *Luftwaffe* planes targeted the city. Day and night in a blitz of fire and doom. Whoever said snakes couldn't fly had not seen them hiss through the darkened London skies in search of a place to bite.

The bastards bombed the hell out of London. Our friends' houses were destroyed. One minute their brick and marble edifices were standing erect, the symbols of their status, and the next they were obliterated, relegating them to the same humanity as those not born of noble blood. The Shaftesbury and Queens theatres took hits, too. The top two floors of our house in Carlton Gardens were blown clear off, and thank goodness we weren't home when it happened.

Charlie insisted we return to Ireland, where Mother had arrived, a comforting balm for the losses, the fear. Socks were no longer enough. I put myself to work, organizing with the farms surrounding Lismore to harvest food for Britain. Drove a tractor myself and chopped hay.

My fingers were covered in blisters and calluses and the muscles and bones of my body ached like they hadn't since I'd been dancing one hundred sets a week. It was good work, work that would help those in England. I was doing my bit.

We sent our staff to see the new Charlie Chaplin picture, *The Great Dictator*, in which the comedian played a version of Hitler. They said it was a scream, and a stroke of genius, but I couldn't bring myself to see it.

I arranged with the Irish Red Cross to host a charity ball at Lismore to raise money for the cause. If I was a lady, then I had to take advantage of what my position offered. Food, money, power, and influence. Although it all seemed trivial in the grand scheme of things, I knew I was making a difference in at least some people's lives.

All we could do was pray that the New Year would bring an end to the war.

But spring held no good news for us or London. In March, our favorite club, Café de Paris, was bombed to hell, and Charlie's nephew Andrew popped the question to the Mitford girl with the dreadful family. The scandals surrounding the Mitfords only seemed to grow greater by the day. At least two of the sisters were known Hitler-lovers. In his devastation at the news of the engagement, Charlie had his will changed to completely cut his nephew out. Poor chap. He and his bride weren't to blame for the foulness of others. I'd never forget sweet Debo's telephone call, her offer of advice.

In any case, I wasn't sure what to expect when we arrived at Chatsworth to help with the war effort. Everything was so solemn. The grand Palladian house had been turned into a dormitory, with over three hundred young girls sleeping in iron beds with lockers for their things. What were once grand staterooms had been reduced to housing for the female students of Penrhos College in North Wales, which had been taken over by the Ministry of Food.

The minister himself, Mr. Woolton, had created a foul pie using rations, which the girls ate nearly thrice weekly. Potatoes, cauliflower, carrots, spring onions, and oatmeal, all cooked together in a pot, then dumped unceremoniously into a pie dish with a sprinkle of parsley, and baked with a flavorless potato-pastry crust, topped with a slimy brown gravy. It at least provided a healthful meal, but the flavor left much to be desired. However, it was far more egalitarian than the gluttony that had gone on there before the war.

Every girl in the school had what they were calling bulletproof Bibles, carrying them in their coat pockets on the way to Sunday services, as if they would stop a bullet or bomb from the *Luftwaffe*.

When the girls weren't helping with household chores and the victory garden, they practiced their typing in the South Sketch Gallery. The sounds of their clattering fingers echoed through the halls until I wanted to march into the gallery and press each of their hands flat, if only to stop the incessant noise. But I suppose learning to type was a nice distraction for the young girls, as opposed to worrying about their loved ones.

Naturally, with bathwater rations of only five inches, and thirteen bathrooms for the three hundred in attendance, the girls were allowed to bathe only twice a week, which meant that Chatsworth's scent was ripe.

A few times the air-raid warnings went off, and we ran to the back gardens, where cold aluminum Anderson shelters—which looked like cans of beans cut in half and stuck right in the earth— were supposed to protect us, though I found it doubtful that the thin structures would stop a bomb.

Less than two weeks later we made our way to London, staying with friends because our house, like so many in the city, had yet to be repaired. One evening we even attended a party at the Dorchester Hotel on Park Lane, where the basement gymnasium and Turkish baths not only provided a safety shelter but were also festively decorated. Massive chandeliers lit up the windowless underground club, and jazz musicians played their hearts out on the makeshift stage. Everything felt almost as if it were at prewar levels of gaiety, except for the uniforms worn by most of the men and even many of the women. We all wanted to forget for a while that war had ravaged so much of our lives.

"You are absolutely dashing," I said to Charlie as he twirled me under his arm. For once, he'd decided not to drink when spirits were presented, and I couldn't have been happier.

The night was full of magic, and if I closed my eyes we could almost be whisked back to the time more than a decade before when we'd danced in Paris.

Charlie pulled me close, his lips by my ear, and I sighed at the pleasant sensation of being held in his arms, wooed by his touch. "Oh, my darling—"

But his words were cut short by a deafening boom followed in quick succession by violent shudders of the entire steel-and-concrete structure. The lights went out. We lost our footing, tumbling to the floor like the others as tiles fell from the ceiling along with the chandeliers. Glass shattered all around us.

Charlie grabbed my waist, sliding me on my rear to a table for cover, shards of glass nicking our skin with vicious stings. People screamed and sirens pulsed in the haze. I tucked myself into a ball, trying to quell the vicious trembling of my limbs. There was only one thing that could have caused that boom—*a bomb*.

While we were down here dancing, and I was reminiscing about the past, the *Luftwaffe* was attacking the city.

Charlie called for our friends, his voice calm despite the chaos. I breathed a sigh of relief when I heard their faint, buoyant replies. The shuddering of the building stopped, though the cacophony did not. I peered into the darkness, trying to make out the damage. Around the perimeter, flashlights flickered on, showing in snapshots the horrific extent of it.

"We have to get out of here!" I shouted to Charlie, gripping his arm for emphasis. "We can't be buried here."

"You're right." He grabbed my hand, our palms slick with sweat and blood, and pulled me to my feet. We raced with our friends to the exit, following the waving beams of a few flashlights. Faces covered in soot, blood, and debris. The stairs appeared to be mostly spared, and we scrambled up, stumbling on bits of rubble as we went.

Out on the street we had to duck as incendiaries dropped from the sky like flaming petals. We dove into Charlie's car, where our faithful driver had waited, sweat dripping from his brow. Now he sped us away from the Dorchester toward Lansdowne House, where we were staying with friends, swerving this way and that. The entire car shook as a bomb thundered down on Berkeley Square. Until first light, we lay on our bellies, hands clutched together, in the shelter that they'd built in the garden. Miraculously, the bombs stopped just before dawn.

Shaken but alive, we left the next day for the country, only to return a few days later to watch Charlie's nephew Andrew tie the knot with Deborah Mitford at St. Bartholomew's in London, an affair with all the pomp and excess that I'd been denied. Even still, Debo was too sweet for me to hold it against her. I found it unbelievable that she could be related to so many Nazi sympathizers.

Although not all the Mitfords were pro-Hitler, her sister Unity, who was as large and blustering as anyone might imagine a Nazi cow to be, had never made her Nazi sympathies a secret. Now she was supposed to have been rendered childlike by a bullet to the brain that she put there herself, but I didn't buy it. Her mean eyes were too keen, and her words too calculated. We were at least lucky not to be subjected to Diana, who had Hitler attend her secret wedding in Germany and who was imprisoned at Holloway for conspiring with the evil dictator.

Their mother, Lady Redesdale, was especially sour in the face as she verbally picked at the eldest girl, Nancy, the authoress who'd gotten a smile out of me with her off-color book, *Pigeon Pie*, which poked fun at fascists.

I suppose, all in all, that I really did like Deborah. She was sweet and pretty and didn't seem to hold an ounce of venom. Even her father seemed like a doting old fool, though Charlie said that at one point he, too, had been a Hitler sympathizer; he'd eventually changed his mind as the war went on.

"Do you intend to go back to Ireland?" Debo asked me sweetly when the ceremony and luncheon had ended and we mingled over champagne and cake.

"We usually do for the winter." Although things had changed. At first I'd agreed that my effort in the war should be relegated to socks, but that wasn't the case anymore.

"I imagine it's lovely there, especially without the bombings." Her mouth twitched a degree, but it was hard to know precisely what she was thinking.

I nodded solemnly. We were quite lucky to have Lismore as a refuge. And I was glad my mother was there, safe and sound.

"I wonder why you keep coming back here?" Debo eyed me curiously. "If I'd a place to go that would keep my head safe, I'd rather be there than here."

Something about the combination of her words and the thoughts rolling around in my head gave me an idea. Lismore Castle *was* the perfect refuge.

That night, as Charlie and I prepared for bed, I said, "I think we should open up Lismore to convalescing soldiers or airmen."

"Oh?" He raised an eyebrow as he fluffed the pillow behind him and then settled in with a book, the latest by our friend Walpole, *The Bright Pavilion*, the fifth in his Herries Chronicles.

"If your parents can do their bit at Chatsworth, what's not to say we can't do the same at Lismore? Besides, you know Mom is an excellent nurse. She would enjoy it, I think."

Charlie set his book on his lap and looked at me then, interest and resignation in the set of his mouth. "And you, my darling saint, had wanted to volunteer at the hospital. I suppose, if we had you nursing soldiers at Lismore, at least I wouldn't have to worry about you falling in a blacked-out street. Or dodging *Luftwaffe*."

"Hopefully not. Nobody wants to see these scrawny legs up in the air." I almost pointed out that Charlie, too, wanted to do his bit but with his recent medical history had been deemed unfit to serve. Considering he'd been doing well of late, I chose not to say anything.

"I beg to differ," he teased, wiggling his brows. "I like seeing your legs up in the air."

I swatted him with my pillow. "What do you say, Charlie? Should we do it?"

"I say, Why not?"

I grinned and jumped onto the bed to give him a big squeeze. "It's settled, then. I'd like to introduce you to Nurse Delly."

"Well, now, Nurse Delly, I've a wound right here that needs tending . . . and need I repeat I wouldn't mind one bit seeing those famous legs?"

CHAPTER TWENTY-ONE

VIOLET

THE LIMELIGHT

Shakespeare said it best in *As You Like It*:

> All the world's a stage,
> And all the men and women merely players . . .

After a lengthy run of *Lady Behave*, following the brief shutdown of theatres at the start of the war, the darling of East End has been called up to play another role in this war of which she could not disclose, leaving London bleaker than it already was. While we are sad to say goodbye for now to one of the greater playhouse geniuses, we pray for a swift victory and an end to the war, anxiously awaiting the day we don our theatre finery and once more enjoy the fruits of Miss Wood's brilliant performing.

In other starlet news, it has come to our awareness that a certain lady of the stage has also been called to action, caring for our wounded soldiers and airmen in palatial style. We heard the prize for recovery was a waltz before send-off.

September 1941

Though calendar might have promised it was summer, but the world seemed to have forgotten. The sky over London had been bleak, draping its darkened clouds over top of the bombed-out buildings and gutted streets. Even in the country, England seemed to have forgotten the months, as the end of summer turned into a dark autumn.

Children had been shipped out of London for safekeeping, a few joining Violet's aunt and son in Perth. Her aunt kept her well up-to-date on their safety, and though Violet had given her son away, she was relieved to know he was thriving and not in danger.

Over the past years, Violet had continued to act onstage. Performing even during air-raid warnings. Guests were free to leave to seek shelter or stay and enjoy the show. When so many warnings passed without them being hit, Violet grew cocky, as did the rest of their crew.

Then the moment they'd thought would never come did. An air-raid siren wailed, and they played on at the encouragement of the crowd, singing louder. Until the building shook violently. A wave of heat hit them as the doors to the theatre burst open. Particles of dust and wood hit their faces. All the players dropped to the floor, and the audience went mad with fear as they tried to rush out of the building. People were trampled in their haste to get away. In the end, the damage had mostly been done to the front of the theatre, but it was enough to knock some sense into Violet.

Pris, too, had been skirting danger, with many near misses, including a bomb dropped right outside Foyles Bookshop on Charing Cross Road. Her employer, Mr. Foyle, treated the city workers to sandwiches as they built a bridge over the crater so eager readers could still come in to purchase books. Every day Pris had crossed herself when she walked over that bridge, praying that she'd walk back over it at the end of her shift. The building itself was lined with sandbags filled with old books, and the roof papered with copies of Hitler's disgusting manifesto, *Mein Kampf*, in the hope that the *Luftwaffe* would avoid the shop because of the books, and at least it was a great big "bugger off" to the dictator if they didn't. Nonsense, of course, because the pilots wouldn't be able to see the minute details of what they were bombing. Coordinates and light seemed to be the only thing they navigated by.

So there they'd been, working like mad, the both of them, to keep people in London entertained while the men were off fighting the bastards in the sky. Able-bodied women without young children were being conscripted into service at home and abroad. It had been lurking in the back of the Wood sisters' minds that it was time to do something to aid in the war effort besides provide entertainment. And then came the telegram.

Violet had ignored the knot of tension building behind her eyes as she read the telegram stating that she and Pris were being conscripted into the Royal Ordnance Factory (ROF) service and were to report to ROF Rotherwas in Herefordshire, along with further instruction about their housing billet.

Inside their rented flat, Violet had kept her voice calm, hoping not to worry her sister. "We'll be together in a munitions factory."

"Munitions?" Pris had plucked a plate from beneath a napkin and set it at Violet's place at the table. "I suppose we should be happy it isn't the fields, like Caty, else the country would be in grave danger with your black thumb."

Violet had snorted, handing her sister the telegram, grateful that they'd remain together. "I am most assuredly not fit for the Land Girl Army. Caty, however, seems to be thriving." Violet could barely keep a houseplant alive, let alone work as a farmer.

So now here they were, munitions women, billeted in a house in the country with two others. Violet rubbed the sleep from her eyes, watching as her sister tried determinedly to snooze for a few more minutes. If she'd been sent here without Pris, it would have been misery, every second spent in worry.

Performing had for a time raised morale and that had seemed good enough for her, but now she was helping fight back. Actually doing something that would make a difference. Every shell she touched was going to take the life of a German who'd tried to kill her friends and countrymen. An enemy who'd bowed to the man who desired to oppress entire communities. Sadly, it was also entirely possible it would take the life of an innocent, as had the German bombs dropped on Britain. But Violet liked to think British pilots had better aim.

She and Pris along with the other women at the munitions factory were doing their bit to make a difference. Daily the "munitionettes"—a name coined during the Great War—in the factory were given pep talks about how the lives of the soldiers depended on them. It was enough for Violet to think about Paul being protected by the munitions she helped create.

With Paul having joined the RAF, she thought making bullets and bombs would be the best way to help him fight the Nazis, end the war sooner, and get him home so they could finally get married. And she was going to demand it this time. No more waiting around.

Though the shifts at Rotherwas were long, Violet walked along the River Wye that bordered the estate when she could. One could never tell that this had once been a grand family estate, considering there were twenty-six sheds built for filling the munitions, more than eighty air-raid shelters, offices, and police and fireman huts. Rotherwas had been used by the Canary Girls during the Great War, too, and every day Pris and Violet checked themselves to see if their skin and hair were turning as yellow as the women in the First World War from handling the Lyddite and TNT that went into the munitions. So far, they each had only a lovely shade of lemon on their fingers and nails, despite the gloves and scrubbing after every shift, but their hair had remained dark.

There were thousands of women there, working in twelve-hour shifts. Those who couldn't billet in town or in a nearby town slept on barracks-like cots that Violet imagined Paul camped out on when he wasn't flying over enemy territory.

For their shifts, they dressed in boiler suits and rubber shoes, their short hair tucked up under felt hats—because one loose strand of hair could cause an explosion. They worked until their yellow-tipped fingers were numb, fitting exploders to shells, then clearing the screwheads and gauging the depth before inserting the detonator. One wrong move and the entire thing could blow up in their faces. Violet never forgot how incredibly dangerous their mission was.

Once the shell was assembled, they stenciled the destructive marks on it and rolled it onto the cart, complete. When her supervisor wasn't looking, Violet put a tiny white *V* under the mark, so if Paul ever saw it he would know it was Violet who'd made the shell, but anyone else might get a kick out of thinking it meant *Victory*, which it did. Some of the other girls would slip notes into the cartridges, telling the boys abroad that they were brave.

Violet got dressed and shook her sister's shoulder, then meandered down the narrow stairs to where their landlady—ironically, named Miss Beech, like their landlady growing up—would serve them breakfast, or, rather, dinner. This week they were working the night shift at Rotherwas, having worked the day shift the week before.

Pris joined her and they ate pease porridge in silence. When they were through, she scraped away the remnants into the bowls that Miss Beech set aside for her dogs. Although the fare was reminiscent of what Mum had made them back in Hoxton, it was filling, and, despite the rationing, they still had plenty to eat. Miss Beech was an avid gardener, so much so that she'd even started to sell or trade some of her extra bounty with the other women in the village. Violet and Pris were lucky to be where they were; besides, it was very close to the factory, and a lot of the girls they worked with spent hours on the train commuting.

They weren't the only women billeting at the house. Two other girls—Sarah and Mary, sisters from the East End working at the factory—had been placed there as well. They were closer to Pris's age, and worried for their brothers, who were soldiers. Their mother and father had been killed when a bomb fell on their house.

The four of them shared the two spare bedrooms upstairs, while Miss Beech occupied a room on the main floor. Taking care of the tenants allowed Miss Beech to remain out of factory work, which she said suited her well enough. She made them breakfast and supper each day, and set up their twice-a-week bathing schedule. On Sundays, after they all trekked to the church service—if they weren't working—Miss Beech made them some sort of treat, whether crunchy biscuits sweetened with a bit of beet juice or a potato-crust pie with apples from the trees in her yard.

Violet put the bowls out for Miss Beech's dogs, noting that if she and Pris didn't hurry the sun would set before they got to work, and she hated walking in the dark.

"Ready?" Violet asked, eyeing Pris, who was cleaning up the table where they'd eaten.

"Yes." Pris always managed to look bright-eyed despite the hard labor and scarcity of sleep.

They trudged up the road with the other women in the village who were either billeting or residents. Nearly to the gate, a loud explosion sounded in the distance.

"The Germans!" one of the women shrieked, causing mass panic.

All of them ran for the ditches at the sides of the road, diving for cover in the few Anderson shelters that had been buried there in case something like this happened.

The earth was still warm from the day, though the sun was setting, and Violet thrust her fingers into the ground, dirt filling beneath her fingernails. Was this what it was like for the men at the front? Diving for cover with soil pressed into their palms?

"It's not even full dark yet," Pris said. "They've bloody doubled the size of their bollocks about when they drop."

Violet nodded. They'd been warned of the risks of working in the munitions factory, told that if the Germans found out the location they would blow them all to smithereens. They were sworn to secrecy about their methods and schedules, but everyone in town knew what they did. Hell, most of the townsfolk were the ones doing it. And those who weren't billeted right there came from the surrounding towns, some commuting as much as three to four hours each morning and night. All of the county knew what happened here, if not the country.

Violet peeked up toward the sky, noticing the lack of buzzing that indicated *Luftwaffe*, as well as the lack of an air-raid siren wailing.

"That's odd." She squinted at the sky, as if that would help her hear better. "I don't hear anything other than shouting from the factory."

The rest of the women peeked up, listening and then nodding, the murmur of their agreement resounding through the ditches.

Slowly they climbed from their makeshift shelters and looked toward the factory, where dark smoke curled toward the sky. There was no doubt an explosion had occurred. *My God*. But it wasn't from the *Luftwaffe*. Not yet. Even still, it was just as dangerous.

Violet took off at a run toward the factory, fearful of what they'd been told since day one—a loose piece of hair, a sneeze, the wrong calculations in the chemical, a day of bad luck.

As they drew closer, they could see that one of the filling sheds where she and Pris normally worked was ablaze. Firemen carried their stirrup pumps and buckets, propelling water onto the flames, but it did no good. The explosion had caused the rest of the shells inside to detonate one after another, pushing the firemen back and making the blaze grow larger. Uncontrollable flaming arms undulated in the air and out to the sides, a fiery toddler in full tantrum.

"What happened?" Pris asked a woman crouched on all fours, her clothes a mess, wiping her soot-smeared brow with a handkerchief.

"Not sure, but they thought it might have been one of the milling machines overheated and caused the shells to detonate. It had been wonky all day, but the sup wouldn't let us turn it off." She started to hack a cough, as tears made flesh-colored streaks in the soot on her cheeks, and Pris attempted to soothe her.

"How many . . . were left inside?" Violet didn't want to ask the question, her mind automatically spinning visions of what had transpired.

"Only a handful, as far as I know." Fresh tears fell from her eyes. "Shift change and all that."

Pris's gaze met Violet's, the fear on her sister's face something foreign. Since the moment of their mother's passing—hell, the moment of Pris's birth—Pris had made the world bend to her will as much as any penniless girl from Hoxton could. But this was something she couldn't work around and fight against. Accidents happened. And here, at Rotherwas, the accidents were deadly.

Violet put her arm around Pris's shoulders and led her away a fraction. "Do you want me to tell the sup you're sick? You can go home and rest. I'll work a double if it makes him happy." With the rest of the sheds unharmed and work to be done, they wouldn't be shutting down.

Pris shook her head. "No. I'll be fine. I can't turn chicken and run when women we knew, women we worked beside, just gave their lives to the cause. I can't honor them by disappearing."

She was right. Their comrades in munitions work were casualties of this war and they both owed it to them to stay and help.

Violet let out a long breath and pressed her cheek to the top of her sister's head, the same way she had a decade ago when they'd been left alone to fend for themselves in this world. "Sometimes I forget how smart you are."

"I did work in a bookshop," Pris snorted, having grown quite adept at making light of situations.

Violet let out a one-syllable laugh. "And as we all know, that makes you genius level, as far as Woods go."

"Mum certainly would have thought so. Told me to get my highfalutin' head out of the bloody clouds." Pris's inflection was dry, but her body trembled slightly as she pulled away and made a show of fixing her hat. As if straightening her cap could somehow straighten out this mess.

"Similar to her telling me to get my fancy good-for-nothing twinkle-toes out of the bloody dancing shoes. If only she could see me now. She'd probably think the rubber boots they have us wear were high fashion."

The sisters laughed quietly, and Pris wiped at her tears. It felt good to joke about the pain of the past in order to mute the pain of the present. It certainly beat sobbing.

"Well, big sister, we'd best get to it. No better way to feel better than to be the cause of some evil Nazi's end." Pris straightened her shoulders, the armor back in place.

Violet grinned, emulating her sister's movements, and surprised at how stacking her spine made her feel more put-together. "Like I said, genius."

October 1942

The unread letter—heavily redacted—trembled in Violet's hand. "Pris! It's about Paul."

The water splashed in the small tub behind the makeshift curtain, where Pris bathed. "Read it to me." Her sister's voice was even, though there was the faintest sharp edge to the first syllable.

Violet's gaze impatiently skimmed the tattered paper, of which pieces had literally been cut out, including all the important details. Why the military felt the need to read all correspondence was understandable, but why cut from it even the most mundane things? Nearly half the letter was cut out, leaving the paper looking like a maze of thin, flat strings magically connected.

Violet's voice was rushed as she tried to quell her own panic. "Something about a dancer and a castle. The balloon popping, and needing a nap with the sheep."

"What in the world?"

Violet nodded, though her sister couldn't see her. "I think it's code. A dancer, a castle, sheep."

"There's only one person we all know where those three things fit—Adele."

"Yes. It has to be. They cut out so much, but I'm guessing he wrote 'a dancer' and a 'castle' and the 'sheep' so I would know he meant Ireland. Lismore."

Oh, how she wanted to book passage right away to get to Paul. She was nearly fainting with relief to know that he was alive, especially after she'd feared him dead when news had come of many airmen being shot down, Paul's letters coming few and far between.

"Vi? You still there?" More splashing, as if Pris was about to climb from the tub.

"Don't get out," Vi rushed to say. "I'm still here."

That night over a small cuppa, she penned a letter to Paul, hoping it would reach him at Adele's castle, then settled into bed with one of the books she'd borrowed from the makeshift library at the factory.

The following morning she stopped at the post office on the way to her shift, and the postmaster waved her down.

"Telegram for you, Miss Wood."

With shaking hands, Violet accepted the yellow note, the blocky black letters blurring in a sudden rush of emotion. Telegrams nowadays only brought news of loss. Never one to have the patience not to look, she sucked in a breath and focused on the words. Prepared for the worst.

PAUL WITH US. RECOVERING WELL. COME STAY TOO. DELLY.

Violet's knees buckled at the words and what they meant, her hand trembling so hard that the paper crinkled. Relief flooded her at the confirmation that Paul was with Adele.

How she longed to drop everything now and run to Ireland. To scoop up Pris and say *The hell with this, let's go be with the ones we love far away from anything that could hurt us.* But the fact was that she might be able to request a day or two of leave, but nothing long enough to make the trek. She'd have to turn around halfway to get back in time for her next shift, which made visiting impossible.

"I need to send a telegram," Violet said, approaching the desk.

The postmaster nodded, sliding her the form to fill out.

THANK YOU. CAN'T COME. CONSCRIPTED. MUCH LOVE. VI.

She prayed that Paul would understand that her hands were tied, and made a vow that when this war was over she was going to make her way to Ireland to stay with Adele, because she'd been invited and had to decline so many times.

The following day, she received another telegram.

UNDERSTOOD. TAKING GOOD CARE OF HIM. WE MISS AND LOVE YOU. DELLY.

After their shift that night, Violet lay in bed, reading the same page repeatedly because she couldn't concentrate. Then the door bounced open and Pris was there, grabbing her hand, forcing her to sit up.

"Downstairs with you." Pris's tone held no argument, reminding Violet of their mother ordering them out of bed on the coldest winter mornings.

"I'm tired." Violet drew out the syllables in the same whine she'd tried on her mum all those years ago. With the same chance it would make a spit of difference.

"You won't be when you see what I've done."

That got Violet up, having memories of some of the pranks that her sister had done in her youth, thinking they were funny—face cream in her dance shoes was decidedly not amusing. "Please tell me that Miss Beech is not going to toss us out."

"She isn't." Pris's smile widened, filled with gleeful anticipation. "Come on."

Violet followed her sister down the stairs, the sounds coming from the front of the house unfamiliar. Gathered in the small sitting room were Miss Beech, Sarah, and Mary.

"We wanted to cheer you up." Miss Beech held up a dusty bottle of wine, and Mary presented her with an old Victrola that Sarah had pulled from the attic, along with several records.

"What better way than to make the sitting room into one of the clubs you used to visit before the war?" Pris exclaimed, clapping her hands.

"I . . ." Violet was struck with emotion, her throat blocking her words from exiting the way the guards at Buckingham Palace obstructed the uninvited.

"Because you've made it your mission to see that we're all happy, and now, when we know you want nothing more than to be with your wounded airman, you're here still putting up the good fight." Pris grabbed hold of Violet's hand and forced her into a twirl, her brushed-under bob loosening to kiss the sides of her face.

"You've taken such sweet care of my Lady and Belle, you're worth celebrating," Miss Beech said, referring to the giant, thick-furred hounds that Violet gave all the scraps to.

Sarah and Mary said similar nice things, warming her heart. She'd not realized until that moment that she might be making a difference in other people's lives besides the ones whose lives she consciously worked to improve—Pris, the airmen, the cast of a show.

Joy clawed its way past melancholy and Violet put her arm around her sister's shoulders, hugging her. "Well, then, if we're to make this into a makeshift dance club, I suppose you'll all have to learn some steps."

"Oh, you mean like this?" Pris struck a pose before doing a full shuffle step and twist, complete with stage smile and wiggling jazz hands.

The move was a complicated one, and Violet was left dumb-struck. "My goodness, where did you learn that?"

Pris laughed and tugged at the end of Violet's hair. "You're kidding, right? I grew up watching you dance my whole life."

"I didn't realize you were paying attention."

"You're hard to miss." Pris winked.

"Show us," Miss Beech implored.

And Violet did, teaching them all the steps until they were laughing and sweating and the last dregs of the wine had been sipped. With every move, her feet had come alive, finding the old rhythms as if she'd never stopped.

"I've another surprise," Miss Beech said. "We all pooled our rations, and I made a cake."

"A cake?" Violet's mouth watered at the sweet syllable; no other senses required.

"Yes. Now, it won't be the same since we had to use margarine instead of butter, and probably half the sugar I normally would, not to mention it's half potato flour, but the strawberry jam in the middle is quite good."

"I am sure it will be heaven," Violet said. Pris, Sarah, and Mary loudly proclaimed their agreement.

Miss Beech served her makeshift cake with a dollop of cream on each slice, and they devoured every delicious crumb with their eyes closed in pure delight and hums of pleasure from every throat.

"This was truly what I needed." Violet set down her plate and met each woman's gaze. "I've not danced in ages. Nor had such a good time among friends."

"We all needed it." Pris reached for Violet's hand and squeezed, her eyes conveying her affection. "Even if we didn't realize it."

Murmurs of agreement sounded.

"Oh, yes," Miss Beech said, the loudest of them all, her entire body leaning forward with enthusiasm. "How about once a week, no matter the time, we learn a new dance routine? What do you say, Vi, are you up to it?"

Violet nodded, a hopeful grin playing about her lips. "More than up to it."

Was it possible they would finally be able to carve some normalcy out of this madness?

CHAPTER TWENTY-TWO

ADELE

THE LIMELIGHT

While Miss Violet Wood is off doing her bit for the war, Miss Bridgette Hughes has made a splash on the stages remaining open. Overheard and not to be printed here were the starlet's harsh comments regarding her rivals Miss Wood and Miss Maya Chopra, the latter of whom has been seen whizzing through London behind the wheel of an ambulance for the Women's Auxiliary Service. Yet to be located is Miss Wood. We can only pray she is thriving wherever it is this war has taken her. And, well, to Miss Bridgette Hughes, all we can say is: break a leg!

In other tragic news, our theatre-loving Prince George was killed when his flight went down during a routine exercise in Scotland. Our condolences to the royal family.

January 21, 1943

Leaving Charlie behind at Lismore had been intensely difficult. But Mom assured me she'd take care of him, and the lunatic himself had waved me off with a smile, as if he were merely remaining behind to attend a hunt instead of lying there incapacitated.

"I'll be fine, darling Delly. Go to London to visit our friends, the same as we planned to do together. Ann and I will keep the castle running as smooth as ever." He'd even had the audacity to wink, as if he were only tucked under the covers as a joke.

Mom had nodded, confident with how adept she'd become at running the estate—management was her strong suit. In fact, the estate had not thrived so well since it had been bequeathed to us. By now, the airmen had gone, so at least I wasn't leaving Mom behind to tend to the wounded.

Every step toward the cab destined for the dock where I'd board a boat to England felt jarringly wrong. Charlie, now stuck permanently in bed, wistfully oblivious to and uncaring about the fact that at thirty-seven years old he had no future to speak of, insisted I leave, even threatening to toss me out a castle window if I remained behind.

His jovial attitude was most assuredly a front, and his insistence was due to guilt.

Charlie's family never visited when he was ill; in fact, they kept their distance altogether of late, angry that he'd allowed himself to succumb to the vicious lure of his vices.

I was angry, too, some days, at being deprived of a husband, a lover, my friend—but I didn't love him any less. Which made my journey to London feel more like abandonment than anything else. When we reached the train station in England, I almost turned around and got back on the boat to Ireland. But I imagined that Charlie was living vicariously through me, and I pushed my way forward on the platform.

We drew to a halt at Piccadilly, and I stepped off the train into the frigid air, pulling my fur stole tighter, feeling the loss of the great hearth in Lismore, my dogs on my feet and lap. The porter carrying my bags behind me had cheeks as red as apples and I swear his eyebrows had grown icicles. I stepped carefully forward over patches of ice to hail a taxi, at the same time as a uniformed American officer.

He swiftly lowered his arm and gestured at the cab. "My apologies, madam; please, you take the cab. There'll be hell to pay if I allow a lady to freeze to death on account of poor manners." His voice was smooth and deep, his cadence assured.

"You're American." My breath came out in white puffs of steam.

"And so are you." There was a slight twitch in his lips at the realization, and he took me in more carefully.

I grinned, friendly, as if both of us being from the States equated to camaraderie. "Lady Charles Cavendish."

"Formerly Adele Astaire," he said. There was no sudden gush, as if the knowledge of who I was would change his future, but rather like I was a curious creature to be studied.

"What a coincidence, so am I," I teased, making light of his pronouncement of my name.

He chuckled with a wag of his finger, at which I made my famous funny face. I don't know what possessed me to be so open with this man whom I'd just met, except that there was something solid about him that made me feel . . . safe.

"Colonel Kingman Douglass." He put out his hand, and I placed my gloved fingers against his palm, feeling the firm shake that was so redolent of Americans, where Englishmen would simply kiss my proffered knuckles.

"Welcome to London, Colonel," I said.

"Why, thank you, though I've been here a few months already." There was something in his stance that was at once as rigid as it was relaxed. As if his body relayed safety but he was also ready to pounce in the face of danger.

"Well, I do hope you're finding the city to be . . . I was going to say welcoming, but, given we're at war, perhaps that's not the right thing."

He smiled but said nothing.

"And where might you be headed?" I asked.

"Ah, the taxi is not for me, I'm afraid, but those gents over there." He pointed to three worse-for-wear-looking uniformed privates who were sitting on the sidewalk.

"They look to have imbibed a bit." I narrowed my eyes at the reminder of my husband, who'd been in similar situations in his day.

"Yes." The man's voice conveyed no judgment.

"It's a bit early." I bit my tongue after saying it.

Colonel Douglass smiled softly, as if he'd not noticed my sour tone, and I was grateful. "Well, to these gents, any time is a good time. And the Rainbow Corner Club serves them all day."

"The Rainbow Corner Club?"

He nodded. "Indeed, madam—my lady—"

"Adele is fine, please, Colonel."

"Then I insist you call me Kingman." He studied me with eyes that felt as if they saw straight into my soul, and I had a hard time not looking away. "The American Red Cross runs it right here, near Piccadilly Circus, on the corner of Princes and Denman."

"The American Red Cross?" I cocked my head and the taxi driver slammed on the horn, to remind us with his rude honk that he'd been waiting this entire time. "Please let those boys have it and I'll find another."

Kingman bowed his head in thanks, then hurried the three privates into the cab, stating an address and tapping the roof as it pulled into traffic.

"So, the American Red Cross has a club here for soldiers?" I pressed, a kernel of a thought sprouting in my head.

"Soldiers, sailors, and airmen like me." The way his eyes missed nothing, however, I wondered if he was more than a pilot. His behavior seemed more suited to spying. "A great club for the fellows before being shipped back to the front."

"Are they looking for more volunteers?" I tried to keep my tone neutral, but I feared my eagerness bled through.

Kingman's gaze sharpened ever so much. "I do believe they are, madam."

"Adele," I corrected.

He pressed his hand to his heart. "Apologies, Adele."

I rubbed my fingers together, trying to bring back some warmth. "I'm not certain I've much skill they could put to use."

"Didn't I see something about you being a land girl in the country?" Kingman asked.

I laughed and waved my hand dismissively. "Hardly a land girl. It was in Ireland. I initiated a minor farming project to help fill the British food stores."

"That's admirable. I'm certain they could use someone like you at the club. Maybe even to teach the men a few dance steps."

It was on the tip of my tongue to say "Oh no, I don't dance anymore." But the truth was that I hadn't been able to dance in ages because my husband couldn't get out of bed and I didn't want to dance with another. And I missed it dearly, as if I'd been stripped of a part of myself.

Besides, it was for a good cause, wasn't it?

"I would like that a lot." Although I said it softly, it was not without conviction. I was in desperate need of a nerve cure, feeling always as if I was just a few jumps ahead of a total breakdown. If I could put myself to good use, caring for the men fighting the war seemed like a good way to plant my feet on the ground.

"Well, how's this—give me your contact information and I'll pass it along for them to get in touch."

I riffled through my purse, my heart flipping at the thought of doing something else for the cause. "I'm sorry, I've not got anything to write with."

Without missing a beat, Kingman said, "No need. I've a memory like an iron vault."

"And no one's tried to crack it?" I teased, closing my purse.

"None have succeeded." He grinned, pride in that subtle curve of his mouth.

I gave him my information, and he repeated it back to me with ease.

"Someone will be in touch soon," he said, as he flagged down another taxi. "It was a pleasure meeting you, madam."

"Adele."

He tipped his hat and took my bags from the porter, loading them into the trunk himself.

"Until we meet again, Adele," he called as I waved goodbye.

I found myself eager to do so. It had been a while since I'd had an American friend to talk to, and that small conversation made me more homesick than I'd been in a long time.

But the headlines in the paper reminded me of how far away I was from New York. Yesterday a German bomber dropped his load on a school not too far from here, Sandhurst Road School. Parents were still digging for their children in the rubble. An untold number were feared dead.

What in the world had made a school a target in war? Children were innocent, harmless, and should not have been put in the middle of a war of good versus evil. But Hitler cared for no living being, no matter how small.

February 1943

Mrs. Whittaker stood before me in her starched uniform, looking me over, straightening my collar, and checking the lines of my jacket to make sure all was in order.

"Well, you turn out nice in your uniform," she said with a perfunctory nod.

"Why, thank you." I hardly think she noticed the sarcasm in my tone.

"First order of business, you'll work at the information desk with Lady Ann Orr-Lewis here, helping any lads out who need it. Pointing them in the right direction and such. This might involve a bit of shopping for their supplies, or sewing socks. You do know how to sew, correct?"

I nodded, thinking of the piles of socks I'd knitted at the beginning of the war.

"Good. Then I'll leave the two of you to it."

"I don't believe we've met," I said to Ann.

She turned a charming smile on me. "I've watched you perform. You're divine."

"Thank you."

Ann led me down to the basement, where the information desk had been placed, and we both settled behind it.

"Do you miss it?" she asked, a curious lilt to her voice.

"Only every day." I surprised myself with the confession. I knew it every morning when I woke, but to express it to a stranger was . . . different. Most people never knew when I was upset—except for my husband—as I always kept up the Good-Time Charlie routine. But over the past few years it had been harder and harder to smile.

"I'm not surprised." Ann shuffled a stack of papers and then straightened a cup of pencils. "To have succeeded and done well, and then give it up, must have been hard."

"Marriage was worth it." I kept my words even, without as much as a wobble. I wanted Ann and anyone else who might wonder to know that I didn't regret one second of my marriage to Charlie, whom I'd spoken to on the phone that morning. With his voice so full of life, it was hard to imagine that he was still lying immobile in bed.

"Not all would agree." Ann laughed, and it was in that trifling jest made mostly to herself that I recalled who she was—the rumored mistress of Prince Bernhard. Supposedly she'd already had two sons by him. Born of German descent, he and his family had opened fire on German aircraft from the palace stairs before running away to the Netherlands. I wondered if his wife, the future Queen of the Netherlands, knew of his affair. It was clear that Lord Duncan certainly despised his wife for stepping outside the marriage bed.

In any case, I'd seen the prince once at our spa in Germany with Charlie. He was very charming, so I couldn't begrudge the woman turning her eyes to him, especially if she was in a loveless marriage not of her choosing.

Ann was quick to change the subject. "Miss Kennedy will be joining us soon on shift. I believe you know her well."

"Kick?" I asked, surprised.

"Yes." Ann's voice sounded bored. "Kathleen."

"Well, that's splendid." I had thought my days would be spent with this sour lady, but to have Kick here would be an added pleasure—and a relief.

A familiar voice, low and confident, sounded behind me: "Lady Charles."

I turned to see Colonel Kingman Douglass standing proudly in his uniform, with the same piercing stare. I was also keenly aware of Ann's eyes on him.

"Colonel. A pleasure to once more make your acquaintance," I said in a neutral tone.

He grinned. "Mrs. Whittaker said you'll be offering dance lessons."

"Yes, after lunch."

"I look forward to it." He tipped his hat, and I worked to shuffle the papers Ann hadn't reached yet on my side of the desk to hide my smile.

The morning flew by, and after eating a rationed, plain lunch of smashed potatoes and sausage—I could hardly stomach the way it had congealed—I turned up at the dance floor as promised and asked the band for something more upbeat.

"You first, Colonel," I said, pointing in Kingman's direction.

He slid across the floor and held out his hands to me.

"Are you familiar with a waltz?" I asked.

"I am, but this music is a bit fast for it."

"Nonsense." I drew out the word, teasing. "The beat is what makes it more fun."

"Shall I let you lead, then?" Kingman had a knack for sounding calm despite the way his body tightened.

"I'm curious to see what you're made of, Colonel. You lead," I countered.

He gave a mock salute, his accent lighter as he proclaimed, "Order accepted."

I laughed in a way that I hadn't done in ages. "Think of it as more of a challenge."

"Ha!" Kingman twirled me into the steps, our feet flying across the dance floor to the heightened beat of the music.

At the end, when he dipped me over his arm, I couldn't help giggling in sheer joy. For all the blathering he'd done beforehand, Kingman was a superb dancer. The lads lined up after that for their turns, wanting a chance to say they twirled Adele Astaire on the dance floor.

Even Mrs. Whittaker seemed to enjoy the show, as she, Ann,

and Kick, who'd finally arrived, pulled several uniformed men out onto the floor. When my legs felt like they might fall off, I sat down, ordered a club soda with lime, and fanned my damp face.

Kick rushed over then and tossed herself into my arms. "Oh, I'm so glad to see you," she gushed.

"You are a darling." I tapped her nose. "And as cute as I remember."

"When Billy said you were volunteering here, I couldn't wait to get back. I'm so glad to see a friendly face." We both looked in Ann's direction.

"She's a bit of a viper, isn't she?" I asked.

"I'll say." Kick rolled her eyes.

"Lady Charles, would you sign this letter for me?" one of the lads asked, pushing a long letter across the table. "It's for my mom back home, and she sure was a fan of yours."

"I'd be delighted." I took his offered pen and scrawled my name at the bottom, in parentheses adding "Fred's sister."

That seemed to start a trend, and the lads lined up for me to sign their letters until late afternoon, when one of them asked me to write one myself. As it turned out, when they wrote letters home, they had to go to the post to have their letters censored.

"Why, sure," I said, true enthusiasm in my voice. "I know just the thing to make your mom smile."

Surrounded by nearly a hundred uniformed American men at once, I felt like I was in heaven. If I hadn't known I was in London, I could have been smack-dab in New York City, or even Omaha, for all it was worth.

Back again the next morning, there was a new sign over the information desk that read, LET ADELE WRITE LETTERS HOME FOR YOU. The boys lined up by the dozens, and it got to the point where I took notes on a stenographer's pad and would spend my nights at home scribbling away. When I wasn't dancing, I was writing. By the end of the week, my fingers were as cramped as my toes.

"They certainly have taken a shine to you," Mrs. Whittaker said.

"I'm merely glad I can use something I'm good at to cheer them up when they're unhappy. Being stuck here when they want to go home or even back to the front has certainly put a good many of them into a sour mood."

"You're a gem to encourage them," Mrs. Whittaker said, leaning close. "In fact, I think next week you can bypass the information desk altogether. Enough of these lads are begging for you to write their letters that perhaps it should be your sole occupation. Besides dancing, of course."

I wrote dozens of letters a week, tallying 130 before calling it quits one Friday when my eyes were crossing. While the Germans tried to tear down our resolve, I rebuilt it one dance and letter at a time.

After the Blitz two years ago, there appeared to be mostly a lull in the bombings over London, aside from the occasional raid. It appeared the giant silver balloons in the sky, the darkening of our lights, and the antiaircraft guns in Hyde Park had helped to counteract their methods, at least somewhat. Or maybe it was due to the Americans, who'd finally joined the fray in December 1941 after the bombing of Pearl Harbor. Men like Kingman Douglass and the boys at the Rainbow Corner. They were part of the reason Londoners could breathe marginally easier.

It appeared the tide of war was turning, and Germany was now more on the defensive. Tucking their tails and running was more like it.

I waited impatiently for Violet on the canteen stairs. On a whim, hoping it would work, I'd gotten in touch with her at the boardinghouse in Hereford, and invited her for a night at the Rainbow Club in London.

Although Violet's smile remained the same, she looked thinner than the last time I'd seen her, and her skin had a slight yellow tinge. She'd warned me about that, and thank goodness, because the hue reminded me too much of Charlie's jaundice and how his liver had turned even his own flesh against him.

My darling husband . . . every morning that we spoke, his voice grew weaker. And when I said that I was going to come back, he bade me stay in London.

"My God, it is so good to see you!" I squealed, hauling Violet into my arms.

"And you—look at this." Violet plucked at the Red Cross pins on my lapel, her eyes luminous. "My uniform is nothing more than a sack with legs, and here you are in a chic skirt."

"Funny how this passes for fashion these days, huh?" I smoothed my hands over the tweed uniform. "Let me introduce you to the boys."

The lads were thrilled to meet another famous dancer, and after we did an impromptu number from *Stop Flirting*, the boys begged for dances of their own.

"We'll promise you one dance, as long as you do something for us," I said, with a wink.

"Anything!" they all shouted, practically in unison.

"When I first met Violet, she was a chorus dancer, and she joined our troupe for *Stop Flirting*."

"'Nonstop Flirting.'" Violet chimed in sarcastically with what we used to call the show when our shoes were wearing thin nearly daily.

The lads got a kick out of that. "So," I said, "we're going to teach you the chorus dance."

"I will kick up my legs anytime for a chance to dance with

you two," one of the soldiers said, performing an impressive high kick.

I started to laugh, and Violet followed, the two of us doubled over in a fit and wiping away tears at the lads' antics. For anyone looking in, you'd not have known a war was on, which seemed to be the precise medicine everyone needed.

"I guess they are ready for their debut," I said.

"More than ready," Violet said with enthusiasm, slapping one of the lads on the back. "Here's what you need to do."

They mimicked our moves, with no amount of tripping or falling over unaccounted for. Even the band was missing a beat or two as they chuckled through the number at the uniformed men's frolics.

That evening, when the Rainbow Corner wound down, Violet and I bundled up and hailed a cab to the Savoy, where I had a room, since our house still lay in disrepair.

"Are you sure you don't mind me staying with you?" she asked, a worried edge to her tone.

"You got leave just for me. Of course I'm not going to make you shell out any of your hard-earned money to stay here. Besides, my suite is massive; I have one with two bedrooms since Freddie's planning a trip in May." Or in case Charlie miraculously got better and he and Mom came to London . . . wishful thinking, I knew, but I had to keep it up or else I'd break.

We changed into our nightclothes and robes, settling on the couch in front of a roaring fire, hot toddies in hand.

"How is it in Hereford?" I asked, the jovialness of the earlier afternoon disappearing as we settled in for a tête-à-tête.

Violet let out a long sigh that expressed more than words ever could. I reached over and squeezed her hand.

"Hard." Her lips formed a straight line. "Besides the normal dangers of the munitions going off, like an explosion a couple years ago, this past summer I nearly lost Pris when a *Luftwaffe* bomber dropped two loads on the site. We lost twenty-two munitions workers. Thankfully, Pris was only injured."

My heart dropped with worry. "And she's fully recovered?"

Violet nodded, though there was a pinched look about her eyes. "I wish there was some way I could get her out of there. Every day we go to work not knowing if we'll make it to the end of our shift."

"Can her injury be used as an excuse to withdraw?"

Violet shrugged. "Possibly, but Pris refuses." Her voice was tired, her shoulders drooped. I guessed from her tone that she'd already suggested it more than once. "She says they tried to kill her, and she wasn't going to let them win. Claims if she dies making only one more bomb, then at least that will be a bomb that takes a life, too."

I shuddered at the thought, and at how many young people were risking their lives to fight in a war against a madman and his thugs. It all seemed so unfair. "And you, how are you doing?"

Violet took a sip of her hot toddy and tucked her legs up under her. "I'm doing all right. I can't thank you enough for helping Paul when you did. He gushed about you and Lismore when he visited me on leave after his recovery."

"You can't imagine my delight when I saw it was him. He was banged up pretty bad, but, boy, was he a trouper. Where is he now?"

"Back in the air. I never know where. But he won't let getting blown out of the sky stop him from retaliating. What is it with the ones I love?" Violet's question came out exasperated, ending with a rueful chuckle, a shake of her head. "Seems we're all full of vengeance."

"Better than being oblivious. Some of the folks in my circle are parading around as if there isn't a war on." I couldn't keep the disgust from my voice. The number of society trendsetters who were sitting in their grand homes while everyone else did something made me sick. Even Princess Elizabeth—the young infant I'd once held grown into a teenager—was digging for victory at Windsor Castle, and rumor had it that she was gunning for a position in the ATS on her eighteenth birthday next year.

"Shameful."

I nodded, draining the last of my warm cocktail. "If only we could wake in the morning and this nightmare would be over," I mused wistfully.

Except mine wouldn't. Because even when the sun rose in the morning, making the Thames look like diamonds, Charlie was still going to be suffering, and the life I'd dreamt of living when he'd first come to see me onstage, when he'd visited me in New York, was merely a fleeting dream. As ephemeral as the wishes for a child, which had only ended in one gutting loss after another.

"It's going to be all right," Violet said, her hand grasping mine, eyes searching into my soul. The calm in her voice soothed me.

I squeezed her hand. "I hope so."

"We have to believe it will." Violet nodded. "Else there's no point in going on. Without hope we are left only with despair."

I smiled, letting out a laugh that sounded almost like a sob. "You always were more optimistic than me."

"Not true at all. I still believe that happiness is waiting for you. Perhaps at the end of this war, when Charlie can get back to the clinics and resorts, he'll be on the mend. When I first met you, Delly, you were the epitome of dreams come true."

"And look how far I've fallen." Bitterness leached into my words, hard to hide from a friend who cared little for my background, and only for me. That was the great thing about Vi; I didn't have to pretend to be someone else.

"I don't know about that." Violet cocked her head, squinting at me. "Just look at all the dreams you made come true tonight."

"Ah," I drew out. "What you're saying is that it's my time to be the dream maker instead of the receiver."

"Sure does sound lovely when you put it like that." Violet grinned and drained her hot toddy.

Well, didn't that beat all? Because it certainly did sound lovely. Perhaps things were not as bleak as I'd thought. If only I could keep my friend here with me awhile longer, to remind me of that.

CHAPTER TWENTY-THREE

VIOLET

THE LIMELIGHT

Signs of life for Miss Violet Wood! Spotted about town with Lady Charles Cavendish, who has been cutting a rug with the uniformed men at the Rainbow Corner Club. Still to be determined is where Miss Wood has been all this time. Alas, we never grow tired of seeing the two glamorous stars together. They are proof that talent is not only born to privilege, and that happiness bears fruit in the hearts of dreamers giving voice to those who might otherwise have been buried. Well, that, and the absence of a significant other . . .

Summer 1943

The deep-bone chill of winter ebbed into a soggy spring, and by summer Violet was ready to leap for joy when she was no longer frozen or wet. Trudging to work day after day in the snow, ice, and rain had been absolute misery. Not that she'd been unused to that in London, but at least there she had doorways she could hop into if it got too bad, and the Tube and its stations, which offered some respite between jaunts.

Walking along the dirt road for the mile or so to Rotherwas was decidedly colder than huddling with dozens of bodies on the train.

As Violet entered the changing room to put on her unform, Pris chatted happily beside her about the latest antics of Lady and Belle, who'd taken it upon themselves to sneak into her room whenever she was sleeping and slowly nudge her out of bed.

Violet was on the last button of her boiler suit when Nora Davis approached and leaned against the lockers, a grin on her face, looking in Violet's direction.

"Good morning, Violet."

Violet glanced over Nora's shoulder toward where Pris was standing, an expression of *I have no idea what this is about* on her face.

"It is indeed, Nora. To what do we owe the pleasure of hearing your voice live and in person instead of on the radio?" Violet kept her tone light and friendly.

Last summer, a few months before the bomb fell on Rotherwas, Nora was recruited from her position in one of the office huts—after having traded up from a munitions position to that job—to become a radio announcer. Rather than filling shells with explosives or filing paperwork, she spent her shifts playing music for the factory workers, especially enjoying their requests, and announcing the news for those on shift who'd missed the BBC broadcasts.

"There's been a lot of talk about you lately." Nora wiggled her eyebrows as if she knew something that Violet didn't.

Violet flicked her gaze away, afraid she'd reveal something she shouldn't. "Me? Why me?" She folded her clothes, tucking them into her locker, then tugged out her rubber shoes and cap.

"You've made a couple of trips to London to dance with Lady Charles Cavendish."

When Violet didn't confirm or deny, Nora prompted, "Adele Astaire."

Violet nodded then, unsure of where this was going and what would have made Nora come all the way down here to talk about it while she was getting dressed for her shift.

"You're holding out on me, Violet." Nora's voice was teasing, but with an underlying hint of pressure. "How do you know her, anyway?"

Violet shrugged, trying to think of the right thing to say. Only the ladies in her boardinghouse and a few others knew about her dancing. Sure, she'd had some big gigs, but she'd not made nearly the name for herself that Adele had.

And, of course, she'd not made an announcement when she came to work at the factory, letting everyone know that she was *the* Violet Wood, the darling of the East End. Without the makeup and flamboyant clothes, she was just like everyone else. Here they were all the same, women doing their bit to help the lads in this fight against a tyrant. "We met when she was starring in *Stop Flirting*."

"Well, do you think she'd come on the variety show?" Nora didn't have to add *pretty please* at the end of her sentence, because her face was doing all the pleading.

"She's off to Ireland for a few weeks to see her husband; maybe when she returns." Violet wasn't about to go into detail about poor Charlie.

"Wow, you know her that well, eh?"

Violet shrugged, not wanting to brag.

"Violet is being modest," Pris piped up, leaning in over Nora's shoulder. Before Violet could shush her sister, Pris added, "She's a famous dancer, too."

The way her sister said the words in the present tense sent a tingle racing up Violet's spine. She was a dancer, *still*. Even if it was only to sway her hips as she hung laundry on the line, or, when she tossed sticks to Lady and Belle, to do a triple step and turn to see them sail, or to provide dance lessons to the women whom she lived with.

"Oh, really?" Nora pushed off the locker with her hip and arched an eyebrow. "Then, if Lady Charles is not available, perhaps *you* could step into her place."

Violet paused, rubber shoes dropping to the floor with a thud. "Me?"

Nora nodded, her gaze taking Violet in with a new interest. "Of course. If you were a dancer, and you danced with *the* Adele Astaire, then you'll be perfect. We've already had Gracie Fields and Anna Neagle, to name a couple. The entertainment managers get really excited when we have interesting people on to interview or perform. You'd be the perfect addition."

Violet had met Anna Neagle, who'd gone by Marjorie Robertson back then, when she starred in *Wake Up and Dream* with Tilly Losch and Jack Buchanan in '29, though she'd been aware of Anna long before that, when she'd seen her dance in *Bubbly*. Gracie, however, she'd heard of only through gossip, mostly that Adele had done a better job of singing "You're Driving Me Crazy" when she'd performed it.

If Violet did this, there'd be no going back. Everyone at the munitions factory would know who she was. She'd not even be able to eat a simple meal without drawing the attention of someone. Then again, she felt as if she'd been repressing a side of herself for so long. She wanted more than anything to perform again. Keeping her tone even, and all her excitement tucked into the back of her throat, she said, "All right, I can give it a whirl."

"Perfect!" Nora exclaimed with three rapid claps. "Come after your shift, and I'll be ready."

Violet touched her hair, which was about to be flattened by the cap that she had to wear. "I'll look a fright."

"It's radio, silly, not a picture." Nora rolled her eyes and gave her a pat on her arm, as if to say that Violet had been stuck in a box too long.

Violet let out a short laugh, realizing that although she'd be performing it would be entirely different. Like a stage with the curtain down, and the audience only able to hear what was happening behind the thick velvet.

"You don't happen to have any tap shoes, do you?" Nora wrinkled her brow.

Violet's belly flopped, and she worried that she was about to lose her chance. "I didn't see fit to bring any." And who would? She'd come to Hereford to build bombs, not dance.

Nora waved away the worry with a negligible *psh*. "No bother, we'll get some. The listeners love to hear dancers tap."

"I appreciate that, thank you."

"No, thank *you*, Vi. You're saving me and the listeners from a boring bit that my manager was trying to push for tonight." Nora grinned like a cat who'd managed to break open the canary's cage.

"I'm looking forward to it." All through her shift, as she filled one shell after another, Violet could think of nothing but which dance number she'd perform. Distracted, she tripped over her own foot when Wolf just happened to be walking by. Wilf Bowen, also known as Wolf, was the supervisor who ran the sheds like a wolf on a bone—necessary, of course, given the dangers.

"What the hell do you think you're doing, Wood?" he snarled.

"I . . . tripped."

Wolf frowned so hard that the hairlines on either side of his head nearly touched. "Get it together or the whole fecking place will blow. Is that what you want? To kill us all?"

Violet shook her head, swallowing nervously and pushing out her words. "No, of course not."

Wolf flung his arm in the direction of the washrooms. "Go wash your face and come back with steady feet."

Pris eyed her as she went, mouthing, "Are you all right?"

Violet simply nodded and hurried into the washroom. She peeled off her gloves, setting them aside as she turned on the taps, splashing cold water on her face. In the mirror she could see that the hue of her once-dark hair had lightened to a burnt orange in places. Cost of the chemicals that they handled day in and day out. Water dripped in slow rivulets down her sallow skin, cutting paths along her jutting cheekbones. The hollows of her face were more prominent from food rationing. She looked sickly. The price of war was more than the boys they lost abroad; those at home lost themselves, too.

Violet let out a disgusted grunt. Those thoughts made her feel incredibly selfish. After all, she was still alive.

She pulled on her gloves. "You're here to help Paul." It was a pep talk that she'd had to give herself more than once lately.

The rest of the shift went by, thankfully, uneventfully. Anytime she found her mind wandering, she simply snapped it back. By the end, she was exhausted, and her feet hurt from standing. The idea of strapping on a pair of dance shoes that were probably too small sounded dreadful, and yet the idea of going home without doing so was worse.

Pris, who didn't want to miss out on seeing the show live, walked with Violet to the radio hut, where Nora and several others waited.

"Perfect." Nora's radio tones were different from her conversational ones, a warmer timbre. "Ladies and gents, allow me to introduce you to the wonderful, the spectacular . . . Violet Wood."

There were a few blank stares, which only made Violet more self-conscious, until one of the men stepped forward and grasped her hand in his. "I saw you in *Stop Flirting* when you performed in Liverpool."

"Oh, but how could you recognize me being so far in the back?" Violet teased.

The gentleman's eyes were warm. "You were the best dancer on-stage."

Taken aback, Violet shook her head. "Certainly not the best."

"Oh, well, if you're referring to Fred and Adele Astaire, they're otherworldly, but for all the others onstage, you were closest to the sky." The older man winked, patting her hand.

Violet laughed, recalling all the reviews that she and Adele had read and gotten a good chuckle over, when Violet was being referred to as an angel. "You flatter me too much."

"Only enough to get you smiling."

"You have succeeded in your mission."

She changed into the tap shoes provided, which were only a tiny bit snug, and with a few practice moves the muscles in her legs came alive.

"Ready?" Nora asked.

Violet drew in a deep breath to calm her nerves and nodded. They directed her toward a small, square wooden platform with a microphone propped in front. After she was introduced, they started playing Glenn Miller. Violet grinned at the memory of dancing to his big-band music at the clubs with her friends. The steps came easily to Violet, and she tapped in time with the melody. Next came the familiar strains of "The Whichness of the What-ness," and as the lyrics fell with playful ease from her lips as she sang, she could no longer contain a nostalgic smile.

There were a few more numbers, and by the time Violet was finished sweat dripped down her spine.

"Miss Violet Wood, folks, absolutely brilliant," Nora said into her microphone. "Before we let you go, I must ask you one thing."

Violet drew in a deep breath and waited.

"Do you think when this war is over, you'll go back to performing onstage?"

"Without a doubt," Violet said, no hesitation. "I love performing, and I miss it terribly."

"Then I have a second question for you—will you come back on the show?"

"Yes, I'd be delighted."

"Oh, no, Miss Wood, it is us who will be delighted."

When they were off the air, Nora's manager beamed and clapped thunderously. "That is going to be one of our most popular shows, I think." His gaze skated over Violet in a way that made her squirm. She looked away, removing the tap shoes to give herself something to concentrate on. "What do you say about becoming an announcer, Miss Wood? Can't tell me you would pass it up to continue filling shells."

The invitation was so shocking that Violet's mouth fell open. Coming on the show as a guest was one thing, but to leave her position altogether? Besides Nora's show, the only other broadcast that Violet listened to was Adelaide Hall's, the dancer whom she'd seen at the Moulin Rouge back in 1932 in Paris.

"I don't—"

"Don't say no," the manager interrupted.

But Nora stepped in before Violet could get irritated with the man for telling her what to do. "You would be perfect, Violet. You have a great speaking voice, as we all heard, and you're funny. Plus, if things got boring or one of our other entertainers couldn't make their slot, you could always fill in. I, for one, could listen to you sing and watch you dance all day."

Violet swallowed, still thinking about Pris and the others. How could she abandon her sister and the rest of her new friends?

Violet glanced toward her sister, who was leaning on the door frame, nodding emphatically, lips pressed firmly over what promised to be a huge smile. "If you say no, you'll be letting Mum win."

"We can't have that, now, can we?" Violet smiled. "But what about you?"

"What about me? You aren't going anywhere, and can you imagine how much more motivated I'll be to work if you're the one talking in my ear?"

Her sister had a point, there, and it wasn't one that Violet wanted to argue with. Curled deep inside her was that itch to break free. To perform and be everything that she'd always wanted. At first working in the munitions sheds had been fulfilling, when she knew she was helping. That sense of purpose had only been reinforced when they were bombed. War work, after all, was helping to save their country and the men abroad.

But who was there for those left at home who were tired, grieving, and ready to give up? She could be their cheerleader.

They needed her.

"We need you," Pris reinforced, as if hearing Violet's thoughts.

And that was all the cajoling it took for Violet to agree.

"We split shifts into three eight-hour segments—Red, White, and Blue. Nora's on White shift. And she's one of our more popular announcers. What do you say about doing Red?"

"All right. Do the girls ever switch?"

"We do," said Nora. "And I'd be happy to switch with you anytime, if you need to."

Violet glanced at Pris one more time. "I won't be able to walk with you if our shifts don't align."

"I won't need you to." Pris grinned. "I've got the other girls at the house, plus the rest of the town, all of us trudging up the road, morning and night."

That was true. The roads were never empty.

"Brilliant," the manager said. "We'll see you here tomorrow morning."

Violet nodded, slipping into her boots, and then handing back the tap shoes.

"Keep those," Nora said, "no one here's going to use them."

"Thank you." Violet stared at the tap shoes in her hand. This wasn't the first time she'd worn someone else's footwear to dance, and she supposed it might not be her last. It was funny how life seemed to happen in circles. And for her it seemed a lot like starting over again and again, when all she really wanted was some stability and the chance to reach the top.

One step forward, and a hundred back. At least this time she was taking her steps forward again, rather than being stuck in the stalemate that had lasted for months.

Arm in arm, she and Pris made their way down the road to town and to Miss Beech's house. A few yards from the diminutive gate that opened onto the short walkway to the front door of the house, Violet stopped, and Pris turned to face her, her expression open and ready.

"Thank you, Pris," Violet said, emotion lacing her words.

"You don't have to thank me. But at some point you're going to have to realize that you're the one holding yourself back. This isn't the first time I've had to push you into doing what you want."

"But—"

Pris held up her hand. "No buts." Her voice was stern, but not unkind. "I'm a grown woman, Vi. It's time for you to take care of yourself. Again." Pris leaned forward, pressing her forehead to Violet's.

At some point Pris had grown as tall as Violet. Staring, eye level, at Violet, demanding that she do for herself.

Why did it always feel as if Violet were being selfish when she wanted to get ahead? As if she were shirking her duties to every-one else by pleasing herself?

"I can still see the guilt pounding around your skull. Tell it to go kick rocks, sissy." And with that Pris grabbed her hand and tugged her inside.

February 1944

"I've an idea," Pris said, her eyebrows bouncing. "What if we con-vince Supervisor Wolf to allow us to host a dance with the lads at Credenhill?"

Several miles down the road along the winding River Wye was a nonflying Royal Air Force base, Credenhill. Lads were com-ing from all over to train at the technical camp. Practically all of Hereford had turned to the business of tending war.

"The likelihood of Wolf allowing us to host a dance is slim." But Violet's toes still curled at the idea. Ever since she'd come home from her leave in London, she'd craved more of what she'd had, and, even though her days were filled with music now, she still wasn't fulfilled. Something else lurked deep inside, clawing to get free.

"But not entirely impossible." Pris hinted that she had an idea. "I bet you could convince him. He always gives everyone a few hours off on Sundays."

And there was the idea.

Violet chewed her lip. "Maybe I'll ask Adele to be a guest on the show, and to stay after to dance with the factory workers and RAF men. Nora would die from happiness."

Pris nodded enthusiastically and clapped her hands. "Brilliant!"

But that afternoon, when Violet tried to telephone Adele, she wasn't at her hotel, and Kick Kennedy at the Rainbow Corner Club told Violet that poor Delly had gotten a telegram from her mother urging her to return to Lismore because Charlie's health was deteriorating. He'd had an attack that had left him incoherent and his heart weakened. The physician worried that it was a heart attack or stroke.

When they'd been together the previous year in London, Delly had confessed to Violet that, if not for her job with the Red Cross and her GI boys whom she was helping, she might have gone nuts from grief and taken to the bottle like Charlie. And almost within the same breath she said that she had so much to be thankful for. It was amazing to Violet that in the face of everything, Adele remained optimistic. A Good-Time Charlie through it all, even if underneath, Violet could tell, she was hurting. Delly had to be beside herself. Violet wished she could hop on the next ferry to Ireland, to be there for her friend.

Violet wrote a long letter to Adele and put it in the post the next morning, hoping it would offer her friend some comfort.

With some haggling from Violet, Pris, and Nora, Wolf agreed to allow them to host not one dance but two—one for each shift. It worked out well for the lads at the air-force base, too, so that they could enjoy a respite between muster calls.

The cafeteria was commandeered for the dance, the tables pushed to the side, and great tubs of punch and snacks fashioned from the stores everyone pulled from their pantries.

Nora operated the radio for the first dance, and one of the other girls was taking the second shift. Pris and Violet gave her a list of all the songs they wanted played for the dance after conducting a poll of some of the factory workers.

The women were dressed in their Sunday best—threadbare getups that had seen better days. Oh, what it would be like to shop for something new when the war was over, and the fabric rations gone. Their hair was done, and they pooled their makeup so each of them could put on a full face, their lips a shade of Victory Red. The airmen wore their uniforms, perfectly pressed, their hair combed neatly and tidily, while the few men who worked at the factory donned their best trousers and shirts.

The press of bodies made the normally chilly mess hall a bit muggy, but, given the cheerful atmosphere, no one seemed to care.

Except Violet. Rather than the joy she'd hoped the dance would bring, a melancholy gripped her in a way she'd not known for a long time. It had been ages since she'd gotten a letter from Paul. She had no idea where he was stationed, and though she checked the papers daily for the announcements of those dead or missing in action, she'd not seen his name listed, and so had hope that he was still alive.

Dancing with other airmen, even if they were the young sprites training to join the more seasoned aviators, still made her sad.

Pris, fresh off a dance, rosy-cheeked and grinning, bounded toward Violet where she sipped a glass of lightly sweetened punch, leaning against the wall.

"Why aren't you dancing?" Pris's voice was labored from exertion, but with a happy note. "I'd have thought this was precisely what the doctor ordered."

Violet passed her punch and Pris swigged the rest, breathing out heavily at the end. "I need more."

They walked together to the refreshments, where Pris gulped wildly.

"Slow down, sis, before it comes back up." Violet laughed and shook her head.

Pris snorted, nearly spitting out another sip. "I'm sorry. So thirsty. Who knew dancing would make my tongue so dry?"

Violet grinned and shook her head.

"Of course, *you* would." Pris slapped her own forehead as if knocking sense into herself.

"Are you having fun?" Violet turned the subject away from herself, hoping that hearing her sister's joy would bring some to her.

"Immensely. Thank you for helping to organize it." Pris put down her cup and hugged her sister.

"My pleasure." Violet put her arms around Pris and squeezed, but her tone wasn't convincing.

"Except it's not really, is it?" Pris pulled away, searching Violet's face, a wrinkle forming between her eyebrows.

Violet drew in a long, ragged breath, not wanting to spoil her sister's fun with her bleak thoughts. "I'm tired, is all."

"Go home, then," Pris said. "You don't have a shift for another twelve hours. Get some rest. I'll walk home with Mary and Sarah."

It was on the tip of Violet's tongue to protest, when another of the young airmen approached, begging Pris for a dance. Her sister flounced off, laughing, calling over her shoulder, "Go!"

For the first time in her life, Violet walked away from a dance.

CHAPTER TWENTY-FOUR

ADELE

THE LIMELIGHT

Did you hear that? That was the sound of Miss Violet Wood on BBC radio! Hosting celebrities of all levels weekly on her show, including her rival Miss Bridgette Hughes. Boy was their conversation a doozy! While we can't fancy-foot it down to the West End to watch her live in person anymore, we can tune in to listen to the sound of her smooth, melodic voice from wherever she's gone to. Better watch out, Miss Hughes, the latest and greatest radio announcer is no wet noodle . . .

They said I should go back to London.

Back to the war work.

They said that Charlie would be fine. Charlie's raspy whisper in the dark of night as I curled up in his frail arms, "Go back to London; you're needed there," had come out more like a plea than a demand.

"But you need me." I'd tried to keep the hysteria from my voice. I'm not sure I succeeded.

He laughed softly, the sound like a scrape against his weakened throat. "Those GIs, as you like to call them, they need you more."

How could he say that? It was absolutely not true.

"I've got your mum here taking good care of me. Sweet Ann is like my own mother."

I knew what he meant, that he'd adopted Mom as his own. I had no doubt she dedicated every moment of her waking hours to his comfort. Ann Astaire shined the most when she oversaw someone else.

Charlie's birdlike hand found mine in the dark. So much had changed in the months I'd been away. The man who lay in this bed, unable to even stand any longer, was wraithlike. A ghost of his former self. In the flashes of weak smiles he sent me, the teasing in a line, I could see the way he used to be. And when he slept, though his breathing was labored, the lines of pain etched into his face faded, and he looked at peace.

Leave him now? When he needed me most?

It seemed impossible. I rested my head beside him, too afraid the weight of my giant skull would crush the delicate bones of his chest.

"Oh, Charlie," I whispered. Fresh tears leaked from my eyes.

I didn't even know what I could say, what I *should* say. I had so much pent up in and around me, like a rope that had been wound eight dozen times around my neck, my chest. I was fairly choking on it all.

"You can't leave me." The entreaty oozed off my tongue, words I'd held back for so long, fearing that if I whispered aloud what I really thought—that my husband was going to die—they would come true.

"I've got a lot of years left in me yet." His voice was jovial and out of place. Absurd, considering the truth that glared between us.

He had days, weeks—months, if he was lucky. But years? No, he'd said goodbye to any years spent with me, to a lifetime of memories we could make, when he'd picked up glass after glass of alcohol, slowly poisoning his body to the point of no return.

But I couldn't say that. Instead I gave his slim hand a squeeze and kissed the paper-thin skin of his cheek. "We'll make the best of what we have left."

"That's right," he agreed. "And you'll go back to London as planned, write some more of your famous letters home for the lads. Have a dance for me, and then come back to visit in the spring so we can watch the garden bloom together."

"I do love Lismore in the spring and summer when everything is blooming and the world smells so fine." I loved it more when we strolled together among the blooms and Charlie plucked a blossom, tucking it into my hair.

"What would you like for your birthday?" he said out of the blue, jarring.

I stiffened and tried to relax, tried not to let him see how scared I was to think of anything that was beyond this moment. "My birthday isn't for months yet."

"I know, but I'm a planner, darling. I want to make sure, with the state of the world the way it is, that your present arrives right on time."

There were so many things I wanted. I wanted my babies back, the three I'd birthed and the one I'd barely felt before he or she was gone. I wanted my husband back. To dance or walk the grounds of our slice of heaven. To play cards or backgammon, or merely to read, as we had, before the fire on so many nights. To ride horses over the moors and cheer during a race for the champions. To go to the theatre and whisper about people at parties.

I wanted all the joy and heart that I should have had. My husband wasn't even forty years old, and here he lay in a bed that would be his last, with Death itself clawing from underneath, biding its time for the right moment to snatch him away.

Was this how Mom felt when she'd left us in London in '24 to go home and take care of Pop? Perhaps that was why she insisted on caring for Charlie now. Still barricading me from the realities of pain, still guarding me from all the things that she thought the world might unfairly and agonizingly wreak on me.

I swiped at the tears now, angry that I'd relinquished these few precious moments to such dark thoughts. Death was the demon that sat in the room with us, stealing our moments as much as it would steal Charlie's breath.

"I think I should like more books," I finally said, in answer to his query about my birthday. "I'll never have a library like they do at Chatsworth, but I think we could have a smaller version. A collection of Brontë, Thackeray. Some Edith Wharton, Anthony Trollope. And, of course, Anita Loos."

"I think that is perfect. Books, it is."

"And what about you, Charlie?" I snuggled closer. "What do you want?"

"I want you to be happy." There was a desperation in his declaration, and in that moment I felt his regret gutting me.

"I already am," I lied, my voice cracking. "Tell me what to get you for your birthday this summer."

"Fresh flowers, cut from the garden, and arranged all over. Especially in your hair. I always adore when you put flowers in your hair." He touched my hair, twirling a lock around his finger. "Your first gift to me was a flower."

I squeezed my eyes shut, willing the tears to go away. "Was it?"

"Yes." His voice grew wistful and took me back in time with him. "You plucked it from a vase at the Ritz in New York and said it was a piece of the city to remember you by."

I laughed softly, afraid to jar him too much with a howl.

"I could never have forgotten you, though, darling Delly. You are the most charming woman I've ever met, and it has been the honor of my life to call you mine." He drew in a ragged breath. "And when I'm gone, I want you to keep on living, darling. I want you to love again."

My throat seized then, and I tried to swallow around the lump that wanted to come out as a wail. I wrapped my arm around his middle, wanting to mold myself against him, aware that even putting the weight of my thin arm on his belly might be too much, but, oh, how I wanted to hold him just a little while longer. To tell him there could never be another.

The following morning, Mom woke me with a shake of my shoulder. "Delly, dear," she was saying. "Let him rest."

I uncurled myself, trying not to notice how ragged his shallow breaths were. I followed Mom from my bedroom down to one of the many refurbished bathrooms. She handed me my toothbrush, a no-nonsense look on her face. As I brushed my teeth, she sat on the edge of the clawfoot tub, her hands folded casually in front of her.

"It's time for you to go back to London, my dear." Although her words came out strong, there was a brittle edge to them, and I felt almost as if she was holding her breath, bearing down for a fight.

I turned around, my toothbrush not what made me feel like gagging. "I can't leave yet," I argued around a mouthful of moistened tooth powder.

"Oh, don't be so silly." She waved away my protest, but I could see in the haunted shadows of her eyes that she did not feel as light as she tried to sound. "Charlie's fine, and Dr. White says he could remain in his present state indefinitely. Don't you lose any more sleep over it. Besides, your husband asked me to arrange your travel yesterday, and so you leave in a few hours."

"A few hours?" I dropped the toothbrush and it clattered on the tile floor. I was stunned, and exasperated.

Horace and Patience started a tug-of-war with my toothbrush, which I normally would have found hilarious, but at that instant I felt as if the world were spinning too fast and I was about to be tossed off.

"Yes." Mom handed me a towel and then wrangled the toothbrush from my dogs, rinsing it under the tap. I tried to wrap my brain around what she'd just disclosed. "Your maid is already packing your bag."

"Mother." I swallowed, feeling like I was being strangled. "No." The word came out a croak.

But she didn't hear me, or pretended I hadn't said a word, at any rate. "It's all settled, Delly. If you want to argue with anyone, you can argue with your husband, though I wouldn't recommend it in his state. He wanted this. He asked for you to leave and go back to London, where you're needed."

I heard the words she was saying, and the ones she wasn't.

Charlie wanted me to go. He didn't want me here. Didn't need me. All he wanted, needed, was for me to leave. In the last hours, days, weeks of his life, he wanted me far away.

A sharp pain stabbed within my chest. My heart was breaking.

"You promise me." I pointed my finger at her and held her gaze so that she'd understand how serious I was. "You promise me that if anything changes you will get in touch with me right away. I want to be here when . . ." But my voice trailed off. I couldn't even say the words. Wasn't supposed to say them or think them or even be living them. My young, vibrant, handsome husband was dying. And there was nothing I could do to stop it.

I'd never even imagined this moment. Thought we had decades to go before I'd have to contemplate losing him. Wasn't it enough that we'd lost our children? How I hated the world at that moment.

"I promise, my darling girl." Mom's voice grew soft as she approached me, the way it had when I was a child, missing Pop in Nebraska. She tugged me into her arms, though I resisted.

And then I couldn't push at her anymore. My arms were weak, my body limp, and I sobbed against her shoulder as I had in childhood, desperate for solace.

March 23, 1944

Mother didn't keep her promise.

Or maybe it was because, when I left in January, it was a shot in the dark to guess when my beloved would breathe his last. And, when it happened, it seemed to have happened quickly.

The telephone rang, and Mother's voice sounded endlessly distant as she said, "Delly, my darling girl." There was a beat of empty space that might as well have been a shout. "He's gone."

I'd not said a word, the receiver feeling as if it were a boulder in my hand, the weight of which I simply couldn't hold. I let it drop. And then I dropped. Sinking to the floor like the flower petals we plucked in a childish game.

Charlie's wish for his birthday came back to me then: *flowers*. He wanted flowers. Because he knew that by the time his birthday in August came around, he'd be long into his grave and that would be the only gift to him that I could fulfill. He'd known he was dying as he told me we had years and years to go. As he forced me away from him.

And I knew it then, as much as I knew my own grief now. I'd not wanted to be aware of what the future held. Wanted to believe what he told me. Wanted to imagine myself coming home in the spring, to a husband fully recovered.

I picked up the telephone, pressing the hard coldness of it to my ear. "Mom?"

"Oh, my darling. I'm so sorry." Her voice was strained, as if she was holding back tears, always strong solely for me.

My lips wobbled, and I swallowed, breathing in through my nose, as I tried to find my voice. "Thank you."

"I know I promised—"

I didn't want her to feel any worse than she must already. "I'll not hold you to it, Mom. There was nothing you could have done. Thank you for taking care of him. And for taking care of me."

It was three days before I could get back to Ireland. The Allied travel restrictions were so stringent and it took pulling so many damn strings that I could have made myself into a sailboat before the wind caught. But finally I was allowed to set sail for Ireland. For Lismore. My husband. My home.

The rest was a haze. The journey. The arrival.

I viewed my husband in bed through blurred eyes, only held up by my mother's strong arms. It looked like he was sleeping. Dressed in his nightclothes, a blanket up to his waist. His hands lay clasped over his middle as if he were simply sleeping. Hands I'd held, that had touched me, stroked my cheeks, twirled my hair, penned marvelous love letters—I wished I could have threaded my fingers with his one more time. I wished they could have been sculpted in marble so I could touch them whenever I wanted. But never would I grasp them again.

Mom led me to the drawing room and settled me in a chair.

"Charlie left you an early birthday present."

"What?" In my confusion I stared up at her, trying to understand what the hell she was talking about. Birthday present?

My husband had just *died* and my birthday was six months away.

"Look around, Delly. He did this for you."

I glanced around the drawing room for the first time, taking in the newly built floor-to-ceiling shelves stuffed full of books. It was gorgeous, incredibly thoughtful. His last gift to me. All I could do was cover my eyes and sob.

Charlie's mother didn't make it to the funeral. Claimed it was the travel restrictions, an excuse that might have been credible, but because she'd not come to see him during his illness, nor seemed to care, I didn't think it was. And given that Charlie hadn't wanted his mother to help him in the first place, I chose not to dwell on it.

In a churchyard that used to be part of the castle, we laid my husband to rest. Hundreds of people followed as he was carried on the shoulders of his longest tenured employees. With the flower-laden casket, they bypassed the hearse, unable to put Charlie down, unable to let him go. None of us were ready for this.

I could barely speak, only clutch the hands of those who gave me their sympathies.

When the last of the guests had gone, I curled up on my freshly made bed, wishing they'd left it alone so there were some remnants of his scent, even as I knew whatever scent had remained wasn't the Charlie I'd loved.

I touched his things. Found in his wallet a letter I'd written him nearly a decade ago, wrapped around the flower from the Ritz, and a picture of me, with his handwriting on the back: *My darling girl.*

I regretted so much the time I'd spent away, even knowing he'd bade me leave, not wanting me to see him as he got sicker and sicker.

Mother let me sulk a few days, bringing me warm milk and freshly made cookies, which I couldn't stomach. My dogs curled up with me, offering sweet licks and nuzzles in their own comforting ways.

Then one morning Mom came into my bedroom and, in the same brisk manner she'd used when I was a child refusing to wake for my lessons, said, "Time for you to go, Delly."

The words were an echo of her telling me to leave Lismore before.

I pushed up on my elbow, tension building between my temples. "How can you expect me to leave? I've just buried my husband."

Mom walked from window to window, wrenching open the blinds. "Because, Delly, it does no good to wallow here in your misery, when you could be making other people's lives better."

"How can I make their lives better when all I want is to lie here and die?"

Mother gasped, whipping around, pressing her hand to her chest. The look of horror on her face almost made me take back my words. "How can you say that? I never want to hear you say that again."

I covered my face with my hands, a fresh wave of tears free-falling. "He was my life."

"Oh, Delly, I know it seems that way." She came closer, sitting on the edge of the bed, her warm hand smoothing the aches from my back. "And grief has a funny way of trying to pull us under. The truth is, Charlie was only part of your life. And his passing will hurt, probably forever, but you can't let it keep you from living for the rest."

My mouth fell open, the tears momentarily stopped short from shock. I prepared to bellow my pain at her, my offense at how casually she tossed away his very existence, but my mother spoke before I had a chance.

"He loved you. And you loved him. Even beyond the pain of loss, the frustration of vices, you never stopped. That's admirable. You don't know how to do anything without doing it fiercely. Without putting everything you have behind it. And you found your match in a man who was the Charlie in your Good-Time Charlie. A man who, even at his end, wanted only your happiness. Don't put his memory to shame by becoming a shell of the woman he loved."

I fell back on the bed, my arms over my face as I heaved a sob.

"It's time to go back," Mom said again, softer this time, and I knew she was right.

I could stay here and cry for the rest of my life, or I could pick myself up and go back to work. My grief was no different from anyone else's. The entire world was weeping for a war that seemed as if it would never end.

"Fine!" I shouted to the ceiling, letting all the pain and anger out in that one roar.

"Good." Mom shuffled quietly from the room, but not without saying one final thing. "There's no one in the world like you, Adele Astaire. Don't deprive them of yourself a single second longer."

I THREW MYSELF into work, giving the world a smiling, laughing Adele Astaire, even while on the inside I grieved. I smiled for the happy bride and groom when Charlie's nephew Billy married Kick Kennedy in May. In June, I prayed our boys would put an end to the war when they stormed Normandy, and sobbed when so many came home broken or not at all.

I penned more letters that summer, assuring wives, mothers, sisters, grandmothers back in America that their soldier, sailor, airman was safe and well. And then, exactly a week after those brave men stormed the beaches of Normandy, Hitler retaliated.

Just before sunrise, with Horace and Patience tethered on their leashes, I walked in the dark, all of us needing the exercise and the brief moments of quiet before the day erupted in torrents of sound.

While Horace sniffed around a tree in Green Park and Patience nipped at his heels, the air-raid sirens wailed, breaking the peace of the morning. The dogs, never seeming to get used to the sound, started to bark madly, and I took off toward the hotel and an air-raid shelter.

Those who were out as early as I rushed in a panic for shelter, while those in uniform seemed to run in the opposite direction. It was damned hard to force men who were trained for war, who wanted to be out there fighting, underground to safety. They didn't want to go down there, they wanted to climb ladders to the sky and yank the bombs from midair.

Outside the Ritz, the windows blockaded by sandbags, I could hear the distant *ack-ack* of the antiaircraft guns firing at top speed. But something was strange about this bombing. Something none of us could grasp. Standing outside the hotel, the sun scarcely touching the horizon, our feet rooted in place, we all tried to understand what that difference was. The usual whirring sound of dozens of *Luftwaffe* was instead a strange buzzing sound. Looking up into the sky, I spotted a single airplane, which didn't look right. Its speed was faster and the body smaller, with short stubby wings compared to the usual German jets. Bright plumes of exhaust trailed behind it, making me wonder if it had been struck already by one of our own.

And then nothing. Absolute, maddening silence. The small aircraft started to plunge swiftly, menacingly, toward the city.

"My God," I choked, recalling vaguely a conversation I'd had with Colonel Douglass the day before at the Rainbow Corner about reports of Hitler's vengeance weapons—rockets that could be launched over the sea toward London. But that seemed like something futuristic, as silly as saying that one day we might fly aircraft up to the moon. Though it wasn't an entirely new concept, given H. G. Wells's destructive scenes from *War of the Worlds*.

Yet, unless there was a pilot flying that suicidal aircraft, it would seem that the rumors were true.

It felt like forever since a bomb had landed in London.

The eerie silence seemed endless until the small airplane disappeared. We waited, listening, until the silence was shattered by a thunderous explosion that shuddered the ground beneath our feet. A massive plume of smoke appeared in the distance, and I prayed that the aircraft had landed on an empty factory, no one yet having gone to work.

I clucked my tongue at Horace and Patience. "Come now, let's get you back inside." The poor doggies used to shiver at the sound of the bombs, tails tucked between their legs; now they raged at the sky, unlike the rest of us, who seemed almost immune to the noise.

Strange how, when faced with so much trauma, it feels like the norm, and the silence is the thing that makes the hair on the back of your neck stand up. What was coming next?

The answer to that was more of Hitler's advanced, pilotless bombs. The devil's goons continued to send their autopiloted missiles for months, striking without rhyme or reason. With the advances in German technology, our boys learned, too, and soon they were taking the pilotless airplanes out of the sky before they had a chance to destroy more innocent lives.

Walking through London . . . it was heartbreaking to see the changes. To stroll with my dogs past a place that I'd seen two decades before as a Bright Young Thing when hope still filled me, and find either a gaping hole in the ground or a mere shell, with the beams and cinderblock exposed. Bodies of buildings stripped bare to the skeletons. The wounded and destroyed edifices that had once made up the city that I loved.

A degree of brightness arrived in London in August, when Freddie waltzed into the Rainbow Corner as part of his USO tour for the American troops. Freddie looked thinner than usual, but so did everyone these days, with the food rations on. His uniform was crisp, and his smile a balm.

"You're getting balder," I teased, rubbing my hand over the smooth skin on top of his head that was covered by fewer wisps of hair since the last time I'd seen him.

"And you, you haven't changed a bit, you scamp."

He was the emcee for an event, and I got to watch him back-stage at London's Stage Door Canteen. The Glenn Miller band started up a set, and cheers boomed in the cramped canteen, packed so thick with servicemen, as Fred danced several sets on-stage. I missed my brother so much. I bounced onto the stage when he was finished and hugged him, joshing him as the crowd begged us to dance. He clutched my hand in his, and I returned the grasp, both of us afraid to let go. Freddie had pleaded with me to go back to Ireland, to stop working in London with all the bombings. And likewise I'd implored him to go back to the States rather than travel the world amid enemy fire. But it would seem neither of us was willing to run and hide, when we knew we could do something to improve the days of those who served. We hon-ored those who gave their everything; it was the least we could do.

"Dance! Dance!" the crowd requested of us as Freddie thanked them all for allowing him to perform. They wanted to see us do a set together, but the thought of it made my belly flip. Freddie was so much better than I was these days. Sure, I danced for fun at the canteen, at clubs, and even in my own living room, but perform onstage? It had been more than a decade since my last time, and the very idea sent my heart thudding with nerves. I shook my head but maintained my smile.

"Oh, no, we can't do that so impromptu." Freddie laughed, re-minding me of the earlier days, how he always stiffened up when asked to perform without having practiced.

I kicked my leg high a couple of times in the back, popping my hip, and teased, "There, you see; we've done it."

But back at the Rainbow Corner Club, when we weren't on a stage with hundreds of people staring, Freddie offered me his hand. "For old times' sake." He grinned.

"I wish you didn't have to leave." I placed my hand in his, trying not to sound as disappointed as I felt, and failing. "I've missed you so much."

"I've missed you, too. I wish you could come with me, sis."

We danced the jitterbug right there in front of everyone, our facial expressions exaggerated for humorous effect. Then we split apart, tugging people who had formed a circle around us onto the floor to join us, until nearly everyone there was dancing.

We danced and talked late into the night, and the way my chest felt, as if it might cave in on itself when Freddie left . . . I wasn't sure I could bear it.

When the time came, I waved him off with a brave face, choking back tears as my other, better, half gave me a mock salute.

"Stay alive!" I shouted to him.

"Keep laughing!" Freddie shouted back, knowing that for me life wasn't worth living without a good hoot.

And I tried, I really tried. For my brother, for myself. For the memory of Charlie. For the lads whom I encouraged to keep going every day. But it was something I actively had to work at. Each day, I woke up, dragged a smile kicking and screaming onto my face, shoved out laughs, and each day it was harder.

The day before my forty-eighth birthday, on the ninth of September, 1944, the telephone in my flat rang, jolting through the silence. I'd barely climbed out of my five inches of tepid bathwater after a long day at the canteen, was rubbing lotion into my legs, and considered not answering. After all, it seemed so rare that anyone called with good news these days. But after a thirty-second pause, during which I breathed a sigh of relief, it rang again. Someone was calling back.

I wrapped my robe around my still-damp body, a chill sweeping through me that had nothing to do with temperature, and padded my way to the telephone.

I picked up the receiver, not wanting to even say hello.

"Adele? It's Anne." Charlie's sister. She sounded strange. Out of breath, her throat thick.

No, God, no. I knew in that instant that something terrible had happened. "What is it?" I rushed to say. "Are you all right?"

Anne cleared her throat, as if trying to find her voice. "It's . . . it's Billy."

My tongue felt thick in my mouth. My nephew Billy was an officer in the Coldstream Guards. From what I understood, his regiment had been engaged in the heavy fighting and liberation of France the previous month. Only a few days before, we'd gotten word that his unit had been the first to liberate Brussels. The town had celebrated him. He'd even written a letter to Kick, which she'd read to me at Rainbow Corner only last week.

Anne didn't say anything; she was quietly sobbing on the other end. My sister-in-law had a heart of gold and a spine of steel. She would not sob, would not have words robbed from her, at a simple injury. Something terrible had happened to sweet Billy.

"Anne, where are you? Let me come to you." I gripped the receiver, willing her to tell me.

"I can't believe he's dead," she said, not having heard me. "Shot by a bastard German sniper. Sweet, sweet Billy."

I clutched the receiver harder, feeling her pain in every word she uttered. It had been only six months since Charlie had passed . . .

The news was devastating. A genuine hero, shot in so cold and calculated a way. To be sighted by an enemy's scope, and then deliberately wiped from existence as if he were nothing.

The following week, I headed to Ireland, taking Kick Kennedy with me. Both of us, now widows, needed the respite, and the care that only Mom could provide, along with the relative peace that blanketed Lismore.

"I want nothing more than to go back to New York," I told Kick as we walked along the moors, our wellies damp from the morning dew.

"I can't imagine anything worse," Kick said, her voice morose, her grief acute. It had taken every ounce of energy I possessed to pull her from bed that morning, and it was only after Mom gave her the speech that she'd given me that Kick finally agreed.

"You really find New York worse than London?"

Kick shrugged sadly. "London is where I had the most fun with Billy."

That I could understand. I suppose part of what drew me to New York, besides all my memories of dancing and friends, was that in New York I'd had Charlie. A better, healthier Charlie.

I remained in Ireland through Christmas, needing the nerve cure the Irish countryside provided. But when the New Year came and it seemed as if the war would never end, I was determined to return to the Red Cross. I wanted to cheer up the uniformed men, see how Kick was doing, along with the rest of my London friends, and I hoped it would cheer me, too.

I stepped off the train, fat droplets of freezing rain pinging against my cheeks. I rushed, the porter behind me with my bags, to the road, waving my hand in the air for a taxi. A sharp gust of wind nearly blew me over, whipping the scarf around my neck up into my face before it flew right off. I reached for it, racing after it, only for the strip of wool to smack a uniformed officer in the face.

He pulled the bright-blue scarf away, revealing a handsome smile punctuated by a deep laugh.

"Adele Astaire." Kingman Douglass drew out my name as though it were a priceless artifact, my scarf still in his hand.

"Funny," I teased, harking back to our first meeting. "That's my name, too."

Kingman chuckled and wagged a finger at me. "We keep meeting like this."

"I've hit you with my scarf before?" I feigned confusion.

He glanced at the train station, an eyebrow quirked, unused to people making jokes, I supposed. "I meant here, in Piccadilly."

"I presume we both find the convenience of the Tube refreshing." I swiped at a droplet of rain running down the tip of my nose.

"As opposed to taxis?" He nodded toward the porter loading up my bags.

I laughed, feeling nervous under the intense scrutiny of his gaze. It was the type of look that made me feel judged, but also that he saw all of me, even parts of me I didn't know existed. "I don't know what I'm saying. I'm exhausted."

"Let me take you for a coffee, then."

"When in London, we drink tea, if there's any left to be had."

"A tea then, Lady Charles." His smile, and his confidence, soothed me, but then it faltered. "Do accept my condolences on the loss of your husband."

It had been nearly a year since I'd lost Charlie, and the pain still lodged in my chest. I nodded. "Thank you. Do call me Adele; we've known each other awhile now, Kingman."

"Fair enough, Adele." He stepped toward me, wrapped the scarf back around my neck, and for the faintest moment I could smell the scent of his aftershave, and it made my heart quicken apace. He stared into my eyes with a concentration that made my stomach lodge itself in my throat.

"Pardon me if this is too forward, but your eyes . . ." The small knot at the front of his throat bobbed. "You are stunning."

My mouth went dry, my fingers tingly. "Thank you." I'd been used to people telling me I was pretty my whole life. But there was something different in the way Kingman said it. A piece of my shattered heart seemed to settle back into place. Whereas I'd once thought I had a face that only a mother could love, somehow I believed him.

It had been so long since I'd felt a flash of hope. And now it felt as if everything was going to be all right. But here, standing on the platform at Piccadilly, where I'd met Kingman for the first time, where I'd run into him again, I couldn't help but think that perhaps hope was still something I could possess. That maybe this was meant to be.

That Charlie's wish for me to be happy was something else that I could give him.

CHAPTER TWENTY-FIVE

ADELE

THE LIMELIGHT

Victory is ours! At long last, Miss Violet Wood will return to the theatre, starring in *Follow the Girls*. Let's hope we can keep her in the West End for years to come. Rumor has it that picture studios have been courting Lord Charles Cavendish's recent widow, Adele Astaire; however, following a brief flirt and rejection of appearing on the cinema screen, our favorite American starlet has continued to maintain her distance as an actress beyond occasional interviews and modeling gigs. We still hold out hope that one day we shall see her perform again. One has not truly lived if they've not witnessed the dancing lilac flame . . .

May 8, 1945

In war, there are the victors and the defeated.

But even on the victors' side there are those who still feel the catastrophic losses of the win. That the end of an era being celebrated by the masses has still brought with it a sense of loss and devastation.

On V-E Day in London, I struggled with those feelings. As people crowded into the streets, as they whooped and embraced, my smile felt as if it might crack. Of course I was elated that the war in Europe was over, beyond jubilant that life could go back to normal, without the threat of a violent dictator over our heads. This was a momentous occasion, it truly was. But although the war might have been over in this part of the world, it was far from over in America. We were still fighting with Japan. Which meant that I was celebrating an end to one part of war, but not another.

Just over a week before, Hitler had committed suicide, robbing the world of serving justice to the man who'd destroyed so many lives. Negotiations started almost immediately for Germany's surrender.

Unfortunately, it was too late for Violet's fiancé, Paul. His Spitfire was shot down over the Baltic Sea near Poland. I'd found out after seeing his name in bold on a list of men presumed killed in action in the newspaper, followed by a tearful telephone call from Violet.

But here I was, smiling a smile I wanted to mean, dancing in the street outside the Rainbow Corner. Hugging strangers. Because, while some parts of me were still in mourning, this was a day for thankfulness, too.

The streets of London filled with people. Drums and trumpet fanfare vibrated in my ears. We danced, we sang, we cheered. Someone had confetti, and they tossed it high in the air, not caring that the tiny paper pieces caught in our hair.

Kingman approached, his smile broad. We'd grown close over the past few weeks, and I felt I could confide in him.

"Care to dance?" he asked.

"Would I ever."

We kicked up our heels, dancing the Charleston right there on the street, our smiles wide. Proof of life.

"Adele Astaire."

I stifled a laugh, tears of joy stinging the corners of my dry eyes when I spotted Violet over Kingman's shoulder.

"Violet Wood!" I shouted, pushing through the throng and stepping over the shredded papers that littered the street.

Violet threw her arms around me. We'd loved and lost so much during this war, and even before. Over the past two decades, we'd held each other up through the rough spots as best we could.

"I can't believe they let you come." I beamed, holding her at arm's length, a smile on her face that could have lit the sun.

"I was also rather surprised. We expected once the surrender was formally announced that Supervisor Wolf would have us dismantling the weapons right away, but he's given us a short leave before we need to start the process."

"Does that mean you'll be done with the radio, then?" I asked.

"I'm not certain, but I definitely want to be there for the women who've shed blood and tears with me over the years."

I nodded, worrying my lower lip with my teeth. The end of the war, the loss of my husband—it meant that I would be returning to the States, once more estranged from a friend so dear to my heart.

"What is it?"

I smiled, shook my head. "Nothing."

Violet took my hand in hers, locked eyes with me, and said, "You can tell me, you know. Your secrets are safe with me."

I hugged Violet again, my body fairly vibrating with happiness. "I do admire how real you've always been, Vi. I've lots of other friends, in all sorts of places, but when it comes to honesty, you're the one I've always known I could count on."

"Right back at you," Violet agreed, then raised an eyebrow, warning me not to change the subject. "So, spill."

"Well, it's just that . . ." I glanced around at everyone celebrating, took in their cheers and hollers and jubilation. "I'll be headed home soon—to New York."

Violet nodded, squeezing my hands softly. "We will keep in touch. We've been through too much to forget each other." She cast a somber glance toward the ground. "We're celebrating, but at the same time we're in mourning. Because nothing will ever be the same."

Several American soldiers whooped past us, tossing their hats into the air.

I nodded. "I suppose it is human nature."

Violet smiled in the soldiers' direction. "To celebrate the victories, even when the war is still being fought."

"Yes." My gaze shifted behind her to Kingman. "I have a wish in my heart that I hope will come true."

Kingman winked in my direction and tipped his hat. We'd become good friends, yes. But there was something else there. The bud of something new. I just wasn't sure if I was brave enough to let myself love again.

"Does that wish have to do with Colonel Kingman Douglass?" Violet raised a brow, a slight teasing note in her voice.

"That's a secret for another time." But my smile said *yes*, because although my brain wasn't yet ready, my heart was. "I say we dance our hearts out for old times' sake."

"I can't say no to that."

I took Violet's hand in mine and we twirled each other around, laughing as we bumped into the soldiers crowding in the street.

EPILOGUE

THE ASTAIRE WAY TO PARADISE

"My sister Adele was mostly responsible for my being in show business. She was the whole show, she really was. In all the vaudeville acts we had and the musical comedies we did together, Delly was the one that was the shining light and I was just there pushing away."

—FRED ASTAIRE, LIFETIME ACHIEVEMENT
AWARD ACCEPTANCE SPEECH

Summer 1954
Round Hill, Jamaica

Although nearly a decade had passed since I'd last seen Violet, time and space seemed not to exist, especially in a tranquil place like Montego Bay.

I leaned back in my beach chair, soaking up the sun that warmed my skin at the Round Hill resort, which we called home for part of every year. A coconut cocktail in one hand, topped with a pocket-sized blue umbrella sporting pink flamingos, and *The Limelight* in the other—with Violet's face on the cover. Lying out on the sun-kissed chairs, with Violet on my left and my husband, Kingman, on my right, life seemed perfect.

There was an intensity to Kingman that I'd gotten used to over the years. While he sat alert, watching, seemingly waiting for something to happen, I just took it all in with a smile. I supposed that underlying tension would come from a man who'd helped form America's Central Intelligence Agency. Without a doubt, some of his taut exterior melted whenever he looked at me. Our adoration was mutual.

"I heard a joke on the plane," Violet said. "You might get a kick out of it."

"Lay it on me," I said, taking a long sip of my cocktail.

"A man at the records office requested to change his name. The officer asked, 'What's your current name?' The man says, 'Adolf Stinkbutt.'"

"Oh, that is unfortunate." I smirked.

"Right, and the officer, feeling quite bad for the man, says, 'All right, sir, I can understand that. What would you like to change your name to?' And the man says, 'George Stinkbutt.'"

My eyes crinkled at the corners as I let out a laugh—lines that hadn't been there the last time I'd seen my good friend. "Ha! That's a good one. I imagine on the heels of the world war there were a lot of men changing their names."

"I heard in America the most popular baby name is Freddie," Violet said with a wink.

"He sure has become America's favorite, though he's always been mine." I glanced at Kingman. "And you, too, dear."

Kingman chuckled. "I would never come between the love of you and your brother. The two of you are a pair, and belong that way."

"Oh, Kingsie." I leaned over and gave him a kiss.

When I settled back against my chair, Violet was watching me with a nostalgic look in her eye. "I like seeing you like this, Delly."

"What do you mean? With a cocktail in hand?"

"Your enthusiasm for life returned."

Magazine discarded, I reached for Violet's hand and squeezed. Throughout the war years, when I'd been suffering from the loss of my babies and Charlie's vices, I'd become a person hardly anyone recognized, including myself. I'd lost touch with a good friend because she reminded me of who I used to be, and the dreams I used to have. In the past decade she'd become one of the most famed stage stars of the age, and a devoted aunt to Pris's children. Paul remained the only man she'd loved to date, though she wasn't always alone.

"I'm so glad you're here." Emotion made my voice wobbly. "I really missed you."

"No war could sever our friendship, and certainly not an ocean." Violet shifted in her chair, fanning herself with her own magazine. "What are you looking forward to next?"

"I'm looking forward to grandchildren to spoil," I said.

Kingman had three sons, all of whom I'd adopted and doted on. They were adults now, venturing out and forming families of their own. But I was endlessly grateful to finally have gotten the family I'd desired after so much pain and loss.

"You'll be a delightful grandmother," Violet said, thunking her coconut with mine, saying, without saying it, that she was happy for me, for finally getting what I'd always wanted.

With an exaggerated sigh, I said, "I suppose I'll have to spend more time at our house in Middleburg, Virginia, than here, but I don't mind. You've got to come visit me. We've the most wondrous horses on the farm. And sheep! We have sheep! And goats. The landscape reminds me of Lismore."

"When do you go back to Ireland?" Violet asked, closing her magazine and tossing it under her chair.

"Later this summer." I gave an exaggerated pout. Truly, I was grateful the Cavendish family still allowed me my summers at Lismore. Kingman and I split the rest of our year between our house in Virginia and the villa in Jamaica. And of course we visited Freddie in California often. Mom was still as energetic as ever, making her home between the two of us, though now she was in California helping care for Phyllis, who'd, devastatingly, been diagnosed with lung cancer. "I wish you could come. Lismore is gorgeous in August. Well, really, it's gorgeous any time of year, but summer is my favorite."

In addition to the Cavendish family generally granting me access to the castle every summer for the rest of my life, they had also given me an annual stipend as the widow of Lord Charles Cavendish. I remained close with the whole family, visiting Chatsworth, even, which pleased me because I'd been quite close to Charlie's siblings and my niece-in-law, Deborah. I'd even remained close to the Kennedy family, following Kick's tragic death in a plane crash several years after the war's end. I needed the connection, and so did they, to the once-vibrant young woman. Kick's brother John, an up-and-coming senator, and his wife, Jackie, had recently visited Round Hill before Violet had arrived.

Later that evening, as we dined on lobster and champagne, and the sun settled below the horizon, there came a beating of drums. The magical sound thrummed in the air; a nostalgic beat that called to something buried deep within the human psyche. A call to nature. In response I began to sway. I might have given up my career as a performer, but the body never forgets.

"Oh, the fire dancers!" I squealed, leaping out of my chair. "I can't resist, and neither should you, Vi."

I grabbed hold of Violet's hand and tugged her away from the table. In our dinner finery, the two of us joined the dancers on the patio, the rhythm of the music sinking into my bones the way it always had. I closed my eyes and let the rhythm take me away. In that instant, I was so filled with contentment.

There was nothing better than living in the moment, embracing joy when it was there to be had, and letting go of all the little things that tried as they might to hold me back. Life was shouting "Encore!" for me over and over each day and for the people I cared to share it with.

If there was one thing I'd learned in all the varied moments of my existence, it was that *life* itself was my most authentic performance yet.

AUTHOR'S NOTE

My journey into the life of Adele Astaire began when, while researching my novel *The Mayfair Bookshop*, I read a letter Nancy Mitford wrote to her sister. Of course I had heard of Fred Astaire many times and knew he had a sister, but I had never really studied her history or realized that at the height of their theatrical career she was the more famous sibling. Nancy wrote the letter in 1933, after having lunch with Adele: "Delly said I don't mind people going off and fucking but I do object to all this free love. She is heaven isn't she?"

After reading that rather shocking statement, I thought, "Oh my, who in the world is this Delly, and how have I not heard of her before?" The footnote stated that Delly was Adele Astaire, sister to Fred Astaire. I was immediately intrigued and spent the next two days in a deep research dive learning everything I could and then determining that I had to write about her. Fortunately, my agent and editor agreed—and now, here we are!

This book, while produced with a heavy dose of research and staying true to much of Adele's life timeline, is also a work of historical fiction. Because it is fiction, I have used creative license in writing the story. The purpose of this author's note is to share with you what I learned and what I may have altered, or things that surprised me. Beyond being a writer, I am a huge history nerd and love to share things I've discovered.

I bought as many books as I could find about Adele and her brother (of which there are many), but what I really needed was to spend some time with the Adele Astaire Collection, which is housed in Boston University's Howard Gotlieb Archival Research Center. Unfortunately, this was during the pandemic, and the library was closed to outside researchers. I contemplated hiring a student, but there really is something about doing the research yourself. I plugged along with my story, emailing the library monthly to see if there was an update on the opening. But they remained closed until November 2021. By that time, I was desperate. I'd written all of Violet's part and most of Adele's, but felt that without getting to dive deeper into Adele's history I wasn't going to have an authentic enough finished project.

At last, the wonderful librarians contacted me, giving me two whole days with the collection the next week, if I could make it. I immediately booked a flight to Boston.

Those two days were amazing, and I wish I could have stayed longer. With the list of things I'd wanted to find out, along with my notebook, pencil, and laptop, I pored through the scrapbooks filled with newspaper clippings, reviews, and pictures. Touched a costume from Adele's Vaudeville days. Read through letters, calendar notebooks, and, best of all, Adele's personal diary. It was through this investigative study that I was able fill a lot of holes in the research I'd done already; for example, a better timeline for her relationship with William Gaunt, as well as the articles that she and Freddie wrote for the London papers. I was able to get a true feel for Delly's voice, and I was pleasantly surprised to see I'd already nailed it in the pages I'd previously written.

There are some audio recordings on YouTube of Freddie and Delly that they did for a couple of their plays: "I'd Rather Charleston," "Fascinating Rhythm," and "Hang on to Me" from *Lady Be*

Good; and "Oh Gee Oh Gosh Oh Golly" and, my personal favorite, "The Whichness of the Whatness" from *Stop Flirting*, to name a few. I listened to them hundreds of times. Unfortunately, the only recording of Delly dancing is from a rehearsal for *Smiles* with her brother and Marilyn Miller—and it's really more of a shuffle. She's on the far side of the recording and you can just barely make her out. Another recording of her with Freddie is from when he visited London with the USO tour, and she greets him onstage. I so wish there were more recordings of her. She was such an incredible person, and I feel as though we are all deprived of not only her dancing genius but her comedic genius, as well. I have watched dozens and dozens of videos of Fred, as well as his movies, which are a treat.

I've been a fan of theatre since I was a little girl and my dad took me to see a Punch and Judy puppet show. In fact, I had a brief stint in theatre myself as a teenager, acting at a local community stage for a couple of years. I've also always loved to dance, though I lack any sort of grace. Writing this book was truly a passion project that allowed me to return to my roots and live vicariously through the characters.

Violet Wood is a fictitious character, though I based some of her history on other performers of the time, like Daisy Violet Rose Wood (aka Marie Lloyd), from whom I borrowed part of her name. I wanted to use the juxtaposition of Violet's character to explore Adele's journey. You'll notice often when one is up the other is down, and vice versa. Both of them started with meager means, and they both struggled in different ways to reach their opposite ends.

The *Limelight* clips at the beginning of each chapter were created by me, as is the name of this fictional theatre gossip magazine. I love to read about celebrities, notable figures, and royals in magazines, and gossip rags have been a part of our history for ages. I used the short clips to update readers about the goings-on of the various characters, otherwise the book would have been eight hundred pages. I also created them for a bit of cheeky fun.

Adele's hair was extremely long early on in her career. Like some other performers of the age, she fashioned it up into rolled curls that made it look like she had a bob. In order to figure out how she did that, I actually consulted a hairstylist. The style of Adele's hair was one of the things I discovered when I went to the archival research center, as I saw her in a picture with her hair down and it came to her waist.

There are a lot of real historical figures who make cameos in the book, and I did this not only to add authenticity to the era, but also because most of them truly did interact with Adele and were a meaningful part of her life. Mimi Crawford, Noël Coward, Marilyn Miller, the princes of England (whom she did date and dance with), Princess Elizabeth (aka Queen Elizabeth II), George Raft, Adelaide Hall, Duke Ellington, Bojangles, the Nicholas Brothers, Texas Guinan (who really did tell people to leave their wallets on the bar), Tilly Losch, Shirley Temple, Prince Aly Khan, and so on. There were a host of others I couldn't put in the book because it would have just been too many.

Though I made Mr. Moore take advantage of the chorus girls early on in the book, I have no proof, nor did I find any suggestion, that the real Mr. Moore did so. However, the abuse we hear of happening today in Hollywood and other performing arts environments was certainly occurring during Adele's time onstage. Many female performers did not feel empowered enough to say no, and were left pregnant, their futures in tatters. Often they'd be sent away for a time, giving their babies up for adoption. Some relinquished showbiz to concentrate on parenting. The majority of them received no help from the men who were partially (if not fully) responsible for their situations. This is why I had Violet fall victim to a preying producer, to bring attention to women being taken advantage of in the arts.

The Shaftesbury Theatre in London's West End was originally the New Princes Theatre, and then Princes Theatre. On its website it says it was renamed Shaftesbury after a renovation in the 1960s; however, the photos from 1923 with Fred and Adele Astaire's *Stop Flirting* billboard show Shaftesbury plainly on the building, as does a copy of the program, so I chose to use this as the name in the book. It is a working theatre to this day, and I had the pleasure of visiting it recently on a trip to London.

Adele and Charlie did lose a daughter first, followed by twin boys, and then there was another miscarriage. The grave markers for the children simply say Baby Girl and Baby Boy. I couldn't find if they named the children on any vital records, and there weren't any christenings because they passed away quickly, so the name "Annie Evelyn" was created by me, using the fairly common naming system of culling from the names of grandparents.

Though I couldn't go into much depth with the Great Depression on account of space, I tried to depict a true representation of New York City during that time. I listed the amount of money that Fred and Adele lost during the crash, which was about $73,000, three-quarters of their savings—a huge amount of money even today! Doing the math, that is equal to roughly $1.2 million now. They were the lucky ones. People lost their homes, roughly 25 percent of people lost their jobs, and they couldn't feed their children. The homeless and unemployed truly did build their own shacks—their squatter communities were called Hoovervilles—in Central Park, and they popped up across the nation. The term was named after President Hoover and was used as a political label to place blame.

"Simpsonitis," in reference to the obsession some of the aristocracy in Adele's circle seemed to have with Wallis Simpson, who married the former King Edward (aka David), was a term Adele wrote in her diary that seemed very fitting for her own feelings and the behavior of her social circle. Additionally, the mention of the quote she'd written on notepaper at the Ritz about a woman being judged by her depth and quality of passion was actually on a piece of blue notepaper from the Ritz in the Adele Astaire Collection, in Adele's hand.

Many of the books mentioned in the novel were ones Adele listed during an interview, as well as writers she counted as friends, such as Anita Loos (*Gentlemen Prefer Blondes*). The one person I couldn't figure out how to include, but wish I could have, was A. A. Milne. Adele was close to him and his son, Christopher Robin, the inspiration for the character of the same name in Milne's Winnie-the-Pooh books. Adele even sent Christopher Robin Christmas gifts. I was able to include Milne's book *Four Days' Wonder* as one of the ones Adele bought at Foyles.

The Cavendishes really did commission two Spitfire planes named the *Cavendish* and the *Adele Astaire* during World War II because Charlie was unable to serve due to his illness. From the severity of Charlie's illness so early on (Charlie and Adele had to postpone their wedding due to his hospitalization), I assume his penchant for drink was quite extensive and likely had been going on for a long time before he and Adele met. He died at thirty-eight years old from acute alcoholism, which was devastating to Adele. A prolific diary writer, there are years missing from Adele's diary in which she suffered alongside him, and she would come back to the journal saying so. I tried to show the slow descent of Charlie's health in the novel, and the heartbreak she must have felt. For as much of a "Good-Time Charlie" as she was, it had to have been absolutely crushing to suffer so much loss after wishing so hard to be a wife and mother. And she never stopped loving him.

In the end, I think Adele found happiness with Kingman, an intelligence officer and assistant director for the CIA. They remained happily married until his death in 1971 due to a brain hemorrhage. Nora Davis (Foster) was a radio broadcaster at Rotherwas in Hereford. Anna Neagle and Gracie Fields were two celebrities she had on the show. As I was doing research for Violet's conscription, I came across Nora's story, and I thought it would be the perfect place, given she was in the entertainment industry. Wilf "Wolf" Bowen was in fact the supervisor of the munitions factory. The accidental explosion as well as the *Luftwaffe* bombing both occurred. I thought it was important to include in the novel some of the lesser-known work that women did, and the risks that came with it.

Adele, Freddie, and their mother, Ann, remained close all their lives. In 1972, the sibling pair was inducted into the American Theater Hall of Fame. Three years later, at the age of ninety-six, Ann passed away. Adele passed away in 1981 at the age of eighty-four after suffering a stroke, and having maintained good health and physical fitness. Freddie passed away of pneumonia in 1987 at the age of eighty-eight, leaving behind two children, Freddie Jr. and Ava.

I hope that you enjoyed the novel and this brief foray into the life of Adele Astaire. Her time on this earth was full of so many fascinating moments that it was impossible to put them all into this book. Additionally, I'm certain to have left out something from this author's note that I altered, omitted, or added to Adele's story. The research process for this book and the writing of it were years in the making, and I promise that every decision made as far as what to add or omit or alter was done with great consideration.

To that end, this is a work of fiction, with the purpose of inviting you into this captivating world full of strong women, their relationships, the struggles they faced, and the ways in which they overcame them, as well as the triumphs they celebrated in their careers and personal lives.

ACKNOWLEDGMENTS

Though I research, plot, and write alone in the confines of my very messy office, no book is ever truly a solitary venture. In addition to the ghosts of the past, there are many people who helped in the creation of *Starring Adele Astaire*.

I want to thank my incomparable agent, Kevan Lyon; my wonderful editor, Lucia Macro; and her associate editor, Asanté Simons. Thank you to the hardworking people in the sales, marketing, publicity, and production departments, including Jessica Rozler. My gratitude to all the remarkable people of William Morrow, including the publisher, Liate Stehlik; my cover designer, Lauren Harms, for the gorgeous artwork; Diahann Sturge for the dazzling interior design of the book, Jane Hardick for the thorough copyedits, and Jen DePoorter and Megan Wilson for the brilliance in marketing, along with my team at Kaye Publicity.

Many thanks to Sophie Perinot, Madeline Martin, and Lea Nolan for reading and critiquing early drafts of this book. I appreciate all your suggestions and guidance. Thank you to Denny S. Bryce for helping me plot and aiding me with dance lingo. Thank you to Katie Brandon for the hairstyling research. Big thank-yous to my writing pals Brenna Ash and Lori Ann Bailey for your enduring support, and the hours you listened and offered advice. Thank you to the wonderful librarian archivists at the Howard Gotlieb Archival Research Center at Boston University for helping me pore over the entire Adele Astaire Collection, including J. C. Johnson and Katie Fortier. Thank you to my brilliant Lyonesses for their sisterhood.

I have always loved to dance, though I lack a certain rhythm. In fact, I gave my eldest daughter the middle name Grace, hoping it would gift her with coordination. It worked. I watched her spin and leap and glide on stage from toddlerhood all the way through high school as she danced competitively with grit, determination, spirit—and grace. It is from her I drew inspiration when writing about one of the most famous dancers of the twentieth century, as well as my fictional character, and from her I understand the aches and pains of doing so, along with the triumphs. So, Ashleigh, I thank you for continuing to inspire me.

Last, but never least, a special thank-you to my awesome husband, Hoff, and our three witty daughters, Ash, Dani, and Lexi, who remind me always to dance whether people are watching or not, and for never turning away from an impromptu kitchen dance sesh. I am forever grateful to you all for joining me on endless trips to the theatre, belting out the tunes to our favorite performances, and supporting me without a second thought. Dare to dream always, I love you all so very much.